PROCEED WITH CAUTION

A NOVEL

PROCEED WITH CAUTION

BETSY BRANNON GREEN

Covenant Communications, Inc.

Cover image *Fear Of The Witness* © Arman Zhenikeyev, Courtesy of iStockphoto.com.

Cover design copyright © 2013 by Covenant Communications, Inc.

Published by Covenant Communications, Inc.
American Fork, Utah

Printed in the United States of America
First Printing: May 2013

19 18 17 16 15 14 13   10 9 8 7 6 5 4 3 2 1

ISBN 978-1-62108-366-5

To Anderson Claire Acker
The glory of God is intelligence, and my is she glorious!

ACKNOWLEDGMENTS

I AM THANKFUL FOR MY husband, Butch, and his continued encouragement, support, and patience. He is the inspiration for all my romantic heroes. We have been blessed with eight nearly-perfect children and (so far) five nearly-perfect in-law children. I am eternally grateful for them and for my nine wonderful grandchildren. (And I just have to say it—they *are* perfect!)

I am particularly indebted to my new editor Stacey Owen and all the other folks at Covenant who worked hard to get this book into print. May we still be working together for many years to come!

CHAPTER ONE

LATE ON A SUNDAY NIGHT in May, Brooke Clayton was in the living room of her off-campus apartment. She stood very still and listened to the knocking on her door.

"Miss Clayton?" A voice penetrated the wood. "We're police officers, and we need to talk to you. It's important."

Brooke stared at the door, barely breathing.

There was another series of knocks, followed by a tense pause. She didn't think they knew she was there. She had slipped in through the back, hoping to avoid notice. The doorknob rattled, and for a minute she wondered if they would force the lock. Then, to her immense relief, she heard them walking away.

She looked out the window at the street below and saw the policemen exit the apartment complex. They stood by their car and talked for a few minutes, occasionally gesturing toward her building. At last, the two men got in their car, but they didn't drive away. Apparently they assumed she wasn't home and had decided to wait for her to return.

Sitting on the edge of her bed, she considered her options. She wanted to call her parents for advice, but she couldn't involve them. She had created this mess and she would fix it. With hands shaking, she started packing. After putting a few days' worth of clothes in her backpack, she pulled on her well-worn hiking boots, put on an old flannel shirt left behind by her ex-boyfriend, and tucked her hair up into a baseball cap.

She stared at her cell phone for several seconds. It had been a birthday gift from her parents. Leaving it would prevent anyone from being able to track her using the GPS. But traveling without a phone would be inconvenient and dangerous. She couldn't let anyone find her, so she tossed the phone onto her couch, shrugged the backpack over her shoulder, and slipped out into the hallway.

She hurried down the back stairs and left the building through the service entrance, which led to an alley. Pulling the cap down to hide her face, she walked away from everything familiar.

It was nearly an hour later when she approached the bus stop. She went into a convenience store across the street to use the ATM and took out the maximum withdrawal her bank allowed per day. She put the cash in her pocket and returned to the corner to wait for the next bus.

There was a streetlight right over the bus stop, exposing her more than she would have preferred. But the police didn't seem to be following her, so she willed herself to relax and check her watch. In just a few minutes she would be safely on the bus. Then she heard someone coming up behind her.

Brooke glanced over her shoulder to see three men approaching the corner where she stood. They were spread across the entire sidewalk so that when they reached the bus stop, one of them would have to step aside—or she would.

She saw one of the men gesture toward her and another one nod. She pulled her flannel shirt close, as if the fabric could provide any protection. She thought about the money in her pocket. They would rob her—and maybe worse. They were drawing closer, moving faster, and she started to panic.

She wanted to run but knew they could easily overtake her. She looked to the store across the street. She could never make it back there before the men reached her.

Suddenly the police didn't seem like her worst option. But since she'd left her cell phone in her apartment, she had no way to call them. Screaming would be inevitable but ineffectual. There was no one to hear her. The men were just a few feet away, and she had never been so scared in her life.

Then with the loud screech of air brakes, the bus came into view. The men stopped, and one made eye contact with her for a few horrible seconds. Finally the men ducked into an alley and were gone. The bus pulled to a stop in front of her, and the doors opened. With her heart thundering in her chest, Brooke climbed on board—unharmed and still in possession of her money.

Her hands trembled badly as she paid the fare. She sat right behind the driver and clutched the rail that separated them, still unnerved by the men who had meant her harm. She looked around at the strangers on the bus. She'd managed to elude the police, but now she had to fear other things, other people. She hated the feeling of helplessness.

Brooke rode the bus all night. The driver eyed her a few times but never insisted that she get off. Finally, as dawn was breaking, he said, "This is my last rotation before my shift ends. I can't turn the bus back in with you still on it."

She nodded. "I'll get off at the next stop."

When the bus rolled to a halt, she stood and moved into the aisle. The driver pulled the lever, which swung the doors open with an unpleasant squeal.

With a whispered thank you, she stepped out into the cool morning air. She pulled up the collar of her shirt, more to hide her identity than to provide warmth. It was unlikely that anyone would look for her here, but she could not be sure. And the stakes were very high.

***

On Monday morning Savannah Dane walked out onto the back porch of the cabin she shared with her husband, Major Christopher Dane, and her daughter, Caroline. Dane had been working in Washington, DC, for a couple of days, fulfilling an assignment for his former commanding officer, General Steele. But thanks to their state-of-the-art security system, she knew that his car had just turned onto the long, gravel drive, and she wanted to be waiting when he pulled up.

She walked to the edge of the porch steps and looked out at the Virginia summer morning, waiting. A mist covered the ground, the result of the sun's attempt to evaporate the dew. Then the old car emerged from the trees, and relief washed over her.

As Dane parked in the yard, he gave her a smile and she rushed down the steps to meet him. He climbed out of the car and caught her into his arms, holding her tight.

"I've missed you!" she whispered.

"You couldn't possibly have missed me as much as I missed you," he murmured back.

"That's probably true. But just barely."

They stood for a few moments enjoying the embrace as the morning mist swirled around their feet. Then the peace was shattered by Caroline.

"Daddy!" she screamed as she came running through the kitchen door. "You were gone forever!"

Dane reached down with one arm and swung the child up so she could join their hug. "It did seem like forever."

4

Betsy Brannon Green

"Mom bought some cookies for your welcome-home surprise. She said we had to wait to eat them until you got home. So can we now, Mom?" Caroline asked.

Dane frowned. "Are you really glad to see me or just excited to eat cookies?"

Caroline clasped her arms around his neck and declared, "I like you better than cookies!"

He laughed. "Then go eat some of my welcome-home surprise."

Caroline wriggled down and started back toward the house. "Come on in and you can eat some too!"

"We'll be there in a minute," Dane promised, wrapping his arm around Savannah again.

"Just eat a couple. It will be time for lunch soon." She pressed her cheek into the crook of his neck.

"If we don't go in and supervise, she'll eat too many cookies and spoil her lunch."

"Probably," Savannah agreed.

Dane gently separated himself from his wife and took her hand. Then they walked into the house.

Caroline was sitting at the kitchen table, eating Oreos.

"How many so far?" Dane asked as he took a cookie from the package.

"Four," Caroline replied.

"That's enough for now." Savannah closed the package of Oreos. "You can have a few more with your lunch."

Caroline washed down the last of her fourth cookie with some milk. Then she said, "Can I go upstairs and play with my trains?"

Savannah nodded. "We'll call you when lunch is ready."

Dane waited until Caroline was gone before he opened the package on the counter, removed another cookie, and popped it in his mouth. "I'm still two short of the four-cookie limit."

She smiled. "You can eat as many as you like. They are *your* welcome-home surprise."

Some of the humor left his face. "I hate being away from home. I'll never take another assignment that requires me to be gone overnight."

Savannah laughed. "Yes you will. If the general needs you, you'll go."

He hung his head in concession. "I'll go, but I'll be miserable."

She put her arms around his waist. "Just as long as you promise you'll always come home."

"I promise," Dane said. But they both knew it was a lie. His work with General Steele was often dangerous, and there were no guarantees.

Dane kissed her forehead and then reached for another cookie. "I don't know how I was able to live on my own without a family. It makes me feel sorry for the other guys on the team."

This was a perfect segue into her announcement, and she made use of the opportunity. "I'm glad you feel that way," she began. Then her stomach rebelled against her. So instead of telling him the good news, she put a hand over her mouth and ran to the bathroom.

Dane followed her and stood in the doorway. When she was finally able to stand, Savannah brushed her teeth and wiped her face with a damp washcloth. Then she walked over to Dane and rested her forehead on his chest.

"You're pale as a ghost," he told her. "Do you have a stomach virus?"

She shook her head and gave him a weak smile. "No, we're going to have a baby."

He looked completely surprised. "You're kidding."

She laughed. "No, I'm not kidding."

"But we've only been married a few months and I just thought, well, I wasn't expecting it so soon."

"We agreed that we should have children right away so the age-gap with Caroline would be minimized as much as possible."

"I know, but still . . ."

"You don't seem as happy as I'd expected." She studied his face curiously.

He pulled her close and stroked her hair. "I *am* happy. You know I don't like surprises. But if there is such a thing as a good surprise, a baby definitely qualifies."

"And you have eight months to get used to the idea."

He nodded seriously. "I'll be ready by then."

They walked into the living room, and once they were settled side by side on the couch he continued. "So many thoughts are going through my head. I'm worried about you. I'm worried about the baby. I'm worried that when you go into labor we won't make it to the hospital on time."

Savannah laughed. "You're worried about that already!"

He nodded. "I can't help it."

"We'll make it on time," she said with confidence.

"I hope so," Dane muttered. Then he thought of something else to worry about. "How long did the morning sickness last with Caroline?"

"I was never sick a single minute when I was pregnant with Caroline," she replied. "So I'm not sure how long this will go on."

He frowned. "Naturally *my* baby would give you trouble."

She laughed. "If your baby is anything like you, he or she will be a lot of trouble—that's for sure! But it will be worth it."

He kissed her and then murmured, "I hope you still feel that way in a few months."

"I haven't told Caroline yet. I wanted you to be the first to know."

"She'll be excited," Dane said.

"Maybe we should wait . . . just to be sure everything's okay."

Dane frowned. "If you're going to be this sick we'll have to tell her soon or she'll think you're dying."

"Who is dying?" Caroline asked from behind them, her voice full of dread.

They turned to see her standing in the doorway. Her face was pale, her expression concerned.

"No one is dying!" Savannah assured her emphatically. "I'm just feeling a little sick because I'm going to have a baby."

Caroline processed this information, looking more interested than happy. "When?"

"In January—right after Christmas."

"Your mom is going to need a lot of help," Dane said. "And the first thing is to come up with a good name."

"Do you know if it's a boy or a girl?" Caroline wanted to know.

"Not yet," Savannah answered. "So you'll have to think of a good name for both."

"Maybe it will be twins!" Caroline said with a grin. "Then if I come up with two good names we can use them both!"

"Double trouble," Dane muttered.

"Don't you like babies?" Caroline asked him.

Savannah answered for him. "You know how your father is. He's nervous about you! Imagine how nervous he'll be about a little baby."

Caroline laughed. "Don't worry, Daddy. I'll help."

Dane pulled the child onto his lap. "We're really counting on that." Over her head, he told Savannah, "I need to call the guys. They were going to come by here to see Caroline. But you're sick, so we don't need company."

"I want them to come!" Caroline cried. "Maybe Mom will feel better!"

"Don't uninvite them," Savannah said. "Just tell Hack to stop and get pizzas for lunch. I definitely can't cook."

Dane looked unconvinced. "You're sure?"

Savannah nodded. "The guys are coming to see Caroline anyway. They probably won't even notice that I'm under the weather."

"Please, Daddy!" Caroline begged.

"Okay," Dane relented.

"Thank you, Mom!" Caroline cried. "Can I tell them about our baby?"

"I guess," Savannah said. Then she turned to Dane. "Unless you'd rather we didn't."

"The guys are part of the family," he said. "They'll want to know."

Savannah started to feel sick again and leaned her head against the back of the couch.

"Maybe we should call the doctor," Dane suggested.

"I just went to the doctor," Savannah replied. "He said I'm the picture of health. I told him about the morning sickness, and he gave me a prescription for some antinausea pills that he said are safe during pregnancy. But I'm afraid to take anything during my first trimester, so I didn't fill the prescription."

"If the doctor said they're safe, I think you should," Dane said. "Otherwise you might not survive your first trimester."

Savannah nodded vaguely, not committing to anything but anxious to reassure him.

There was a knock at the door, and Dane checked his watch with a frown.

"They're here sooner than I expected. You're sure you don't want me to send them away?"

Savannah shook her head. "They can stay. If I start feeling too bad, I'll go upstairs."

Caroline ran toward the door. "Can I let them in?"

Dane stood and followed her. He unlatched the dead bolt and then nodded. "You can open the door."

Caroline swung the door open, but it wasn't Dane's band of merry men standing on the porch. It was his older sister, Neely.

"It's just Aunt Neely!" Caroline cried.

Neely gave them a self-deprecating smile. "Yep, it's just me."

"Apparently this is my day for surprises," Dane muttered.

"Good ones, I hope," Neely said brightly.

Savannah walked over to give Neely a hug. "Wonderful surprises. But why didn't you tell us you were coming?"

"It was kind of a spontaneous decision," Neely explained.

Dane leaned down to take the overnight bag from her hand. "I presume this means you're staying."

His sister stepped into the living room. "Maybe overnight if that won't be inconvenient."

Dane narrowed his eyes at her. "It's your birthday, and Mom said your kids were coming home to help you celebrate. So why are you here?"

"No one in my family could come, so we had to cancel," Neely told him. "It's not that big a deal. By the time you get to be my age, it's foolish to celebrate birthdays anyway."

Savannah was not fooled by Neely's flippant tone. "I know you're disappointed. I'm sorry."

Neely looked away. "I did feel a little sorry for myself. So instead of sitting around my house alone, I decided to come here."

"It's your birthday?" Caroline asked.

Neely nodded. "I wanted to bring my birthday cake to share with you, but I didn't think they'd let me take it on the plane."

"Italian cream from Denati's Bakery?" Dane asked.

"Yep. Almost as good as the cakes Mom used to make." Neely sighed. "It's a shame to waste it."

"We can make you a new cake!" Caroline offered. "One from a box."

Neely smiled. "That's very nice of you."

Caroline took Dane by the hand. "Let's go make Aunt Neely a cake!"

Dane gave them a pained look and allowed Caroline to pull him into the kitchen.

Once Caroline and Dane had gone, Neely turned to Savannah with an unnaturally bright smile. "I'm excited to see the renovations you've done. Can you give me a tour?"

Savannah wasn't sure she could without throwing up, but to be polite she nodded. "Don't expect too much. It was important to your brother to maintain the simplicity and rustic feel of the cabin."

"I wasn't expecting anything grandiose," Neely assured her.

Savannah smiled. "Then you shouldn't be disappointed."

They climbed the stairs, and when they reached the landing, Savannah led the way into the new addition. "The room on the right is Caroline's."

Neely peeked into the room where trains and tracks were scattered on the floor. On the walls were framed pictures of old locomotives and a shelf that displayed model trains. "Let me guess," she said. "Caroline decorated this room herself."

"She did," Savannah confirmed. "With a little help from me."

"The pink gingham curtains are a nice touch. They soften the room. And the patchwork quilt is exquisite."

"The curtains are from our house in Washington, DC," Savannah said. "Wes's mother made the quilt."

Neely smiled. "You're blending all the parts of Caroline's life in her room."

"That was the goal."

Neely moved on to the next door. "A bathroom!" she exclaimed.

"Having one upstairs has been a huge convenience." Savannah said.

"You shouldn't have settled for just one!" Neely cried. "You've got Christopher wrapped around your little finger. He'd do anything for you!"

Savannah sighed. "I didn't want to be greedy."

"I'm afraid you may have just missed your only chance to get a master bathroom."

"At least I don't have to go downstairs to take a bath."

"You are way too easy to please."

Savannah smiled as she pointed to the empty bedroom on the other side of the bathroom. "And obviously we haven't gotten around to decorating this room yet. But you'll be pleased to know that we completely remodeled the kitchen."

"It's about time! Did you put in a dishwasher?"

Savannah nodded. "And a garbage disposal and a huge refrigerator."

Neely shook her head. "Now *that* I've got to see. A modern kitchen in this cabin."

Savannah led the way to the stairs. "Oh, it *looks* exactly the same—except a little bigger. The new refrigerator and dishwasher are hidden behind wooden cabinets. Dane searched everywhere until he found an old house in Kentucky that had been destroyed during a tornado. The wood matched ours close enough, so he bought it and used it for the additional cabinets and flooring. Of course he had them take apart our old kitchen floor and mix the other wood in so it would look uniform."

"That does not surprise me at all," Neely told her as they descended the stairs. "What did you do with that old refrigerator?"

Savannah said, "Oh, we kept it too. Dane had the parts replaced, and now it works perfectly."

"I'm still excited to see the new kitchen, even if it looks the same."

When they reached the stair landing, Savannah pointed in the opposite direction from the kitchen. "Let's go this way so I can show you Dane's new office."

They walked through the living room and into the downstairs portion of the addition where a home office was set up.

Neely ran her hand across the desk. "This antique fits perfectly in here."

"And the corner of the living room where it used to be is now full of Caroline's toys." Savannah led the way through a door on the right into a small hallway. On the left was a new bathroom, complete with a shower, and on the right was a small bedroom with two sets of bunk beds. Savannah said, "Since Dane's team stays here whenever they work with him on an operation, it's nice to have a place to put them besides the back porch."

Neely nodded. "Very wise."

The hallway ended, and they walked through the laundry room and into the newly enlarged kitchen. It still looked like it was straight from the 1930s. Caroline had a big bowl on the counter, along with a cake mix and other baking paraphernalia.

"We're making your cake now, Aunt Neely!" Caroline informed them.

Dane looked up from the pan he was dusting with flour and told Neely, "I hope your expectations are low."

Neely smiled. "I'm sure it will be delicious."

"Let's get this thing in the oven," he told Caroline. Then he held the pan steady while the child transferred the batter from the bowl to the pan.

"How long will it take?" Caroline asked.

"The box says twenty-eight minutes," Dane told her. "I'll set the timer on the oven."

Caroline moved toward the kitchen door. "I'm going back upstairs to play with my trains. But call me when the cake is done. I want to wear the mitts and lift it out myself."

"We'll call you," Savannah promised.

Caroline gave Dane an impish grin. "Then me and Daddy can make frosting."

Dane groaned and looked at his wife. "Frosting too?"

Savannah mustered a wan smile. "What kind of a birthday cake would it be without frosting?"

Caroline left but poked her head back around the doorframe a few seconds later and said, "You want to come and play trains with me, Aunt Neely?"

"I'd love to," Neely said. "But I'd like to visit with your parents for a few minutes first."

"I'll be waiting!" Caroline called over her shoulder before running up the stairs.

"Would you like me to make something for lunch?" Neely offered. "I'm famous for my potato salad."

Just the thought of hard-boiled eggs made Savannah's stomach revolt. "I'm sorry, but I'm going to have to go . . ." And she made a hasty exit.

She heard Neely ask Dane, "She doesn't like potato salad?"

The sickness was worse this time. It was a while before Savannah could leave the bathroom, but when she did, she found Dane and Neely in the living room.

Neely walked over and gave her a gentle hug. "Congratulations! Christopher told me your wonderful news!"

"I'd hoped to make the announcement in a more dignified way."

Neely waved this aside. "You can't help being sick. And the baby is coming in January?"

Savannah nodded. "I just went to the doctor today, but after I took the home pregnancy test a few days ago I started feeling sick. Maybe it's all in my head. I was never sick with Caroline."

"This is Christopher's baby," Neely reminded her unnecessarily. "Nothing can be simple in his life, and I guess babies are no exception. Do you have some saltine crackers? Sometimes they can help settle an upset stomach."

"We do have some crackers, but I'm afraid if I eat anything I'll throw up again."

Neely stood. "It's worth a try. I'll go find the crackers. You sit here, and don't think about potato salad."

Savannah controlled a gag. "I'll certainly try not to."

Once Neely was gone, Dane whispered, "Do you want to go up to bed? Neely means well, but if she's bothering you . . ."

"She's not bothering me," Savannah assured him. "And maybe the crackers will help."

Savannah rested her head on his shoulder. Neely joined them a few minutes later and placed some crackers on the table beside the couch.

"Just nibble," she advised.

Savannah managed a small bite and then leaned back against Dane.

"Do you want a boy or a girl?" Neely asked.

"I guess it doesn't really matter," Savannah said.

Neely considered this. "It seems like Caroline might like a sister, but it would be nice to have the Dane name continue—so a boy would be good too."

"We'll be happy with either one—as long as it's healthy."

"And I promise to mention only foods that don't have objectionable smells from now on."

Dane told his sister, "The doctor gave her a prescription to help with the nausea that we're going to get filled." He turned to Savannah. "Do you want to go to the hospital in Fredericksburg and let them check you out?"

Savannah shook her head. "This is not an emergency. Pregnant women throw up. It's nothing to worry about."

Dane did not look reassured. "Well, I'm worried."

Neely laughed. "It's going to be a long nine months."

"Eight," Savannah said. "We've already got one under our belt."

Neely settled in a chair near the fireplace.

"Now, tell us why you're really here," Dane said. "Because I know it wasn't just so we could sing happy birthday and make you a cake."

Savannah wasn't at all surprised that Dane doubted his sister's story—he was suspicious of everything.

"Is it Adam?" Dane pressed. "Didn't he finish his commitment to the Peace Corps?"

Neely nodded. "I am concerned about Adam. He is finished with the Peace Corps and was supposed to leave Zimbabwe yesterday morning. That would have put him here in time for my birthday. But he called last night and said there is some kind of tribal war and the borders are closed. No one goes in or out."

Savannah saw Dane's shoulders tense. "Where is he now?"

"He was at the airport when he called me, but they were planning to go to the US Consulate's office and wait there."

"Have you called the consulate's office?"

"Yes," Neely confirmed. "I can't get through. The Peace Corps officials assure me that he is okay, but I don't think they actually know that—they're just assuming."

"First we need to find out where he is." Dane was already strategizing. "If he's not in a secure location, we need to get him to one. Then we can figure out how to get him out of the country."

"And you can do all that?" Neely asked. "For someone in Zimbabwe?"

Dane frowned at her. "Of course."

Savannah said, "That is exactly the kind of thing he does for the army. He's the best in the world."

"That might be an overstatement," Dane murmured.

"I never have really understood all that covert operations stuff," Neely said, "but I'm glad you can help Adam."

"My team is on the way, and as soon as they get here we'll start working on it."

"Thank you," Neely said. "That alleviates my concerns about Adam."

"You're concerned about someone else?" Savannah asked in surprise.

"Yes, I'm worried about Raleigh."

Neely's husband, Raleigh, was the most steady, stable man Savannah had ever met—maybe to the point of boring. So Neely's concern was surprising.

"What's wrong with Raleigh?" Dane asked.

"I don't know for sure," Neely said hesitantly. "He called me this morning from the office and said that representatives from one of the company's biggest clients had come into town unexpectedly, claiming there is money missing from their accounts. They brought some private auditors to go over all the records—the investments, transactions, fees—all that kind of thing."

Dane nodded. "Auditors would want to examine everything if they think money is missing. Raleigh wasn't aware of any irregularities in this big client's accounts?"

"No," Neely replied. "He was shocked and anxious to prove that everything is in order. He said the client didn't want him or his partner to leave the office until the money is accounted for, and he agreed."

"Which meant he had to miss your birthday party," Savannah said.

Neely nodded.

"But you said you're worried about Raleigh," Dane said. "Surely you don't think he had anything to do with it?"

"Oh, no! Raleigh is so honest," Neely prefaced her answer, "but sometimes that can be a bad thing."

"How?" Dane wanted to know.

"It makes him too trusting," Neely said.

"You think someone at his company might have stolen the money?" Savannah asked.

Neely nodded. "I don't think the client would come roaring into town unannounced with private auditors unless they had good reasons to be suspicious."

"Do you suspect anyone in particular?"

"No," Neely said. "But his partner recently went through a messy divorce and has been having a lot of financial problems."

"You think he might have embezzled money from the company?"

"I hate to think that," Neely replied, "but I wouldn't be shocked."

Dane nodded. "When the guys get here, we'll start an investigation on Raleigh's company."

Savannah expected to see all tension leave Neely's face, but instead, her sister-in-law chewed her lower lip and wrung her hands.

"Don't worry, Neely," Savannah said. "If someone is stealing money at Raleigh's company, the team will catch them."

"What else is going on, Neely?" Dane said. "I presume it has something to do with Brooke, since she's the only family member left?"

Neely nodded. "Brooke was actually the first one to back out of my birthday party. She called a couple of days ago and said she was scheduled to work and couldn't get anyone to cover her shift. So she was going to miss the party but said she would come this weekend and see Adam."

"And?" Dane prompted.

"I haven't been able to reach her by phone since then," Neely said. "There may be a good reason, but she's usually good about answering, or at least returning, my calls. She knows I worry."

Family trait, Savannah thought to herself.

"And I wasn't *really* worried until this morning," Neely continued, "when the police came to the house looking for her."

Those few words changed everything, and Savannah could see new anxiety reflected on Dane's face. "Why are the police looking for Brooke?"

Neely spread her hands. "They said they just needed to ask her some questions. According to them, she isn't in any kind of trouble, but they've been watching her apartment. They said her car is parked out front but she hasn't been home for two days. They checked the yogurt shop where she works too. Not only was she not there, but according to the manager she quit a few days ago. She just called and said she wouldn't be back."

"So she'd already quit her job when she told you she had to work?" Dane asked.

Neely nodded. "And that's just not like Brooke. She always tells me the truth, even if she knows it will upset me. The police are still parked in front of my house."

"The police wouldn't invest all those man hours watching her apartment and your house if the questions they want to ask her weren't important," Dane said. "We've got to figure out where she is and why they want to talk to her—fast."

"Actually I think I might know where she is," Neely interrupted, surprising Savannah.

Dane raised his eyebrows. "You *think*?"

"She volunteers for an animal rights group, and they've been planning a big march protesting the treatment of chickens and turkeys on poultry farms.

The group was scheduled to leave from Nashville this morning. They're going to camp near the chicken farms and hold a big rally all week. She was disappointed that the march conflicted with my birthday celebration. So when I found out she'd lied about needing to work, I thought maybe she did it so she could go to the rally."

"Then she doesn't even know that the police are looking for her?" Savannah asked.

"That's my guess," Neely answered, "but I figured it would be best to find her before the police do."

"You're right about that." Dane stood and started toward his new office. "Finding Brooke is an emergency and so is getting Adam secured in Zimbabwe. I'm less worried about Raleigh, but if someone has stolen money from one of his clients, we need to figure out who the thief is before the police get involved. Because whoever it is, they surely covered their tracks."

"And the police might think Raleigh did it?" Savannah guessed.

Dane nodded. "That's what I'm afraid of. I'm going to call my team and tell them to get here fast. And I'll start setting up a three-pronged strategy so we'll be ready to hit the ground running when they get here."

After Dane disappeared into his office, Neely turned to Savannah. "I thought I would feel better when I turned all this over to Christopher," she said. "But he seems so concerned, I wonder if things are even worse than I thought."

"You know your brother is no optimist," Savannah said. "But that's a good thing. It makes him thorough. He'll leave no stone unturned and will solve all three problems at once."

"I hope so." Neely's eyes drifted anxiously to the closed office door.

To distract Neely, Savannah said, "So Adam likes Africa?"

Neely nodded. "He *loves* Africa. I don't know if he'll ever come home to stay. He's starting a job with the Church there in a few weeks—a job he hopes will be permanent."

"It's wonderful that he's so dedicated to helping others," Savannah observed, "but I know you miss him."

"I do." Neely reached up to wipe a tear from her cheek. "And it's hard having him so far away. I worry about him constantly."

Realizing that this topic was not going to cheer Neely up, Savannah abandoned this line of questioning and broached another subject. "And Brooke's still in school?"

"And volunteering for causes," Neely replied. "We don't see much of her."

"Didn't she transfer to Juilliard?"

"Just for one semester," Neely said. "She's back at Vanderbilt and will graduate next May. She's already applying to master's programs."

"She's a smart girl."

"She worries me," Neely confided. "Not just this current situation—whatever it is—but her judgment in general. She *is* smart and in some ways seems to know exactly what she wants and what she believes in. But her relationship with that awful ex-boyfriend, Rex, makes me wonder if she's as sensible as she seems."

"Whatever happened to him?"

"All Brooke told us was that he moved to California. We assume that she wasn't invited to go with him. That's when she signed up for the semester at Juilliard. She claimed it was the opportunity of a lifetime to study with some of the best pianists in the world, but it was very sudden and I think she just wanted to get away from everything that reminded her of Rex."

"Dane says she's extremely talented musically," Savannah said. "So I'm sure the semester at Juilliard wasn't a waste."

"She said it was six months she'll never forget," Neely acknowledged. "But I don't think she would have even considered going to New York if Rex had still been around."

"You didn't like him?"

Neely shook her head. "I despised him and the effect he had on Brooke. If I never see him again, it will be too soon."

This was a stronger reaction than Savannah was expecting. "Then thankfully it didn't work out and he's gone."

"I'm sorry that Brooke had to go through a painful breakup, but yes, I'm very glad that Rex is out of her life and ours. I wish Brooke could feel that way too. She still has a sad look in her eyes." Neely cleared her throat. "But enough about my family. Is Caroline enjoying public school?"

Savannah nodded. "She loves it."

"Has Christopher stopped sitting outside the school every day?"

"Yes, but one of Hack's men is there whenever Caroline is. At first it seemed excessive, but it's better to be safe than sorry. I've learned that the hard way."

"So now that he's been relieved of guard duty, my brother works for your foundation?"

"He does some work at the Child Advocacy Center," Savannah confirmed. "And he takes an occasional search and rescue case from the army."

"He seems happy."

"It's been a long time coming, but at the moment, life is good."

"You and Christopher have both had your share of hard times," Neely said. "You deserve some happiness."

Dane walked back into the living room. He stopped behind the couch where Savannah was seated and put a hand on her shoulder. She knew he was worried about her. She pressed her cheek against his hand in silent reassurance.

"I put a call into General Steele to find out what we can do about Adam," he told them, "and there are no outstanding warrants on Brooke."

Neely looked horrified. "You thought there might be a warrant for her arrest? Even though the police said she's not in trouble?"

"Sometimes the police are selective in the information they give mothers of suspects," he replied. "But no warrants is good. There are also no accident reports on her."

"That's a relief," Neely said.

Savannah gave her an encouraging smile.

Dane said, "My team members should be here soon, and I told them they'll be staying for a couple of days. Hack located Brooke's phone using GPS. It's still at her apartment. She probably left it behind, but Hack's got some guys on the way there to check it out just to be sure."

"Hack has guys in Nashville?" Neely asked.

"Hack has guys everywhere," Savannah told her sister-in-law.

Neely looked at Dane. "So will you send some of your men to the march to look for Brooke?"

Dane nodded. "And we'll check with the Nashville police to find out why they want to talk to Brooke."

"Do you want the names of the policemen who came to the house this morning so you can work together?"

Dane shook his head. "We'll keep our investigation separate from the police's until we find Brooke and she tells us what's going on. Then we'll decide how much information to share with them. Our contact today will be just to get information *from* them."

"Does Brooke need a lawyer?" Neely's voice was full of dread.

"Not yet," Dane replied. "Steamer just passed the bar exam, so we have access to legal advice within the team. If we decide she needs counsel, I'll let you know."

Neely wrung her hands. "This is starting to sound very serious."

"Legal advice is a precaution, not an admission of guilt." Dane checked his watch. "The guys should be here any minute."

As if on cue, the alarm system reported that a car was approaching. On the monitors they could see Hack pull up and park in the back. A few seconds later, he walked through the door.

Dane stood to greet Hack. "Where are the rest of the guys?"

"I gave them the pizza assignment," he replied. "They should be here soon."

Caroline came running down the stairs. "Hack!" she cried. "I'll get the fishing poles!"

"Give Hack a minute to get settled," Savannah requested on Hack's behalf.

Hack put his duffle bag on the floor by the door. "I'm settled." He grinned, exposing his gold tooth.

"Just until the others get here." Dane gave limited permission to the fishers. "Then I'll need Hack to work."

"Fishing *is* work—it's catching food." Caroline took hold of Hack's ham-sized hand and pulled him toward the kitchen. "Come on, we have to hurry!"

"And I'll have my laptop with me on the dock," Hack said. "I can work and fish at the same time."

After they left, Neely stood. "I'll go crazy if I don't keep busy. Maybe I could make frosting for the cake. Hopefully it won't make you nauseous."

"Don't waste your time worrying about that," Savannah said. "Everything makes me nauseous."

Neely gave her a sympathetic look as she went into the kitchen. Dane returned to the couch, but Savannah shook her head. "Go back to finding Brooke and helping Adam get out of Africa and proving that Raleigh didn't steal any money," she told him. "I'll be fine."

"What if you get sick again?"

"I will get sick again," Savannah predicted. "But I can find my own way to the bathroom."

He grimaced. "Well, call me if you need me."

"I will," she promised, closing her eyes. She prayed it would be a while before her stomach rejected the crackers Neely had given her.

Savannah dozed but woke up suddenly when Caroline came in and announced, "We caught three fish! Then Dad said we had to stop, and Hack said that was probably good because the mosquitoes were about to eat us alive."

Savannah sat up straight and stretched. "You should have put on insect repellent."

Caroline scratched a red welt on her arm. "Naw, Hack says that's for sissies."

Savannah made a mental note to talk to Hack about diseases carried by mosquitoes.

"Hack is cleaning our fish, and Aunt Neely said she would fry them for dinner."

"Wow," Savannah replied, trying not to gag at just the thought.

There was a commotion by the door. Savannah turned to look as Steamer burst in with his usual fanfare. He was very tan, as always, and his jet black hair was smoothed back in his signature little ponytail at the back of his head. He was wearing designer jeans, a fluorescent orange polo shirt, and a gallon of pungent aftershave.

"I'm here, baby! Let the party begin!" he declared.

Hack walked in from the kitchen. "We smelled you before we saw you."

"It's very expensive French cologne," Steamer informed him. "Not that I'd expect a Neanderthal like you to appreciate the finer things."

Dane came out of his office and fingered the fabric of Steamer's brightly colored shirt. "You working for a highway construction crew now?"

"Very funny. This is the year's most stylish color," Steamer claimed. "If you don't want to be left out in the fashion-cold you'd better buy you a shirt just like this."

Dane shook his head. "I don't care that much about fashion."

Steamer took one look at Caroline and whistled. "Savannah, this kid is gigantic! What have you been feeding her? Magic growing beans?"

Caroline giggled.

Steamer studied Savannah for a few seconds. Then he said, "You, on the other hand, look terrible."

"You shouldn't say people look terrible!" Caroline objected with a smile. "It's rude!"

"No offense," Steamer replied, "but you know us folks from Vegas got to call it like we see it."

Savannah said, "I'm not offended. I've been . . . sick."

"Mom's having a baby!" Caroline announced. "After Christmas."

"Congratulations!" Steamer said.

"And you didn't tell me?!" Hack thundered.

"We were going to tell the whole team at the same time," Dane said.

"Oops!" Caroline covered her mouth but did not look repentant.

"I have a special recipe that is guaranteed to alleviate nausea," Steamer claimed.

Dane raised an eyebrow. "Guaranteed?"

Steamer nodded. "It works every time. You mix lemon-lime Gatorade and Sprite—equal parts. I call my invention Spriteorade. I considered Gatorite, but that just didn't roll off the tongue as nicely."

"That is not an invention, and you can't name it!" Hack scoffed. "You haven't created anything. You're just mixing together two drinks that other people invented."

"There are precedents!" Steamer claimed. "Bleach in household cleaners, Oreos in ice cream, Reese's cups! All I've got to do is get the involved parties together and cut them in on the action without stepping on any copyrights or patents. And now that I'm a lawyer, well, that's a piece of cake. I'll probably make millions. "

"I hope you do," Savannah encouraged. "And we'll be able to say we knew you when."

Steamer gave her an approving smile. "You can do my infomercials!"

"I can't think of anything I would hate more," Dane said without a hint of a smile.

"Before we start marketing this magic elixir, I'd better try it," Savannah told him. "If it can stop me from throwing up, it should help anyone."

"Sip it and your sick days are over, baby!"

Caroline pulled on Steamer's arm. "Will you help me set up my train tracks?"

Steamer smiled. "I'd love to, but there is a crisis and you know everyone is counting on me to save the day, as usual."

Hack growled.

Steamer ignored him. "But I brought you something." He reached into his bag and pulled out a rectangular box. "It's another switching station."

She took the box from his hand with near reverence. "Now we can split the tracks into two different routes!"

"I can't thank you enough," Savannah murmured. "Just what I need, more things to trip over."

"Just *one* more thing," Steamer said with a grin. "And you gotta admit another switching station will be so cool."

"It will be pretty cool," Savannah acknowledged.

Then Steamer saw Neely and said, "Hello!"

"Hi," she returned.

"So you're the reason we're getting to extend our time together?"

"I am," Neely said. "I'm grateful for your help, and to show my appreciation I'm going to cook for the team."

"Well, we all appreciate that—especially Hack," Steamer said with a glance at the big man. "Be sure and make a *lot* of food."

Hack growled again.

There was a knock on the door. Dane pulled it open to admit Doc and Owl. They were each carrying three pizza boxes.

"You think you got enough?" Dane asked.

"Hack placed the order," Doc replied.

"Enough said!" Steamer quipped with a smile.

Caroline welcomed them both with a hug. Doc accepted the exuberant affection patiently, juggling the pizza boxes to keep from dropping them. Owl allowed Caroline's hug but seemed embarrassed by the attention.

"Mom's having a baby!" Caroline announced. "And I'm thinking of two names in case we have twins!"

Doc's eyes widened. "That is exciting news!"

"We're only planning on one baby," Savannah assured him. "But Caroline does have to think of two names since we don't know if it will be a boy or a girl."

"Congratulations," Owl added awkwardly.

Savannah always felt bad for Owl. He was quiet and reserved, which kept him separate from some of the natural camaraderie that existed between the other men. She didn't know him as well as the others, but she could tell he was uncomfortable around her. She wanted to make him feel welcome, but she was too sick.

Steamer immediately started teasing him. "Even Owl came to help out! I guess the president was able to do without his best pilot for a few more days?"

Caroline gasped. "Do you really fly the president in your plane?"

"Well," Owl began carefully, "actually the plane is owned by the United States of America. And I can't tell you if I fly the president. It would be a breach of national security."

"Wow." Caroline was sufficiently impressed.

"Enough of this," Dane said. To Caroline he added, "Steamer has some work to do right now. He can help you with the trains later."

Caroline's disappointment was obvious. "Does everybody have to help you work?"

"Yes. Everybody that is part of my team," he confirmed.

"I'll work fast so we can play with trains sooner," Steamer promised.

"Go get a piece of pizza," Dane told Caroline. "I need Steamer to focus."

"Hurry!" Caroline whispered to Steamer. Then she ran into the kitchen.

CHAPTER TWO

ONCE CAROLINE WAS GONE, STEAMER pulled an iPad out of his backpack and set it on the coffee table. A miniature view of a courtroom appeared on the small screen. "I'm following a trial; hope you don't mind."

"And what if we do?" Hack asked.

"Then I hate it, but I'm a lawyer now and I've got to keep up with current legal events."

Hack scowled.

Neely said, "I heard that you just passed the bar. Congratulations."

"Yeah, when the real estate market in Vegas started going bad, I figured I'd better hedge my bets, so I enrolled in an online program."

Hack shook his head. "As much as I love computers, even *I* think there are some things that should be taught in person—like how to be a doctor or a lawyer." He looked at Dane. "I don't accept his online credentials, and I won't trust a legal word he says."

"He couldn't have passed the bar exam if he didn't learn what he needed to know," Dane pointed out.

Hack wouldn't relent. "His legal skills are still questionable."

"Come on, Hack," Steamer cajoled. "If you let me be your lawyer, I'll give you a discount."

Hack frowned. "I've already got plenty of lawyers, and all of them went to real law schools."

Dane interrupted, moving them toward the kitchen. "We've got to get our initial meeting going."

"What about the pizza?" Hack asked.

"We'll eat while we talk," Dane decided. Then everyone stood and walked into the kitchen.

Savannah trailed behind the others. She wanted to hear the discussion but wasn't sure she could stand to be near the food. Everyone else settled around the table. Savannah chose to pull a chair over by the window, as far as possible from the smells.

Caroline was finishing her pizza as the oven timer went off. With Neely's supervision, the child removed the cake from the oven. Then she waved to the team and ran upstairs to play with her trains.

Steamer opened one of the boxes, "I'm starving, and this pizza smells delicious. The cake too."

"Christopher and Caroline made the cake," Neely told them.

"I'm less excited about eating it now," Steamer admitted.

Neely laughed. "I made the frosting."

"We appreciate that," Doc said.

"That might make it edible," Steamer agreed hesitantly. "Thanks."

"It's the least I could do," Neely replied.

Steamer winked. "If you need any help with meals, just let us know. We all like to be on good terms with the cook. Especially Hack."

Dane looked cross. "Steamer, quit aggravating Hack. I need him concentrating on our operation instead of thinking about ways to kill you."

Steamer's expression immediately became serious, "Operation? So this is official?"

Dane nodded. "Fix your plates and we'll talk."

Once all the men were eating, Dane began the meeting. "I think everyone knows my sister, Neely. If not, you can now consider yourself introduced. She lives in Nashville, and she's been married to the same man for twenty-five years. Her husband, Raleigh, owns his own investment firm. She has a son, Adam, who has been working for the Peace Corps in Zimbabwe. Her daughter, Brooke, is a music major at Vanderbilt."

"Who's in trouble?" Steamer asked as he picked up a piece of pizza.

"All of them," Dane responded.

Hack frowned. "Seriously?"

"I wouldn't joke about something like that," Dane assured him. "Adam is stuck in Zimbabwe because a tribal war has closed the borders and airports. Doc, I want you to work with General Steele on this. We want Adam in a secure location while we arrange to get him out."

Doc nodded.

"Neely's husband might have some trouble at work," Dane continued. "I'll handle that. And then there's Brooke, who is missing. She told her mother that she couldn't come home because she had to work, but this morning Neely got a visit from the Nashville PD. They claim they've been watching Brooke's apartment for two days and she hasn't been home during all that time. And apparently she quit her job suddenly, so that's not the real reason she couldn't come to the party. There's a squad car parked in front of Neely's house, waiting to see if Brooke will go there."

"Is she hiding from the police?" Hack asked.

"Maybe," Dane said slowly. "Or she might not even know they're looking for her."

"Why are they looking for her?" Steamer asked.

"We don't know that either," Dane said.

"Any reason to think she's in danger?" Owl wanted to know.

"Not that we know of," Dane said.

"What steps have you taken so far?" Owl asked.

"Using her phone's GPS, we've determined the phone is at her apartment," Hack said. "But I sent a couple of guys over there and the apartment's empty."

"Any signs of struggle?" Dane asked.

Savannah waited tensely for the answer.

Hack shook his head. "No. They said everything is neat as a pin."

Savannah could see the relief reflected on Dane's face.

"So now what?" Steamer asked.

"First we need to move our command center to Neely's house so we can be near Raleigh's office, Brooke's apartment, and the Nashville PD." Dane turned to Savannah. "If you don't feel well enough to make the trip, you and I can stay here and Hack can run the operation."

Neely needed Dane's help, and Savannah couldn't let a little morning sickness stand in the way. "Once I get my prescription filled I should be fine."

Dane looked worried, but he nodded. "Hack, I need you to secure the area around Neely's house before we get there. See if anyone else is watching it, set up a computer room—all the regular stuff. And snipers in her trees."

"Snipers?" Neely repeated with obvious alarm. "My neighbors are already upset about the police car outside. I don't know what they'll do when they find out about the snipers. They'll probably report us to the homeowners' association."

Steamer said, "It's standard operating procedure."

"Snipers in trees are *standard?*" Neely asked incredulously.

Dane nodded. "My team is always thorough, and the snipers provide more than firepower should that even become necessary. They're lookouts who will see if anyone approaches the house."

"And look on the bright side," Steamer added. "With police officers *and* Hack's people guarding your house, you'll be the safest woman in the world!"

"I'll try to consider that a good thing," she murmured.

Dane reclaimed control of the discussion. "We want to find Brooke before the police do, and we have reason to believe that she's participating in a march protesting the treatment of poultry. So I need two volunteers to join a chicken march. Steam and Owl, are you up for that assignment?"

The two "volunteers" exchanged a glance.

"Sure," Owl said after a brief pause.

"A chicken march?" Steamer inquired with obvious distaste. "How will a bunch of people marching help mistreated chickens?"

Neely explained, "They walked from Nashville to a large chicken farm in the country. They plan to hold rallies all week to draw a lot of media attention, which should translate into a public outcry."

"It seems like there would be an easier way," Steamer muttered.

Hack gave him an evil grin. "You're just afraid you'll get your fancy shoes dusty."

Steamer looked down at his loafers with concern. "These are handmade from Italian leather!"

"You'll need to wear something less noticeable," Dane said. "There's a thrift store near the airport in Fredericksburg. Stop there and buy some old stuff."

Steamer paled. "You want me to buy shoes from a thrift store?"

Hack laughed. "I'm so glad you volunteered for the chicken march!"

Doc smiled, and even Owl seemed less solemn than usual.

"They're camping, so you'll also need to get some tents," Dane said.

Steamer looked distraught. "We're going to have to camp with them overnight?"

"Right beside a chicken farm," Hack was pleased to remind Steamer. "And I'll bet it smells terrible."

"You don't have to spend the night if you find Brooke fast," Dane said. "But the march involves thousands of people, so be prepared just in case. I've got two private planes waiting at the airport in Fredericksburg. You guys go now. I want Owl and Steamer at that march as soon as possible. And guys, Hack will be in charge until I get to Nashville."

"And my first order as team leader is to outlaw senseless legal jargon," Hack said.

"I'm so glad you specified 'senseless,'" Steamer replied. "I'll take that under . . . *advisement.*"

Hack turned to Dane. "I may kill him before you get to Nashville."

"Try to restrain yourself," Dane requested without a trace of humor. "We're already shorthanded."

"When will you be coming?" Hack wanted to know.

"It all depends on how Savannah is feeling, but hopefully in a few hours."

Steamer looked unhappy, and Savannah tried to cheer him up. "The chicken march might be fun."

"Fun?" Steamer repeated. "I can smell the chickens already."

"I'm sorry about the march and the primitive conditions," Neely apologized. "Brooke did say they were setting up portable bathrooms and outdoor showers for the campers."

Steamer groaned.

"I'm tempted to volunteer to go on the march myself just to see you as an unhappy camper." Hack was thoroughly enjoying Steamer's misery.

"Why can't Doc go camping with Owl?" Steamer asked. "I'll work with the general on getting your nephew out of Africa."

Dane held up his hand. "In addition to working on Adam's removal from Zimbabwe, Doc is going to take Caroline to her grandparents in Colorado." He looked at Savannah. "If that's okay with you?"

The proposal seemed extreme to Savannah. "Why?"

"A combination of reasons," he replied. "You're not feeling a hundred percent. The guys are great soldiers but probably not the best influences on a six-year-old girl. And besides, they'll be busy and I don't want to constantly be telling her they can't play. And last—and most important—is security."

Savannah frowned. "But Hack's going to secure Neely's house before we get there. He'll have snipers in the trees. I don't think even a mountain in Colorado is safer than that."

"I'm not just worried about someone from outside getting in. I'm worried about Caroline falling down the stairs or getting hurt while we're not watching her. Our house is compact; Neely's is not. I like being able to find her easily."

"I just follow the train tracks on the floor," Savannah said.

"You know what I mean."

She nodded. "I do. And I'm fine with sending her to Wes's parents. She'll be happy about it, and so will they."

He looked relieved. "If you'll call the McLaughlins, I'll arrange transportation."

"How soon?"

"Now."

Savannah wasn't surprised. She'd known Dane long enough to realize that when he decided safety was an issue, he acted quickly.

She called for Caroline, and when the child rushed into the kitchen, Savannah told the girl, "I've got some exciting news."

Caroline's eyes lit up. "What?"

"You're going to visit your grandparents in Colorado for a few days."

The happiness left her little face, and she cut her eyes at Dane. "What's wrong?"

Savannah reassured her, "Nothing's wrong. Aunt Neely needs Daddy's help, so he and I are going to Nashville and he's nervous about you being in a strange house with a lot of rooms and stairs. You know how he is."

Caroline relaxed a little. "He worries."

"And your grandparents have been asking for you to visit."

Caroline nodded. "I know. You're sure it's not because someone's going to shoot at you?"

"Nobody is going to shoot at us," Savannah said and hoped it was true.

"Doc is going with you," Dane said.

Doc and Caroline exchanged a smile.

"Run upstairs and start packing," Savannah instructed. "You're leaving right away."

"Neely, will you help Caroline pack?" Dane requested.

"Of course." Neely finished frosting the cake and wiped her hands on a dish towel. Then she took Caroline upstairs.

Once they were gone, Savannah said, "Thanks, Doc."

He nodded. "I got the best assignment of all."

Dane asked, "Hack, the pilot will drop Steamer and Owl at an airstrip near the chicken march and then take you on to Nashville. After that, he'll fly Doc and Caroline to Colorado. Do you have a guy who can copilot from Nashville to Colorado and provide additional security?"

"I do," Hack said. "I'll arrange for him to meet us at the Nashville airport."

Dane turned to Doc. "Report regularly. Let me know what you find out about Adam and your plan for getting him out."

"I will," Doc promised.

"Steam, Owl, once you join the march, look for Brooke, but be careful not to scare her off. If she's there and we lose her, we might not be able to locate her again."

"What if she's not at the march?" Steamer asked.

"If you search the entire crowd and don't find her, let me know so we can make a new plan."

"Can we eat some of the cake before we go?" Hack asked.

Dane nodded. "But remember that I made it, so you're eating at your own risk."

"I'm a brave man," Hack said as he cut a piece of the cake.

***

When Neely and Caroline returned, each of them was holding a suitcase.

"Two suitcases?" Dane questioned. "You're just going to be gone for a couple of days."

"One has clothes, and the other is for my trains!" Caroline explained.

Savannah smiled. "Of course."

There were hugs all around.

As Hack was preparing to leave, Dane said, "Hack, after the driver drops you all off at the airport, will you have him stop by the drugstore and fill Savannah's prescription?"

"And to get Sprite and Gatorade," Steamer added. "Make sure it's lemon-lime. That's the only flavor that comes with a guarantee."

Hack rolled his eyes. "Are you sure you want to follow his advice?"

Dane nodded. "We're willing to try anything to help Savannah feel better."

Hack didn't argue.

After the guys and Caroline left, Neely started cleaning the kitchen while Savannah and Dane went upstairs to pack. Dane did most of the packing for both of them while Savannah concentrated on not throwing up. Their suitcases were packed and sitting by the front door—and Savannah was coming out of the bathroom after having lost her most recent battle against the nausea—when Hack's driver returned. He handed Dane the antinausea medication, several bottles of lemon-lime Gatorade in assorted sizes, and a six-pack of Sprite.

"I wasn't sure what you wanted, so I got one of everything they had," he explained.

Savannah thanked him as Dane carried the Gatorade and Sprite to the kitchen. Dane arranged the bottles, along with measuring cups and a glass pitcher, like a mini-laboratory on the counter. Then he carefully mixed up a batch of Steamer's Spriteorade and poured it into the various-sized bottles. Finally he put one of the bottles in front of Savannah, along with the small prescription bottle.

Savannah swallowed a pill and then tasted the Sprite-Gatorade mixture. "Not bad," she decided, taking another sip. "Maybe it's all in my head, but I think I feel better."

Dane gave her a small smile. "As long as you're feeling better, I don't care if it's in your head. Now why don't you go lie down on the couch and give it a chance to work."

"If I lie down, I'll fall asleep," Savannah predicted.

"That's okay," Dane assured her.

"Maybe when you wake up you'll be a new woman," Neely added.

Dane stroked her cheek. "I just want you back to your regular old self."

Savannah smiled as she settled on the couch. "That's a more attainable goal."

Two hours later they climbed into their car and headed for the airport in Fredericksburg, with Savannah clutching a small bottle of Spriteorade in her hands.

***

Brooke stood in line with the rest of the marchers to get a brown bag dinner. Her body was exhausted after an entire day of walking in the sun. Her nerves were frazzled from constantly checking over her shoulder, always on the lookout. She didn't even want any food but knew she had to eat to keep up her strength. So she shuffled forward until she reached the front of the line. A volunteer handed her a brown bag and a bottle of water.

She took her meal to her little tent. She had loosely attached herself to a group of protesters she knew. They were really Rex's friends, not hers. But they tolerated her presence, and being with a group made her feel a little less vulnerable. The group had chosen to set up their tents on the side of a hill overlooking the main camp. So while sitting on her sleeping bag, she ate the sandwich from her brown bag and surveyed the scene below through the tent door.

There were two lines of portable toilets, one on each side of the large field where the marchers were camping. Outdoor showers, surrounded by blue plastic tarps, were set up as well. With thousands of people milling around, privacy would be minimal, so Brooke determined to deal with being dirty for another day.

A band was warming up in the center of camp. Tonight there would be speeches and dancing and drinking. It was just the kind of chaotic environment where a girl could go unnoticed. Just the kind of place where she needed to be.

Beyond the camp she could see the poultry farms—the reason for the march. She shuddered, thinking about the poor chickens huddled inside the coops, awaiting their fate. She felt an unhappy kinship with the miserable, defenseless animals.

She had just taken a bite out of the oatmeal cookie from the brown bag when she saw the man. He was walking casually through the crowd, but his eyes were searching. He was dressed right but seemed wrong—like an undercover cop trying to fit in with a bunch of chicken protestors. The bite of cookie in her mouth turned to dust. Brooke took several deep breaths to calm herself. Maybe he was there at the request of the march organizers to keep the peace. Or maybe he was looking for her.

She stood and walked down into the small forest that separated the campers from the chicken farms. Safely hidden from view by a large tree, she studied the man more closely. He had a deep tan, and his dark black hair was pulled into a little ponytail at the back of his head. He looked vaguely familiar, and she was trying to place him when she noticed his shoes—Gucci loafers. And then she knew. He was one of the men who worked for her uncle. And she was certain he had been sent to find her.

Brooke ducked further behind the tree as he walked by. She figured the only way to keep him from seeing her was to stay behind him. She pulled her hat down and stepped out of the trees, following the man with the expensive shoes. She walked fast to keep up and was so focused on him that she didn't see the man who walked directly into her path until they bumped into each other—hard.

Brooke stumbled, but the man reached out and caught her before she hit the ground. She was grateful until his other hand snaked around and covered her mouth while he dragged her into the woods. Helpless to escape, Brooke felt defeat and fear cascade over her.

CHAPTER THREE

BROOKE FOUGHT WILDLY, BUT HER captor held her tight as he dragged her deeper into the woods. She couldn't see what he looked like, but she knew that he was tall and strong. When they were far enough away from the camp that the band's music was just a distant hum, he stopped and turned her around.

With her arms pinned to her sides and his hand over her mouth, Brooke tried to express her fury with her eyes. She judged him to be in his mid to late twenties. He had short brown hair and gray eyes that were regarding her steadily. His facial features were sharp but not unattractive. Slowly he removed his hand from her mouth, and she began to hope that he didn't intend to kill her.

"Are you a policeman?" she rasped.

He shook his head. "I'm a soldier."

She squinted at him. "A soldier . . ." Then she felt weak with relief. "You work for my uncle too! Your name is Bird or Hawk or Eagle or something!"

"Owl," he provided. "Why were you following Steamer?"

"Is that the man with the expensive shoes?"

Owl nodded.

"I was just walking behind him so he wouldn't see me," Brooke said. "I didn't think about my uncle sending backup."

Owl's already solemn expression became more so. "He sent both of us here to find you and bring you back to your mother's house. Some Nashville police officers came looking for you this morning, and your mother's worried, especially since you left your phone in your apartment, which the police have been watching."

Brooke was actually relieved that it was just the police who had visited her mother. But she acted indignant. "I haven't done anything wrong, so I'm not going to talk to them."

Owl looked confused. "But if you haven't done anything wrong, talking to them is the logical thing to do so they'll quit bothering you and your mother."

She shook her head. "I'm going to stay here at this chicken march where they can't find me. Will you tell my uncle that for me, please?"

"But I'm supposed to bring you back. Your mother is worried," he reiterated.

Brooke decided it would be best to speak to him in a commanding tone. "Call my uncle. Once you get him on the phone, I'll tell you what to say."

Slowly, Owl reached into his backpack and pulled out his phone.

She used this opportunity to ease away from him.

"Don't you want to tell him yourself?"

"I can't do that." She acted as if this was the most ridiculous suggestion. "Then if the police question him, he couldn't honestly say he hadn't talked to me."

Owl kept his eyes on her as he placed the call.

She continued to back away, feeling her way cautiously over the uneven ground. She heard him explain the situation. After a moment, he moved the phone slightly away from his ear and asked her, "What else do you want me to tell your uncle?"

"Tell him that I didn't do anything wrong but that if I talk to the police they might think I did." She waited for Owl to relay this information, and then she continued. "Tell him I've considered the situation carefully and have decided that the best course of action is for me to hide out for a few days."

Owl repeated this to her uncle.

"Tell him I need him to trust me," she said.

Slowly he delivered the message.

She took another step back and determined that she was now out of his grabbing range. "And last of all, tell him if he won't respect my wishes, I'll scream rape and have you thrown in jail."

She was poised to run, but Owl didn't try to recapture her. Instead, he told her uncle every word she'd said, as calmly as if he'd been giving a weather report. Then he added, "I'm willing to bring her in against her will if that's what you want me to do, sir. What are my orders?"

She held her breath, hoping her uncle wouldn't force the issue—or at least want to keep his soldier out of jail.

After a few seconds, Owl ended the call and put the phone in his pocket. Then he nodded. "Your uncle says you can stay."

She smiled. "Good. It was nice meeting you." She turned and walked back toward the camp. When she reached the edge of the clearing, she expected him to veer off in search of the fancy-shoe guy and then head back home to her uncle. But instead, he continued to follow her. Turning to face him, she asked, "What are you doing?"

"Protecting you," he replied.

"I don't need your protection!" she hissed, exasperated. "I need you to leave me alone!"

"Your uncle agreed to let you stay here, as long as I stay too."

"I didn't agree to that!" Brooke protested.

"I don't need your permission to go on this march," he replied.

She knew she had been bested, and it made her angry. "I'll tell the organizers that you aren't really a sympathizer!"

His eyes scanned the area around them. "And I'll tell them the police are looking for you."

Realizing they were at a stalemate, she decided to give in, at least until she could come up with a way to get rid of him. "Okay, you can guard me. But don't make it obvious."

He stepped up beside her. "So is there anything else you can tell me about your . . . situation?" Owl asked. "It will help me protect you better if I know what I'm dealing with."

She pursed her lips. "The police want me to testify in a trial, but I don't want to. And I don't have to—unless they serve me with a subpoena. That's why I'm hiding."

He frowned. "And why won't you testify?"

"Because if I do, they'll twist my words and I'll end up in trouble—even though I'm innocent."

He was still frowning. "It sounds like you should get a good lawyer."

"I don't need a lawyer. I just need to stay out of sight for a few days. Then it will all be over."

He shrugged. "That seems like the hard way to me, but if that's what you want to do . . ."

"What I want to do is go to my campsite, and I hope you have a tent because I don't intend to share mine," she told him. Then she started walking back toward the hillside, with her unwelcome bodyguard following close behind.

***

Apparently drowsiness was a side effect of the antinausea medicine because Savannah couldn't keep her eyes open. She slept during the short drive to the airport in Fredericksburg and fell asleep almost as soon as she got on the small plane. She woke up as they began their descent into Nashville. Gingerly she sat up and waited for a wave of nausea, but it didn't come.

"Are you okay?" Dane asked her from the copilot's seat.

She nodded. "I don't know if it's the Gatorade and Sprite mixture or the medicine or the combination of both, but I'm pretty much normal."

He gave her a relieved smile. "I'm glad. And we just need to make sure we never run out of either one."

Savannah yawned. "Have you heard from Doc?"

"He reports in regularly. Caroline is fine."

"What about Brooke?"

"Owl found her."

Savannah was surprised and relieved. "Well! That is very good news. Are they going to meet us at Neely's house?"

Dane shook his head. "No, Brooke wants to stay at the march, so Owl is going to stay there with her."

"Why doesn't she want to go home?" Savannah asked.

"Apparently she knows something that she doesn't want to share with the police. She asked me to trust her, so that's what I'm going to do—even if it gives me an ulcer."

Savannah was surprised but pleased. "And what made you decide to generously allow Brooke some freedom?"

"I believe in freedom," he claimed. Then he gave her a quick smile. "Within reason."

In front of the airport, one of Hack's men was waiting for them in a dark van with tinted windows. It was a short drive to Neely's neighborhood, a gated community with a swimming pool and golf course.

Savannah had never been there before, and she was very impressed. "This is lovely," she said as they approached Neely's beautiful Georgian-style home.

"Thank you," Neely said.

The garage door opened like magic, and Savannah laughed. "Hack must have seen us coming."

Dane was scowling at the police car parked at the curb. "He wants to get us away from prying eyes as quickly as possible."

Savannah doubted that anyone could see through the van's tinted windows, but she did feel a little better when the garage door closed behind them. They walked into the kitchen, where Steamer and Hack were waiting.

"I thought you were at the chicken march," Savannah said to Steamer in surprise.

Steamer grinned. "Owl sent me back—said he didn't need me. And you can be sure I didn't argue. I got out of there quick, before he could change his mind!"

"Lucky you," Savannah said.

Steamer winked. "So how is the Spriteorade working for you?"

"It's working great." Savannah took another sip. "Maybe you really should market this stuff."

"I told you it was guaranteed!" Then he turned to Neely. "And I love your house!"

Dane rolled his eyes, but Neely smiled. "Thanks."

"Seriously, it is the most beautiful place I've seen lately," Steamer continued. "You have a real gift for interior design. Would you consider coming to work for me in Vegas? With your help I might actually be able to sell a couple of the houses I'm listing!"

"I'm flattered, but that's too long of a commute from Nashville."

Steamer laughed. "I guess you're right. But you know how to make a house look exactly the way it should. It's spotlessly clean and perfectly organized and tastefully welcoming. The only thing I'd change is that floral curtain over the sink in the kitchen. I think a Roman shade in a nice copper tone would be better. Sleek without calling attention away from the more important features of the room."

Neely gasped. "You're right. I've wanted to make a change there but couldn't figure out what to do."

Dane interrupted at this point. "Let's cut the decorating talk. We're running an operation here."

"Sorry," Steamer said.

"I promise not to discuss my house or curtains anymore," Neely vowed. "But Steamer obviously has good taste—he likes mine."

They heard Hack groan. "Please don't encourage him, Neely!"

Dane cleared his throat. "Everybody sit down and report."

They all took seats around the kitchen table. Anxious to avoid being sick again, Savannah tried not to think about food and sipped Spriteorade double-time.

"May I say something?" Neely asked.

Dane nodded his permission.

"I just want to thank all of you for coming to help my family."

"They are all on the McLaughlin Foundation payroll," Dane reminded her. "It's their job to come whenever I call them."

She smiled. "I know, but I'm still thankful."

"We're glad to help," Hack assured her.

"Saving people is what we do," Steamer contributed, "being military heroes and all."

"Enough of the mushy stuff," Hack declared.

"Before we give our reports, I have an important matter of team business that I'd like to discuss," Steamer said.

Dane frowned. "What kind of team business?"

"It better not have anything to do with curtains," Hack warned.

Steamer ignored him. "Since Neely is a part of our team, I think she needs a nickname."

Hack demanded, "That's important business?"

"I don't want Neely to feel left out," Steamer defended himself.

"We can use the one she had as a child," Dane suggested. "Crybaby."

"Nobody called me that but you!" Neely objected. "And I always hated it."

"Since she's our cook we could call her Chuck-Wagon," Steamer suggested.

"I'd rather be Crybaby," Neely muttered.

"Ladyfinger?" Steamer proposed. "Nightingale?"

"Can't you just call me Neely since I'm only a temporary member of the team?"

"It doesn't seem right," Steamer sounded hesitant.

"Savannah doesn't have a nickname," Neely pointed out.

"We'll just call you Neely," Dane decreed. "Let's quit wasting time with this and get back to business. Hack, has Owl checked in?"

"Every hour on the hour," Hack replied.

Neely cleared her throat and then asked, "So Steamer, did Brooke look okay?"

"I never actually saw her," Steamer admitted. "She spotted me and hid. My shoes gave me away."

Dane frowned. "I thought I told you to buy old shoes at a thrift store."

"I just couldn't do it, sir," Steamer replied. "Wearing someone else's discarded shoes is asking for a toe fungus."

"You can't compromise an operation over shoes," Dane reprimanded.

"Even you should have known better than to show up at a chicken march wearing Gucci loafers," Hack contributed with obvious disdain.

"Everyone makes mistakes," Steamer said. "Even you, big guy."

"Back to Brooke," Dane redirected them again. "So you never saw her, but she saw you?"

Steamer looked embarrassed. "Yes, sir. Owl said she was following me when he intercepted her."

"How long are we going to wait before we tell him to bring her home—whether or not she wants to come?" Hack asked.

Dane considered this. "We'll reassess the situation regularly."

"Because we believe in freedom, you know," Savannah said with a wink at her husband.

"Freedom?" Hack repeated.

"Huh?" Steamer grunted.

"We're allowing Brooke the *freedom* to stay at the march . . . under close supervision," Dane said. "For now."

"I appreciate your efforts to respect Brooke's privacy, but can she at least call me on Owl's phone?" Neely asked.

"Owl suggested that," Steamer said, "but Brooke declined. She wants you to be able to honestly say you haven't talked to her if the police ask."

"I don't love this plan," Hack said. "Brooke's freedom is not as important as her safety."

"If the police show up at that chicken march looking for Brooke, they don't pose a threat to her safety. The worst that will happen is she'll be served with a subpoena. I'm willing to accept that risk if Brooke is."

Hack's tone eloquently expressed his feelings about this decision. "That's it? We're just going to sit around and wait?"

Dane nodded. "There's plenty to do while we sit around here waiting. The first thing we need to figure out is why Brooke attracted police attention."

Neely frowned. "I thought we were respecting her privacy."

"Within reason," Dane said. "But we can't fly blind. We need to know what we're up against in case we do have to get more involved." He turned to Hack. "Have you been able to find out anything from the Nashville police about why they want to talk to Brooke?"

"Not yet; I was planning to head over there now," Hack replied.

"Let Steamer take that assignment," Dane suggested, "since he and his expensive shoes are back with us."

"And he can wear his fancy loafers to the police station without arousing suspicion," Savannah said with a smile.

Steamer grinned. "Intimidating the Nashville PD in any kind of shoes sure sounds better than camping near a chicken farm."

"We need to talk to Brooke's neighbors and classmates—see if any of them know what might have caused some interest from the Nashville PD."

"I'm on it," Hack said.

"I'm a little uneasy with that," Neely told them. "Brooke will hate it when she finds out we pried . . ."

"She can't have it both ways," Dane said. "I won't force her to come home if she doesn't want to, but we need information and that means sacrificing some of her privacy. However, we'll try to keep our probing minimal."

"Remember, I'm from Vegas, Crybaby," Steamer said. "And you know our saying: 'What happens in Vegas stays in Vegas.'"

"That makes no sense," Hack objected. "We're not in Vegas."

"It speaks to my ability to investigate without compromising privacy," Steamer explained. "They taught me that in law school. It means I can keep a secret."

Hack groaned.

"We just agreed that you would all call me *Neely*," Dane's sister reminded Steamer, "not *Crybaby*."

Steamer grinned. "Sorry." Then he turned to Dane. "In my spare time, do you want me to file some motions or make some formal complaints against the Nashville PD to put a little pressure on them?"

"Not yet," Dane replied. "We'll try to keep our relationship with them friendly for now."

"Any news about Adam?" Savannah asked.

"He's safe at the American Consulate in Harare. We're working on getting him out legally. If that doesn't work, we'll sneak him out," Dane said.

"And what about the independent audit at Raleigh's company?" Neely asked.

"I'm still working on the best approach for that situation," Dane replied. "And since it's the least pressing of our three situations, I have the luxury of taking my time to think it through."

Neely stood and said, "Is anyone hungry? I can fix some sandwiches for dinner."

"Hack is always hungry," Steamer said.

Neely walked to the refrigerator. "Well, I love to cook, so we're a perfect combination."

***

Brooke was relieved when the sun set. Darkness settled around her, and she felt safe, anonymous. Owl pitched his tent a few feet from hers. She steadfastly ignored him.

When it was announced over loudspeakers that the evening's entertainment was about to begin, the surrounding campers started making their way down the hill. Brooke didn't want to go with them, but she knew staying at the campsite alone would be conspicuous. So she stood. Owl did the same. Then she took his hand and rushed to catch up with Rex's friends.

"Act like you're my boyfriend," she whispered as they trotted down the hill. "That's the only logical explanation for your presence here."

His hand was stiff in hers, and he looked very uncomfortable but nodded.

When they reached the others, a girl with a long blond braid pointed at Owl and asked, "Who is this?"

"My boyfriend." Brooke stopped herself right before she said *Owl.*

"Hunter," he filled in for her quickly.

The girl drew her eyebrows down in a little frown. "I thought you were with Rex."

Brooke shook her head. "Not anymore."

The blond girl shrugged. "Oh. Well hey, Hunter."

He gave her a little wave.

Brooke pulled him a few feet away. Then she whispered, "You're my boyfriend, remember. So don't flirt with other girls."

He looked at her like she'd accused him of mass murder. "I was not flirting."

She rolled her eyes. "Come on."

They stayed in the middle of her group of quasi-friends during the rally, trying to be unnoticeable. She couldn't concentrate on the plight of helpless chickens. Her eyes were continually darting from shadow to shadow, watching for someone who was watching her. She saw Owl doing the same.

Finally the speeches ended and the dancing began. Brooke's circle of protective friends paired up and moved onto the makeshift dance floor of trampled grass, leaving Brooke and Owl alone. She turned to him and placed her hands on his shoulders. "Put your arms around me."

He stared at her.

"We can't just stand here," she hissed. "We have to dance."

He put his hands out so that they barely grazed her waist.

She hauled him closer and said, "Now we have to move, at least a little."

He shuffled his feet, completely out of rhythm with the music.

Just as Brooke was beginning to wonder if she should have sent Owl home and kept Gucci Loafers, Owl bent down and whispered, "There are two guys by the bandstand flashing badges and showing a picture. I couldn't get a good look, but it's a girl with long brown hair like yours."

Brooke resisted the urge to look behind her. "My friends don't trust the cops. They won't turn me in."

"Not all the marchers are your friends," he said.

"But they're all suspicious of the police."

He shook his head. "You can't depend on that. It's just a matter of time before they find someone who will point you out."

She bit her lower lip, considering. Owl could be wrong, but she couldn't take the risk. It was imperative that she not end up in police custody. So she said, "We need a place where we can stay for a few days. Somewhere the police won't think to look."

Owl glanced over her head at the teeming crowd around them. "I'm not sure where that place might be, but we're going to have to get out of here now."

Brooke's heart pounded. "The police will be watching for people who try to leave. How can we avoid them?"

"We will get as close to the parking lot as we can, create a distraction, and then leave during the confusion."

"But you won't tell my uncle where we're going?"

"I don't *know* where we're going," Owl replied. "We'll cut through the woods to the field where all the cars are parked. I'll hot-wire one and get us out of here."

Under the circumstances, the prospect of breaking the law did not bother her. "What kind of a distraction are you going to create?"

"I'll figure that out later." He took her arm and pulled her into the woods. As they moved through the thick brush, he warned, "Try to walk softly."

"I'm trying."

It seemed like they were in the woods for a long time. Then finally they stepped out into the field on the other side. Just a few yards separated them from the closest poultry farm. The smell was terrible, and the mewling of the chickens made Brooke's heart ache.

Owl paused, listening. Then he pointed at the cars parked in the distance. "That's where we're headed, but we'll go along the far side of the farm so we'll have some cover."

She nodded. They left the shelter of the trees and moved to the fence line. Careful to stay in the shadows of various structures and equipment, the pair moved toward the parking area. They were about to walk into the open when Owl stopped and pointed into the distance. Brooke's eyes followed his finger and saw two men approaching.

He put a finger to his lips and pointed to an old shed on the other side of the fence. Brooke and Owl made their way to it; he opened the door, and they slipped inside. The interior of the shed was pitch-black, and the stench was horrible. Brooke put a hand over her mouth to keep from retching. After a few seconds, her eyes adjusted to the darkness. She could see rusted tables and grappling hooks caked with gore. Owl had taken her into an old slaughterhouse. Her head started to spin, and she was afraid she would faint.

"Stay with me," Owl encouraged. He wrapped a hand around her waist to help her remain upright. In his free hand he held a gun. She was terrified and reassured at the same time.

He half carried her to a corner where brown rubber suits were hanging. Owl and Brooke hid behind the suits as the door to the building opened. They saw a man enter the shed. He left the door open so light from the moon could aid his search.

Hiding behind the sticky rubber suits, Brooke tried not to think about what might be on them. She could no longer see the man, but she heard him as he walked closer and closer to their position. Owl's fingers moved over her mouth, and he gave her a warning look; then he shifted his foot and kicked something out toward the man.

The man yelped in surprise, and a gunshot reverberated through the small space. Brooke pressed her eyes closed and tried to control her trembling. She heard the sound of more footsteps approaching the shed—fast. Then a voice asked in a harsh whisper, "What are you shooting at?"

"I thought I heard something, but it was just a rat."

The men argued over the wisdom of firing a gun at a rodent as they walked out of the shed and slammed the door behind them.

Owl removed his hand from Brooke's mouth but motioned for her to remain silent.

They sat in the dark, stinking shed for what seemed like a very long time. Brooke's leg muscles were cramping, and she was afraid her sense of smell was permanently ruined. Finally Owl stood and pulled off his backpack. He took out some flares then taped and bound them together. Then he attached a small timing device to the bundle with wire.

"What is that?" she whispered.

"A flare bomb," he replied. "I'll set it to go off in fifteen minutes."

She looked around. "Will it destroy this place?"

"I hope so," he replied.

He put his explosive device inside a crumbling cardboard box filled with old rags. Then he motioned for her to follow him out. They left the shed, stopping frequently to be sure no one was following them.

When they reached the parking lot, they crouched down behind a pickup truck while Owl surveyed the options.

"I may never get that stench out of my nose," he whispered as he scanned the field full of vehicles.

"Now you know why I'm a vegetarian."

"I won't say I'm giving up meat completely," he replied, "but I doubt I'll be eating chicken anytime soon." He pointed to a battered Chevy Cavalier. "That's a stick shift. If it's not locked, it's the car we're going to borrow."

After one last look around, Owl stood and they walked toward the car he had chosen. They were almost there when two figures stepped out from behind a maroon-colored minivan.

Brooke couldn't control a small scream before she realized that the two figures were not police but a married couple she knew vaguely.

Pressing a hand to her heart, she said to them, "Sorry! You startled me!" Then she turned to Owl. "These are friends of mine, Scott and Elizabeth Cauthen."

He nodded, still not completely at ease. "Nice to meet you."

Scott studied Owl for a few seconds. "I don't remember seeing you before. Are you a part of the movement?"

"He's my . . . boyfriend," Brooke told them. "Hunter."

Elizabeth said, "I thought Rex was your boyfriend."

Brooke looked at the ground. "No, that's been over for a while."

"You folks leaving?" Owl asked them.

Scott looked sheepish. "I know it looks bad that we're sneaking out early, but we have summer jobs in Gatlinburg, and our new-employee orientation is tomorrow afternoon. So, well, we just need to go."

"We're cutting out a little early too," Owl said. "But my car won't start. Would you folks give us a ride to the first town with a car repair shop?"

The Cauthens looked uncertain.

"We could give you money for gas," Owl offered.

This seemed to sway them from any reservations they might have had.

"Sure," Scott said. "Here's our car." He walked up to the old Chevy Owl had chosen as their getaway car. "I know it doesn't look like much, but it runs great."

Brooke hid a smile.

Scott opened the trunk and put his and Elizabeth's things inside. Owl said he preferred to keep his backpack with him in the backseat, so Brooke did the same.

It took Scott several tries before the old car finally started. And just as the engine roared to life, they heard an explosion behind them.

"What was that?" Elizabeth cried as they turned and looked out the rear window.

Brooke stared at the fireball that used to be a stinky slaughter shed. "Fireworks," she said.

Once they were on the road, heading away from the camp, Owl seemed to relax. He settled back against the car seat and asked, "So, what kind of jobs do you have in Gatlinburg?"

Scott replied, "It's a Civil War resort opening for the first time this year. It's near Dollywood."

"We really do care about the cause," Elizabeth said. "But we have to make money over the summer to pay our rent during the school year. We don't want to be kicked out of the organization. I hope Freddo will understand."

Freddo Higgins, the animal rights activist in charge of the march, was a good friend of Rex's, and he didn't understand anything other than his own best interest. "Freddo will complain when he finds out, but he won't kick you out of the organization," Brooke comforted Scott and Elizabeth. "He needs dedicated people like you."

"Maybe you can put in a good word for us," Elizabeth suggested, "since you're friends with him."

Brooke had made a point to stay away from him during the march because he always had members of the press around him and the last thing she needed was to have her picture on TV. But she nodded. "Next time I talk to him," she promised. She resisted the urge to look behind them to see if they were being followed but couldn't help listening for sirens in the distance.

"So, you two will be working at a Civil War resort?" Owl asked.

"Until the end of August," Scott confirmed.

Owl frowned. "I'll admit I don't see why people would want to go to a place like that. I mean, what's fun about the Civil War?"

"Apparently a lot of people think it will be fun," Elizabeth said. "The place is booked solid through the entire summer. And it's not cheap. It costs about three thousand dollars a week for a couple. The resort may eventually include activities for children, but for this first year it's adults only."

"What do they do while they're at the resort?"

Brooke didn't really think Owl was that curious about the Cauthens' summer job. She assumed he was just filling the time.

"They spend a week living exactly the way people did in the 1860s," Elizabeth continued. "They wear period clothing, eat period food, and enjoy period entertainment like dances and recitals. And every day they reenact a battle from the Civil War."

"I wouldn't pay three thousand dollars for that," Owl said.

Scott laughed. "Me neither, but I'm glad there are people who will. It's easy work, and the money's good."

"We're in the market for jobs ourselves," Owl said. "I wonder if there's a chance we could get on at the resort too."

Elizabeth shook her head. "I don't think so. It was a pretty long application process, and the deadline has passed. Maybe next year though."

"The name of the company is Charter Vacations, and they own all kinds of resorts and a cruise line. It's possible they have openings somewhere else. We'll give you the number, and you can call them," Scott offered.

"We'd appreciate that," Owl said.

Elizabeth fished in her backpack and found a number, which she gave to Owl. Brooke listened to all of it without interest. She knew Owl would not be looking for a summer job with Charter Vacations—not this year or any other.

"There's a big truck stop about an hour ahead," Scott told them. "We stopped there on the way down. They have a hotel and a bus station and a mechanic shop. So you can have your car towed in and stay there while they fix it."

"Sounds good," Owl said. He pulled out his phone. "That gives me time to play a couple of games."

That left Brooke to make small talk with the Cauthens. She sent him an annoyed look, but he ignored her, focusing totally on his phone.

Fortunately it wasn't hard to keep the Cauthens talking, and the hour-long ride to the truck stop passed quickly.

As Scott pulled into the parking lot, Owl said, "I need to break a big bill so I can give you money for gas. Will you let us buy you folks a cup of coffee?"

The Cauthens didn't look thrilled. "We have hotel reservations near Gatlinburg for tonight and want to get there as early as possible."

"A cup of coffee won't take long," Owl said with a smile.

Good manners required them to accept the token of gratitude, so the Cauthens nodded. They walked together into the truck stop and found the restaurant. They all ordered coffee except Brooke, who chose orange juice. She felt exposed with glass windows on every side—like a fish in a bowl. The Cauthens looked uncomfortable too, and Brooke was mad at Owl for causing this awkward situation. But he seemed perfectly at ease.

While they were waiting for their drinks to be brought to the table, Scott's phone rang.

"Who would be calling you this late?" Elizabeth asked crossly.

Scott shrugged and stepped a few feet away from the table before answering the phone. When he returned, Brooke could tell from his expression that he was slightly upset.

Elizabeth intuitively demanded, "What's wrong?"

"Nothing's wrong, exactly," Scott replied. "That was the human resources department at Charter Vacations. They said they overhired at the Civil War resort so our assignment has been changed."

"Changed?" Elizabeth's voice was strident. "Changed to what?"

"Instead of working at the Civil War resort, we're going to be on an Alaskan cruise ship."

Some of the anxiety left Elizabeth's face. "But we'll still get paid the same amount?"

Scott flashed her a grin. "Actually, we get *more* money."

She smiled back. "What will we do on the cruise ship?"

Her husband said, "Hospitality—which means being friendly and making sure the customers are having fun."

"That sounds easy."

"That sounds like a three-month vacation instead of a job!"

Elizabeth was already worrying about the next thing. "So we have to get to Alaska?"

"No, the cruise leaves from Los Angeles," Scott said. "They've got plane tickets waiting for us at the Nashville airport, so that's where we've got to go." He looked over at Owl and Brooke. "I hate to cut this short, but we need to get there fast."

The tension had returned to Elizabeth's face. "What are we going to do with the car? We can't leave it at the airport all summer!"

"Would you want to sell it?" Owl asked. "I think my car is a lost cause. So if you'd be willing to make me a good deal, I could take it off your hands."

Brooke turned to stare at him.

"We can't just give it away," Elizabeth hedged. "We'd need to get at least two thousand for it."

Brooke was about to say that this was a ridiculous amount for the old car, but Owl spoke first.

"That sounds fair to me."

"You've got that much cash?" Elizabeth asked suspiciously. "We can't take a check from someone we don't know."

Owl nodded. "I have that much in cash."

"We don't have the title with us," Elizabeth said.

"I'll just get you to sign a bill of sale, and you can mail me the title later," Owl told them. "And we need someplace to stay tonight—so I'll even take that hotel room near Gatlinburg off your hands."

Elizabeth pulled an online receipt from her purse. "We paid $76.50."

This didn't seem to bother Owl. "I'll add that amount to the cost of the car."

Elizabeth pushed the receipt across the table, looking very pleased. Brooke was uneasy. She didn't know why Owl had attached himself—and her—to this couple she barely knew. She didn't understand why he was buying their car and their hotel room and why they were all sitting in a huge truck stop in plain view of anyone who might want to arrest her or give her a subpoena.

She gave him an annoyed look, and he nodded. Whether he was just acknowledging that she was aggravated or telling her to be patient, she wasn't sure.

"But we need to get to the airport," Elizabeth reminded them. "Can you drop us off there?"

"I'm paying you $2,076.50," Owl said. "You can use some of it on a taxi."

"I guess that will be all right." Elizabeth turned to her husband. "Scott, call a taxi."

While Scott made his call, Owl rounded up a couple of pieces of paper and wrote out two identical bills of sale. Once the signatures were in place, he counted out $2,000 in hundred dollar bills. Then he added exactly $76.50. He passed the money across the table to Elizabeth.

"I wrote my address on the bottom of your bill of sale so you can mail me the title," he said, "at the end of the summer, when you get through taking Alaskan cruises."

Scott announced, "A taxi is on the way." He stowed the money in his wallet and tipped his head at Owl. "Thanks."

Owl nodded. "It worked out good for both of us. I hate to leave you before your taxi gets here, but we really need to go."

Scott waved this aside. "There's no need for you to wait. We'll get our stuff out of the car, and then you two can go."

Elizabeth stayed inside the truck stop while Scott walked out with Owl and Brooke. The old Cavalier looked the same, but now it belonged to Owl instead of the Cauthens. Owl unlocked the trunk, and Scott got his and Elizabeth's stuff out.

Owl slammed the trunk closed. "Thanks for the ride, and good luck to you."

"Same to you," Scott said over his shoulder as he walked back toward the truck stop.

As Brooke watched Scott leave, she asked Owl, "Where are we going now?"

Owl opened the door for her, and when she was settled in the passenger seat, he leaned down to whisper, "To the Civil War resort. From this point on, you're Elizabeth Cauthen and I'm your husband, Scott."

Then he closed her door, walked around the car, and climbed in behind the wheel.

CHAPTER FOUR

Brooke stared at him as he started the old car. "What do you mean?"

"That's how we'll hide," he replied calmly. "We'll go to the resort and pretend to be the Cauthens."

"But their job at the resort isn't available," she reminded him. "The people from human resources called and changed them to the cruise."

He gave her a sly look.

She gasped. "You weren't really playing games on your phone, were you?"

He shook his head. "I was setting things up with Hack for us to take over the Cauthens' identity. The taxi driver coming to get them is really one of Hack's men."

Brooke looked back at the truck stop. "He won't hurt them, will he?"

"No," Owl replied. "He will take them to the airport and make sure they get on that plane to California. Impersonating them is only safe if the real Cauthens are out of the picture."

"You promised you wouldn't tell my uncle where we're going!"

"I didn't exactly promise that," he corrected. "You said you didn't want your uncle to know."

"I told you, we have to leave my family out of this!"

Owl looked more cross than usual. "My contact was only with Hack, and he's not your family."

Brooke was more hurt than she should have been by Owl's betrayal. "And you think Hack won't tell my uncle?"

"He will report contact and that all is well with you, but he won't give them details like where we are or who we are pretending to be."

Brooke didn't believe this for a minute. "Right. Because you and Hack respect my privacy so much."

Owl said, "No because your *uncle* respects your privacy. He's agreed to limited information since that's the way you want it."

Brooke was both surprised and pleased. "Is that true? Please don't lie. I really need to know."

Owl turned to her. "I don't lie."

Brooke nodded. "Good."

"So now you trust me?"

"I don't mean to hurt your feelings, but not really," she said honestly.

"You didn't hurt my feelings," Owl assured her. "I'm a professional soldier. I don't have feelings."

She raised an eyebrow at this declaration. "Well, you may be heartless, but I'm not and I appreciate all you're doing to help me."

"I'm not helping you; I'm working for your uncle," he clarified bluntly. "But I do hope you learn to trust me. It will make things easier."

They drove in silence for a few minutes, and then she asked him something that had been worrying her. "Do you think any of the chickens got hurt because of the explosion?"

He shook his head. "That shed was pretty far away from the coops."

"Unless we gave them heart attacks," she muttered.

"Why do you care so much about chickens?" he asked.

She looked over to see if he was making fun of her, but she didn't detect any ridicule in his expression. So she said, "It's not just chickens. I care about all defenseless animals that get mistreated. You probably think that's stupid."

"No, as a soldier I think I have a responsibility to defend the helpless too—usually people instead of animals—but it's the same principle. I admire your dedication and your willingness to spend your spare time fighting for it."

"Most people think this is just a phase I'll outgrow. But I won't."

"I hope you don't. Defenseless animals need people like you."

He seemed completely serious, so she relaxed. "What do you do when you're not protecting people for my uncle?"

"I fly planes for government VIPs."

"How VIP?"

"Very."

"Like the president?"

"I can't say."

She smiled. "Wow. How did you get an amazing job like that?"

"I have an unusual combination of talents."

"Which are?"

He was quiet for so long she was afraid he wasn't going to answer. She risked a look over at him in the darkness and found him scowling at the road.

Finally he said, "I hate to admit this to an animal activist—but in addition to being a pilot, I'm also proficient with guns."

"How proficient?" she asked.

"I can shoot just about any gun with a very high rate of accuracy from a very long distance."

"You shoot *people*?"

"I protect people," he corrected. "I would never shoot anyone who didn't pose a threat."

Under normal circumstances, being in the presence of a professional gunman would seem like a bad thing, but at the moment she had to admit it had its benefits. "How long have you had this talent?"

"My father discovered my shooting ability when I was a little kid. I have better than 20/20 vision and a photographic memory, which give me a huge advantage over any prey."

His jaw was clinched and his voice tense, so Brooke knew this was an emotionally charged topic.

"I come from a long line of hunters," he finally continued.

"I'll bet your father was proud."

"He was," Owl confirmed.

"You don't sound too happy about it."

"I hated hunting," he said simply. "My father couldn't understand. We ate everything we killed, so it wasn't just sport. That was all the vindication he needed."

"But that wasn't enough vindication for you?"

"No, but I didn't want to disappoint my father. So I kept hunting and improving my skills. Then we discovered shooting contests, and I liked those better. My dad liked the trophies I won, so we were both happy for several years. Then an army recruiter saw me shoot at a big competition and convinced my dad that I should join the military. My dad loved that idea. So as soon as I graduated from high school, I joined the army. They turned me into a sniper, and I was back to hunting."

"So how did you get to be the president's pilot?"

He gave her an impatient look. "I am not the president's pilot. Your uncle arranged for me to take flying lessons. I love flying. The only downside is that I don't get to work with the team as much anymore."

"The VIPs keep you busy."

He nodded. "Very busy. So what about you? What do you do when you aren't marching for chickens?"

She shrugged. "I'm a music major at Vanderbilt. I play the piano."

"Are you good?"

"Very."

"But it doesn't make you happy?"

She searched for the right words. "I love music and the piano in particular. But I want to make a difference in the world, and I don't see how I can do that as a pianist. So I became an animal rights activist." She looked away. "But I don't see myself doing that all my life either."

"You don't have to be an activist to help animals," he said. "You can become a famous pianist and donate money to animal causes."

"That sounds so lame—just donating money. In our group we make fun of people who only care from a distance." She frowned. "And even though I love playing the piano, I don't really enjoy performing."

"So you don't want to be a famous pianist?"

She shook her head. "No."

"What do you want to be?"

"I might like to teach piano lessons," she said. "I can see myself enjoying that. And eventually I want to be a wife and a mom." She waited for Owl to laugh or ridicule her in some way, but his response surprised her.

"When you get married and have kids, you'll teach them to play the piano and to care about defenseless animals. Then you really will have made a difference in the world."

She sighed. "We've only known each other for a few hours and you already know me better than my own family."

"I'm sure that's not true," he said. "I just don't make judgments about people. I accept them at face value."

"That's a good character trait," she assured him. "Do you mind if I call you Hunter?"

"If you do, I probably won't know you're talking to me. I've been Owl forever."

She laughed. "You'll get used to it, and pretty soon you won't answer to anything else."

He obviously didn't think that was funny because he didn't so much as crack a tiny smile. "I doubt that. The best thing to do when we're in front of other people is to avoid calling me anything. Just look at me and say what you need to say. But if you have to use a name, remember to call me Scott. And you're Elizabeth."

She nodded. "I'll remember."

***

It was two o'clock on Tuesday morning when Hunter pulled the Cauthens' car into the parking lot of a motel near Gatlinburg.

"We're staying here?" Brooke asked with a yawn.

"This is where the Cauthens had reservations," he confirmed. "We're only about an hour away from the Civil War resort, and there's a mall down the road where we can buy some clothes and suitcases so we don't show up for a summer-long job looking like hobos."

Hunter left her in the car while he checked into the motel. When he came back with keys, he said, "I would have gotten two rooms, but in case someone checks out the Cauthens, I want it to look like the real Scott and Elizabeth stayed here. They only reserved one room, so . . ."

"I guess it's okay, since I'm trusting you and all."

"You can," Hunter said. "Trust me, that is."

"I know."

He led the way up the sidewalk to the door of their motel room. The paint was peeling, and the tarnished number five was hanging slightly askew. Inside, the decor was shabby without being chic. The air was damp and smelled of cigarettes despite the prominently displayed No Smoking sign.

Brooke was exhausted, so she walked straight over to the double bed closest to the bathroom. She pulled back the bedspread, with its faded geometric print, and snuggled under the top sheet. Closing her eyes, she tried to forget she was in a seedy motel room with a man she barely knew.

Brooke heard Hunter double-checking the locks on the door. She opened her eyes just a sliver so she could see him sitting on the far side of the other bed, choosing to put as much distance between them as possible.

He took out his phone and started typing.

"Playing games again?" she murmured.

He nodded without looking up.

When it was obvious he wasn't going to defend himself, she said, "I know you're not really playing games."

"I'm reporting," he said. "If Hack doesn't hear from me every hour on the hour, your uncle will send reinforcements."

"Oh." She knew she shouldn't be surprised. Her uncle was very thorough. "Do you have to do that during the night too?"

"Twenty-four hours a day."

"You won't get much sleep, then."

"I'm here to guard you," he said. "Not to rest."

"Thank you," she whispered. And then, for the first time in almost a week, she fell asleep without fear.

***

When Savannah woke up on Tuesday morning in the guest room at Neely's house, she reached across the bed for Dane, but he wasn't there. This was not surprising. He no longer had nightmares, but he didn't sleep long or well, and since the sun was pouring in through the bedroom window . . . It wasn't even that early.

She got dressed and went downstairs. Dane and Hack were in Raleigh's office. "So, what's going on?" she asked them.

"Caroline is good. I've already talked to Doc this morning."

Savannah had confidence in Doc, but the news was still good to hear.

"Owl reported that everything is fine with Brooke," Dane said as he crossed the room. He pressed a kiss to Savannah's forehead. "How are you feeling?"

"Okay," she said, raising the Gatorade bottle that contained the Sprite mixture. "I just keep sipping."

"After breakfast we'll have a meeting and go over the plans for today."

They walked into the kitchen, where Neely was cooking breakfast.

"I'd offer to help you," Savannah said, "but I'm afraid I just couldn't do it without vomiting."

"That kind of help I don't need," Neely said with a smile. "Besides, I like to cook, and I like to stay busy. It keeps me from worrying."

One of Hack's men walked in and said that two detectives were on the front porch wanting to talk to Neely.

She looked at her brother. "Do I have to?"

He nodded. "That's the best way to figure out what they want. I'll be there with you, but I don't want them to know we're investigating. Just tell them we're visiting."

Neely turned off the stove and set her pancakes aside. Then she led the way to the front door, clutching the collar of her robe, pulling the sides together. She opened the door and invited the two policemen inside.

"Hello, Mrs. Clayton. My name is Detective Napier," one of the men said.

Savannah stared at the detective. He was an older man with frizzy, gray hair. He was wearing a rumpled suit, and even from across the room Savannah could see a stain on his tie.

He hooked a finger toward his companion. "And this is Detective Worrell."

The other man was younger and neater. Savannah immediately liked him better.

Both men simultaneously pulled out badges and presented them to Neely. "We're from the Nashville Police Department."

Neely gave the badges a cursory glance and nodded.

"I see you have company." Detective Napier's beady eyes moved over to Dane and Savannah.

"My brother and his family are visiting," Neely said stiffly. "My birthday was yesterday, and they came to help me celebrate."

The officer grinned, exposing coffee-stained teeth. "Well, happy birthday."

"Thank you," she said. "Now what can I do for you?"

"We'd like to speak to Brooke Clayton."

"I told the other officers who came yesterday that my daughter doesn't live here anymore. She has an apartment in Nashville."

Detective Napier bobbed his frizzy, gray head. "And as the officers who visited yesterday told *you*, your daughter hasn't been to her apartment in several days. We thought you might know where she is."

"I don't."

Detective Napier gave Neely a look of exaggerated surprise. "Are you sure about that?"

"Positive."

"You don't sound too concerned that your daughter is missing."

Detective Napier had made a negative first impression. Savannah wasn't sure what bothered her most—his unkempt appearance or his arrogant tone.

Neely responded, "I am quite anxious to talk to my daughter, but I trust she will contact me when she's ready to talk."

Detective Napier rubbed a hand across his fuzzy hair. "You have a little family spat or something?"

Neely frowned. "We've been having a spat since she turned thirteen. Sometimes I don't hear from her for weeks."

Detective Worrell gave her a sympathetic smile. "I have teenagers too."

"Why do you want to talk to my daughter?" Neely asked.

"We just have a few questions." Detective Napier held out his card. "Please let us know if you hear from her."

Neely took the card but didn't actually commit to call them. She escorted them to the door and closed it behind them then walked to the living room window, where she could watch them leave.

Dane and Savannah joined her there. Together they watched as the policemen got into their car but remained parked at the curb in front of the house.

Dane put an arm around his sister's shoulders. "You handled that perfectly."

Neely gave him a tremulous smile. "I hate this."

"I know."

"And my neighbors hate it too. There are already six messages on my answering machine asking why the police came yesterday. When my neighbors see the police still parked in front of my house, well, there will be more messages until they decide not to talk to me at all."

"Your neighbors are the least of your worries."

"That's easy for you to say; you haven't lived here for twenty years."

Dane pulled her away from the window. "Let's go eat those pancakes."

***

After breakfast Savannah went upstairs and called Caroline. Savannah had a nice, long conversation with her daughter and then spoke briefly with Doc and the McLaughlins. When she ended the call, she felt reassured. Caroline was safe and happy, and Dane wasn't worried that Caroline would fall down the steps and break her neck. So Savannah would deal with the separation for a few days.

Savannah was headed to the kitchen to refill her Spriteorade and found Neely standing in the family room, staring at the picture hanging over the fireplace.

"It's a beautiful picture of a beautiful family," Savannah said.

Neely gave her a sad smile. "I poured all my heart and soul into my family. Adam grew up with a huge capacity for loving others. He wants to serve and sacrifice—but he wants to do it so far from home. I feel selfish, but I want him here, near us."

Savannah nodded. "That's perfectly understandable."

"And Brooke." Neely paused to shake her head. "I feel so separated from her—and not just because I don't know where she is. I always say the wrong things, and she's usually angry or distant." She hugged her arms with her hands. "I need Raleigh to be here! He's always been the one who could reach out and pull us together. But he still can't leave work."

"You talked to him?"

She nodded. "He called this morning, and I told him that the police had come looking for Brooke again. I thought he'd come straight home even if it cost him that big account or even the company. But he just said he was glad Christopher is here."

"There's not really anything he can do here. In fact, there's not really anything any of us can do except sit and wait for Brooke to decide she doesn't want to hide anymore."

"I guess."

"Everything will be okay." Savannah tried to sound optimistic.

Neely sighed. "I hope you're right."

They started walking toward Raleigh's office, where they could hear the men talking. As the women entered the office, Neely's phone rang.

"It's Mother," she told Dane.

"Answer it but don't mention," he twirled his finger, "any of this."

Neely nodded and pushed the speaker button on her phone.

"I tried to wish you a happy birthday yesterday, but I kept getting your voice mail!" Her mother's voice filled the room.

"Sorry, Mom," Neely said. "It was a busy day, and I didn't get a chance to call you back."

"I hope it was incredible! Did you get our card?"

"I did get the card," Neely confirmed. "Thank you so much."

"It doesn't seem like it's been forty-five years since you were born." The voice sounded a little wistful.

"Are you calling me old?"

Her mother laughed. "When you get to be my age, you'll realize how young forty-five really is!"

"Now that's something to look forward to."

"You were such a pleasant baby. I've always been thankful that you were my oldest. If Christopher had been born first, he probably would have been an only child."

"He wasn't that bad," Neely murmured with a glance at her brother.

"You must be losing your memory now that you're approaching old age," her mother teased. "I give him credit for all my gray hairs!"

Neely forced a laugh. "Christopher has always been the daring one."

"He's brave and brilliantly fearless, which makes him a great soldier, but these are not traits that warm an old mother's heart!"

"I should tell you that Christopher and Savannah are visiting, and he just heard every word."

Her mother was nonplused. "Hello, Christopher!"

"Hello, Mom," he answered.

"Well, I've got to go. Your father and I are going for our morning walk. I love you!"

"I love you too."

"Tell Raleigh I said hello."

"I will," Neely promised.

When she ended the call, Dane said, "Okay, enough of this birthday nonsense. It's time to go over the plans for the day." They all settled around the desk, and Dane continued. "Since Doc is watching out for Caroline and Owl is with Brooke, we're two men short. That means the rest of us have to work twice as hard."

"I'm as good as two men any day," Steamer came back, "and Hack, well he's as big as two men every day!"

Dane fixed Steamer with a stern look. "Concentrate on your responsibilities, and don't distract Hack from his. First, Adam. Doc is working with General Steele on two different ways to get him out of Zimbabwe. One is legal, with the cooperation of the local government. The other is illegal and involves a special ops team going in and removing him. We'll go with whichever plan is ready first."

"And Raleigh's situation?" Steamer questioned.

"I haven't started on that yet," Dane said. "Now tell us what you learned from the Nashville PD."

"They have no open case involving Brooke," Steamer said. "They are looking for her at the request of the district attorney. She's a material witness in a case he's trying to make."

"What kind of case?"

"I couldn't get any details," Steamer replied. "Either the police don't know or they aren't saying. My guess is they don't know."

"So we need to talk to the DA," Dane concluded.

"I tried yesterday and again this morning. His secretary keeps giving me the runaround," Steamer said. "I talked to some law clerks and secretaries, but I never got anyone to admit that they'd ever heard of Brooke. She's not on any witness list or mailing list. She's not even on their Christmas card list."

Hack scowled at him. "Quit joking around."

"I'm serious," Steamer said. "Whatever she's involved in must be top secret."

Dane ignored the exchange. "And important if the DA has asked the police to camp out here and at her apartment."

"Actually it's not unusual for the DA to keep details pretty close to his chest while trying to build a case," Steamer said.

Hack looked at Dane. "Is that true or is he just spouting off legal opinions like he's a real lawyer?"

"It's true," Dane confirmed. "In the early stages, secrecy is to be expected. The DA doesn't want to tip off a guilty party or scare any witnesses away. But usually the staff has some idea of what he's working on."

"Well," Steamer said, "if they know, they aren't talking."

Dane frowned. "Steam, go back again, and this time make a lot of noise. Tell them you're Brooke's attorney and want the police harassment stopped. Demand a face-to-face with the DA, and if you get it, ask him what he wants with Brooke."

"Got it," Steamer said.

Dane turned back to Hack. "What did you find out from Brooke's neighbors?"

"Nothing," Hack reported. "She keeps to herself. No one has seen signs of another boyfriend since that Rex character moved out. They didn't notice the police watching the building and have no idea what she might have witnessed or been a part of to attract police attention."

"You looked up crimes that took place near her apartment over the past six months?"

Hack pushed a report across the desk. "There were several, but they've all been either settled or dismissed."

"Nothing waiting for a star witness?" Dane muttered as he looked through the report.

"Nope."

"How about near her work or the college?" Steamer suggested.

"Several near the yogurt shop where she used to work, and two are still under investigation, but it's minor stuff—nothing that would attract the DA's attention. Same with the crimes committed on campus."

Dane nodded. "We'll see what Steam can do at the DA's office. Now, Hack, give everyone an update on Owl and Brooke."

"They left the chicken march late last night," the big man reported. "Men with badges came looking for Brooke. We assume they were Nashville PD, but Owl didn't actually see the badges. Brooke didn't want to come home, so he took her to a secure location."

"Where are they?" Neely asked.

"Dane has given me permission to keep that to myself for now," Hack said. "That's the way Brooke wants it, so that's the way we're playing it."

Neely and Hack both looked equally unhappy about this decision.

As the meeting broke up, Neely asked Savannah, "So what do you hear from Caroline?"

"She's got her grandfather and Doc building her a playhouse," Savannah said. "Wes's mom is even making curtains and a rag rug."

Neely patted her arm. "Wish you were there?"

"I miss Caroline," Savannah replied carefully. "But I don't really wish I was in Colorado. My place is with Dane, to offer my support—even if it's mostly just moral support. And things are always a little awkward with the McLaughlins."

"Because you remarried?"

"I don't think they mind that. They're glad Caroline has a father. They're just private people, and when I'm there we're all uncomfortable. But I have to say, building a playhouse sounds fun."

"Maybe you could have Dane build one at your house," Neely suggested.

Savannah nodded. "That's what I was thinking. I can make curtains. I don't know about a rag rug."

Neely waved this aside. "You can buy a rug. Of course, if Christopher is building this playhouse, it will probably have a security system."

"And one of Hack's guards standing by the door," Savannah added. "And maybe a moat."

"With little alligators!"

Savannah laughed. "And maybe a Plexiglas dome over the whole thing so he can control the weather!"

Dane looked up from the computer, where he was consulting with Hack, and frowned. "Are you two making fun of me?"

Savannah walked over and put her arms around him. "Yes."

"I don't know why," he said. "If I built Caroline a playhouse, I'd never put alligators in the moat . . . Maybe piranhas . . ."

***

Brooke was awakened by the sound of someone calling her name. She opened her eyes and saw Hunter's face hovering above hers. Sunlight was streaming in through the holes in the window shade behind him, making him seem almost angelic. His eyes were red-rimmed with fatigue, and she felt guilty for the sleep he had given up to protect her.

"What time is it?"

He checked his watch. "Nine o'clock."

She sat up and rubbed her eyes. "I thought we would want to get an early start."

"I looked up the Civil War resort online, and the orientation meeting for new employees isn't until this afternoon. So you've got time for a shower."

"Are you saying I look terrible?"

He didn't even grin, so her attempt at humor fell flat. "No, I'm just saying you have time for a shower." He held out his hand. "These are some shampoo samples I got from the guy at the front desk. It's cheap stuff, but that's all he had."

"Thanks, but I've got shampoo in my backpack."

He closed his fingers around the samples and let his hand drop to his side.

She grabbed her backpack and went into the bathroom. After a quick and refreshing shower, she towel-dried her hair and pulled it into a ponytail. She put on a change of clothes from her backpack. It was just jeans and a T-shirt, but they were clean and she felt amazingly better. Then she stuffed her ponytail into the baseball cap and shrugged on the old flannel shirt before leaving the small bathroom.

Hunter was standing by the window when she came out. He gave her a quick visual assessment. She could tell by his expression that he didn't particularly like what he saw.

She spread her hands. "This is the best I could do under the circumstances."

"You need to take off that men's shirt and the baseball cap," he said. "There's nothing we can do about the combat boots until we get to the mall."

"They're hiking boots," she corrected him. "And I have on the flannel shirt and baseball cap because I'm trying to keep people from recognizing me."

"Clothes that are inappropriate draw attention instead of diverting it—like wearing Gucci loafers at a chicken march," he replied. "It's a common rookie mistake."

Stunned, she looked down at herself. "What's inappropriate about my clothes?"

"The weather is too warm for a flannel shirt," he began. "But that's only one of the things wrong with that shirt. It's made for a man, and you are a woman."

She fingered the fabric of the shirt. It had given her a sense of security—apparently a false sense.

"And a baseball cap is like sunglasses," he continued. "If you're looking for someone who doesn't want to be found, you start with the people wearing the world's most obvious disguises."

She was a little offended but mostly embarrassed. She removed the flannel shirt and cap and handed her rookie disguise to Hunter.

"Do these have sentimental value?"

The shirt and hat had both belonged to Rex, the man she thought she would spend the rest of her life with. He was also the man who had left her without a backward glance. She shook her head. "They don't mean anything to me."

Hunter put them into his backpack. "I'll get rid of them later. We can't leave a trail."

She nodded, trying to keep the painful memories at bay.

He led the way to the door and then stopped. He pressed his cell phone into her hand. "I'm going to go out first. When I give you the all-clear signal, follow me." He demonstrated with a low-key thumbs-up. "If I don't give the signal, lock the door and press *one* on my phone. Help will be here in seconds."

"What about you?"

"That's not your concern." He opened the door and stepped outside. She watched as he approached the old Cavalier. He didn't make a show of searching the area, but she knew he was doing exactly that. He unlocked the trunk and tossed their backpacks inside. Then, closing the trunk, he moved his thumb toward the sky. Brooke stepped out immediately. He had the passenger door open by the time she reached the car. Moments later they were on their way.

"Are you starving?" he asked.

"I'm hungry," she replied as she returned his phone, "but not near death." Most people would have smiled at this comment, but not Hunter.

"There's a big mall twenty minutes ahead where we'll stop. If you can wait that long, we'll eat there."

"I can make it twenty minutes," she assured him.

She was pleasantly surprised by the size of the mall when they arrived. It had several major department stores, and even at the early hour, the parking lot was almost full.

"It looks pretty crowded."

"Good," he replied. "Crowds will help keep us from being noticed, and busy people are less likely to remember faces."

He opened his door and got out. He had told her to wait for him to come around and open her door. She realized this was not good manners but a security measure.

Once they got inside, Hunter asked her opinion on the available eating establishments. They settled on a family-style restaurant, where she ordered a whole-wheat bagel and lite cream cheese. Hunter ordered eggs, bacon and sausage, buttermilk biscuits, and gravy.

"How can you eat like that and stay so thin?" she asked him when their food arrived.

"I have a high metabolism," he replied in between bites of egg. "And I don't always eat like this. Just when I get the chance."

After breakfast he took her through the mall and stopped across and down from a huge hair salon. "That's your first stop."

She eyed the glitzy sign that read *Shear Elegance* and then turned back to him. "You really do think I look awful."

"I think you need to look like Elizabeth Cauthen. Your hair has to be shorter and dyed blond. That is a *real* disguise."

Brooke definitely wanted to avoid detection, but she'd hoped that she could wait things out and then go back to her normal life. Cutting and dying her hair seemed so permanent—like she would never really be the same again.

Hunter was watching her. "You don't want to dye your hair?"

"It's okay if you're sure it's necessary."

"The more you look like Elizabeth Cauthen, the better," he said.

She decided to defer to his greater experience. "Okay, I'll dye my hair."

"I'm not going in. The salon people might remember you, since you'll be in there awhile, so I don't want them to see us together." He pulled out his wallet, but she shook her head.

"I have cash."

He put his wallet away without argument. "We can't show up at the resort without luggage and clothes. So while you're in the salon, I'll do some shopping. If you'll give me your sizes, I'll pick out things for you."

"I've got enough clothes in my backpack. Just get me a suitcase. Something cute."

He sighed. "I can't promise cute, but I'll get you a suitcase. Now let's get this process started. While you're in the salon, keep a low profile. Don't leave a large tip, and don't give them your real name."

"I'm not an idiot," she whispered.

He gave her his exasperated look. "I'm just trying to help. This is serious."

"I know perfectly well how serious this is," she retorted. Then she turned and walked into the salon, with him scowling at her back.

There were four long rows of stylists—each wearing black pants and a hot-pink tunic—and all of the stylists had customers in their chairs except the one in the far right-hand corner.

"Can we help you?" the stylist closest to the counter asked.

"I'd like a cut and color," Brooke told her.

"Do you have an appointment?" she asked.

Brooke shook her head.

"I can do it when I get through with this customer, but you'll have to wait about an hour."

Brooke knew she couldn't wait that long. "I'm in sort of a hurry. Is there anyone else who could do it sooner?" Her eyes strayed to the girl in the back with unnaturally black hair.

The stylist's eyes followed the direction of Brooke's gaze. "Nyla is available if you want to risk it." She lowered her voice and whispered, "She's new."

Brooke chewed her lip and quickly considered her options. Then she nodded. "I'll take my chances."

Brooke walked to the back corner of the salon and settled herself in the chair. Nyla's hands were shaking as she put a cape around Brooke's neck.

"What color were you thinking of?"

"I want to go blond," she told the girl. "I've heard they have more fun."

Nyla nodded solemnly.

Since no one was laughing at her jokes, Brooke was beginning to wonder if she just wasn't funny.

"My final exam in beauty school was three-tone blond. I got an A."

"That is good news," Brooke told the girl. "I need a trim too. Can you handle that for me?"

Nyla took a deep breath. "I think I can."

Clinging to the exam grade and trying to forget that Nyla was fresh out of beauty school, Brooke leaned back and closed her eyes.

Nyla sprayed Brooke's hair to dampen it and then combed it out. After facing her client toward the mirror, the stylist asked, "So how much do you want cut off?"

Brooke looked at her long brown hair, cascading nearly to her waist. Then she thought of Elizabeth Cauthen and bravely pointed to a spot just below her shoulder.

"It's a shame to cut it," Nyla ventured. "You have beautiful hair."

"I wanted to try something different," Brooke told her. "And the good thing about hair is it always grows back."

"If you want, I can donate it to the people who make wigs for cancer patients."

Brooke was touched by the thought. "I would like that very much. Thank you."

After a moment the girl asked, "How blond do you want to go?"

"Just sort of a honey color," she said. "And I want it to look natural."

Concentrating like she was about to do brain surgery, Nyla said, "I'll use a combination of three colors—if that's okay."

"You're the one who graduated from beauty school," Brooke said. "I trust you."

The girl gave her an odd look, and Brooke guessed she didn't hear those words often. Then Nyla went to work. She was nervous but efficient and, more importantly, silent. Brooke was relieved that she didn't have to make small talk while pretending to be someone she wasn't.

While she was sitting under the dryer, her hair sticking out like an aluminum alien, Brooke saw Hunter walk by pulling two suitcases. One was black and the other was brown. She wasn't sure which he considered *cute*. He let his eyes stray casually into the salon, and to his credit he controlled his reaction when he saw her.

The process of removing the foils was long and nerve-wracking, especially since Brooke was very anxious to see the finished product. Once the foils were out, Brooke tried to turn around and look in the mirror, but Nyla stopped the chair's spin with her hand.

"I'd like you to wait until it's dry, if you don't mind."

Brooke nodded. She'd waited this long; she could wait a few more minutes.

Nyla dried and styled her masterpiece. Finally she turned Brooke toward the mirror.

Brooke stared at her reflection. The color was a perfect blend of three different shades of blond. The shorter length would take some getting used to, but it was stylish and she thought she would eventually like it. And most importantly, she looked a lot like Elizabeth Cauthen.

She smiled at Nyla in the mirror. "You get another A."

The girl smiled back. "I hope you like being a blond."

"Thanks." Brooke paid Nyla, giving her a generous tip in spite of Hunter's instruction to the contrary. Then she walked out of the salon.

Hunter was loitering in front of a jewelry kiosk two stores down. She started walking toward him. As she approached, he eyed her hair but didn't comment on it. Brooke was disappointed and afraid that maybe her confidence in the perfection of her hair was unfounded. So she was subdued as she followed him to the end of the mall. He stopped at the entrance to a large department store.

He leaned close and said, "I got you a few pairs of jeans and some shirts. You may never wear them, but they'll help to fill up your suitcase. I also bought you a pair of tennis shoes and some leather sandals. I estimated that you wear about a size seven."

"You estimated exactly right," Brooke replied.

"This store should have anything else you need—something to sleep in, makeup, whatever."

She frowned. "All these remarks about my hair and makeup are starting to give me a complex."

He ignored this altogether and continued, "You've got fifteen minutes, so shop fast. Do you need money?"

She shook her head.

With a nod, he moved to a position on the perimeter where he could watch her without being obvious.

Taking her time limit seriously, Brooke walked from section to section grabbing anything she thought she might need—a pair of cotton pajamas, some socks, a hairbrush, some perfume. She stopped by the Clinique counter and got some mascara and moisturizer. Then she paid and joined Hunter by the door.

"Did you get everything you need?"

She nodded. "You should see an improvement in my appearance very soon."

"All that matters is that you look like Elizabeth Cauthen and show up at the war resort with everything she would bring."

Brooke rolled her eyes. It was impossible to joke with this man. He had no sense of humor.

When they got to the Cavalier, Hunter opened the brown suitcase in the backseat so Brooke could pack her purchases.

"This is the cute one?" she asked him.

"This is yours," he replied. "Remove the tags from everything." He watched over her shoulder to be sure she didn't miss anything. The things he'd gotten her were not ugly and were amazingly close size-wise. It made her wonder if he had looked through her backpack while she slept.

"Go ahead and take off those boots," he pointed at her feet. "I'll toss them when I get rid of your hat and shirt."

She took off the boots and slipped on the sandals. The cool leather felt wonderful on her feet, but she wouldn't admit that to Hunter and give him any undeserved satisfaction.

He was zipping her suitcase closed when a black sedan with tinted windows pulled up behind them. Brooke froze with fear, but Hunter didn't seem alarmed. He turned calmly as a tall, heavyset man wearing a purple jogging suit got out of the car.

"Don't worry," he whispered to her. "It's one of Hack's guys. He has driver's licenses for us in the Cauthens' names."

"Man, I got more than that!" the purple-suited man said. He shook hands with Hunter and nodded politely at Brooke. Then he showed them an envelope. "I've got credit cards, insurance cards, report cards." He paused to grin at them. "Not really report cards, but I do have a copy of all the correspondence the Cauthens received from the Civil War resort—including their employment contracts—just in case you need them."

"These are great," Hunter said. "Thanks."

"Let us know if you need anything else," the man added as he walked back to his car. Then he drove off.

Once they were sitting back in the Cavalier, Hunter said, "Take out everything that has your real name on it."

She sorted through her wallet and finally handed him a stack. He added her stack to the things he had taken from his own wallet. He put them in a hidden compartment in the bottom of his backpack and then started the car.

As they left the parking deck at the mall, Brooke organized the new cards in her wallet. Staring at the Tennessee driver's license with her picture and Elizabeth Cauthen's name, she asked, "How did he get all this stuff?"

"Hack's got special talents, and he trains his guys well."

"They're computer hackers?"

"That's how he got his name."

Through the Cavalier's cracked windshield, she could see the black sedan parked along the curb up ahead. After they passed it, the sedan pulled in behind them.

"Is he coming with us?"

"Just to the entrance of the resort," Hunter confirmed. "Hack will have men stationed around outside in case we need them."

Normally an announcement like that would have made her feel that her privacy was being invaded, but under the circumstances it was a comfort.

CHAPTER FIVE

SAVANNAH SPENT ALL MORNING LOOKING through the police records that Hack had pilfered from the Nashville PD, searching for some mention of Brooke or a college student that met her description. Savannah was pretty sure that this assignment fell into the category of busywork, but she did it just in case there was a chance it would help.

Neely made chicken soup for lunch and insisted that Savannah try some. "Mom always made it for us when we were sick. And you can't live off Gatorade and Sprite for the next eight months."

Savannah pushed herself away from Raleigh's desk and said, "I'll give it a try."

When they had all gathered in the kitchen, Dane asked her, "So, did you find anything that matches our criteria?"

"No," Savannah said. "I've lost all confidence in the human race, but I haven't found a case that involves Brooke."

Steamer walked in and sat heavily in a chair.

"So," Dane said as Neely put a bowl of soup in front of Steamer. "I'm guessing it didn't go well?"

"You guess right. I didn't get anywhere. I mean, they're more than not talking to me," he said as he spooned soup into his mouth. "They're completely ignoring me. When I complained, they told me to leave and threatened to call security."

Dane frowned. "I'll go with you after lunch. And if they still won't talk, we'll get General Steele involved with this situation too."

Savannah carefully swallowed some soup. It didn't come back up immediately, so, encouraged, she took another small bite.

"How is Caroline's playhouse coming along?" Neely asked.

"Too slowly to suit her," Savannah replied. "So Caroline is learning a lesson in patience."

"We're all getting a little dose of that," Hack muttered.

"Patience is a virtue," Savannah said.

"Well then, we're all going to be real virtuous by the time this operation is finished," Steamer predicted.

When the meal was over, Savannah tried to help clean up the kitchen, but Neely refused the offer.

"Go back to reading about all the crimes committed in Nashville," Neely insisted. "I'll handle this."

Savannah was in the middle of a case involving a drug ring run by elementary school teachers when Dane came over to tell her good-bye.

"If that's depressing you, I'll tell Hack you don't want to do it anymore."

She shook her head. "I want to help Brooke."

He pressed a kiss to her forehead. "I'm driving into Nashville to see if I can convince the DA to talk to me. Steamer's going with me, but Hack will be here if you need anything."

"Be careful," Savannah instructed. "And good luck."

After the men were gone, Savannah worked until a crack of thunder startled her from the case file she was reading.

Hack walked in, looking more grim than usual. He flipped the light switch and said, "The sky has turned as dark as night. We may be in for bad weather."

"We have a storm cellar in the basement if it gets too bad," Neely told him.

Hack seemed relieved. "Let's turn off the computers in case we lose power."

They were sitting in the family room watching the rain beat against the windows when Dane and Steamer returned.

"Man, it's like a monsoon out there!" Steamer cried.

"Has the power been out?" Dane asked.

"No, we just turned everything off as a precaution," Hack replied.

"How did it go?" Savannah asked.

"The DA won't meet with me either," Dane said. "I made as big a commotion as I dared, but the secretary steadfastly insisted that the DA was not available. So finally we left not knowing any more than we did when we arrived."

"They are being very uncooperative."

Dane frowned. "It's time I made a call to General Steele."

"No, you can call the general later. Right now we're going to eat my birthday cake before it gets stale," Neely announced.

"You won't have to tell me twice," Hack said.

"Me neither," Steamer agreed, sitting on a barstool by the kitchen island.

Neely took the bakery box out of the refrigerator and said, "I've been dreading the cake-cutting moment since Raleigh and the kids aren't here, but I've been blessed with a wonderful brother, sister-in-law, and friends! I'm glad I could share this moment with all of you."

Savannah gave Neely a quick hug. "We're glad to be here with you too!"

"Let's eat some cake," Hack said.

Savannah sat beside Steamer while Neely stuck four pink candles in the middle of the cake. "Since I don't want to risk a house fire, we'll just commemorate each decade I've been alive instead of each year."

Savannah laughed. "Make a wish, Neely! And blow out the candles."

Neely closed her eyes and wished fervently.

Savannah had no doubt what Neely's wish, or prayer, had been.

Neely put slices of the cake on dishes and passed them out. Savannah nibbled while the men ate with relish. Neely didn't eat any cake at all.

***

When Brooke and Hunter arrived at the entrance to the Civil War resort, a uniformed guard instructed them to follow the signs to the employee parking lot. Once the old Cavalier was parked, Hunter opened the trunk and unloaded their new luggage.

Brooke took the not-so-cute brown suitcase by the handle and dragged it as she followed Hunter toward the door marked Employees Only. A woman was standing there to greet them. She was almost as tall as Hunter and twice as wide. Her period costume included a hoop skirt, which made her seem even more substantial. Her hair was an unnatural color of red and twisted into a mass of ringlets that encircled her head.

"I am Wilma Frye, the employee coordinator," she said when they reached her. "And you are?"

"Elizabeth and Scott Cauthen," Hunter provided.

She referred to her clipboard. "Oh yes, the couple with the incorrect measurements. I'm so glad you realized the mistake and notified us. Costuming has been working to alter your clothes, so you need to get up there fast."

She thumbed through a boxful of large manila envelopes and pulled out one with "Cauthen—Room 203" written across it in bold letters. "Here is your orientation packet. It contains your room key. There is a map of the facility and a list of rules. All of this will be discussed during orientation." She pointed down the hallway. "You'll find the elevators this way. Go to the second floor and drop your luggage off in your room. Then go to the basement and find the door that says 'Costuming.' You can't miss it. And hurry, because you have to be in costume for the orientation meeting!"

Brooke and Hunter followed Wilma's pointing finger down the hall and rode the elevator to the second floor. Hunter looked in the envelope and pulled out a plastic key. They stopped in front of the door to room 203, and Hunter slid the plastic key through the lock. Brooke turned the handle, and they stepped inside the room.

Their temporary home was composed of a little kitchenette; a sitting area with a couch and television; and the bedroom, tucked into an alcove, with an attached bathroom.

The room seemed very small, too small for Brooke and a man she barely knew. Brooke had a moment of panic, but Hunter didn't seem bothered at all. He put their suitcases in a corner and looked around.

Finally he said, "It looks secure." He walked to the door. "Now let's see if we can find costuming."

The minute they stepped off the elevator in the basement, they became part of the crowd of new employees congregated around the door to costuming.

"Looks like we found it," Brooke murmured.

"But I don't know how we'll be ready in time for the meeting," Hunter replied.

They watched the couples in front of them enter the room and come out pushing rolling racks full of old fashioned clothes. The process did seem to be moving quickly, and in less time than Brooke had anticipated they were at the front of the line.

"Name?" a woman demanded.

"Cauthen," they answered in unison.

"Oh, we've been waiting for you! It's a good thing you noticed that the measurements you'd sent earlier were wrong. Although I'm not sure our head seamstress, Mrs. Tabor, thinks so. She's had to spend the last few hours altering your things."

"I'm sorry," Brooke felt obligated to say.

"Don't worry about it. Follow me!" She headed off into the large room. Over her shoulder she added, "I'm Dylanne, by the way."

"Nice to meet you," Hunter answered for both of them.

Hunter and Brooke trailed after her, dodging clothes racks and sewing tables.

When they reached a far corner, Dylanne yelled, "Mrs. Tabor! The Cauthens are here!"

Brooke braced herself for complaints from the seamstress about the erroneous measurements, but Mrs. Tabor turned out to be very good-natured. With a tape measure around her neck and straight pins inserted randomly across her apron, she welcomed them with a hug.

"Oh, you're such a handsome couple," she gushed. "I just know you're going to look beautiful in the costumes we've made for you! But you're going to have to try them on before you take them since we're not sure about the fit."

Dylanne returned pushing two racks out of the back room. One contained three dresses, and the other had four gray uniforms lined up side by side.

"I'm a Confederate soldier?" Hunter asked with obvious dismay.

Mrs. Tabor nodded. "Most of our guests are Southerners, so most of our employees have to be Union soldiers to make up the difference. But a few get to be part of the Confederacy. Aren't you lucky!"

Hunter nodded. "Lucky me."

"One uniform is a formal or 'dress' uniform," Mrs. Tabor told Hunter. "It's made of linen, and you wear it at night when you'll be dancing or watching a play—where it won't get damaged. The other three are made from broadcloth, which is not as pretty but is sturdier and intended for battles. Nothing makes me angrier than to see an employee out on the battlefield in one of my formal uniforms, so pay close attention and pick the right one for the right occasion."

He nodded. "I'll be careful."

Then Mrs. Tabor directed him toward the dressing room a few feet away on her left. "The uniform parts are all hung together and in order so you shouldn't have any trouble figuring out what goes where, but if you do, just ask."

Hunter nodded.

She continued, "If one uniform fits, they'll all fit, so just try on one."

He pushed his rack into the dressing room to the left.

Brooke was staring at her clothes. "These are beautiful," she whispered, fingering a dress made of gray silk. It had rows and rows of delicate lace.

"In the old days this lace would have been handmade in France," Mrs. Tabor told her. "Now it's made by machine."

"It's hard to imagine that it could look *better*—even with French lace."

Mrs. Tabor seemed pleased by Brooke's appreciation of the high-quality costume. "Thank you. We try hard to make our costumes authentic and beautiful."

The pink calico dress was ridiculously girly with ruffles and flounces, but oddly it was Brooke's favorite. However, Mrs. Tabor chose the red-and-yellow plaid dress for Brooke to wear that evening.

"Come and let's get started," she said. "For women in the 1860s, getting dressed was quite a process."

Dylanne grabbed hold of the rack and pushed it to the dressing room on the right.

Brooke followed with trepidation. Once they were inside the dressing room, Mrs. Tabor took some items from the rack.

"Here is a pair of black hose, pantalets, and a camisole," she said. "Put these on, and then we'll help you with your hoop, a petticoat, and the dress."

Brooke accepted the stack of 1860s underclothing and put them on the small bench inside the dressing room. She was about to pull off her T-shirt when she realized that Mrs. Tabor and Dylanne were standing in the open doorway watching her.

"Don't be shy!" Mrs. Tabor said. "No one can see you except Dylanne and me—and your husband when he comes out of his dressing room!"

Brooke wasn't prudishly modest, and she probably would have been okay with changing in front of the wardrobe ladies, especially since she might need reassurance that she was putting everything on right. But the thought of Hunter opening the door of his dressing room and seeing her in some state of undress was more than she could bear. So she stood there, paralyzed.

Mrs. Tabor frowned. "We don't have a minute to waste. The new-employee orientation meeting starts very soon!"

Brooke was trying to think of a way to explain why she didn't want her "husband" to see her undress when the door to Hunter's dressing room opened. He was standing there wearing the pants of his uniform. His well-muscled chest was bare. Only the faint pinkish tint to his cheeks indicated his embarrassment.

"Can you ladies help me?" he asked although his eyes were on Brooke. "I can't figure out how to get this uniform on." This was a blatant attempt on his part to lure Mrs. Tabor and Dylanne away with both his impressive physique and feigned male incompetence. It worked like a charm.

Mrs. Tabor threw her hands in the air and laughed. "You silly boy! Of course we'll help you."

Then both women left to rescue him and, no doubt, admire him at closer range. And Brooke was left alone. She smiled her thanks and closed the door of her dressing room. Quickly she put on the items Mrs. Tabor had given her. Even though they were technically underwear, they covered more than modern outer clothes, so Brooke didn't feel too self-conscious when she opened the door and walked out into the main room.

Mrs. Tabor and Dylanne had helped Hunter get his shirt and uniform coat on. He was an incredibly handsome sight, standing straight and tall like the soldier he really was. Brooke whistled in appreciation.

He jerked around, startled.

"Hold still, sir! I need to get these pants pinned up," Mrs. Tabor instructed Hunter while holding straight pins between her lips. "Then we'll get your wife's dress on."

Brooke watched in fascination as the pins moved with Mrs. Tabor's mouth, and she wondered how the seamstress kept from swallowing them.

Once Hunter's pants were pinned to Mrs. Tabor's satisfaction, she stood. "Slip those off, and Dylanne will hem them."

As Hunter headed to his dressing room, the women turned their attention to Brooke.

"Grab that hoop," Mrs. Tabor told her assistant.

Brooke stood still as they placed it on the ground. She stepped into the center, and they lifted it up to her waist and then tied it. Next they added the petticoat.

"In the 1860s you would have worn one petticoat underneath your hoop skirt and at least one petticoat on top," Mrs. Tabor informed her. "But here we let you get by with just the one on top."

"To keep you from heat exhaustion," Dylanne explained.

Hunter returned wearing his jeans and the loose, open-necked shirt that was apparently worn under the jacket. He handed the pants to Dylanne, who hurried off to hem them.

Mrs. Tabor waved to Hunter. "Let me show you how to help your wife put on her dress. There are some tricks to it, and you'll be the only help she has from now on."

Hunter stepped up beside Brooke. He didn't seem uncomfortable with the idea of helping her dress. He was all business, paying close attention so he could do his job well. Nothing personal. She wished she could learn to be so detached about everything. Life would hurt less for someone who didn't take things to heart.

Mrs. Tabor began her instructions. "You bunch the skirt up from the bottom." She demonstrated. "Not enough to wrinkle it, but just so you can get a firm hold on it."

Hunter bunched the skirt fabric as instructed.

"Once you have the skirt up to the waist, you lift the dress over her head. She can help you bring it down into place."

As Hunter leaned above her and dropped the dress over her head, Brooke was thankful for the substantial underclothing of days gone by.

"Put your arms into the sleeves," Mrs. Tabor said to Brooke.

Brooke complied. Then she pressed the bodice of the gown tightly against her chest.

"Now, Mr. Cauthen, help the fabric settle into place. Just give it a few gentle tugs."

Mrs. Tabor showed him how to arrange the yards of red-and-yellow plaid fabric down over the hoop. The dress had rows of black ribbon and lace along the hem and sleeves.

"And now for the buttons." Mrs. Tabor pushed back a ringlet that had escaped from her bun and then pulled a little metal tool, which resembled a crochet hook, from her pocket. "This is an ingenious little device that they invented to make buttoning easier. Don't expect to be able to do it as fast as I can, but your speed will increase with practice."

Mrs. Tabor told Brooke to stand straight. Then Hunter observed the buttoning process.

Once the dress was on, Mrs. Tabor pulled Brooke's hair up into a loose bun and secured it with hairpins.

"Next door is hairdressing," the woman told Brooke. "In the morning you'll go by there and let them fix your hair. But we don't have time for that now so this will have to do."

Mrs. Tabor put a bonnet on Brooke's head and tied the ribbons into a bow under her chin. Then the woman stepped back and admired her handiwork. "Don't you look nice! You have the perfect figure for the gowns of the Civil War era—a tiny waist and curves in all the right places!"

Brooke carefully kept her eyes away from Hunter to avoid dying of humiliation.

As Mrs. Tabor smoothed the fabric of the skirt, she explained, "This is a day dress and so is the pink calico. You will wear them on alternate days so they can be washed in between. You'll find a laundry bin in your room. Just put the things in it that need to be laundered, and roll it outside your door."

"And I wear the gray silk at night?" Brooke asked.

"Yes, it is your evening gown. You'll wear it to dinner and other night-time activities. Since it will get less wear, you can probably make it all week between launderings. You may wear your bonnet indoors if you'd like, but it must be worn if you go outside. And there is a shawl on your clothes rack. Here in the mountains the evenings are sometimes cool."

"It's a lot to remember," Brooke said.

"If you get confused, you can come here and ask us," Mrs. Tabor said. "Or just ask any of the other girls."

Dylanne returned with Hunter's pants. He took them into his dressing room while Mrs. Tabor and Dylanne helped Brooke with her slippers and gloves.

Mrs. Tabor said, "You can put your slippers on first tomorrow. It's much easier when you aren't working around that hoop. Or just let your husband put them on for you."

When Hunter came out wearing his full uniform—including the properly hemmed pants and a long, shiny sword—Mrs. Tabor studied him critically. Finally she nodded. "The alterations look perfect. Step over here in front of the mirror so you can see the transformation."

Mrs. Tabor sent Brooke to a three-way mirror at the far end of the room. Hunter met her there, and together they studied their reflections. His high cheek bones, square jaw, and sober gray eyes made him look just like a soldier headed to war. And wearing her beautiful dress with her newly blond hair pulled back in a bun, Brooke felt as if she, too, had stepped back in time.

"We don't look like ourselves anymore," she whispered.

Hunter scowled at his reflection. "I don't feel like myself either."

She smiled. "I'm sorry you can't be a Yankee."

"I really am a soldier in the Union Army," he whispered back. "Wearing this uniform makes me feel like a traitor."

Mrs. Tabor came rushing over. "You've admired yourselves long enough. Now go on to the meeting! We'll get Mr. Cauthen's other pants hemmed and then deliver your clothes to your room."

"Thank you," Hunter said.

Brooke nodded. "Yes. Thank you."

"You're welcome." Mrs. Tabor followed them to the door. "I'm sure Wilma told you, but you cannot walk around outside your room unless you are dressed in full costume. It's a fire-able offense."

"She told us," Brooke said.

"Which way is the meeting?" Hunter asked.

"First floor," Mrs. Tabor replied. "Just follow the crowd." She reached up to straighten the gold braid on Hunter's shoulder. "And conduct yourself proudly since you are a Confederate officer."

Hunter nodded. "I'll give the uniform the honor it deserves."

They were about to step out into the hallway when the seamstress stopped them.

"Here, let me show you how a gentleman and his lady walked in the 1860s." She tucked Brooke's hand through the crook of his arm.

With her gloved palm pressed against the fabric covering Hunter's forearm, Brooke could feel his muscles tense.

Mrs. Tabor beamed at them. "Lovely. Now go on."

So they walked to the elevators arm in arm—his brass buttons shining and her hoop skirt swaying.

***

When they exited the elevator on the first floor, there was indeed a crowd for them to follow. They filed into a large room where many other new employees were already seated in folding chairs lined up in neat rows. Wilma Frye was there with her clipboard, checking everyone off as they entered.

"You're the Cauthens, right?" she asked as Brooke and Hunter approached.

They nodded in unison.

Wilma pointed to an exquisitely beautiful little woman beside her. "This is the director of our resort, Jovette Weeks."

"Nice to meet you." The director's dark brown hair was arranged in a complicated series of ringlets. Her brown eyes were large and friendly. And her red silk dress was breathtaking.

Hunter spoke for both of them. "I'm Scott, and this is my wife, Elizabeth."

"Welcome," the director said. "I hope this will be the best summer of your lives."

This seemed unlikely, but Brooke smiled. "Thank you, Ms. Weeks."

The little woman waved a dainty hand. "Call me Jovette, please. Do either of you play the piano?"

Brooke said, "I do."

"If you'd stay after this meeting for a few minutes, we're going to audition for a pianist to play for our guests during dinner and to accompany the band during the after-dinner balls. If you're chosen, it's an increase in pay and a lighter daily schedule since you have to work at night."

Brooke nodded. "I'd be glad to audition."

Jovette smiled. "Now it's time for the meeting to begin. Find a seat."

Hunter and Brooke located two empty chairs together and sat down—no easy task with his sword and her huge hoop skirt.

Jovette walked up to the front of the room and tapped a microphone. "If you'll be seated, we will get things started."

She welcomed everyone and then turned the time over to Wilma, who showed them a never-ending PowerPoint presentation of the resort, including details of the amenities, activities, and regulations. Even in pictures, the resort was impressive. It was built in horseshoe shape, with a beautifully landscaped park area in the middle called The Commons. The edges of the horseshoe were made up of shops, restaurants, and other historically correct buildings—like an old-timey cul-de-sac. Between the shops and The Commons was a wide brick walkway. At the open end of the horseshoe was a large battlefield with bleachers on each side for spectators.

Wilma's presentation was informative but much too long, and Brooke had to struggle to keep her mind from wandering. She glanced at Hunter, expecting to see him looking as bored as she felt. But he was alert and looking covertly around the room—no doubt searching for trouble. She was glad that he took his job so seriously, but sometimes she wished he would just relax and act normal.

She leaned close and whispered, "Are you regretting your decision for us to impersonate the Cauthens?"

He turned his head slightly so that his lips were pressed against her ear. "I've been regretting that decision ever since I saw the Confederate uniform."

She smiled even though she knew he wasn't joking.

The PowerPoint presentation finally ended, but the meeting did not. Wilma then gave them a virtual tour of the administration building, using a laptop to project the images on a screen. With the cursor she pointed to a room to the right of the building's entrance. "This is the cafeteria. Lunch and dinner are served here for the staff. A continental breakfast is provided, but if you prefer something more substantial, you have a small kitchen in your room and there is a little grocery store on The Commons. As employees you get a ten percent discount on anything you buy there."

Wilma moved the cursor to the image of the next room.

"This is the laundry room where you can wash your personal items. Costumes are laundered by the resort. If you have any problems with your clothing, see Mrs. Tabor in costuming."

Wilma navigated on the screen to an office area down the hall. "Here is where you come if you have questions about your salary or employee benefits." The cursor moved down to the basement. "Here is a a lounge with a big television and a game room that has a pool table. These areas are to be used only when you are off duty and always still in costume. The only time you are allowed to dress in your regular clothes is when you are in your private room."

Jovette stepped forward and spoke into the microphone. "I know this may seem a little extreme to some of you, but we want everything to be as authentic as possible so we can give our guests a genuine feel of the Civil War era. And clothing is a big part of that."

"During the pilot stages of this resort, costumes were the favorite part for the guests," Wilma inserted. "So even though you might get a little tired of wearing them, remember it's all about our guests and making their experience positive."

Jovette smiled. "We want you to stay in your assigned character, but we realize that there are times when you will need to relax. That's why we've provided the TV and game room. But we do ask that you wear your costumes, just in case one of the guests wanders in."

"Technology was not a part of life in 1860, so it can't be a part of your life here," Wilma went on. "No phones, computers, handheld games, iPods, iPads—*i* anything!"

"You can keep your cell phones with you for emergencies as long as you keep them silent and out of sight," Jovette said.

Wilma just had to add, "If you are seen texting or talking on a cell phone in the presence of guests, you can be fired on the spot."

"We do need your cooperation on this matter," Jovette said with a friendly smile.

Wilma continued, "The upper floors of this building are made up of housing for employees." She turned away from the screen and addressed the group. "You all have schedules in your packet telling you where to be at what time. You also have a map of the resort to help you until you learn the layout. Guests leave on Saturday night and come in on Monday morning, so everyone is off on Sunday. You all get an additional day off each week—check your schedule for when. This week is abbreviated since you're being trained, so you have no day off until Sunday."

Jovette said, "You'll get a new schedule each Sunday. We try to mix up the assignments to give you variety, but we do have to match duties with skills. If you aren't happy with something on your schedule, see Wilma and she will try to accommodate you."

Wilma didn't look very happy about this. "But in the meantime, go where you're scheduled. We can't have areas unmanned because someone doesn't like their assignment."

"We're trying to keep things simple to make sure everything will run smoothly," Jovette explained. "And we can't do that without you!"

"The guests have a schedule too," Wilma announced, pointing at another chart on the screen. It listed breakfast times, followed by a few optional activities before the Battle of the Day, which took place from ten until noon. Guests were given an hour for lunch, and then classes were available during the afternoon.

"The Battle of the Day is the main event, so to speak," Wilma said. "Your packets contain information each soldier needs to learn about the battles we re-create and about your roles in particular."

"During the battles, the women sit in the bleachers and watch, cheering for their teams, as it were," Jovette said. "It's hot, so bring your parasols."

"That's why we do the battles in the morning. It's hot now, but it will be more so in July and August, so read the section on heatstroke in your employee handbook and take the necessary precautions.

"After the Battle of the Day, there's an hour lunch break. Some of you are scheduled to eat the first half of the hour, and some the second. These are staggered so we can staff all work stations during meals. Then in the afternoon we provide a variety of classes and activities. The sewing and cooking classes are for the women, and the fox hunts, fishing, et cetera, are for the men."

Jovette gave everyone a bright smile. "The resort does not discriminate on any basis, though, so if men want to take the cooking classes, they are welcome. Likewise, the women may hunt and fish if they wish."

Wilma continued. "All the classes end by four o'clock, and dinner isn't served until seven, so this is considered discretionary time for the guests. This will be a good opportunity for them to shop in our fine souvenir and gift stores, which provide income and help pay your salaries."

"Technically, *all* time is discretionary time for guests," Jovette inserted. "We are not going to make them go to classes or activities. However, the classes do have to be staffed, so schedules are important for our employees."

"So don't think that 'discretionary time' applies to you," Wilma reiterated sternly. "You cannot leave your station early or even switch your meal time without permission."

Brooke was getting used to the good cop/bad cop way of presenting information.

"Each evening there is a special activity for our guests," Wilma said. "We hold two formal balls, host a play by a troupe of professional actors, have a hoedown in The Commons, and offer a musical recital. Some of you will be off duty during these activities; others will be assigned to help. Refer to your schedules."

Jovette reclaimed the microphone. "Now we'll hear from Dr. Sambosa, our activities director. Dr. Sambosa has a doctorate in history, specializing in the Civil War era. He has helped us develop the activities we will provide for our guests. He has also set up reenactments of five battles that took place in the state of Tennessee during the Civil War. Tomorrow's battle— Chickamauga—took place not too far from here and was one of the most well-known Confederate victories."

There was applause from the predominantly Southern crowd, along with a smattering of boos from the others.

Brooke glanced at Hunter and saw that his jaw was tightly clenched. He didn't join in the boos, but she didn't have any doubts about where his loyalties lay.

Jovette pointed to the man who had joined her. "I'll turn the time over to him now."

Dr. Sambosa was a stereotypical academic wearing a tweed jacket and glasses, and he had a passion for his chosen field. He was not a particularly good speaker, so even though Brooke was interested in the concept for the resort and wanted to know what they would be doing for the next week, she found it hard to concentrate on his long-winded discourse.

Finally he concluded and Jovette asked, "Any questions?"

Unfortunately there were some. Hunter and Brooke sat quietly while a few of their fellow employees posed questions, most of which had already been answered at some point during the comprehensive orientation.

Brooke was relieved when the director called the meeting to a close.

"And now we have a special treat for you," Jovette told them. "You are invited to eat dinner in the formal dining room at the Plantation House, which is usually reserved only for our guests. After the meal we'll have music and dancing."

"We thought it would help you slip into character if you could experience a night like one that would have taken place in the 1860s," Wilma added. "But after tonight your meals will be served in the employee cafeteria."

"When the dancing is over, feel free to walk around the grounds and familiarize yourself with the layout if you haven't done so already." Jovette waved toward the door. "We will reassemble at the Plantation House. Consult your map or just follow the crowd."

Hunter and Brooke waited until most of the others had left the room before joining the small group of musicians who wanted to audition for the piano-playing job.

Jovette rushed over and breathlessly said, "Thank you for your willingness to help us out musically! There's a piano in the dining room at the Plantation House. I thought I'd let you each play a few songs, then I'll choose the person I think is best suited for our purposes." She gave them a smile and started walking. "Come with me, please."

They went out into the pleasant evening air and strolled along the brick pathway toward the Plantation House—a Tara-looking redbrick building with six white columns. Crystal chandeliers sparkled through the front windows, which were flanked by black shutters. A neat green lawn, manicured shrubs, and a variety of multicolored flowers completed the 1860s look.

Wilma met the group at the large wooden doors and led the way into a huge room with round tables covered by floor-length white cloths. An arrangement of candles, surrounded by flowers, decorated each table. The lighting was bright enough for Brooke to appreciate the beauty of the room but dim enough to be romantic.

As their fellow employees were settling down at the tables, Wilma showed Brooke and the other musicians to a fabulous baby grand piano set up on a little stage in the corner of the room. It looked antique, with yellowed ivory keys, and Brooke felt an immediate appreciation for the musical instrument.

Jovette ran her hand along the edge of the piano. "There's a notebook full of old music—period correct, of course—that was compiled by Mr. Sambosa. So pick out whatever tickles your fancy and play!"

A nervous-looking young man went first. He played a couple of songs with textbook accuracy. When he was finished, Jovette thanked him and asked for the next person.

Brooke noticed that the waiters were beginning to deliver salads to the other employees, and her stomach growled. It had been a long time since breakfast at the Family Café.

A middle-aged woman went next. She played with more heart but made several obvious mistakes. Jovette gave her a polite smile and thanked her. Then she pointed to Brooke.

"Your turn."

Brooke settled herself on the piano bench and thumbed through the notebook until she found a piece she liked. She was vaguely aware of all the people sitting at the tables and acutely aware of Hunter. For some reason, his opinion of her musical ability mattered very much.

Her fingers began flying over the keys. She infused emotion into the music by adding compatible chords and occasionally even changing keys. She was absorbed by the music, at one with the baby grand.

Finally she felt a hand on her shoulder, and she looked up to see Hunter standing beside her. "The audition is over," he said softly. "You got the job."

Brooke brought the piece she was playing to a graceful end. Then she looked behind her, where three other people should have been waiting for their turn to play.

"Where are the others?" she asked Hunter.

"They surrendered," he replied as the diners gave her rousing applause.

"You play magnificently!" Jovette complimented. "Like a professional."

"Thank you," Brooke replied.

"Where did you learn to play like that?" Wilma wanted to know.

"My college major is piano, so someday soon I hope I will be a professional."

Jovette patted her arm. "I'm sure you have a very bright future ahead of you."

"I hope so." Brooke picked up the book of music and said, "Can I take this with me so I can familiarize myself with the pieces?"

"I've got several extra copies, so you can have that one," Jovette offered. "We appreciate you sharing your talent with us this summer."

Brooke felt a little guilty knowing that as soon as her impersonation of Elizabeth Cauthen ended they'd be looking for a new pianist. But she said only, "I'm glad to do it."

"Your schedule will have to be altered to accommodate playing for choral practice, square dancing classes, and dinner," Wilma said. "On a regular week we have dances after dinner here in the dining hall on Monday and Friday, so on those nights you'll also play with the band. And I believe the choral performance is on Thursday."

"I'll never be able to remember all that," Brooke said.

"I'll work out a new schedule and print it for you," Wilma promised.

"If my wife's schedule is being changed, mine will have to change too," Hunter said. "The resort agreed to keep us together in case she has an asthma attack."

Wilma frowned as she flipped through the papers on her clipboard. "I don't see any notation to that effect."

"We submitted medical information," Hunter replied.

"I don't have your full file here, of course." Wilma didn't look happy. "I'll double-check that in the computer, and if it's true I'll adjust your schedule too."

"But for now, come eat!" Jovette commanded. "The band will want you to play with them during the dancing, so this is your small window of opportunity."

Hunter escorted Brooke to a table with two empty chairs. The six people already seated there paused from eating their salads and introduced themselves.

"We're the Dooleys from Memphis," said an elderly lady with steel-gray, sausage-style ringlets hanging on both sides of her thin face. "I'm Doreen and this is Bob." She pointed at a bald-headed little man in a Confederate uniform sitting beside her. Then she waved toward a young couple across the table. "And these are the Mengenthals from Mississippi. Elliott and Jada are newlyweds."

The Mengenthals smiled pleasantly as they exchanged greetings with Hunter and Brooke. But they were more interested in each other than in competing with Mrs. Dooley for conversation time.

Doreen waved toward the last two people at the table—two tall, red-headed young men. "Last but not least, Trent and Tate Bouyer. They're twins, so don't ask me to tell you which is which."

"I'm Trent," the one on the left said.

"And I'm Tate," his brother added as they both stood and extended their right hands toward Brooke and then Hunter. "We wanted to be the Tarleton brothers from *Gone with the Wind* since we've got red hair and all. But they made us Yankees!"

Brooke cut her eyes over at Hunter. "I know you're disappointed."

Tate hung his head. "Man, we sure are."

Hunter frowned. "You know that the *Yankees* won the war?"

"Yeah, but that was when the South was fighting without us!" Trent proclaimed.

"We might have had a chance to rewrite history!" his brother added.

Doreen Dooley took exception to this. "You can't change what happened! The battles are *reenacted*—which means they have to turn out the way they did during the Civil War."

The young men exchanged a disappointed glance. "Man!" they said in unison.

Brooke found their optimism and exuberance irresistible. She leaned in and whispered, "Maybe you can sabotage the Union Army and help the Southern boys win the war that way."

Hunter and the Dooleys looked appalled. The Mengenthals couldn't have cared less.

The brothers exchanged a glance. "Now that's a good idea," Trent said.

"That is a terrible idea," Doreen reclaimed control of the conversation. "In order to be authentic, the South has to lose the war. And if you all want to get hired next year, you'd better follow the rules."

"It might be worth my job to change the course of history, don't you think, Mrs. Dooley?" Tate teased.

Doreen shook her head. "I do not. Besides, the South won the battle that we're reenacting tomorrow, so the Confederates don't need your sabotaging help. Now why don't you men tell us about your military responsibilities? Bob is a munitions expert. Cannons." She narrowed her eyes at the brothers. "I particularly want to know where you two will be assigned so I can warn your commanding officer that he might be in for some trouble."

"No, Miss Doreen. Please!" Trent begged. Then reluctantly they admitted that they were assigned to an infantry unit. "I wish we could shoot cannons or at least ride a horse."

"I'm in the infantry too," Hunter told them.

"But you're an officer," Trent said.

"And a Southerner," Tate added with obvious envy.

"Infantry is a dangerous place to be, even if you're an officer," Doreen informed Brooke. "Just go ahead and prepare now. By the end of the week, you'll be a widow!"

Brooke's eyes widened in surprise.

Doreen grinned at what she had apparently meant as a joke. "Fortunately he won't stay dead for long. That's the beauty of reenactment!"

"And how did you get to be a cannon expert?" Hunter asked Bob politely.

Doreen was only too happy to answer for her husband. "He's been involved in reenactments for years. He started out as a private but worked his way up to lieutenant. We're so excited about this opportunity to actually live like people from the Old South. I enjoy watching the battles, but I love the clothes and the dancing and, well, all of that!"

Bob nodded in agreement with his wife but didn't comment. He was apparently used to not getting a word in edgewise.

The waiter arrived with plates on a rolling cart. "You have the choice of beef or chicken," he announced.

Brooke's stomach roiled.

"We're vegetarians," Hunter said, kindly including himself in the noncarnivorous category. "Can we have meat-free plates?"

"Sure," the waiter responded. "I'll be right back."

"Why are you vegetarians?" Doreen demanded. "Don't you know that there are essential nutrients in meat?"

"Some meats trigger my wife's asthma, so we just avoid them all." Hunter sounded so sincere Brooke nearly believed him herself. "But that's not a very interesting topic. Why don't you tell us about the reenactments you've participated in?"

Doreen didn't require any convincing. For the next ten minutes she detailed a redo of the Battle of Gettysburg, with Bob—the actual participant—listening in.

The vegetarian plates were delivered, and Brooke ate the rice pilaf, salad, and yeast rolls. Doreen talked all through dinner, which was a good thing as far as Brooke was concerned since it eliminated the need for her to say anything.

When the group was finished eating, the waiters cleared away the plates and served everyone a piece of pecan pie with a dollop of homemade vanilla ice cream. "Can you eat nuts?" the waiter asked before he placed a plate of pie in front of Hunter.

He glanced at Brooke, who nodded. So he said, "Yes, we can."

While they ate pie and listened to Doreen describe imaginary Civil War carnage, a four-man band came in and set up near the piano. And when dessert was over, Jovette stepped to the microphone.

"We hope you enjoyed your dinner. Now you'll have a chance to enjoy some music and to dance if you'd like. Let's give our band a round of applause!" Jovette pointed toward the musicians.

The fiddle player waved his bow to the crowd.

Brooke clapped along with everyone else.

"We'd also like to thank Mrs. Cauthen for sharing her incredible piano skills with us!"

More enthusiastic applause. Reluctantly Brooke nodded in acceptance.

The band started playing a square dance, and several couples hurried onto the dance floor.

"Are y'all coming?" Doreen asked as she pulled Bob from his seat.

The Mengenthals shook their heads in unison. "We'll wait for a waltz," he explained.

Trent declined for the brothers. "We can't dance with each other, and we haven't had time to meet any girls here yet!"

Brooke stood. "I'm supposed to play with the band, so I'd better get to the piano."

Hunter rose to his feet. "And even though I have no musical abilities, I'll go sit by the band so I can be near my wife."

"Oh, isn't that sweet," Doreen said with a smile. "Are you newlyweds too?"

Two little pink spots appeared on Hunter's cheeks. "No, ma'am."

She gave him an approving nod. "That's even better. It's easy to be romantic when you first marry. Learning to maintain those tender feelings after the honeymoon is the key to a long and successful marriage." She glanced fondly at her husband. "The way Bob and I have."

Brooke would not have described the Dooleys as a perfect couple. But Doreen's words reminded Brooke of her own parents, who did have a successful marriage. She was surprised at how much she missed them and how, for the first time in many years, she longed to be home. Feeling lonely and a little pathetic, she walked to the piano.

"Are you okay?" Hunter, ever aware, asked.

Brooke was embarrassed that she had allowed her emotions to show. She gave him one short nod. He settled in his chair behind the piano, and she turned her attention to the band.

She saw the list of songs leaning against the music rack. "We'll play the songs in this order?" she asked.

The man holding a fiddle nodded. "With one fifteen-minute break in the middle. Miss Jovette chose the order. Then at the end of the evening, they'll divide the room into North and South. The North sings the first verse of 'Battle Hymn of the Republic,' and then the South sings 'Dixie.' After that we're done."

Brooke opened her book of music to the first song on the list. "Okay."

"We do little solos—just to break up the monotony. If I hold up my hand, that means for you to stop playing so we can highlight a band member."

"And how will I know if you want me to play alone?"

The band members exchanged a glance. "I won't assign you any solos tonight."

Brooke knew he meant until he determined how well she could play.

"Since this is your first night and we haven't had time to practice together, just follow along and do the best you can. If a song is too difficult, you can sit it out."

"I've looked through the music, and I think I can play everything."

He seemed a little taken aback. "You can sight-read that well?"

She nodded.

With a little shrug, he put his bow to the fiddle strings. "Show me what you've got."

During the third song, the fiddle player gave Brooke a solo, and she knew she had won his confidence. By the break the band members were treating her like an old friend, insisting that she call them by their first names. The fiddle player was Charlie, and he was accompanied by his brothers Daryl and Dexter. The fourth member of the band was named Rick, apparently no relation.

When the break ended, the band members returned to their instruments while Wilma and Jovette got the "guests" lined up for the Virginia Reel. Charlie leaned toward Brooke and said, "This doesn't have a piano part, so you and your husband go dance." He glanced at Hunter. "He's been patient, but he deserves a little time with his wife."

Brooke doubted that Hunter wanted to dance but knew he wouldn't refuse, and she was tired of sitting. So she scooted the piano bench back and stood.

She held her hand out to Hunter. "Let's go."

After the briefest hesitation, he put his hand in hers, and she led him to the dance floor, where the couples were lining up. Wilma and Jovette gave some quick instructions, including a hilarious demonstration in which they were a couple.

"There, I hope you get the idea," Jovette said a little breathlessly when they were through. "You beginners watch the more experienced dancers and try to follow them. You'll all be experts in no time."

"And that is important," Wilma chimed in. "To help the guests learn, we need a certain number of people who can do the specialized dances like the Virginia Reel. So if you catch on quickly, some evenings you might be assigned to attend the dance, which is a very easy duty."

The dance began, and Brooke loved every minute of it. Hunter tried his best but was completely out of his element. Finally she looked away from his awkward attempts to follow the steps, afraid she'd start laughing hysterically if she kept watching him. When the dance was over, she reluctantly turned toward the piano, but he caught her by the hand and turned her around as the band started playing a slow waltz.

Jovette and Wilma were again demonstrating the proper steps, but this time Brooke had no desire to laugh. She wanted only to enjoy the feeling of Hunter's arms around hers. He pulled her close, and they swayed to the music, not even attempting to actually waltz.

"We should try to be like the Mengenthals," he said softly against her ear. "They can be our model for what a loving married couple acts like."

His words brought her back to reality. They were not a loving couple, and it would be very dangerous for her heart to pretend that they were. She stood a little straighter, separating herself from him physically and emotionally as her gaze settled on the Mengenthals. They were staring into each other's eyes. It was too private to watch, and Brooke turned away.

When the waltz ended, Brooke returned to the piano and started playing again.

Just before ten o'clock, Jovette came to the microphone and asked all those assigned to the Union Army to stand on one side of the room and all those who were part of the Confederacy to stand on the other. She announced that the band was going to play songs for the respective groups and everyone was to sing their hearts out.

"It's a contest, a battle of voices, so to speak."

"Which one do we do first?" Brooke whispered to the fiddle player as the crowd separated into two groups.

"We alternate," he said. "We'll start with the North."

So they played "Battle Hymn of the Republic" first and followed it with "Dixie." Both were rousing and made Brooke feel oddly patriotic.

Hunter didn't have the same reaction. "It's a good thing we won't be here all summer. If I had to hear that 'Dixie' song every week . . ."

She smiled as the band members came over to congratulate her. Charlie said, "You didn't miss a note even though you haven't had time to practice! And that music is not easy!"

Brooke accepted the compliment and didn't tell him that the music in the notebook was not nearly as difficult as the classical pieces she played at school.

Jovette came to the microphone and announced that the evening's activities were at an end. She invited them to walk about the grounds if they felt so inclined and reminded them to be at their appointed places on time the next morning.

"Even though the guests who will be arriving tomorrow are not *paying* guests, we expect you all to take your duties very seriously. We have four days to practice our parts and work out all the kinks before the actual guests arrive. They have paid a premium price to attend this resort, and we intend to give them their money's worth!"

There were cheers and shouts of encouragement from the crowd. Then everyone dispersed. Trent and Tate challenged some other young men to a pool-playing contest. The Dooleys were going to watch a movie and invited Brooke and Hunter to join them.

"We'd like to be alone for a while, so we're going to take a little walk around the resort," Hunter said. "But thank you anyway."

He tucked Brooke's hand through his arm in the 1860s way and led her toward the door. "Hurry," he whispered. "Before they decide they want to walk with us."

That possibility was more than enough to spur her on. As they slipped outside, she saw the Mengenthals walking toward the elevators. Brooke watched them a little wistfully. She didn't miss Rex, but she did miss being in love.

Hunter noticed the direction of her gaze and said, "I guess we should be going upstairs too—if we want to act like a loving couple. But I need to walk around the grounds so I can get my bearings."

She nodded. "Loving couples take walks too."

It was a beautiful early summer evening. They walked arm in arm, looking at the shops and restaurants that lined the brick lane.

He seemed to recognize that she was in a melancholy mood, if not the reason for it. "Are you tired?" he asked.

"Yes," she admitted. It was true.

"Is that huge dress uncomfortable?"

"Surprisingly, it's not. How about your uniform?"

"I'm used to wearing a uniform, so it's fine."

"Except the color?"

He frowned. "And the sword. This thing banging against my leg all the time is annoying."

Brooke smiled as Wilma rushed up to them. "There you are!" she said as though she had been searching for hours. "You were right about the medical information. I don't know how I missed that when I was making assignments. But to avoid legal liability, the company did agree to have you two assigned together." She pressed a sheaf of papers into Hunter's hand. "Both of your schedules have been adjusted. Call me if you have questions. My number's on the bottom." Then she hurried off.

Brooke peered at the schedule. "So, what will we be doing?"

Hunter read aloud, "From nine until ten, you will play the piano for a choral group at the Town Theatre." He looked around The Commons and pointed out a bright yellow building. "Then you watch the Battle of the Day for two hours in the grueling sun. I will only be a few feet away, pretending to fight against my country. Either Jovette or Wilma will sit beside you during this time in case you have an asthma attack. We have the early lunch, and then you play for two dance classes."

"And what will you do during all this?"

"I have to sing with the choral group and provide a dance partner for any unattached women during the dance lessons." He didn't sound thrilled.

"Do you sing?"

"I'm not tone-deaf," he replied.

"Dance?"

He cut his eyes over at her. "You saw me demonstrate my dancing abilities during the Virginia Reel."

She laughed. "Then dance classes should be entertaining."

"From two until five, we work in the ice cream parlor."

His eyes searched again, and he pointed out a cute little pink building with white, wrought iron tables and chairs arranged outside so guests could eat their ice cream alfresco.

"We get an hour break for dinner and to change into our evening clothes. Then you provide musical accompaniment for the guests' dinner while I sit behind you, looking romantic and tragic."

Brooke laughed but Hunter didn't.

"I'm serious," he said. "Those are my exact instructions."

"I don't know about the romantic part, but if tragic looks anything like grim, you've got it down pat."

He seemed mildly offended. "I'm not grim. I have a responsibility, and I don't take it lightly."

"Well, you could relax a little," she said. "Maybe even smile occasionally. My uncle is the most serious person I know, and even he smiles every now and then."

His frown deepened. "I'll try."

She shook her head in despair. "You'll have to try harder than that."

He turned back to the schedule. "And at the very bottom it says you'll need another formal gown—something a little more 'showy' than the gray silk since you're a performer. Costuming will deliver it tomorrow."

She liked the gray silk and wasn't too excited about wearing something showy, but before she could comment, another couple passed them, headed the other way. They stopped and politely introduced themselves. Hunter put his arm around Brooke during the exchange, giving the impression that they were a loving married couple.

As they moved on, she noticed that his eyes were scanning the area.

"What are you looking for?"

"Exits," he replied. "In case an escape becomes necessary. I don't mean to scare you, but I have to be prepared."

"*You* didn't scare me," she said.

He stopped walking and looked down at her. "But you are scared?"

"I'm nervous" was all she was willing to admit.

"Because the police might find you and give you a subpoena, which means you'll be required to testify in a trial?" He itemized the excuses she'd given him with obvious suspicion.

She could not defend herself without telling him more than she wanted anyone to know. So she nodded.

He frowned. "Are you sure there isn't something else you can tell me about this trial and what you witnessed?"

She shook her head. "I've said all I intend to say."

He sighed as they started walking again. "Well then, I'll just do the best I can to protect you, although this whole piano-playing thing makes things more difficult."

"Why?"

"Because Elizabeth Cauthen doesn't play the piano," he said. "But Brooke Clayton does. If anyone looks here for you, that will be a pretty big clue."

"I'm sorry," she murmured, feeling stupid.

"It was just a small mistake, and I know you're new at this, but it's best not to veer too far from our assumed identities."

"I'll be more careful from now on," she promised. "No volunteering." She felt so safe here, so insulated from the real world. But looking out at the darkness that surrounded the resort, she asked, "Do you think the police will look here for me?"

"We've done all we can to cover our tracks," he replied. "They are looking for an individual, and you are part of a couple. But if the police are really determined, they might figure out that you were on the chicken march. They'll check out all the registered march participants. When they can't contact the Cauthens, they'll come here looking for them."

Even though the weather was mild, she felt a chill. "What will we do then?"

He shrugged. "We'll leave. That's why I'm mapping out the exits."

They were quiet for a while as they walked around The Commons. Brooke looked at the shops while Hunter searched for exits. The battlefield loomed in the distance, like a grim reminder of the unhappy reason for them being there.

"How long do you need to hide?" Hunter asked.

"Just until Monday," she said. "After that it will be safe to go home."

He nodded. "We'll probably be okay here until then."

A couple came up and complimented Brooke on her piano playing and Hunter on his good fortune in landing the role of an officer in the Confederate Army.

Once the couple had moved on, Brooke said, "It might help us seem more like a loving couple if we know each other better. Why don't you tell me about yourself?"

"What do you want to know?" He sounded wary.

"Anything. Your favorite color, your favorite dessert . . ."

He said, "I don't have a favorite color, and I eat just about anything."

Brooke cut her eyes over at him. "That doesn't help me get to know you better."

"Sure it does," he argued. "Colors and food aren't important to me. That's something a wife would know."

She shook her head. "Maybe we'll just have to do everything the Mengenthals do."

"They seem a little too much in love."

She sighed. "I don't think there is any such thing."

"I'll take your advice since you know about love and I don't."

She teased, "Well then, I'd better get ready because it's only a matter of time until I get called to testify as an expert witness on love." When he didn't smile, she said, "That was a joke."

"Your safety isn't funny."

"You've really got to work on your sense of humor," she muttered.

"I'll work on my deficient character traits when you're not hiding from the police." Then he turned her around and started back toward the administration building. "I've seen enough to develop a couple of emergency escape plans. So let's go back to our suite and get some rest."

She walked along beside him, her hand on his strong arm. She felt safe with him, and that was a feeling she hadn't experienced in quite awhile.

When they got back to their room, they saw that their costumes had been delivered on rolling carts. They moved the outfits to the closet. Then Hunter offered to let Brooke take the first shower.

He unbuttoned the plaid dress for her. She held it in place until he had worked through all the buttons. Then he lifted it over her head. Even though the underclothes were very substantial, she felt embarrassed. This situation was too intimate for people who barely knew each other. He politely kept his eyes averted as she crossed the room to hang up her dress in the closet. The outfits looked so comfortable side by side—unlike their temporary owners.

She carried her suitcase into the bathroom and took her shower. When she came out wearing her new pajamas, she saw that Hunter had covered the empty rolling carts with a blanket to create a makeshift room divider.

"I'll take my shower now," he said. "You go on to bed and try to get some rest."

"You're sleeping on the couch?" she guessed.

"Yes."

"Or dozing in between calls to Hack," she added.

He nodded as he picked up his suitcase and walked toward the bathroom. "Good night."

Brooke climbed into bed wondering what it would take to actually make Hunter smile. It wouldn't be easy—she was sure of that. But she'd always loved a challenge.

CHAPTER SIX

SAVANNAH GOT UP FROM THE desk in Raleigh's home office and walked to the kitchen to refill her Gatorade bottle with Steamer's magic elixir. When she returned, Savannah heard Neely asking about Brooke.

"Hack, any news from Owl?"

"He sends me texts every hour using a prearranged code, and he hasn't missed one."

"Even during the night?" Savannah asked in surprise.

"Even during the night," Hack confirmed. "Soldiers have to sleep with one eye open."

"You still don't know where they are?"

Hack shook his head. "It would be easy for me to find out, but my orders are to leave it alone."

Dane said, "We'll assume Owl has things under control until he lets us know otherwise or he misses a check-in."

Neely nodded. "I'll trust your judgment."

Dane leafed through the files on the desk. "So have you found any more cases that could involve Brooke?"

"We've found a few that fit your criteria. We gave them to Hack, and he checked them out."

"Nothing," Hack contributed without looking up from his computer.

Dane frowned. "I'd say we could just stop worrying about it, but the police are still parked in front of the house and outside Brooke's apartment. Their determination makes me think we'd better keep looking."

"We know how you hate surprises," Savannah teased wearily.

"Especially surprises involving my niece and the police," Dane replied.

Steamer yawned. "Is that it, Major? I'm ready for bed."

"That's it," Dane said. "Everybody get some rest."

"And be looking forward to breakfast." Savannah smiled at Hack. "Neely is going to make biscuits."

***

Dane walked with Savannah and the others to the stairs.

"Do you think it's too late to call Caroline?" she asked him. "Since it's an hour earlier in Colorado than it is here?"

Dane shook his head. "You know the McLaughlins go to bed when the sun sets. You could call and talk to Doc, but if you want to speak to Caroline you should probably wait until morning."

She nodded. "I'll wait. I'm anxious to see if the cat has had kittens." She cut her eyes up at him. "You know Caroline's already asked if she can bring one home with her."

"I'm allergic to cats," Dane claimed.

"You are not," Neely said. "You just don't like them."

"Same difference," he claimed. "Caroline is getting a brother or sister—that's as close as she's going to get to a pet. She can visit the kittens at her grandparents' house."

Savannah yawned. "That's probably for the best."

Dane kissed her and said, "Go on to bed. I'll be right there."

"Don't be too long," Savannah requested. He hadn't gotten any significant sleep since they'd arrived at Neely's, and she was starting to worry about him.

"I'll come as soon as I can," he promised. Then he returned to Raleigh's office.

Savannah started up the stairs and then changed her mind. If Dane was going to stay up half the night, she would too. So she went back to the office.

Dane was sitting behind the desk, looking solemn.

Savannah walked around the desk and sat on the arm of his chair. "What's wrong?"

He wrapped his arm around her waist and said, "One of Hack's guards just called. We have a visitor."

"Who is it?"

"Nashville's District Attorney."

Being married to Dane, Savannah had learned to expect the unexpected. But this was almost alarming. "Why would the DA refuse to talk to you all day and then come to Neely's house in the middle of the night?"

"That is the question," Dane said. "My guess is to prevent anyone from knowing that he's talking to me."

They both stood as they heard the garage door open. A few seconds later, three men walked into the office. Two were huge, obviously employed by Hack. One was a normal-sized man wearing a raincoat with the collar turned up. Since it wasn't raining, Savannah assumed that Dane was right. The DA didn't want anyone to know that this meeting was taking place.

The man stepped into the office and said, "Major Dane?"

Dane nodded. "Yes."

"I'm Kirk Shaw, district attorney for Davidson County." His sandy blond hair was windblown, and his blue eyes were circled with fatigue. He looked to be in his late thirties, and he spoke with a heavy Southern accent. "I appreciate you meeting me under these dramatically clandestine circumstances."

Dane dismissed the guards and then addressed his guest. "I am confident that you would not take such measures unless they were necessary."

"You are correct," Mr. Shaw replied. "But I'm grateful nonetheless."

Dane waved toward the chairs that were still arranged in a semicircle in front of Raleigh's desk. "Have a seat."

The DA glanced at Savannah. "I'm sorry to ask, but may we speak in private?"

"That won't be necessary," Dane said. "I keep no secrets from my wife."

Mr. Shaw didn't look particularly pleased, but he sat down. Dane sat in the chair behind the desk. Savannah sat on the couch across the room. She hoped that by removing herself slightly from the conversation she would make Mr. Shaw more at ease.

"I came here for two reasons. First, to request that you stop asking questions about Brooke Clayton at the police department and at my office. Doing so endangers a very important case."

"What kind of case?" Dane asked.

Mr. Shaw stole a look at Savannah. "I don't need to remind you that everything I say must be kept in strictest confidence?"

"You don't need to remind us of that," Dane assured him.

Mr. Shaw began his story. "A few weeks ago, Brooke Clayton went on a tour of the new Nature Fresh facility near Nashville. They claim it's the future of the poultry industry—more humane treatment of the animals and more environmentally friendly disposal of the by-products. Anyway, when the new plant opened they invited some animal rights activists in to see it, hoping to earn goodwill and reduce the protests."

"Obviously it didn't work since the protests continue," Dane guessed.

"The company's conciliatory gestures were in vain," Mr. Shaw agreed. "But all that aside, according to Miss Clayton, after leaving the chicken plant she stopped for a picnic lunch in the woods that surround the Nature Fresh property. She drove her car in as far as she could and walked the rest of the way to Willow Creek, which eventually feeds into the Tennessee River. When she was ready to leave, her car wouldn't start and she didn't have cell service. She decided to go back to the Nature Fresh plant, where she could borrow a phone. She knew the plant ran past the creek, so to save time she followed it instead of hiking all the way back out to the road." Mr. Shaw paused.

"Go on," Dane encouraged him.

"She said she'd intended to follow the fence that encloses the Nature Fresh property but when she reached it, the trees were growing too close and would have made walking along it difficult if not impossible. Then she noticed that the water level of the creek was low enough for her to slip under a part of the fence that would ordinarily be underwater. She kept walking on the dry edge of the creek bed up to the plant. Approaching it from the back, she said she saw portions of the chicken plant that had not been a part of the tour."

"Let me guess," Dane said. "This back part of the plant was not environmentally friendly or humane."

Mr. Shaw nodded. "She found chickens packed in coops with inadequate ventilation, and even worse, there was an iron pipe a foot in diameter spewing chicken gore directly into the creek."

"If the creek had been at a normal level the pipe would have been covered by water?" Dane asked.

"Yes," Mr. Shaw confirmed.

"And this creek they are polluting eventually becomes drinking water?"

"It is processed first, of course."

"But dumping chicken waste products into the creek has got to be illegal," Dane said.

"It is," Mr. Shaw confirmed. "Additionally for Nature Fresh, it's a public relations problem. They have recently spent millions of dollars trying to convince the world that they are the greener, kinder choice when buying poultry. If it became known that they were still using inhumane housing methods *and* willfully polluting a creek while running ads about how caring and environmentally responsible they are . . . it could ruin them."

"Through lost sales, fines, and possibly even lawsuits," Dane said.

Mr. Shaw nodded. "At the very least, it would cost them a fortune in legal fees. Miss Clayton took pictures with her phone, turned around, and left the Nature Fresh property the same way she came in. She walked to the road until she got cell service and called a tow truck. She reported what she had seen to the leader of her animal activist group, Freddo Higgins. He brought her and her pictures to me."

"So you agreed to prosecute?"

Mr. Shaw cleared his throat. "I want to impress upon you the seriousness of the situation. Bringing the charges Miss Clayton has leveled against a very well-respected and powerful company must be done with great care."

"You said Brooke gave you pictures she took with her phone."

"Those pictures could have been taken anywhere," Mr. Shaw replied. "I need to get a warrant to search the Nature Fresh property, and the judge won't issue one without Brooke's testimony. When I contacted her she seemed happy, even anxious, to do whatever was necessary to bring Nature Fresh to justice. I arranged a private hearing in the judge's chambers to keep it quiet so the evidence wouldn't be destroyed before we could search the premises. But then Miss Clayton called and told my secretary that she would not be available to testify—ever. She claimed a trial would interfere with her schoolwork."

"When was this?"

"About a week ago," Mr. Shaw said. "I tried to call her back, many times, but never got an answer. So I sent a clerk from my office to her apartment."

"She wasn't home."

"No," Mr. Shaw said. "I asked the Nashville PD to help me find her, but they have been unsuccessful as well. The judge is running out of patience, and that means our case is running out of time. He has set a deadline of Monday at noon. If she doesn't present her testimony by then, he will close the case and it will never come to trial."

"Why can't you go ahead without Brooke's testimony or a search warrant," Dane suggested. "You might not be able to make a great case against them, but even if your case is dismissed they would still pay a price in the things you mentioned—goodwill with customers, lawsuits, and legal fees."

"I care about the environment," Mr. Shaw claimed. "But to accuse a company like Nature Fresh without adequate evidence would be, well, professional suicide."

"And you want Brooke to be the only person who risks anything," Dane said.

Mr. Shaw's face turned red. "I'm not a coward, and neither is the judge. The fact that we're even considering an explosive case like this proves that."

The men stared at each other for a few tense seconds. Finally Dane nodded. "I'll look for her." Then he stood, indicating that the late-night meeting was over.

Mr. Shaw stood too. "When you find her, will you tell me one way or another about her testimony so I'll know how to proceed?"

Dane gave him a little half nod that Savannah knew was short of a commitment. "We'll be in touch."

The men shook hands, and then Dane led Mr. Shaw to the garage door, where Hack's guards were waiting to escort the DA to his car.

When Dane returned, Savannah asked, "What do you make of that?"

"I'm not sure," he replied.

"When are you going to tell Neely?"

"In the morning." Then he pressed a kiss on her cheek. "Why don't you go to bed for what's left of the night."

"What are you going to do?"

"I'm going to check out Nature Fresh."

Savannah sighed. "Wake me up when it's time to tell Neely. She'll need moral support."

"I can provide moral support. I'm her brother."

"You're also a hard-core soldier. Promise you'll wake me up."

"I promise," Dane agreed.

Savannah didn't think she'd be able to sleep, but at Dane's request, she went up to the guest room Neely had assigned to them. She knew he'd work better if he wasn't worrying about her. She climbed into bed, and she did sleep. Dane woke her up at six o'clock on Wednesday morning.

She was instantly alert. "You're ready to tell her?"

He nodded.

"I'll be down in a minute," she said. "Don't start without me."

"I won't."

As Savannah stood and stretched, she noticed that it was still dark outside. But the first few orange rays of sunlight were visible along the horizon. To Savannah they looked like hope.

When she got to Raleigh's office, the guys were sitting in the chairs arranged in front of Raleigh's desk, waiting. She sat in the first empty chair she came to.

A few minutes later, Dane walked in with Neely beside him. She glanced around the room nervously. "Is Brooke okay?"

Dane nodded. "She's fine."

"Raleigh? Adam?"

"Everyone is fine. But we do have some new information. Sit down and I'll tell you."

She took the chair beside Savannah while Dane went behind the desk.

Then, with complete disregard for Mr. Shaw's request that everything he'd said be kept confidential, Dane told Neely about his nighttime visit from the DA and the implications for Brooke.

He concluded with, "What we don't know is why she doesn't want to testify."

"Do you think the people from Nature Fresh could have found out about the pictures she took and threatened her in some way?" Savannah asked.

"I think that's possible," Dane said. "Or maybe they offered her a deal if she wouldn't testify and she accepted. That would explain why she's avoiding the DA."

Neely looked appalled. "Brooke wouldn't take a bribe!"

"It might not be that simple," Dane said. "If they found out she had evidence that could destroy the company, they might have approached her and asked her not to testify."

Savannah was confused. "But why would she agree?"

"Nature Fresh employs a lot of people nationwide," Hack said. "If the company goes under, all those folks lose their jobs."

"So if they promised to clean up the plant . . . I can see Brooke agreeing not to testify," Dane said.

"I guess I can too," Neely agreed, "if you put it that way. But why wouldn't she just tell us?"

"I don't know," Dane said. "And that might not be what happened at all. She really might think that getting involved with a trial would interfere too much with her schoolwork. But whatever her reasons, we're going to respect them. Our job is to keep her safe."

"And you're sure we can do that long distance?" Savannah asked.

"At the moment, yes," Dane answered. "Owl will let us know if that changes. We've beefed up her security detail a little as a precaution." He turned to his team members. "Hack, I've been researching Nature Fresh, but you have resources that I can't access. So I'd like to turn that over to you. I'll give you everything I've got."

Hack nodded. "I'll get right on it."

"Savannah, I need you to help me research the animal activist group that Brooke is a member of. I think it's called Joined Forces or Joint Forces, something like that."

"What am I looking for?" she asked him.

"I don't know," he replied. "For now just give me everything you can find, and I'll sift through it."

"I can help too," Neely offered. "When I'm not cooking."

Dane nodded. "We can use an extra researcher."

Neely stood. "It's time for breakfast. Everyone come to the kitchen and eat before we start working."

While they were gathered around the table eating buttermilk biscuits and homemade blackberry jelly, Neely got a phone call. "It's Raleigh," she told them as she left the table and went into the family room for some privacy.

Raleigh checked in with her every morning, so Savannah didn't think anything about the call until Neely returned, looking pale.

"What's wrong?" Savannah asked.

Neely sat down and addressed her brother. "There *is* money missing from some of the accounts at Business Services."

Savannah felt a little queasy at this announcement and took a swig of Spriteorade.

Dane, never one to overreact, calmly said, "Okay, I guess that means it's time to give that part of your problems a little attention. Tell us about Raleigh's company."

Neely frowned. "I don't know much about his business, and talking about it always makes me feel stupid."

"We're not writing an article for the *Wall Street Journal* here," Dane said. "Just tell us what you know."

She cleared her throat. "He has a partner, Finn Hopewell. They've been in business together for about fifteen years. They were both auditors at Freedom Mutual Life Insurance and decided to go out on their own. They provide a lot of different services for their clients—auditing, of course, but also accounting and insurance and investment advice. Maybe other things as well."

"Company's been doing okay?"

"As far as I know. They both work hard, and Raleigh makes a very good salary."

"They must physically handle some of the investments for their clients themselves since money is missing and the client is holding Business Services responsible."

"I don't know," Neely replied. "I guess."

He turned to Hack. "We need to know more about the company. I want to know assets and net worth at the end of each quarter for the past two years. And we need to know specifically what money is missing. You and I will work together on Business Services and Nature Fresh."

"Like research buddies," Steamer teased.

Hack gave him a menacing look.

Steamer scooted his chair a few inches farther away from Hack.

"Why do we have to investigate Business Services?" Savannah wanted to know. "Can't we just let the auditors handle it?"

"If we wait until the independent auditors decide who they are going to blame for the missing money and it's Raleigh, we'll be behind in the game. And you know I like to stay out front. The worst that could happen is we'll waste some time on an investigation that isn't necessary."

"And time is something we've got plenty of, since we're just sitting here waiting for Brooke to decide she's ready to come home," Hack muttered.

Dane ignored this. "We need to find out who at Business Services had access to the funds in question. And we don't want the auditors to know we've taken an interest in the situation, so be discreet in your research."

Hack rolled his eyes at this unnecessary warning.

"Steam, you go to Raleigh's office."

"Do you want me to tell them I'm his lawyer?" Steamer asked.

"No, tell them you're there to service their copy machines," Dane said. "Then learn what you can without making them suspicious."

"Are we going to tell Raleigh that we're looking into the situation?" Savannah asked.

Dane shook his head. "Not yet. At this point we're just doing a little snooping."

CHAPTER SEVEN

BROOKE WOKE UP ON WEDNESDAY morning to Hunter gently shaking her shoulder. Sunlight was streaming in through the window in the bedroom. He looked tired but not alarmed. All was well.

She smiled and said, "Good morning."

He nodded in response. "You need to get dressed so you can get your hair fixed before we eat breakfast."

Brooke put a hand to her head. "My hair?"

Hunter held up a piece of paper. "This was pushed under our door sometime during the night."

Brooke took the paper and read the heading. "Exceptions."

"It's a personalized list of things we need to do better. I assume everyone got something similar."

"Except for the perfect people."

He didn't smile. "Except for them."

"So they didn't like my hair."

"It just says they want something a little more elaborate since you'll be playing the piano for the guests."

"Did they have any complaints about you?"

"Not today," he said.

She narrowed her eyes, wondering if he was attempting a joke. But his next words dispelled the notion.

"But the exceptions list we get tomorrow will be complaining that we were late if you don't hurry."

"Why do you care so much about keeping the schedule?" she complained. "It's not like this is really our summer job."

"We don't want to stand out, remember? People who are perpetually late—or otherwise cause problems—are memorable."

"What about people who are perpetually grouchy?"

"There are plenty of us; we blend in."

With a sigh she climbed out of the very comfortable bed and trudged to the bathroom.

It didn't take her as long to get into her chemise, hose, pantalets, petticoats, and hoop this time—she was becoming experienced. She walked into the bedroom and took the pink calico dress from its hanger. Carefully she lifted it over her head and dropped it into place. At this point, she had to ask Hunter to help her with the buttons. He worked the little hook until he had the dress secured. Then he lifted the skirt and billowed it a few times the way Mrs. Tabor had done to smooth the fabric over the hoop.

Finally he stood back and studied her. "I like this one better than the plaid from yesterday."

She knew she looked cute in the calico dress and was determined to make him give her a compliment. "So I look nice?" she twirled a little so her skirt would flounce.

"You looked nice yesterday too," he replied. "I just said I like this dress better."

She clasped her hands and did her best impersonation of a Southern Belle. "Why, sir, I do believe you have given me not one compliment but two!"

His pressed his lips together as his cheeks turned pink—indicating both embarrassment and exasperation. She was hoping for a smile but decided that any emotion at all was a small victory.

"You look very nice too," she told him. "You might have been more comfortable in Union blue, but Confederate gray matches your eyes."

"My reasons for not wanting to be part of the Confederate Army have nothing to do with my eyes."

"You've got to learn to look on the bright side," she chided him.

He ignored this. "Are you ready to go?"

She leaned forward and hooked her arm through his. "I am, sir."

With another sigh he opened the door to the hallway. They walked to the elevators and rode down to the basement, where the hairdressing room was located.

Brooke was expecting the hairdressers to use curling irons and industrial strength hair spray to force her hair into tight ringlets. But instead they pulled her hair up into a bun not that much different from the one Mrs.

Tabor had fixed the day before—the one that had gotten bad reviews on the exceptions sheet. Then they attached a premade ringlet hairpiece. It took less than thirty minutes, and the result was amazing.

Brooke leaned forward and stared at herself in the mirror. "I love it!" She twisted around so she could see the back. "How did you match my hair so perfectly?"

"We have all colors," the hairdresser said. "And it does look nice."

"So do I come back here every day?"

The girl nodded. "If you like. And you can come back in the evening before dinner if your hair needs a touch-up. They particularly want you to look nice when you play the piano. I was there last night—you play great."

Brooke smiled at the girl in the mirror. "Thank you."

"Just take the hairpiece off before you go to bed so it doesn't get squished."

Brooke climbed out of the chair. "I will!"

Hunter was waiting for her by the door.

As they walked down to breakfast, she patted her new curls. "How do you like my hair?"

He glanced at her. "I prefer it the regular way."

She decided to count that as compliment number three.

The continental breakfast was nothing special, but Brooke got some fruit and a bagel. Hunter piled his plate with doughnuts. He started to get some bacon, but Brooke reminded him that he had declared himself a vegetarian the night before.

He made a face, indicating that he now regretted that decision, and scraped the bacon back into the warming pan. Then he picked up three cartons of chocolate milk with one hand and led the way to a table in the corner.

Brooke pulled out a chair and sat down. "If we're lucky, maybe we can eat and get out of here before the Dooleys find us."

The words had no sooner left her mouth than the Dooleys walked in and approached the pretend Cauthens with purpose.

"So much for luck," he muttered.

"Good morning!" Doreen greeted. Bob was standing right beside her, silent but smiling for all he was worth.

"Morning," Brooke said. Hunter had his mouth full of doughnut so he just nodded.

"Did you sleep well?" Doreen wanted to know.

"Pretty well," Brooke confirmed. "How about you?"

"Oh, we slept great!" Doreen replied. "The mattress on our bed was the perfect firmness." She studied their food for a few seconds. "And breakfast looks delicious. Bob, go get us something to eat." She settled herself down at their table, and Brooke thought she heard Hunter whimper.

"The employee accommodations at this place are so nice I can't even imagine what the guest suites must be like."

"They are probably very nice," Brooke replied.

"I'm just thankful for air conditioning," Doreen said as Bob returned with two plates. He placed one in front of her and then sat down beside his wife.

Eating food did not limit Doreen's ability to carry on a conversation. Between bites she said, "One reenactment we attended made the participants sleep in little huts with no electricity and on straw mattresses! A bed of nails would be more comfortable. And we had to wear period clothes even at night. Mine was a cotton gown, but Bob had to wear a nightshirt." She shook her head. "Very uncomfortable."

Bob Dooley made a rare contribution. "Nightshirts are the worst idea in the history of the world. It gets twisted around you; it's like trying to sleep while you're tied up."

Doreen seized control of the conversation again. "He threatened to take it off, but I said, 'Don't you take it off! What if there's a fire!'"

Bob blushed crimson, and Brooke had to laugh. "Some things are worse than trying to sleep while you're tied up in a nightshirt!"

"Definitely," Bob agreed.

"Are you finished eating?" Hunter asked Brooke hopefully.

When she nodded, he stood and held out his hand. "Well, we'd better get going then."

She took his hand and let him help her up.

"What's your first assignment?" Doreen asked.

"The theatre," Hunter replied. "Elizabeth has to play for the choral group."

It took Brooke a split second to realize he was talking about her.

"If we'd known that, we would have asked Wilma to change us so we could be together," Doreen said with obvious disappointment.

This time Brooke was positive she heard Hunter whimper.

"Oh well," she said brightly. "Maybe we'll see you later today!"

Then they hurried out of the cafeteria.

"That woman is a nuisance," Hunter said.

"She's just friendly . . . and nosey . . . and talks incessantly."

"Like I said, a nuisance."

They walked out of the administration building and to The Commons, which was teeming with people.

"Pretend guests?" she whispered to Hunter.

"I guess," he replied. "Crowds can be dangerous. Stay close to me."

They walked along the store fronts, careful to stay in the shadows. When they did come face-to-face with someone, Hunter nodded, Brooke smiled, and then they moved quickly by.

The interior of the Town Theatre was as beautiful as Brooke expected. There were chandeliers and red velvet curtains with gold tassels. The wooden stage was lined with lanterns that, in the 1860s, would have been filled with kerosene. Fortunately, because of the fire code in the modern age, they were safely illuminated by electricity.

The choral director settled Brooke at the piano and showed her the music they would be rehearsing. Then he welcomed the combination of fake guests and employees—which included Hunter—to his choir. Next he led them all through a series of voice-warming exercises. Brooke sneaked peeks at Hunter as often as she dared. He looked so uncomfortable, and she found it hilarious. It was a testament to her musical skills that she was able to perform adequately with this level of distraction.

When the choral session was over, Hunter led her outside. "That was worse than any combat assignment I've ever been given," he claimed. "I'd rather shoot people than sing."

She was aghast. "You don't mean that!"

"Well, almost," he relented. "Now let's go get this battle over with."

He led her to the bleachers that lined the field, which was not unlike a football field without the hash marks. All kinds of equipment was set up around the field—fake trees, fences, hills, even livestock. It looked like an old-timey obstacle course.

"How do you know what you're supposed to do?" she asked Hunter.

"I don't," he admitted. "I read the synopsis of the battle, so I know basically what happens. And I know what regiment I'm in, so I'll just get with my group and do what everyone else does."

"That sounds pretty haphazard."

"They aren't expecting perfection on the first try." He squinted at the sky and then at the overhang that provided shade for the bleachers. "I'm not sure if the shade will last, and you forgot to bring your parasol."

"I won't melt," she assured him.

"And I've got my parasol; I'll share if she needs it," Wilma said as she joined them. "Heat can trigger an asthma attack."

"I'll be fine," Brooke insisted.

"I can still keep an eye on you from the field," Hunter told her softly. "So if you need me, stand up and I'll come."

"I wouldn't do that," she warned him with a teasing smile. "They used to shoot deserters."

"I'm serious," he replied.

She nodded. "Oh, I know."

"I'll take care of her," Wilma promised. "You concentrate on beating the Yankees."

At this remark Hunter's expression became resentful as well as concerned.

The Dooleys and Mengenthals walked over to join them. Hunter stood quietly while the other men made small talk. When the announcement was made for the men to line up by regiments, Doreen announced, "It's traditional for the ladies to kiss their men for luck as they go into battle!"

The Mengenthals were only too happy to support this tradition. They embraced and kissed passionately.

Brooke looked away from the excessive public display of affection.

Doreen gave Bob a peck on the cheek and sent him on his way. Then she turned to Brooke. "Come on now and give your husband a kiss. If you don't, he might get shot."

"I'll kiss him if you won't!" Wilma volunteered.

Hunter looked so horrified by this possibility that Brooke had to laugh. "Thank you very much, but I'll kiss my own husband!"

Doreen said, "There's something about sending a man off to war—even if it *is* a fake war. It makes you think what it would really be like, and you appreciate each other more."

Brooke leaned over the railing toward Hunter, who was standing on the ground below. She intended to give him a little kiss just to satisfy Doreen. But when their lips met, she thought of the Civil War women who really did send their men off with no guarantee that they would return, and she found herself clinging to Hunter for longer than was necessary or appropriate.

Finally the teasing cheers from the pretend soldiers around them brought Brooke to her senses and she pulled away, a little shaken. She wasn't sure what it meant, but the kiss definitely wasn't the businesslike encounter she'd expected.

"Sorry," she said. "I didn't mean to embarrass you in front of your soldier friends."

"I'm not embarrassed." He seemed to be affected as well. Or maybe he was just concerned for her safety while he was off, a few feet away, at war.

"He's not really going to get shot!" Doreen comforted.

"I'll be back soon," he whispered solemnly. "Stand if you need me."

"Go on," she said. "I told you I'll be fine."

With a nod he moved over to the growing group of uniformed men at the left end of the field.

"No one will tease you if you cry," Doreen told her. "The first battle is the worst, but I've been to almost a hundred and even I tear up occasionally."

"I'm not going to cry," Brooke said. Then she looked out at Hunter. She had grown accustomed to his humorless company and his protective presence. One day in the not-too-distant future they would say good-bye and go back to their real lives. The thought made her incredibly sad.

He saw her staring at him and waved his hat. She waved back. Then she settled down to watch the Battle of the Day—Chickamauga.

The battle reenactment was more impressive than Brooke had expected. The loud speakers blasted out music and sound effects. There was a narrator who dramatically described what had actually happened while the men on the field tried to replicate it.

"They're a little unsure of themselves now," Doreen observed, "but in a few weeks they'll be familiar with their roles, and they'll perform with impressive accuracy."

Cannons fired, infantrymen marched, and cavalries charged to bugle accompaniment. The action might have been hard to follow if Doreen and Wilma hadn't been sitting beside Brooke, giving the play-by-play. It was exciting, and the time passed quickly, even though they had to stop occasionally and redo something that had gone wrong. But in the end, when the battle was over and the cannon smoke cleared, Brooke stared at the field littered with bodies from both sides. It was a sobering sight.

She searched for Hunter, hoping he wasn't among the fallen. Dying the first day seemed like a bad omen. She was pleased when she saw him waving his hat. Not only was he still alive, he knew she would be concerned and wanted to reassure her. In all the months she was with Rex, he'd never shown as much perception or consideration.

The soldiers were dismissed, and Hunter came over to collect her, his face sunburned and covered with dust. She was afraid it might be awkward between them, after their Mengenthal-ish prebattle kiss, but he seemed just the same—serious to the point of grumpy.

"You look a little worse for the wear, soldier," Brooke teased him.

"War is hard work," he replied. "Especially in this Tennessee sun."

"Did you enjoy it?"

"It was interesting," he allowed. "And I much prefer war where no one actually dies."

She whispered, "Don't let the Confederate generals find out you are an expert shooter. If they use your talents it really might change the course of history."

"We're all using blanks, which pretty much makes my shooting skills worthless. And the script is set. The North won the war, and that's the way it's going to stay."

"Not very suspenseful," Brooke murmured.

"No, history is badly lacking in suspense," he agreed.

They walked across to the administration building so Hunter could take a quick shower and change into a clean uniform. Then, after lunch in the employee cafeteria, they went to the Plantation House, where Brooke played for two square dance classes. Hunter helped set up chairs for dinner until they needed another man for the dancing. Then he provided a partner for a silly woman from Little Rock, and again Brooke was thoroughly entertained at his expense.

After the square dancing classes were over, she practiced with the band for a few minutes. Then they hurried to the ice cream parlor since Hunter was determined to make the Cauthens look like model employees.

At the ice cream shop, they were both issued pink aprons and warned that their jobs could be messy. Brooke put her apron over her head while Hunter removed his uniform jacket and rolled up the sleeves of his loose-necked, full-sleeved 1860s shirt. She turned away for a few seconds to let their trainer tie her apron and then turned back toward him, prepared to make fun of him, but the laughter died on her lips. The pink color actually seemed to enhance his masculinity, making him more handsome than ever. Their eyes met, and from his expression she could tell he thought she looked pretty in her apron as well.

Because Brooke had worked at a yogurt shop, she was assigned to the front counter, scooping homemade ice cream into little parfait dishes. Hunter, who had no frozen dessert experience, was assigned to work in the back room, watching several freezers and bringing the batches of ice cream into the front when they were ready to eat. The shop had lots of customers, and staying busy made the time pass quickly.

When their shift was over, Brooke took off her apron and washed her hands. Then she walked into the back, where Hunter was keeping watch over his flock of ice cream freezers. She looked around at the barrels of rock salt stacked against the wall and the bags of ice in a huge glass-front freezer. The freezers whirred in the background. "Time to go."

"We'll have to wait for my replacement to get here," he said. "I can't leave the ice cream unattended."

She smiled. He was even loyal to freezers of ice cream.

A young man walked in and announced that he was there to take over. Hunter showed him the supplies and explained the process. Then, with something that seemed very much like regret, he removed his apron and they went outside.

"I feel guilty that I was just scooping ice cream while you had to work so hard."

"I didn't mind," he surprised her by saying. "I like doing things the old fashioned way."

She stopped and smiled up at him. "I finally know something about you—something personal. Even if you won't tell me your favorite color."

He gave her his exasperated look. "I don't have a favorite color."

She was determined to consider this a breakthrough in their relationship. "But you do like old-fashioned things! Before long you'll probably be boring me to death with details of your life."

He stared at her, uncertain.

"I'm kidding," she assured him, taking his arm and propelling him forward. "You couldn't bore me, and goodness knows there's no chance you'll start babbling about your personal life. But let's pursue this topic. So you're not a big fan of modernization and technology?"

"No."

"But without your phone you couldn't text Hack—or anyone else for that matter."

"I hate texting," he said. "I believe that people were meant to communicate face-to-face—or at least voice-to-voice."

"So you're saying when this is over I shouldn't expect a text from you asking me out to dinner?" She meant to say it playfully, but it came out a little more sincere than she intended.

He looked at her solemnly. "No."

She swallowed around the lump of sadness that rose in her throat. "Anyway, I'm glad we're working at the ice cream shop. It's fun."

"I wish we were working somewhere that gets less business, like a bookstore or something. If I wasn't afraid it would call too much attention to us, I'd tell Wilma you have an allergy to ice cream."

Brooke forced a smile. "If you do that she'll think I'm too sickly to even be here."

He shrugged, accepting that their assignment could not be changed. "Do you want to eat dinner before we put on our formal clothes for your musical performance tonight?"

She nodded. "I don't want to end up on the exceptions list over food stains on my gray silk dress."

They walked into the cafeteria and were pleased to see that the Dooleys were nowhere in sight. Dinner was served buffet style. Brooke got a salad that she didn't really want, and Hunter got enough fried chicken to feed a family of four.

"I don't have to be a vegetarian now since none of the people from our table last night are in here," he explained.

"What will you do if one of them walks in?"

He shrugged. "I'll say I fell off the wagon."

She shook her head. "I can't believe you're going to eat chicken so soon after our experience in that slaughter shed."

"I just won't think about that shed while I eat."

"Apparently the Dooleys don't have the same dinner time that we do." She stabbed a piece of lettuce with her fork. "Luck finally smiled on us."

"It's about time," Hunter mumbled as he went to work on a drumstick.

They saw the Mengenthals and the Bouyer brothers, but only from a distance. So Brooke and Hunter were able to finish their meal in peace.

Afterward they went up to their room. The plaid dress and the uniform Hunter had worn the day before were on the hanging rack—clean, pressed, and ready for the next day.

"I hate that I have to wear this tomorrow since I know it's not your favorite," Brooke teased him.

"You don't have to fish for a compliment," he said. "You know you look good no matter what you wear."

She smiled. "Since I'm teaching you about women and love, let me give you some valuable information. It doesn't matter if we already know we look nice, we still like to hear it."

He frowned in concentration as if he really were filing the information away for future use.

"Don't men like to be complimented?"

He looked down at his uniform. "I can't speak for all men, but I don't like compliments, especially if they aren't sincere. And I don't look nice. All my clothes are the same—dull gray."

"You do look nice, even in dull gray," she said with a sigh. "But since this love lesson isn't going very well, let's get changed."

After a long day in and out of the hot sun wearing several layers of clothing, her shower was wonderfully refreshing. She felt so much better that she actually hummed as she put on her 1860s underclothing. And the prospect of playing the piano all evening was not something she dreaded.

When she came out of the bathroom, Hunter was sitting on the couch, holding a fresh uniform, waiting his turn. While he was in the bathroom, Brooke managed to get the gray silk over her head and was waiting for him to button the back. He came out wearing his uniform pants and one of the open-necked shirts, which showed a good portion of his muscular chest.

"I think you're supposed to tie that shirt closed." She indicted to the strings hanging down.

"I've tried," he responded. "It just comes back untied, so I gave up."

She turned around so he could button her dress. This process required him to be very close to her. His short hair was still damp from his shower. He smelled pleasantly like soap and toothpaste—a combination she'd never found particularly appealing before. When he was finished she shook the yards of fabric over the hoop and posed for him in the mirror.

"Well?" she asked.

He put on his uniform jacket. "You look nice."

She was pleased but not completely satisfied. "Eventually, if I'm a successful teacher, you will say things like that without me having to ask you first."

He nodded—ever serious.

She rolled her eyes as they walked out into the hallway, headed toward the elevators.

When they arrived at the dining hall, Brooke walked straight to the piano. She was peripherally aware that Hunter had taken a seat behind her. She gave herself to the music, leaving her worries behind for a time.

Brooke paused while Jovette welcomed the guests and told them that there would be dancing after dinner. Then Brooke resumed her playing.

A few minutes later, Doreen Dooley, accompanied by the long-suffering Bob, came up to the piano.

Brooke was surprised to see them. "I thought only guests were allowed to be here tonight."

"They needed a few of us to fill in the tables and help keep the small talk going."

Brooke and Hunter exchanged a look. No surprise that they chose Doreen for a talking assignment.

"Don't you two look lovely tonight," Doreen continued.

"Your costumes are great too," Brooke returned.

Doreen blushed. "Oh, you're just saying that."

That was true, but Brooke smiled, happy that Doreen had taken the comment as a compliment.

"But we can't compete with a young couple, glowing with love!"

Hunter's eyes widened, and Brooke had to put a hand over her mouth to keep from laughing.

"Well, we don't want to keep you from your duties," Hunter murmured.

Doreen looked disappointed but nodded. "Yes, we'd better find our assigned seat. We'll probably have to sit with some annoying people."

Brooke steadfastly avoided making eye contact with Hunter.

"We're having a little get-together in the game room this evening after all the regular activities are over," Doreen said. "Promise you'll come by for a few minutes. Even the Mengenthals have agreed to be there!"

If the lovey-dovey newlyweds could sacrifice some of their alone time to attend the gathering, Brooke didn't see how she could politely refuse. So she nodded. "We'll come by."

Then, thankfully, Doreen led Bob off to find their table.

Hunter leaned close and whispered, "If I was paying money to be here and had to sit with the Dooleys at dinner, I'd demand a refund."

Brooke turned to him. "You've got to control your expressions! I almost laughed right in their faces!"

"Why do you think everything is so funny?"

"Why don't you think *anything* is funny?" she countered.

"We're opposites," he said as Charlie and the band arrived.

They greeted each other, and then the band warmed up. Once they were ready, they began playing together as they had the night before. Since she was doing something she loved, the time passed quickly for Brooke. She worried about Hunter, who had to sit for hours just listening to her play. But he didn't complain.

Toward the end of the evening, as a waltz started, Charlie came over to the piano and closed her music binder. "It's cruel to make your husband sit there all night, looking at you in that gorgeous dress, without giving him a chance to spin you around the dance floor at least once."

Brooke turned to Hunter and batted her eyes at him. "Are you asking me to dance, sir?"

"I guess I am" was his less-than-gallant response.

Frowning, she let him escort her onto the dance floor. But she forgot her irritation quickly as they moved together with the music. She enjoyed being close to him—the feel of his arms around her and his soapy, toothpaste smell. Their eyes met, and she wished she could read his mind—and hoped he couldn't read hers.

The moment was interrupted by the Dooleys, who came dancing up beside them.

"We're going to start calling you the Mengenthals if you keep acting so romantic!" Doreen hollered.

"You two look pretty romantic yourselves!" Brooke teased back.

Doreen tossed her sausage curls as Bob twirled her off to another part of the dance floor.

"I'm sorry you have to sit for hours while I play the piano," she said. "I know you must be bored out of your mind."

"Actually, I'm not," he replied. "I like watching you play."

She wanted to question him more on this topic, but a couple danced over to compliment Brooke on her musical performance. Soon there was a whole group of "fans" surrounding them. Finally Hunter told them she had to get back to the piano and led her away.

"This is not the low profile I'd hoped we could keep," he murmured into her ear as they walked. "It's like you're a Civil War celebrity."

She smiled up at him. "That was such a nice thing to say."

He frowned. "That you're ruining our cover?"

She nodded.

He shook his head. "Well you'd better be working on that testimony you don't want to give because a subpoena could come at any moment."

She knew she should be scared, but hearing him compliment her seemed worth the risk.

When they reached the piano, Brooke settled on the bench and Hunter sat back in his chair. It was time for the North against the South singing contest. When she started playing "Dixie," Hunter muttered, "Oh, not that again."

She smiled without taking her eyes off the music. "Put your hand over your heart and sing, sir!"

When the dance was over, they said good-bye to Charlie and his band, then they walked through The Commons. Even though Brooke was in a fake town, under an assumed identity, with a man she barely knew, she felt happy.

"Isn't it pretty?" she said. "The lights and the charming little buildings and everyone dressed in beautiful clothes."

Hunter frowned. "I don't like it."

She was so stunned, she stopped in her tracks. "How can you possibly not like this lovely place?"

"I don't like it because it romanticizes war," he told her. "War is terrible. People die, homes are destroyed, and lives are changed forever. This place highlights all the charming things about the Old South and leaves out all the ugly things—like death and slavery. It's wrong to make a party out of battles where men suffered and died."

Brooke watched him with awe. "I don't think they are making a party out of death; they just want to experience how it felt to live back then."

"You can't take the good without the bad," Hunter said. "That's all I'm saying."

She smiled. "Now I feel like I know you even better. You're an old-fashioned man who scorns technology and has scruples."

"Are you making fun of me?"

She wrapped her hand more tightly around his arm. "I definitely am not. I wish there were more men like you." Then she started walking again, and he moved along with her.

They passed the ice cream shop, which now had a line out the door.

"Thank goodness we didn't have the late shift," she murmured. "Although ice cream does sound good. They're probably serving the batches you made this afternoon."

"Do you want to stand in line and get some?"

She shook her head. "Maybe after our shift tomorrow. Right now we have to get to the Dooleys' party in the game room."

He groaned. "Do we have to go?"

"We'll just put in a short appearance," she said. "But if we don't go at all, we'll draw attention to ourselves and I know how you hate that."

"You'll probably have people wanting your autograph."

She smiled. "As long as I sign Elizabeth Cauthen, we should be okay."

The Dooleys' party was in full swing by the time they arrived. The Mengenthals were cuddled on a couch, seemingly oblivious to the people around them. Trent and Tate both had female companions.

"This is Jackie," Tate introduced the girl on his arm.

"And this is Sabrina." Trent pointed to the young lady by his side. "We've been sitting here quoting lines from *Gone with the Wind*."

Sabrina smiled up at him. "Trent and Tate have the whole movie memorized!"

Brooke couldn't understand why Sabrina considered this a good thing. But before she was forced to come up with some kind of polite response, Brooke felt Hunter's hand tighten on her arm.

"Well, it was nice meeting you," he said to Jackie and Sabrina. Then he steered Brooke over toward the Dooleys. Once they were far enough away, Hunter whispered, "We're going to speak to our host and hostess, and then we've got to get out of here before I lose my mind."

"Party pooper," she muttered back. "I was dying to hear the Bouyer brothers recite all the lines from a three-hour movie."

"For once I actually *hope* you're joking," Hunter responded.

When Doreen saw them approaching, she hollered, "Come get some refreshments." She waved toward a table behind her. "I made bean dip."

Hunter said, "Thanks, but we're going to have to go. Elizabeth isn't feeling well."

Brooke was annoyed that he'd used her as an excuse.

Doreen frowned in concern. "Oh dear. Do you want me to tell Wilma? She has all kinds of over-the-counter medications in her office."

"I'm sure I'll be fine," Brooke assured her. "I just need some rest."

"Well, come get me if you need me," Doreen offered. "We're just down the hall from you in 207."

"Thank you," Brooke said, and Hunter pulled her toward the door.

As they rode the elevator up to the second floor, she asked, "Why did you say I was sick instead of you?"

"If we leave because I'm sick, it makes me look like a wimp. If we leave because you're sick, it makes me look like a considerate husband."

Brooke put her hands on her hips. "What about my image?"

"We've already established that you're sickly," he said. "So your image is unaffected."

She narrowed her eyes at him. "It will serve you right if Doreen insists on spending the night with us to nurse me back to health."

His look of horror was all the vindication Brooke needed.

When they walked into their suite, Hunter's uniforms and the calico dress were clean and pressed, hanging side by side on the rolling cart that would eventually divide the bedroom and sitting area.

There was also the new evening dress Wilma had promised. It was made of ivory silk embroidered with pale green and pink flowers. There were even tiny seed pearls stitched into the bodice. "I love this dress!" she said, pressing it against her. "I think it's my new favorite."

"It's pretty," he agreed. "But I still like the pink one best."

She shook her head. "I like the pink dress too, but this is a masterpiece." Reluctantly she hung it in the closet, already looking forward to the next evening, when she could wear it.

Then they went through their evening routine just like the married couple they weren't. Hunter helped her take off the huge dress, and after they put all their dirty clothes into the laundry bin, he rolled it out into the hallway. Then, exhausted after a long, full day, Brooke went to bed.

Even though the rolling rack covered with a blanket was between them, she didn't feel separate from Hunter the way she had before. She was sure it was just the fear combined with the months of loneliness that had drawn her to him. She wouldn't even allow herself to consider that she might be falling in love.

CHAPTER EIGHT

SAVANNAH FINISHED READING YET ANOTHER boring article on Joined Forces and their animal activism. She now knew more than she ever wanted to about how Nature Fresh chickens were raised, transported, and slaughtered and how they finally ended up in the meat section of local grocery stores. And she knew she would never look at a piece of chicken the same way again.

Dane came into Raleigh's office and announced that they needed to have a team meeting. Once they were settled around the desk, he said, "Steam, we'll start with you."

Steamer said, "Well, they wouldn't let me in to work on the copy machines at Raleigh's company, but I had a good conversation with the receptionist at the insurance agency across the hall. She said the independent auditors have basically shut Business Services down. They seized their books and insisted on sending home most of the employees. They set up cots so the remaining folks don't have to leave to sleep. She said they're having food brought in—like a siege."

"The receptionist didn't know anything about the missing money?" Dane asked.

Steamer shook his head. "She said everyone in the building has been talking about it, of course, and they assume some money was stolen by an employee."

Neely looked pale, and Savannah reminded her, "That's just the opinion of a receptionist across the hall."

"But it is the logical conclusion," Dane said. "We need a more reliable source."

Hack said, "I think I have a better source. I was able to track down a couple of the employees who were sent home. Based on what they told me,

I've determined that as a benefit to their clients, Business Services allows clients to participate in an investment fund called Sterling Strategies."

"Is it a mutual fund?" Dane asked.

"Sort of," Hack confirmed. "They accept investment capital from their members on the first of every month. At the end of the month, they value the fund's assets and distribute gains or losses per dollar. They have been in business for over twenty years and have historically done well, even in down markets. One of the secrets to their success is that they keep things manageable by limiting their membership."

"So Business Services is an exclusive member and they give their clients the chance to invest with Sterling Strategies through them?" Dane summed up the situation.

Hack nodded. "Right. Based on the information I collected from the employees, I started an investigation of Sterling Strategies and their association with Business Services."

"How do clients of Business Services invest with Sterling?" Savannah asked.

"Every month the clients send Business Services the money they want invested with Sterling. It's kept in a holding account until the first of the next month, when it's transferred to Sterling for investment. But one of the clients hasn't been getting credit for all the money they've sent to be invested with Sterling. After a short investigation, the auditors determined that the entire transfer amount for this month is missing."

"And by missing you mean that the money is not just misplaced, but actually stolen?"

Hack nodded.

"How much money are we talking about?" Dane asked.

Hack said, "A hundred thousand dollars."

Dane frowned. "So the embezzlement rumor is probably true, and it's just a matter of time before the police get involved."

"It pretty much had to be either Raleigh or the partner," Steamer said. "Who else would have the information necessary to transfer that much money?"

"Raleigh is the most honest person I know," Neely said. "He would never steal anything, especially not from his own clients."

"I agree. We'll base our investigation on the premise that Raleigh did not take the money." Dane glanced at his sister. "For now."

Savannah said, "Then we need to build a case against Finn Hopewell."

"And that shouldn't be hard," Steamer said. "According to office gossip, Hopewell has money troubles thanks to a divorce last year—caused by his college-student girlfriend."

Dane nodded. "Neely mentioned that he had a messy divorce." He turned to his sister. "Tell us everything you know about Hopewell and his marital problems."

"About all I know is that Finn and his wife of twenty-five years got divorced because he was cheating." Neely frowned. "Raleigh isn't much for gossip. I never thought that was a bad thing until now—when we need information on Finn's personal life."

Steamer said, "According to my receptionist friend, the ex-wife got a very generous divorce settlement and the girlfriend is demanding."

"How generous was the settlement?" Dane wanted to know.

"Generous enough that she was able to afford a house in Key Biscayne."

Neely said thoughtfully, "And Raleigh did mention a week or so ago that Finn might be interested in selling his half of the business. He said Finn wanted to simplify his life, but the sale may really have been motivated by his money problems."

"So Hopewell is our guy?" Hack asked.

"He's the most obvious," Dane agreed. "But I don't want to ignore other possibilities at this point. So let's look for a couple of other suspects."

"You know our team motto," Steamer said. "Follow the money."

"I don't know if it's a motto exactly," Dane hedged, "but it usually works."

Steamer persevered, "If we can figure out who will benefit financially from the current situation, we'll have our guilty party."

"That brings us back to Finn Hopewell," Hack said. "He's the one with money problems. He had access and opportunity."

"No one is questioning that," Dane said. "But other people involved may need money."

Savannah nodded, "And there are other reasons that someone might have taken money from Business Services—like revenge. If Finn cheated on his ex-wife, she might want to get back at him."

"Or jealousy," Dane contributed. "The ex-wife would be a good suspect for that motive too. The girlfriend needs to be checked out as well."

Steamer shook his head. "I still say money is more compelling and we should look for someone who benefits."

Hack gave him an impatient look. "Will you quit saying the same thing over and over?"

"Just making an argument. For those of you without law degrees, that doesn't mean I was fighting, it means I was stating a valid point."

Hack growled.

Dane turned to Hack. "Find out everything you can on Hopewell and his financial situation. I also want to know about his divorce and the settlement. I don't like the feel of this. We need to get a handle on it quick."

***

When Brooke woke up on Thursday morning, the suite at the Civil War resort felt familiar and the knowledge that Hunter was just a few feet away seemed natural. She walked out of the bedroom and found Hunter dressed in his uniform pants and one of the open-necked shirts. As usual the strings were hanging loose. And he was studying the Battle of the Day.

"Which one are you reenacting today?"

"Chattanooga," he replied.

She stood behind his chair so she could read over his shoulder. "Did the North win that one?"

"We did," he said.

She smiled at him. "I know you're happy about that."

He nodded. "I am."

She gave up on engaging him in a meaningful conversation and went into the bathroom. She brushed her teeth, put on her makeup, and dressed in her 1860s undergarb. Then she came out, and he helped her put on and button the plaid gown. He'd gotten so good with the little button hook that it only took a couple of minutes.

After a stop at hairdressing to have her ringlets professionally affixed, they went to breakfast. The Dooleys ate with them, but Brooke didn't find them overly annoying. Maybe she was getting used to Doreen's constant chatter. It did, however, force Hunter to eat like a vegetarian, which was amusing.

They went to choral practice, and Brooke played but Hunter did not sing. He told the director he had a sore throat and couldn't participate. Then he sat by her on the piano bench and turned the pages for her.

"You don't have a sore throat," she accused on the way to the battlefield. "You lied!"

"It was self-defense," Hunter claimed. "No one would blame me."

She couldn't really disagree with that, and she almost liked knowing that he had a human foible. Constant perfection was hard to relate to.

They reached the bleachers, and she greeted the other women. Then they all stood around and made small talk for a few minutes. When it was time for the men to line up, no one had to force her to kiss Hunter for good luck.

But when the battle began, it was more nerve-wracking than the day before since she knew this time he was on the losing side. Throughout the reenactment, her eyes were constantly searching for him, and she even caught herself praying that he wouldn't be shot. Then she quickly apologized to the Lord.

Finally, as the battle intensified and her heart was pounding with fear, she faced the fact that she had feelings for Hunter. Once she had admitted this, she tried to decide the best way to handle these inconvenient and unwelcome emotions. She could keep her distance from him emotionally and possibly spare herself some pain. Or she could enjoy the time she had with him and deal with the inevitable grief once he was gone.

She spotted him on the field, and he waved his hat. With a sigh she realized the choice had already been made. She would make the best of the time they had together and deal with the consequences later.

After the battle, they went to lunch and then worked their shift at the ice cream parlor. When it was time to dress for dinner, she put on the beautiful, ivory-colored gown. While Hunter buttoned the back, she admired herself in the mirror. The dress contrasted nicely with her tanned shoulders, and it accentuated her small waist. The green and pink embroidery was subtle and helped to break the monotony of all that white. And the tiny pearls sprinkled across the bodice made her sparkle. She had to agree it was "showy," but she liked it.

Lifting the skirt, she curtsied to Hunter. "Don't you have something you'd like to say to me?"

"The dress is beautiful."

She frowned. "Just the dress."

He shook his head. "I've never met a woman who looks as good as you do and still needs so much reassurance."

She laughed. "I know I look nice. I just want to be sure *you* know it."

His eyes met hers in the mirror. "I know."

Brooke wanted to make a playful reply, but her mouth had gone dry and she couldn't find the words. Finally she looked away and said, "If we want to stay off that exceptions list, I'd better be playing the piano in the dining room at the Plantation House before they start serving dinner to the guests."

He nodded solemnly and opened the door for her.

She played during dinner as usual, with her gorgeous new dress flowing all around her. But when the meal was over, Jovette came over to tell her there would be no dancing that evening. "Tonight the guests are invited to go watch a play at the theatre. There's plenty of room, so you and your husband should go."

Brooke looked over her shoulder at Hunter. "Is that okay with you?"

"It's fine." He stood and tucked her arm through his. Then they walked out of the Plantation House and over to the Town Theatre. The old-fashioned performance hall looked even more beautiful at night. The play was silly and predictable, with a dastardly villain, a lady in distress, and a gallant hero. Brooke enjoyed it, but Hunter seemed preoccupied.

On the way back to the administration building, she said, "The only thing I didn't like was the taped music."

"Don't mention that to Jovette or you'll be providing music for the play too."

"I wouldn't mind."

"Well, I would," he said. "They would probably make *me* be in the play."

She smiled up at him. "I can see you as the gallant hero." Then she thought about the love scenes the hero shared with the lady in distress and changed her mind. "I guess you're right. I won't say anything to Jovette."

They continued in silence for a few minutes, and then she asked, "What's the matter? Were you worried that one of the actors would leave the stage and come running over to give me a subpoena?"

"This white dress worries me," he admitted. "Especially in the dark. It makes you too easy to spot if anyone wanted to give you a subpoena—or whatever."

"I'm not worried about a subpoena, but we might get an invitation to another game room party."

He shuddered. "Let's hurry back to our suite."

She laughed. "Heaven forbid that we have to socialize!"

"That's not socializing—it's torture," Hunter muttered.

It started to rain just as they reached the administration building. Hunter pulled Brooke, and her huge dress, up into his arms. He hurried up the stairs, and she wrapped her hands around his neck, holding on for dear life. When they were under the protection of the roof, he slowly put her down. As her feet touched the floor, Brooke remained inside the circle of his arms. She was a little breathless and clung to him for balance.

The rain intensified, pummeling the roof above them. A damp, gardenia-scented breeze tousled her ringlets. Raindrops glittered in Hunter's hair like diamonds. She waited for his kiss, confident that it would come. And then the spell was broken by squeals and screams from people caught in the sudden storm. They ran across The Commons from all directions, in search of cover.

Hunter stepped back, leaving Brooke feeling bereft. Then she saw Wilma slip in a puddle and fall in a heap on the muddy grass.

Laughing, Brooke looked up at Hunter and said, "You *know* that is funny."

His eyes were amused even if he didn't actually smile. "Let's get inside before she sees us and calls for me to come help her up."

"So you're old-fashioned but not necessarily chivalrous," she remarked as they hurried inside.

"I'm just not stupid," he corrected.

When they got back to their suite, he helped her out of the damp dress.

"I hope the laundry people don't kill me," she murmured as they put it in the laundry bin.

"After they see Wilma's mud-covered dress, I don't think yours will bother them at all."

She smiled as she headed for the bathroom to change out of her other wet things.

Once she had on her pajamas, she ventured out into the sitting area, which was essentially his bedroom. Aware that she was invading his space, she said, "I'm not sleepy. Do you mind if I stay out here with you for a while?"

He looked wary but nodded his permission.

She sat on the opposite end of the couch. "We've done a pretty good job of acting like a loving married couple, don't you think? Considering that we barely know each other?"

He thought for a second and then said, "I don't think we've given anyone reason to be suspicious that we're not the Cauthens."

She turned toward him on the couch. "I'd like to know more about you, if you don't mind."

"I promise I don't have a favorite color," he insisted.

She smiled. "How about brothers and sisters? Do you have any siblings?"

He shook his head. "I'm an only child, and both of my parents are dead."

"Oh, I'm sorry."

He shrugged. "It happened a long time ago. I'm used to it now."

She felt like they had passed an important hurdle. "Okay, now it's your turn to ask me something."

"And you have to answer because I did?'

She nodded.

He said, "Why won't you testify?"

She rolled her eyes. "Something personal."

"I've never known anyone who changes the rules to suit themselves as much as you do."

"It's my game," she reminded him. "That makes me in charge of the rules."

He frowned. "Okay, if you won't talk about the trial, tell me about your boyfriend."

Brooke's smile disappeared. "I don't have a boyfriend."

"But you did," he said.

"His name is Rex."

Hunter nodded. "I know that much. Are you still in love with him?"

She considered how to describe the relationship that had changed her life forever. "I met him when I was a sophomore in college. He was much older than me, handsome and smart. And he had causes."

"Like chickens?"

"Yes. He was the kind of person I thought I wanted to be. So I started going to rallies and meetings where I knew he'd be. I think he realized I was stalking him, but he didn't mind."

"I'm sure he didn't," Hunter muttered.

"Finally he invited me to join the organization. From that point on, I was his assistant, and eventually he moved in to my apartment."

Hunter's eyebrows rose. "Your parents were okay with that?"

"I didn't tell them until later," she admitted. "At first it was just platonic. His lease was up at his place, and he said it made financial sense for us to share expenses."

"He helped pay the rent?"

She shook her head, feeling ashamed of her gullibility. "No."

"So what he really meant was that it made sense for him—financially— to let you pay his expenses."

"I guess." She looked away. "I know I was a fool where Rex was concerned. I'd never met anyone like him before. He was so charismatic and important.

When I was with him, I felt smart and worthwhile. I felt like I was making a difference in the world."

"So eventually the relationship became more than platonic."

She nodded. "We were together for almost a year. Then he got the job offer in California. I assumed I'd be going too. I'd already looked into universities that would accept my transfer credits. Then he told me I was not invited." She dragged her eyes up to meet Hunter's. "It sounds cliché, but he broke my heart."

"He was an idiot to leave you behind."

She smiled. "Thank you."

"But one idiot shouldn't make you give up on all men. You should have another boyfriend by now."

She raised an eyebrow. "This from a man who doesn't have time for relationships?"

"I'm different," he claimed. "I was never social; you were."

"I haven't given up on men and relationships, exactly." She bit her lower lip. "It's hard to explain."

"We've got plenty of time."

She sighed. "When Rex left, I couldn't even really be mad at him. He told me from the start that he didn't believe in marriage. I thought I could change him. I created this whole pretend Rex in my mind and ignored every bit of evidence that was contrary to my dream." She searched for the right words because she really did want Hunter to understand. "I hoped I could make him love me so much that he wouldn't want to leave me."

"But he did."

"When I had to face the truth about him and his feelings for me, it was terrible. I never want to feel that much pain again."

"You still miss him?"

She nodded. "I miss being in love. I miss the life I thought we were going to have together."

"If he knocked on our door right now, would you take him back?"

She shook her head. "Oh no, I would never do that."

His stoic expression made it hard to tell if her response pleased him or not. "But you're lonely?"

"Yes." She looked out the window at the rain. "Are you?"

"I've been on my own for so long that I'm comfortable with it."

"You don't have to be alone," she said. "You're a handsome man. You could get a girlfriend—if you'd just learn to smile."

"I'm never in one place long enough to establish any kind of meaningful relationship."

It was a clear warning, but her heart ignored it.

"The right girl will force you to make room for her," she predicted. Then she stood up before he could argue with her. "I guess I'll go on to bed now."

***

On Thursday night Savannah was headed to Raleigh's home office for the final meeting of the day. As she walked passed the French doors that led into the living room, she saw Neely standing in the dark, looking out one of the windows.

"Are you okay?" she asked.

Neely's nod was less than convincing. "My daughter is hiding from the district attorney, my son is stuck in Africa, and my husband is trying to prove he didn't steal money from his clients. I have a police car parked in front of my house and snipers in my trees. My neighbors aren't speaking to me, and even the wind blowing through the dogwood trees seems vaguely threatening."

"Try not to worry."

"I'm not worried exactly," Neely said. "I know Adam will make it home eventually. I know Dane will protect Brooke and that Raleigh didn't steal any money. But I can't help feeling that my life as I've known it up to this point is over."

Savannah moved closer. "What do you mean?"

"This is a close-knit, snobby sort of community. I don't think we'll be welcome here after all this is over—even if Raleigh is proven innocent of any wrongdoing."

"You can live wherever you want to," Savannah pointed out. "And if your snooty neighbors don't like it they'll just have to get over it."

Neely smiled. "They can't make me move, but they can make me want to. And even if I could stand being snubbed and ignored, once word gets out about the missing money and the independent audit, Raleigh might lose all his clients. In which case the business won't survive and we'll have to sell the house."

Savannah was about to disagree when Dane walked in. "That's true. Selling this house may be necessary. And if it is, don't look at it as a bad thing. Look at it as a fresh start."

Neely stared at the street in front of her house. "I can't imagine living anywhere but here."

"Come on, Crybaby. Let's go meet with the guys." As they moved down the hall toward Raleigh's office, Dane said, "You don't have to make any drastic decisions right now—like whether or not to sell your house."

When the trio walked into the office, Steamer said, "Did I just hear you say that Neely is selling her house?"

"I said that if Business Services goes bankrupt she might have to consider it," Dane clarified.

Steamer turned to Neely. "If you do decide to sell, I'd be glad to be your real estate agent, and I wouldn't even charge you a commission. I had a very successful career as a Realtor in Vegas before I dedicated my life to the law."

"How can you sell her house?" Hack demanded. "You aren't licensed in Tennessee!"

"I can get licensed, or just work with a local agent to sell the house," Steamer replied.

"That's stupid," Hack said. He turned to Neely. "Promise me if you sell your house you won't let him handle it. I'll pay the commission if you'll use a *real* agent."

"I'm as real as it gets, baby!" Steamer insisted.

"No more real estate talk." Dane sat down at the desk. "Hack, report on what you found out about Raleigh's partner, his financial situation, and his personal life."

With one last malevolent glance at Steamer, Hack said, "I confirmed that Hopewell is in serious financial trouble. He's got almost no cash reserves, and he's borrowed to his credit max. In addition to his own massive expenses, he's making payments on a car he bought for his girlfriend, and he pays her rent."

"Were you able to talk to the ex-wife?"

Hack nodded. "I met personally with the former Mrs. Hopewell, and may I say, she is a real knockout even though she's in her midforties." There was a brief pause, and then he added, "Sorry, Neely."

"Neely knows she's ancient," Dane said, dismissing the comment. "Go on."

Neely smiled at Hack to reassure him. "I wasn't offended."

"Seriously," Hack emphasized. "Marjorie Hopewell is the spectacular kind of beautiful—Miss America beautiful."

"She was Miss Tennessee, back in the *olden* days," Neely inserted.

Hack sighed. "She was very nice and politely made time in her busy schedule to talk to me. But she doesn't look like a good suspect."

"Why, besides the fact that she's so pretty that she has you bedazzled?" Steamer asked.

Hack responded through clenched teeth. "She said she has no contact with her ex—everything is handled by their lawyers now. So she didn't have access to the missing money."

"Does she get alimony?"

Hack shook his head. "She got their house, which she sold, and a lump sum in the divorce, about two million dollars total. She used part of the settlement to buy her house in Florida and some to set up a little travel-planning business. So she's in good shape financially."

"And her lifestyle isn't tied to the financial health of Business Services," Savannah pointed out. "She could destroy the company and get revenge against Finn Hopewell without suffering any ill effects herself."

"So she's a reasonable suspect, despite her beauty?" Steamer asked.

Dane nodded. "I think so."

Hack shrugged. "I sensed some bitterness when we were talking about Hopewell. But she got her revenge with the divorce settlement. She has a good, new life. I don't see why she'd waste her time and risk what she has trying to get back at him."

"Never underestimate that woman-scorned thing," Steamer advised. "If we're accusing someone based on revenge, my money's on the ex-wife."

"If you *had* any money," Hack taunted.

"Hey, things are looking up for the guy from Vegas!" Steamer claimed. "After all, I'm a lawyer now."

"That's disputable," Hack said, "which means 'in question,' if they didn't teach you that word during your online courses."

"I'm going to have to send one of you home if you can't stop this constant bickering," Dane told them.

"We'll behave!" Steamer promised. "I'm in it to win it!"

Hack growled at Steamer but addressed his comments to Dane. "If I had to pick a revenge suspect, it would be the weird new girlfriend. She is young and smart but just average looking at best."

"Beauty isn't everything," Savannah said, oddly offended in behalf of the girlfriend.

"I know," Hack was quick to assure her. "It's just that after meeting the ex-wife and developing an opinion of Hopewell's 'type,' I don't think the girlfriend fits it, if you know what I mean."

Savannah nodded. "I think I do."

"How would it benefit the girlfriend to put Hopewell in worse financial shape, possibly even jail?" Dane asked. "He's paying her bills, so that would be like biting the hand that feeds her."

"Hopewell's continued ability to support her is in serious question, and a smart girl like her would realize that. If she saw an opportunity to take some money and pin the blame on him, I think she'd do it. She seems like the cold, calculating type."

"Would she have the information necessary to transfer money from the holding account?" Dane asked.

Hack nodded. "I think there is a good chance that she would. In addition to pillow talk, she also works part time for the firm."

"Raleigh wasn't happy about that," Neely contributed, "but Finn insisted."

"So she would have known about the monthly money transfers to Sterling Strategies," Savannah said. "And she would have had the opportunity to clean out the account."

"Which is something else that clears Marjorie Hopewell," Hack said. "She didn't have the opportunity."

"We can't make that assumption just because she says she no longer has contact with Hopewell," Dane replied. "She might still have access to financial information."

"Or a key to the office," Savannah added.

"Right." Dane made a note on his legal pad. "So we've got three reasonable suspects besides Raleigh. Anything else?"

Hack said, "The girlfriend might have a police record."

Dane's eyebrows shot up. "What makes you say that?"

"She was very concerned about getting involved in any kind of litigation," Hack replied. "It's just a hunch."

"Your hunches are usually pretty accurate," Dane remarked. "Check it out."

"I've got someone working on it now," Hack said. "I'll let you know when I hear something."

"Did we ever find out where the money went after it was transferred from the holding account at Business Services?"

"To an offshore account," Hack said. "It's probably been moved twenty times by now, making it very hard to find."

"But the auditors are trying, right?"

Hack nodded.

Dane stood. "Good. Now everybody get some sleep."

CHAPTER NINE

BROOKE WOKE UP ON FRIDAY morning looking forward to the day. She was anxious to see if Hunter would sing with the choral group or make up a new ailment. She wanted to watch him fight for the Confederate Army during the Battle of the Day and dance with unaccompanied women during the square dance classes. She wanted to work with him at the ice cream shop and waltz with him at the dance that night. The real world with all its problems seemed very far away.

She climbed out of bed, knowing he was already up and dressed and reading about the day's battle. After a shower she put on her layers of 1860s underclothes. She smiled when she pulled the pink calico dress over her head—since it was Hunter's favorite.

Then she made her way into the living area and greeted him. "Good morning!"

He put down his battle synopsis and said, "Good morning."

She handed him the little button hook and turned around so he could secure her dress. When he was finished, she spun and raised her eyebrow. "Well?"

"Nice," he said.

She smiled. "You look very nice too, sir."

"Thanks."

She didn't let his lack of enthusiasm subdue her. "What is the battle for today?"

"Stones River."

"Does the North win that one?"

He shook his head. "The South won, sort of, but didn't follow through, so it turned out to be a short-lived victory."

"Good," she said. "I like for you to be on the winning side. It makes it seem less likely that you'll get shot."

He gave her his exasperated look. "Lots of soldiers on the winning side get shot."

She clutched both lapels and told him, "When the bullets start flying, duck."

He reached up and covered her hands with his, and for just a second she thought he was going to kiss her. But instead he gently pried her hands from his jacket and smoothed his lapels. Then he took a step backward to put a little distance between them. "Let's go get some breakfast."

Brooke nodded, determined not to let the missed kiss opportunity ruin her day.

When they walked into the employee cafeteria, Doreen Dooley spotted them and started waving wildly.

"We saved you a seat!" she hollered.

Hunter leaned close and whispered, "You go on and sit with them before she makes more of a spectacle. I'll get you a bagel and fruit."

As she crossed the room to join the Dooleys, Brooke took an illogical amount of pleasure in the knowledge that Hunter had noticed what she ate for breakfast.

"Don't you look lovely!" Doreen exclaimed when Brooke reached their table.

"Thank you," Brooke replied.

"So are you ready for today's battle?"

Brooke nodded. "I'm getting used to them."

Doreen frowned. "I don't know if you can ever completely get used to them. You are familiar with them, and you know what to expect with the shooting and all. But your husband hasn't died in battle yet. That's something you still have to face. Today's battle isn't too bad, but wait until tomorrow. That's the Battle of Shiloh, which was very bloody. So prepare yourself that your husband might not survive that one."

Brooke looked up to see Hunter coming with two plates of food. He was so handsome in his Confederate uniform. The thought of him dying, even just during a reenactment, was almost unbearable. She was blinking back tears as he reached them.

Hunter studied her for a few seconds. Then he looked between her and the Dooleys in obvious alarm. "Is everything okay?"

Doreen laughed. "Yes, I just scared her by mentioning that a lot of men were going to die in the battle tomorrow, and she doesn't want to lose you!"

As Doreen said the words, Brooke knew it was true. She didn't want to lose him, now or ever. She turned to face him, but his expression was unreadable.

While they were walking to choral practice, he said, "I'm getting a little nervous. We may not be able to stay here until Monday."

"You mean we'll need to find another place to hide?"

He nodded.

She looked around The Commons and tried to imagine leaving it forever. Then she looked at Hunter and tried to imagine how she'd feel when they finally said good-bye. When she didn't see him every morning and dance with him every night. Reality came crashing down, and the joy she'd felt since waking up disappeared.

During choral practice she didn't steal glances at Hunter as he tried to sing. And she was quiet as they walked to the battlefield. He didn't ask her what was wrong. She suspected that he knew but didn't have any words of comfort.

When the time came, Brooke kissed Hunter for luck, but she was careful not to meet his eyes and to keep the kiss quick and almost businesslike. Watching him walk away to join his regiment, Brooke felt a tension in the air that she hadn't noticed before. She mentioned it to Doreen, who nodded.

"It's because the men are learning their roles better and taking it more personally," she said. "It will be worse tomorrow with Shiloh. It was a particularly difficult defeat for the South, sort of the beginning of the end, if you know what I mean."

Brooke looked out at Hunter and nodded. "I know exactly what you mean."

"I hope Elliott doesn't die," Jada Mengenthal said. "I just don't know if I could stand it."

Doreen patted her shoulder. "Don't take it so hard, now. Just be glad we didn't really live in the 1860s. Then this would be much more serious."

Brooke watched the men line up. She could see the Bouyer brothers— thanks to their red hair—Elliott Mengenthal, Bob Dooley, and Hunter. Music blared through the sound system, and the narrator began describing the events that led up to the Battle of Stones River. Cannons boomed, and shots were fired. Brooke covered her ears, wishing she could stop it.

Hunter waved his hat to reassure her, and she waved back.

"Your husband is very considerate of your feelings," Doreen said. "You should appreciate that."

"I do," Brooke said. And she did appreciate Hunter very much.

Doreen rattled on. "It's nice to see young people so in love. I was talking to Bob last night about how, when you're playing the piano, your husband can't take his eyes off you."

"He was probably just afraid I was going to have an asthma attack," she said.

Doreen laughed. "I know the look of love when I see it! And that boy is smitten!"

Doreen was not an expert on love or a qualified judge of Hunter's character. But just the thought that he might have feelings for Brooke gave new life to her dream that they might have a future together after Monday. Brooke looked back at the battlefield, where Hunter was crouched and ready to fight. This was an issue that had to be addressed. Brooke folded her arms and gave her full attention to the battle, determined to confront him later.

***

During lunch Hack asked, "So, does Caroline have kittens yet?"

Savannah nodded. "Five. They were born in her new playhouse overnight, and she's already named them. And now she wants to bring them all home."

"I told you how I feel about cats," Dane reminded her. "We aren't having one cat, let alone five."

"Cats are sneaky," Hack added illogically.

Savannah said, "Well, who's going to be the one to tell Caroline she can't have a kitten."

"I could tell her," Dane claimed.

She raised an eyebrow. "Oh really?" Then she turned to Hack. "And I know you're not even going to try and say you could tell her."

Hack's shoulders slumped. "If she wants them, I say let her have them. You can keep them outside. They kill rats."

"Not the most pleasant comment to make while we're eating," Neely pointed out.

Savannah laughed. "We'll decide about the kitten later, and if the answer is no, I'll tell her."

"I miss that little girl," Steamer said. "It doesn't seem natural to be walking around without tripping over a single train track."

Savannah sighed. "I miss her too."

"This will all be over soon," Dane said. "Or if it's not, we'll have Doc bring her back."

Savannah was relieved to hear that the separation was going to be over soon—one way or another.

After lunch Dane announced, "We've arranged appointments with Finn Hopewell's current girlfriend and ex-wife this afternoon, is that right?"

Hack nodded. "The girlfriend will be here in about thirty minutes, followed by the former Mrs. Hopewell an hour later. We'll have to talk quick because she's working us in before a tennis match."

"Coordinate that carefully," Dane advised. "We want to make sure they don't cross paths."

"Why are they coming here?" Savannah asked

Dane frowned. "There really wasn't a better option since I won't leave you—or take you with me to do an interview. And I want to meet our suspects personally."

"How did you get them to come?" Neely wanted to know.

Hack answered, "The girlfriend is trying to sublease her apartment, so we told her Neely was interested in renting it for her daughter but was too elderly to come there."

Steamer grinned. "After all, she did just turn forty-five."

Savannah rolled her eyes. "Nobody thinks forty-five is *elderly*."

"And Marjorie is coming as a personal favor to Neely," Dane added.

Neely sighed. "Now I'm indebted to her. There's no telling what I'll have to do to pay her back."

"If this helps Raleigh, no matter what she asks for will be worth it," Savannah predicted.

"You're right," Neely said. "But you might have to remind me of that again when she calls in her favor."

"The girlfriend's name is Selma Estes, correct?" Dane asked.

Hack nodded. "And I was right about her police record. It's not much—just juvenile stuff—but she's been arrested more than once."

"I don't know if that makes her more suspicious or not," Dane said. "But we'll keep it in mind."

Hack's phone beeped. He checked it and announced, "Ms. Estes is here."

After a few minutes, one of Hack's men escorted a tall, thin young woman with long, dark hair into the room.

Dane stood and extended a hand.

"Ms. Estes?"

She nodded.

"I'm Major Dane from the US Army."

Dane almost never used his rank, so Savannah could only assume he was trying to intimidate their guest. He went around the room, giving names—as well as ranks—for everyone. When he reached Neely, Ms. Estes nodded.

"I've seen your picture on Raleigh's desk." She glanced nervously around the room. "You're the one who is interested in subletting my apartment?"

Neely turned to Dane for an indication of how she should proceed.

"Have a seat," Dane pulled out a chair and gave her one of his most charming smiles. "May I call you Selma?"

"If you like," she granted permission guardedly.

"Thank you." Dane resumed his seat behind the desk. "So, Selma, we've brought you here today under slightly false pretenses."

She tensed immediately. "What do you mean?"

"Neely doesn't really want to rent your apartment. But we do want to ask you a couple of questions. You may have heard that there are some financial problems at Business Services."

"I heard," Selma confirmed.

"We want to help Raleigh, obviously, but the auditors are not being very . . . generous with information. So we'd like to get some background information from you."

"I don't want to get involved in an investigation, so I'm not sure how much I can say to you. Not to be rude or anything."

"I understand your concerns," Dane said. "Nothing you say here will be legally binding or incriminating. But it could help to save Business Services, so we hope we can count on your cooperation."

She gave him a noncommittal shrug. Apparently Business Services did not mean the world to her.

"First, if I could ask a few questions about you and Finn Hopewell. According to my information, you've been together for about a year. You met at a bar near campus, and a friendship grew from there."

"Yes, it's been about a year," she confirmed, completely skimming over the less-than-auspicious beginnings of the relationship.

Hack said, "He pays for your apartment and recently bought you a new car."

Selma's face settled into a frown. "Finn offered to help me out until I finish school. There's no law against that."

Hack flashed her a gold-toothed smile. "Not one that I know of."

"You work at Business Services too—is that correct?" Dane asked.

"Just part time."

"What are your responsibilities?" Dane sounded like he was truly interested.

"I'm Finn's personal assistant. I do a little of everything."

"Like mange his client accounts, deposit checks, return phone calls, transfer money?" Dane asked.

"Only on his authorization," Selma said carefully.

"Do you ever handle things for Raleigh?"

"Sometimes if he's really busy, but not often."

"What about the holding account for Sterling Strategies? Do you know anything about that?"

"I know there is a holding account for Sterling, but I've never handled the monthly transfers."

Dane asked, "Is there anyone else who could have transferred that money out of the holding account?"

"Besides Raleigh or Finn? No one," Selma sounded certain. "A transfer of that magnitude would require both of their authorization codes."

"Could someone have stolen the codes?"

"I doubt it." Selma stood. "I hope you can help Raleigh. He's a nice man. But I have studying to do, and I don't know anything about the missing money. So I want to leave now."

Dane nodded and Hack rose to escort her to the door.

"Thank you for your time, Selma," Dane said. "And I'm sorry we didn't tell you the real reason we wanted to talk to you."

"It's okay," she said, accepting the apology. Then she nodded to the room in general and followed Hack out into the entryway.

Once Savannah was sure Selma was gone, she said, "Well, she's very composed."

"She had an answer ready for every question we asked," Hack said.

"We know she's your favorite suspect," Steamer said. "Since she's not much to look at."

"I don't have a favorite suspect," Hack denied. "And I don't care how she looks!"

Dane looked at Neely. "Tell me what you can about Hopewell's ex-wife."

"I've known Marjorie for years and, at one time, would have even called her a friend. But we haven't seen each other much in the last few years. Once our children were grown, we didn't have much in common. As Hack said, she's stunningly beautiful and still looks much younger than her forty-plus years."

Steamer winked. "Yes, Hack has told us, several times."

"Just wait until you see her," Hack defended.

They didn't have to wait long before one of the guards escorted Marjorie in.

"Neely!" the woman cried as she pulled Neely into a warm embrace.

Marjorie was not just thin like Selma Estes; she was fit and tan and dressed for tennis in a very flattering outfit. Her blond hair was perfectly highlighted so that if there were any gray strands, they were well hidden.

Neely said, "It's good to see you."

"I'm glad I was able to work it in. My schedule while I'm here is insanely busy."

"Thank you for coming," Dane said. Then he introduced everyone and explained the reason for the meeting.

"I'm glad to do anything for Neely," Marjorie assured them as she settled in the chair recently vacated by Finn's girlfriend.

"This won't take long," Dane began. "But we wanted to ask you some questions about your ex-husband."

"I'm the wrong person to ask about him," Marjorie said. "As I told Mr. Hack yesterday, I rarely talk to Finn anymore and never see him."

She flashed Hack a smile, and Savannah was afraid the big man would faint.

Dane continued the interview. "Hack told you that there have been some problems at Business Services?"

She nodded. "I was sorry to hear that. Raleigh has worked particularly hard to build up the company, and it would be a shame if it goes under because of poor money management."

"Would you mind answering some questions about your personal life?" Dane asked. "It might help us figure this out."

"You mean about Finn and how he cheated on me?" Marjorie's smile dimmed slightly. "I lived with that man for almost twenty-five years; we had two sons together, and how did he repay me? By fooling around with a younger girl! I work out! I watch what I eat! But that wasn't good enough for him. He had to have the one thing I couldn't give him: youth!"

Dane nodded. "Selma Estes?"

"Yes," Marjorie confirmed. "To tell you the truth, though, she did me a favor. I spent all those years in Finn's shadow, always putting him first.

Now I have a nice little house on the beach and a travel business that keeps me busy. I don't clean up after anyone, and I couldn't be happier. I wish I'd caught him cheating years ago."

Savannah had to admire Marjorie Hopewell. Her life had been ruined, through no fault of her own, and she had picked up the pieces and made another life, one she seemed to like just as well if not better.

"I understand that you did well in the divorce settlement," Dane said.

"I took him for everything I could," she admitted. "He cheated on me; I figured I deserved it. I got the house and a nice lump sum. My lawyer told me after it was over that she'd never gotten such a good settlement before. I think Finn was embarrassed about getting caught with that college girl and anxious to put the whole thing behind him. Later he regretted not contesting some of my demands."

"How do you know?"

Marjorie laughed. "Because he told me! He basically accused me of robbing him—me! He asked me to go back to court and renegotiate."

"But you refused."

"Of course I did."

"So you haven't talked to Finn lately?" Neely joined in.

Marjorie shook her head. "No."

"Apparently he's been having severe financial difficulties."

"I wish I could say I felt sorry for him," Marjorie said. "But he made this bed—literally—so he can lie in it. And if he is having cash flow problems, he can put his little girlfriend in a cheaper apartment instead of asking me to give back some of the money the court awarded me."

Savannah was inclined to agree.

"Is there anything else?" Marjorie asked. "I hate to rush you, but I've got an appointment with a tennis pro in ten minutes."

"You worked at Business Services some when you were married to Hopewell," Dane said.

"I volunteered there sometimes, when they were busy," she confirmed.

"Did you ever handle money transfers?"

"Occasionally."

"So you know Hopewell's code," Dane continued, "the one you'd need to move a large amount of money."

"I *knew* it," she said. "I'm sure he's changed it since our divorce."

"What about Raleigh's code?"

"I never knew his." Marjorie was starting to look impatient.

"Do you think Selma Estes knows the codes?"

Marjorie's smile was now more of a grimace. "I'm sure she knows Finn's. It's unlikely Raleigh would tell her his, but she's a resourceful young woman so she could have figured out a way to get it if she wanted to."

Savannah saw Hack and Dane exchange a glance.

"But honestly, if you're looking for a suspect, you might want to check out the receptionist that Selma made Finn fire last week."

"How do you know Hopewell fired someone last week," Dane asked, "since you aren't in communication with your ex-husband anymore?"

"I said I didn't talk to Finn," Marjorie clarified. "I still have friends at Business Services."

Dane nodded, digesting this information. "Why did Selma want the receptionist fired?"

"She said the girl was rude to clients, but the consensus is that the girl was just too attractive and Selma was afraid Finn's famously roving eye would eventually turn the girl's way."

"The receptionist would know the codes?" Dane asked.

"She worked closely with both men—doing what I used to do. So it's possible, even likely."

"Can you give us her name?" Hack asked.

Marjorie smiled. "I could, but I'd rather not. I'm sure you have ways to find that out in a matter of seconds." She stood. "And now I've got to go."

Dane walked her to the office door, where one of Hack's guards was waiting. "Thanks for making the time to see us."

Neely joined them. "Yes, thank you very much."

"It was good to see you, and I hope everything works out for Raleigh. I'm only in town for a few days, but next time I come we should get together for lunch."

"Call me," Neely invited.

Savannah watched the exchange with sadness. It was unlikely that Neely would ever eat lunch with Marjorie Hopewell again.

After Marjorie was gone, Neely asked, "Well?"

Steamer addressed the room, "I'm about to say something I never thought I'd say: Hack was right. Marjorie Hopewell is gorgeous. Her ex-husband must have been an idiot to cheat on her."

"Well, it sounds like she's certainly making him pay for his mistakes," Savannah murmured.

"Darn right," Hack replied.

"But did she steal money from Business Services?" Savannah asked. "Life on the beach may be more expensive than she realized."

"I can see her stealing from Finn," Neely said thoughtfully, "and even feeling like he deserved it. But not Raleigh."

Dane said, "How about Selma?"

"You know how I feel," Hack said.

"I can definitely see her as our thief," Savannah agreed.

"And the fired receptionist?" Dane asked.

Hack stood. "I'm going to check into that now."

***

It was after dinner before Hack returned. They gathered in Raleigh's office for a report.

"So," Dane said to him. "What did you find out about the fired receptionist?"

"Her name is Cindy Marsh," Hack replied. "She's cute, but not gorgeous like Marjorie. She's young, but not quite as young as Selma. And she claims that there was nothing going on between her and Finn Hopewell. She said there was no way she'd be interested in an old man like him. She described Selma as mean and petty. She's considering a wrongful dismissal lawsuit and working at her mother's beauty salon until something better comes along."

"Was she ever involved with the Sterling Strategies money transfers?" Dane asked.

"She says no, and I believe her. I doubt the girl could memorize her own phone number, let alone bank security codes. But the most interesting thing I learned was that the ex–Mrs. Hopewell still drops by Business Services from time to time."

Dane raised an eyebrow. "Really?"

"According to Cindy, Marjorie not only has a key, she comes by about once a month and is very close friends with the personnel manager."

Steamer raised his eyebrows. "So the ex–Mrs. Hopewell is back on our suspect list?"

Dane nodded. "I would say so."

"I hate that I found incriminating information on her," Hack said. "I really don't want it to be her."

"I just want it to be anyone besides Raleigh," Dane replied.

"What have you found out about Nature Fresh and Joined Forces?"

"The investigation is still ongoing," Hack reminded him. "But so far we haven't found anything helpful."

"Keep looking," Dane requested. "Now let's go into the kitchen. Neely made a pie."

After dessert Savannah went back to reading about Joined Forces and their animal rights efforts. Once the kitchen was clean, Neely joined her. A little while later, Dane walked in looking serious.

Savannah was immediately worried. "Is something wrong?"

He shook his head. "No, but the district attorney is back. You two wait here. We're bringing him in through the garage."

Savannah saw the deep concern on Neely's face as they waited for Dane to bring in Mr. Shaw. They heard movement at the door and looked up anxiously, but it was just Hack and Steamer.

Finally Dane ushered the district attorney in. Mr. Shaw was wearing the same raincoat he'd had on when he'd visited previously. His sandy blond hair was windblown, just as before. And his eyes still looked tired. When he saw the people assembled in the office, he looked back at Dane. "I thought I made it clear that what I have to say is for your ears only."

"Talking to my team is just like talking to me." Dane pointed to a chair directly across from the desk for Mr. Shaw. Once the newcomer was seated, Dane settled behind the desk.

Mr. Shaw cleared his throat. "Have you been able to find Brooke Clayton?"

Dane shook his head. "I still don't know where she is."

Mr. Shaw gave Dane a narrowed look, as if he doubted this were true.

"Please tell us the reason for your second unexpected visit," Dane requested.

"There's something I thought you should know," the DA said. "I have reason to believe that Freddo Higgins sold Miss Clayton out to Nature Fresh."

Dane frowned. "What makes you think that?"

"My office received word this afternoon that Mr. Higgins has left the country. Further investigation showed that he withdrew large amounts of money yesterday and bought a ticket for the Cayman Islands."

"He got the money from Nature Fresh?" Dane asked.

"We haven't been able to prove that yet, but I think it's safe to assume. If they knew she was scheduled to testify in the hearing on Monday, they probably threatened Miss Clayton, causing her to back out."

"But on Monday, when the case is closed, she'll be safe?" Savannah asked.

Mr. Shaw shook his head. "I wouldn't count on that. They won't want to worry about the pictures or Miss Clayton's testimony resurfacing at some point in the future. So if they can't buy her off . . ."

Savannah could barely breathe. "You're saying Brooke is in danger?"

"I'm saying it's a possibility," Mr. Shaw corrected. "Ironically, the best and safest thing Miss Clayton can do is to come in and testify. Nature Fresh will be a much weaker opponent when they are facing criminal charges and being crucified by the press."

Dane nodded. "I appreciate you coming and telling us your concerns. If I communicate with Brooke, I'll tell her what you've said. Then if she wants to testify, I'll be in touch with you." Dane stood. "Hack will escort you out to your car in the garage."

The DA looked around. "I hope I can count on all of you to keep this strictly confidential. Brooke Clayton's life may depend on it."

"You can," Dane answered for everyone.

Mr. Shaw stood and followed Hack out.

No one said anything until Hack returned.

Then Neely asked, "So it's not just the police and Mr. Shaw who are looking for Brooke? Nature Fresh is looking too?"

"And Brooke is not on the top of the police priority list," Steamer predicted. "But for the Nature Fresh guys, she's numero uno!"

"Speak English," Hack demanded.

"Now that I have my law degree, I'm taking some online Spanish classes," Steamer replied. "You can never have too much education."

Hack muttered something under his breath that Savannah didn't even try to hear.

"What Steamer said is basically true, in any language," Dane inserted. "The Nature Fresh people will try harder to find Brooke since there is more to lose from their perspective."

"There is everything to lose," Savannah said. "According to Mr. Shaw, a scandal like this could completely put them out of business."

"So what will they do if they find her?" Neely asked.

Dane sighed heavily. "I don't know, but one thing is for sure. It's time to bring Brooke home. Now."

CHAPTER TEN

BROOKE STOOD ON THE EDGE of the outdoor dance floor at the night's entertainment—a hoedown. She swayed with the music and tapped her foot. Hunter had made it clear that he didn't like square dancing. They had danced once to a slow song, and since then they had been spectators. He was standing beside her, alternately checking the crowd and his phone. She knew his vigilance should make her feel safer, and it did. But it also made her feel like a job.

She was about to risk rejection by asking him to dance when he put his arm around her waist. She thought he had read her mind, but instead of leading her to the dance floor he pulled her away from the crowd, into a dark spot between the theatre and a souvenir shop. Holding her tightly, his face descended toward hers. With her heart pounding, she closed her eyes and waited for a kiss that never came.

Instead he whispered, "We have to leave here immediately."

Heart still pounding, her eyes flew open. "Why?"

"I just got a text from Hack, and they have reason to believe that you're in danger."

"What is the reason?"

He frowned. "Don't we have this a little backward? You should be the one explaining it to me."

She tried to remain calm. "I just want to know what has changed."

"You uncle had a visit from the DA. He says a company called Nature Fresh knows you have information that could ruin them and they might not care if you're dead or alive as long as you can't testify at the hearing on Monday."

She closed her eyes briefly. "But I'm not going to testify. That's why I left. If I don't show up for the hearing, the case will be closed and they won't have anything to worry about."

"Apparently they aren't willing to risk the future of their company on your word. Major Dane thinks they will kill you if they find you. And I agree. Remember that guy with the gun in the slaughter shed?"

"How could I forget?"

"He heard a noise and he shot. Fortunately all he hit was a dead rat. Next time it could be you."

"I thought those men were the police!"

"The police don't shoot first and ask questions later," he said. "But the important thing is if they knew you were at the march, they may have found out that the Cauthens left the same night we did."

"And they might be coming here to find me?"

"Or to ask the Cauthens if they saw you. But either way, this place is not safe."

"What are we going to do?"

"First we're going back to our room to change into regular clothes. Then we're going to get out of here—one way or another."

He took her hand and pulled her through the shadows along the storefronts, moving slowly but steadily away from the hoedown. As they walked inside the administration building, they ran right into Wilma Frye.

She fixed them with a frown. "Why did you two leave the hoedown early? You're assigned to be there until ten o'clock."

"Elizabeth is having trouble breathing," Hunter said. "I want to get her to a hospital before it progresses into a full-blown asthma attack."

Wilma turned to Brooke with a concerned expression.

Brooke had no idea how to fake an asthma attack, so she just tried to look scared.

"I'll drive you to the hospital," Wilma said. "The guards at the gate won't give me any trouble about leaving—even this late. Go ahead and change clothes quickly, then meet me by the back door of the administration building. I'll grab my keys and be there in a minute."

"Thank you," Hunter said. Then he took Brooke's arm and hauled her toward the elevators. Hunter took off his jacket while they rode up to the second floor. When they walked into their suite, he dumped the coat on the couch and started unbuttoning her dress. She pulled out the hair clips that attached her ringlets to the back of her head and yanked the hairpiece loose just as he finished with the buttons. He lifted off the dress and tossed it onto the couch beside his jacket.

"Hurry," he whispered, pointing toward the bedroom. "Wear jeans and a dark-colored shirt."

She grabbed her backpack and went into the bathroom. She removed her 1860s underclothing for the last time and put on the pair of jeans and navy blue T-shirt Hunter had purchased for her at the mall near Gatlinburg. Once she was dressed, she glanced at herself in the mirror. She looked as terrified as she felt.

Slinging her backpack onto her shoulder, she rejoined Hunter in the living room. He was waiting by the door. Gone was the Confederate officer she had halfway fallen in love with. In his place was the humorless soldier who had been sent to guard her.

"So, after we get out of here, where will we go?"

"Hack's guys are waiting by the front entrance to take us to your parents' house."

Brooke shook her head. "I can't go home," she said flatly. "I won't endanger my family."

Hunter frowned. "Hack's got the place secured. Nothing will happen to you or your family. He won't let it. *I* won't let it."

"You don't understand," she said, feeling a little desperate. "If they see me at home and think I've come back to testify, then no one will be safe. Not me or my parents or my brother or even my uncle! The only thing I can do to protect them is stay away!"

"Your uncle is an officer and my superior. He's given me an order," Hunter explained. "I have to take you home or I'm in trouble—and not just with your uncle but with the army too."

"Please," she begged.

He spread his hands in obvious exasperation. "Please what? Let you get yourself killed?"

"I want you to keep me safe," she said honestly. "Just don't take me home. Take me somewhere else."

"Is this worth risking my military career?"

She wiped impatiently at a tear that slipped out onto her cheek. "You hate shooting anyway."

She expected more demands from him, more questions, more fight. But he seemed unaccountably affected by her tears. His shoulders slumped and he said, "Okay. But that means we won't have any help from Hack's men."

More tears slipped out—this time tears of relief. "You don't need any help. You can keep me safe and hidden for a few more days."

He nodded, reluctant but committed. "It will be harder now since we'll be running not only from the Nashville PD and these people from

Nature Fresh who want to kill you, but also from your uncle and his team of experts, who will want to kill *me*."

She winced. "I'm sorry if this gets you in trouble, but there's no other way. And I'll explain to my uncle when this is over."

"I doubt he'll be very understanding," Hunter muttered. "But if you're sure this is the only way, then it's what we'll do."

She held him close. "Thank you," she whispered.

He let her hold him for a few seconds and then pulled away. "Now let's go tell Wilma she's going to have to take us out another way since Hack's guys are waiting for us at the front entrance."

They heard a faint tapping on the door, and Hunter put his fingers to his lips. Then he opened it slowly. Doreen and Bob Dooley were standing in the hallway.

"Can we come in?" Doreen asked.

Hunter pulled the door open, and the elderly couple slipped inside.

"We heard you had an asthma attack," Doreen said. "So we came to check." Her eyes scanned their civilian clothes.

"How did you know Brooke was having an asthma attack?" Hunter asked.

Doreen looked confused. "Brooke?"

"Elizabeth," Hunter corrected himself.

"I heard Wilma talking to some men," Doreen replied. "She said she was sure your original application didn't mention asthma, but when you got here she looked again and there were medical forms and a letter from your doctor."

Brooke and Hunter shared a worried glance.

"Are the men she was talking to employees here?" Hunter asked.

Doreen shook her head. "No, they looked like policemen. She told them she'd bring you out the front entrance in just a few minutes. I was worried about you, but now that I see you're not having asthma problems . . . well, I don't know what to think. Are you in trouble with the police?"

Hunter considered his answer for a few seconds. Brooke knew he'd decided to trust them when he said, "We will be in trouble if those men find us," he said. "They are not policemen. They are here to harm . . ." he looked at Brooke, "my wife."

The couple digested this information. Then Doreen said, "Oh dear."

"I witnessed something," Brooke explained. "And they've threatened that, if I testify, they will hurt me and my family."

"Just like in the movies," Doreen said breathlessly.

"You could leave this building by the side door and go out the service entrance at the back of the resort," Bob suggested.

Doreen nodded. "Bob has a key since he's responsible for moving all those cannons."

Bob fished in his pocket and produced a single key. "This works on the gate and the equipment shed right beside it. They keep a couple of dirt bikes in the shed too. The keys are stuck in their ignitions. And helmets are hanging on the handlebars."

Hunter smiled. "Thanks."

"Will you tell Jovette I'm sorry that we had to leave?" Brooke requested. "And we'll send money to pay for the dirt bike?"

"Of course," Doreen promised. "But dinner sure won't be the same without you."

Brooke gave both the Dooleys a hug. "Thank you." And to think there had been a time when she would have done anything to avoid them.

"Don't stay here," Hunter said. "When the men who were talking to Wilma realize we aren't coming, they'll look for us here. If they know you've helped us, well, it could be dangerous." He looked at Bob. "If anyone asks you about this key, tell them you lost it during the battle today."

Doreen's eyes widened with fear, but Bob stood a little taller. "I'm not scared of them."

Hunter frowned. "Well, you should be."

"We'll leave," Doreen promised.

"If you could watch though," Hunter added, "and when some other men come—some huge men like football players—you can tell them how we left and why."

The Dooleys nodded in unison.

"And if you'd give them this." Hunter handed Bob his phone.

"I'll guard it with my life!" he vowed.

Hunter put a hand on his shoulder. "Thank you, Lieutenant Dooley." Then Hunter opened the door and looked into the hallway.

While he was making sure the coast was clear, Brooke took one last look at the suite that had been their home, the costumes they had worn, and the Dooleys, who were their friends. She gave them a little wave as Hunter pulled her into the hall.

They hurried to the stairs and descended as quietly as possible. Brooke was terrified that they would be discovered, but they made it to the side exit without anyone noticing. After checking outside, Hunter led the way into the darkness. She immediately felt safer, less exposed.

As they walked she asked, "How do you know Hack's men won't be watching the back entrance?"

Hunter replied grimly, "Because it would never occur to them that I would disobey an order."

They moved at a quick but cautious pace, staying in the shadows as much as possible and going into the open only when absolutely necessary. When they reached the back entrance, Hunter told her to wait by the trees until he had the gate open and the dirt bike ready.

She nodded. Then she watched as he approached the shed and unlocked it. A few nerve-wracking minutes later he came out, pushing a dirt bike silently beside him. He rolled it to the gate and unlocked it. Then he motioned for her to come with him. She ran forward through the small opening. Then Hunter closed the gate and relocked it.

They walked for a while in silence, him pushing the bike and her looking nervously around the dark woods. Finally he decided they were far enough away from the resort to risk starting the bike. After helping her secure her helmet, he put on his own and climbed onto the bike. Holding it steady with both feet, he said, "Now it's your turn."

She swung a leg over the bike and sat behind him. She leaned against his back and wrapped her arms around his waist.

"Hold on tight," he instructed.

She pressed even closer against him. "I will."

He turned the key, and the bike roared to life. The noise seemed incredibly loud in the dark, quiet woods. Hunter leaned into the bike, and they took off, spraying dust behind them.

After a while she asked into his ear, "Where are we going?"

Hunter turned his head slightly. "They'll expect us to get out of the mountains as quickly as possible—to go to a metropolitan area like Knoxville or Chattanooga, where we can lose ourselves in the crowds."

"So we should stay in the mountains?"

"I think so, but once we've committed to that plan, there will be no going back. When they realize we've left the resort, they'll start watching all the roads that lead out of this area, so we'll be trapped."

"It will take a long time to search all these mountains," she said.

He nodded. "If we're lucky, no one will find us until the danger has passed. Our first step is to leave a false trail."

"Make them think we're going to a big city?" she guessed.

"No, we're going to buy camping equipment and make sure they get us on camera. They'll know I wouldn't let that happen unless I wanted it to. And hopefully they'll assume the opposite—that we left the woods. That should buy us a couple of days."

"It's a good plan." She pressed her cheek against his back and held Hunter close, listening to the hum of the bike's engine and enjoying the cool breeze on her face.

***

It was a few minutes after ten o'clock on Friday night, and the rest of the team was in Raleigh's office when Hack walked in with the bad news.

"When will Brooke and Owl be here? Are they on their way?" Neely asked.

Hack shook his head. "They never showed up at the meet with my men by the resort entrance. And Owl just missed his check-in."

"What does that mean?" Neely asked in alarm.

Dane walked over and put an arm around her. "We're trying to figure out what it means." He turned to Hack. "Did you send your guys inside?"

He nodded. "The director is showing them to the room where Owl and Brooke have been staying." He pressed his phone to his ear. Then he held up a finger, requesting that everyone be quiet.

The office was silent as a tomb.

Finally Hack said, "The room is empty. It looks like they left in a hurry."

"Signs of foul play?" Dane asked.

"No evidence of it." Hack held up his finger again.

Savannah saw the relief on Dane's face.

This time the silence seemed to last forever. Then Hack turned off his phone and addressed the group. "My guys talked to an elderly couple— well, really just the wife. They claim to be friends with Brooke and Hunter. They said they helped them escape by giving them a key that let them out the back gate and gave them access to a dirt bike."

"And do we believe them?" Dane asked.

Hack nodded. "They had Owl's cell phone. On the screen was a message he never sent. Our code for 'All is well.'"

Savannah felt her body relax. "So Brooke is with him and they are okay?"

Dane nodded. "I think we can assume so."

"But now they are hiding from us too?" Neely asked.

Dane made a face. "It looks that way."

"But we'll find them, right?" Neely looked from Hack to Dane.

The two men were steadily regarding each other, communicating without words.

Hack finally answered. "We probably could, but in the process we might lead the Nature Fresh folks right to them."

"I'd trust Owl with my life," Dane added. "In fact, I have—many times."

Savannah frowned. "So you believe he's doing what is best?"

"I believe he's doing what he *thinks* is best," Dane modified slightly.

"So you aren't going to look for them?" Neely's tone was tense.

"We're going to look very carefully," Dane said. "Hack's already got men working on it. But we're going to assume Owl has things under control with Brooke. Which brings us to Raleigh."

Neely rubbed her temples. "Why does that bring us to Raleigh?"

"I've had an uneasy feeling since I heard about the audit at his office. The whole thing about sleeping on cots and no one leaving until the money was found sounded odd. But I couldn't put my finger on it until just now," Dane said slowly. "Think about Brooke's reaction to the threat from Nature Fresh. If someone threatened you, what would you do?"

"I'd call you," Neely replied promptly.

Savannah nodded. "Me too."

"But Brooke didn't call me. She didn't call anyone," Dane reminded them. "Why would she do that when she had resources to help protect her and maybe even take down Nature Fresh too?"

"Because they didn't threaten just her." Savannah's throat felt tight. She knew very personally how it felt to have a family member in jeopardy. "But coming to you would still be the best option. You could protect her family too."

"Not if they already had someone," Dane said grimly.

And then it all became clear. "Raleigh?" Savannah whispered.

"Raleigh?" Neely repeated in confusion.

"That's my theory," Dane confirmed. "I think that the missing money and the independent audit at Business Services is all just a sophisticated form of kidnapping. Brooke knows they have her father. Maybe they told her they had him or maybe she realized it when Neely told her that he was going to have to work through Neely's birthday. Brooke knows that if she testifies, they will ruin her father financially—and possibly even worse."

"So what can we do?" Neely wrung her hands.

"If we can help Raleigh, we'll help Brooke too," Dane said.

"Nature Fresh must have had assistance from someone inside Business Services to set this all up," Steamer pointed out. "So we can go back to our investigation, but this time we'll check out all the employees."

"That's a good idea," Neely sounded encouraged.

Hack was less enthusiastic. "That could take weeks."

Dane was frowning, a look Savannah had come to associate with deep thought. He said, "Neely, can you give me that card the detective from the Nashville PD gave you? I want to call Detective Napier."

"Can't you call the other one?" Savannah asked. "The nicer one?"

Dane shook his head. "It's Detective Napier that we need."

Neely retrieved the card and handed it to him. "Why do you want to call the police?"

He said, "Because I need to get Raleigh arrested."

Neely paled. "Arrested!"

Savannah was shocked herself. "Dane?"

He explained, "Raleigh would be in considerably safer hands at the police station than being held hostage at Business Services."

***

On the outskirts of Gatlinburg, Hunter found a Wal-Mart Supercenter that was open twenty-four hours. He and Brooke purchased some camping equipment, a few groceries, a map of Tennessee, and two disposable phones. They made a point to shop quickly and to get in range of several security cameras.

On the way out, Hunter picked up a free magazine that advertised rental cabins. Then they walked back to the dirt bike. They stowed as many of their purchases as possible in their backpacks and tied the rest onto the bike. Then, with the aid of a streetlight, Hunter looked through the rental magazine and studied the map.

"Are we going to stay in one of those cabins?" Brooke asked, pointing at the open magazine.

He shrugged. "Right now I'm just looking for areas that have a lot of cabins."

"Because the more cabins there are around us, the harder it will be to find us? Like a needle in a haystack?"

"Yep. We want our haystack to be as big as possible."

Finally he closed the map and the magazine. "Okay, I think I know where we're going."

So they climbed back on the bike and headed for the hills.

After an hour of driving through winding mountain roads, Brooke was getting very sleepy. When she would relax her hold on Hunter's waist, he would rouse her.

"Hold on tight," he called over his shoulder.

She reestablished her hold on his waist and promised to stay awake. But minutes later she was nodding again. She didn't know how long they had been riding before he finally drove up a steep driveway to a cabin hidden from the road by huge trees. It was built of brown-stained wood so that it blended into the countryside. Brooke was sure Hunter liked this nearly invisible quality.

"So this is it?" she murmured against the back of his neck as he brought the bike to a stop.

He put both feet on the ground, one on each side, to steady the bike. Then he looked up at the house. "Yes, I think this is perfect."

"What if a renter shows up?"

"Then we'll leave." He eased away from her and swung off the bike. He held out a hand to assist her. Then he rolled the bike up to the front door.

"Is there is a security system?" she whispered.

He nodded. "Yes, but no cameras or motion detectors."

"That's good?"

"It's very good." He parked the bike on the front porch. "Now I need you to stand over here by the bike, and don't make a sound until I get the lock opened and the alarm disabled. Okay?"

"Okay."

He opened his backpack and took out a small pouch. Inside was a set of tiny tools. He went to work on the lock and had the door open in a matter of seconds. Then he moved inside. Brooke could see the alarm panel flashing red on the wall. He walked up to it and popped off the cover. Moments later the light turned to green.

Brooke sighed with relief as Hunter came out to get the bike. "How did you learn to do that?" she asked, pointing to the alarm panel.

"Special Ops training."

Brooke frowned. "A skill like that would come in handy if you ever decide to try a life of crime."

"I guess."

"That was a joke," Brooke muttered.

"Maybe you can start telling me in advance," Hunter suggested as he lifted the front wheel of the bike over the threshold onto a gleaming hardwood floor.

Brooke followed him inside. "Will you laugh if you know it's coming?"

"Probably not." He parked the bike by the door.

Brooke couldn't be annoyed with him. She was too busy admiring the cabin. It was more spacious than it seemed from the outside. Brown leather furniture arranged around a huge stone fireplace added to the rustic appearance. There was a wall of windows along the front of the house, providing a breathtaking view of the mountains, where the first rays of sunlight were breaking over the horizon. "Isn't this beautiful?"

Hunter joined her by the windows. "The view is nice, but the best part is that no one will be able to sneak up on us."

She smiled up at him. "Especially since you've got good eyesight."

He nodded. "But windows work both ways, so we can't turn on any lights."

"I'm starving." She looked toward the kitchen.

"We'll eat and then get some sleep."

She yawned. "Sounds good to me."

They walked into the kitchen and unloaded their groceries onto the granite countertop. Brooke made peanut butter sandwiches while Hunter poured glasses of milk. Then they sat at the table and ate with relish.

When he finished his third sandwich, Hunter said, "Okay, now I think I deserve to know what's going on. Everything."

She faced him across the table. Not her boyfriend, but no longer just her uncle's employee. He had put his career on the line for her. That was more than Rex had ever done.

Slowly she told him about Nature Fresh and finding the hidden part of the plant and the gory pipeline. "I knew it was my civic duty to report it," she said. "And I was glad. I felt like I was getting a chance to prove my dedication to the cause." She gave him a self-deprecating smile. "So I showed my pictures to Freddo Higgins. Once he saw them, he took me straight to the DA."

"Not the police?"

"He said if we took the pictures to the police, word might get back to Nature Fresh and they could destroy the evidence. He said he'd worked with the DA before and knew we could trust him."

"What did the DA say?"

"He said he would get a warrant to search the Nature Fresh property and once they had proof, they could file charges. So I left my pictures with him and thought that was the end of my involvement. Then a few days later, he called and said the judge wasn't willing to issue a search warrant unless he had my corroborating testimony. That didn't seem like a big deal, so I agreed. That night, when I got home from work, two men were waiting for me in the parking lot."

"Did they hurt you?"

She rubbed her wrist. "One of them twisted my arm behind my back and told me I'd better not testify for the DA. He said they knew where to find me and my family." She took a shuddering breath. "I promised that I wouldn't." She looked up at him. "I didn't feel like I had a choice. I still don't think so. The case against Nature Fresh is not more important than my family. So I decided the district attorney would have to prove his case without me. I called him the next day and said I had changed my mind. He didn't take that very well."

"What exactly is 'not well'?"

"He said I had to testify and that if I wouldn't do it voluntarily, they would subpoena me. He asked if I had been threatened and I denied it, but I could tell he didn't believe me. He said he could protect me if I would come in, but I couldn't risk it. So I disappeared."

He shook his head "Why didn't you just call your uncle? He could protect you and your family."

Brooke bit her lip. "I wanted to, but he has a family too. I couldn't put them at risk either. All I could do was hide until the DA closed his case. I guess that makes me a bad citizen and a coward."

"I think it makes you a good daughter and sister and niece," Hunter responded.

Relief cascaded over Brooke. She hadn't realized how important Hunter's opinion was to her.

Finally he said, "That Freddo guy sold you out to Nature Fresh."

"Freddo?" she repeated incredulously. "But he's dedicated his life to protecting helpless animals and the environment. Why would he help a company that is torturing chickens and contaminating drinking water?"

"Well, apparently he's retired. Hack said he left the country with a lot of cash."

Brooke was intensely disappointed. "I guess that explains how the Nature Fresh people knew I was going to testify. But it never occurred to me that I couldn't trust Freddo."

Hunter scowled. "I never liked him."

"You've never met him."

"I don't have to meet him to hate him," Hunter claimed. "His name is Freddo, and he was friends with your stupid ex-boyfriend."

Brooke gave him a weak smile. "Honestly, I never liked him much either."

They cleared away the sandwich things, and Hunter packed them in his backpack. "We always have to be ready to go on a moment's notice," he told her. "Just in case."

She put her backpack beside his, near the dirt bike.

"Right now we need to get some rest. I can go a long time without sleep, but I've reached my limit."

"You haven't had a good night's sleep since you were assigned to protect me. And now you've put your career in danger. I don't know how I can ever thank you."

"You just did." He pointed to a bedroom to the left. "You can sleep there. I'll be out here on the couch. You've got your little throwaway phone, but I don't have to remind you to use it only in an emergency."

She nodded and yawned at the same time. Then she walked into the bedroom and pulled the door mostly closed before stretching out on the bed and closing her eyes.

Brooke allowed herself to doze but resisted the deep sleep her body longed for. After an hour, she stood and tiptoed to the bedroom door. Peeking out she saw Hunter lying on the couch near the windows, sound asleep. His lips were parted, and he was snoring softly. A handgun and his disposable phone were on the coffee table beside him—both within easy reach.

She stood there watching him for a few minutes, memorizing his features. Relaxed by sleep, he looked younger and much less grim. Over the past few days, he had grown very dear to her. She was going to miss him and hated that she couldn't even say good-bye. But she wouldn't let him destroy his career for her.

Walking softly, she went to the door and picked up her backpack, stacked neatly beside Hunter's. As she shrugged it onto her shoulder, she saw raindrops hitting the front windows. Discouraged but determined, she walked through the kitchen to the back of the house. This was unfamiliar territory and since she couldn't turn on any lights, Brooke had to feel her way through a mudroom and into the garage. She closed the garage door and stood still, waiting for her eyes to adjust to the darkness.

Once she could see, she found the door that led outside. And she saw that there were two bicycles hanging on the garage wall. A bicycle would make her trip down the mountain much quicker and easier. Her plan was to get back to civilization and catch a bus or get a taxi. By the time Hunter woke up and realized she was gone, she would be too far away for him to find her.

In the dim light, she chose the bike that looked the lightest and lifted it off the wall rack. Then she pushed the bike to the door. She stopped there and stared at the alarm panel. Her finger was moving toward the disarm button when a hand snaked out and wrapped around her waist.

She screamed in terror.

"It's just me," Hunter said.

She collapsed against him in relief. "You scared me to death!"

"You shouldn't have been trying to run away."

"I didn't want to get you in trouble for helping me," she admitted. "I figured I could handle it from here by myself."

And then for the first time since they'd met, she saw Hunter laugh.

CHAPTER ELEVEN

Brooke scowled at him. "What's so funny?"

"You actually thought you could slip out of here without me knowing? And that you could protect yourself against criminals all alone?"

She tried not to be distracted by his beautiful and rare smile, concentrating instead on her righteous indignation. "I was trying to do you a favor! I didn't want you to get in trouble with Uncle Christopher!"

His smile faded and then, to her dismay, completely disappeared. "I'll be in trouble with your uncle for taking off on my own, but if I let you get away I'd be in much *worse* trouble."

Her shoulders sagged as she watched him return the bicycle to the rack on the garage wall. She couldn't do anything right.

"Don't feel bad." He sensed her thoughts without even turning around. "There aren't many well-trained soldiers who could get by me—even when I'm asleep."

She was not comforted by this knowledge. He walked back into the house, and Brooke trudged behind him.

Hunter went straight to the wall of windows and looked out, searching for uninvited guests. She sat on the couch and looked at the rain. The day was dreary, much the way she felt.

"See anything?" she asked finally.

"All is peaceful and quiet," he replied. "Now why don't we go back to sleep—for more than an hour this time."

***

When Savannah woke up on Saturday morning, Dane was sitting up in bed beside her. She asked, "How long before the detective gets here?"

"About an hour," he replied. "How are you feeling?"

"I'm sick of drinking Spriteorade, but otherwise good."

He smiled. "There are worse things than Spriteorade—like throwing up."

"How about you? Are you getting used to the idea of a baby?"

"The thought of raising my own child terrifies me," he admitted. "There are so many things I would do differently if I could go back and do my own childhood over. I was a willful and stubborn kid."

"You are a willful and stubborn man."

He didn't smile. "It will serve me right if this baby is as bad as I was."

"Our children will get traits from both of us, and I was a good child."

The remark earned her a little grin.

"And you have so many incredible traits, like bravery and integrity and protecting the helpless."

"Disobedience, recklessness, irreverence," he added to her list. "I was raised by good parents, who started me on the path of righteousness, and I purposely veered off. Looking back now, I don't even understand why. I could have been good like Neely—and you. Then I wouldn't have all this guilt and dread."

"You wouldn't have met me, and we wouldn't be about to have Christopher Jr. or Christina."

"You know what I mean."

"I do. We all have regrets. You think I don't wish I could go back and treat my mother differently? I was so resentful of her; I hated her sometimes. Now I understand that everything she did was to protect me. She literally gave her life for me. I could have made things a little happier for her if I'd had a different attitude. And I won't even start talking about Wes."

"I don't really want to talk about Wes either," Dane agreed. "But that wasn't your fault either. He tricked you."

"And he gave us Caroline." Her voice trembled a little. "I can never regret that."

"Your experiences are things that happened *to* you. You might regret some of your reactions, but I'm talking about conscious choices I made that were against what I had been taught. What if that is a character trait? What if our child won't listen and makes bad decisions?"

"Then we'll love them and pray for them and wait for them to come to their senses—just like your parents did."

Dane drew her into his arms. "Parenthood terrifies me more than anything I have ever done."

She laughed. "And that is saying something."

When they made it downstairs, they found Neely making breakfast as usual.

"Good morning," she greeted.

"Good morning," Dane said as he passed through toward Raleigh's office.

Savannah sat at the island in the beautiful kitchen and sipped Spriteorade while trying not to watch Neely scramble eggs. On the table were two plates—one piled with biscuits and the other with at least two pounds of bacon. Savannah looked away from the mound of glistening meat.

Neely finished with the eggs and called out, "Breakfast is ready."

Once they were all seated around the table, Neely asked, "So have we heard anything from Brooke or Owl?"

Hack said, "Not directly, but they were caught on security cameras buying camping gear at a Wal-Mart near Gatlinburg."

Savannah nibbled on a biscuit. "So that means they are camping in the woods?"

Hack shook his head as he spooned a huge serving of eggs onto his plate. "It means that's what Owl wanted anyone checking the security tapes to think."

"He probably took her to a big city where they can hide in a hotel room until Monday," Steamer said.

"That's the obvious thing to do," Dane agreed. "But since he knows how we think, he might do the opposite and hole up in a small rental cabin."

Hack frowned. "And there are so many rental cabins, it would be nearly impossible for us to search them all."

"But if we can't find them, that means the Nature Fresh guys can't either," Dane said.

"I've got everybody I can spare working on it," Hack said. "We've narrowed the list to cabins and vacation homes that are not currently rented out, which is still thousands. Now we're watching for anything unusual in places that are supposed to be unoccupied—a spike in utility use or a report from a security alarm. And I've got a couple of planes up, looking for heat signatures. For now that's all we can do."

"So we aren't worried about them?" Savannah clarified.

"I wouldn't go that far," Dane replied. "But we'll concentrate on Raleigh and getting him out of trouble. Then Brooke might agree to come home, and protecting her will be simpler."

"Is there any way we can put some pressure on Nature Fresh?" Savannah asked. "Like tell them we have Brooke's pictures and will take them to the press?"

"Not without endangering Raleigh," Dane replied.

Savannah was disappointed. They really were stuck between a rock and a hard place.

"When is the detective coming?" Neely asked.

Dane checked his watch. "Thirty minutes. Everybody eat fast and meet in the office so we'll be ready and waiting for him."

They finished the meal, and then Savannah insisted that Neely allow her to clean up so Neely could prepare for the arrival of the police. Hack and Steamer pitched in, and they had the kitchen returned to order in no time.

And exactly at the appointed time, the doorbell rang.

"It's the policeman from the other day," Hack confirmed with his phone to his ear.

Dane and Neely walked to the front door. Savannah stood at the office door so she could see without being in the way.

Neely opened the door. Detective Napier was standing between the potted ferns on the front porch.

"Good morning, Mrs. Clayton," Detective Napier said.

She nodded. "Good morning. Please come in."

Dane was waiting in the entryway. "I'm Neely's brother, Major Dane."

The detective nodded. "We sort of met the other day."

Dane waved for him to come into the office. "This way, please."

Once everyone was seated, Detective Napier said, "I have to tell you, ever since your late-night phone call, I've been full of suspense."

Dane placed his elbows on Raleigh's desk and said, "I'm sorry we haven't been very cooperative up to this point, but we weren't sure what we were dealing with. Now we think we know, and we'd like to explain."

The detective nodded.

"We do not know where Brooke is, but one of my men is with her."

Detective Napier frowned. "If you have a man with her, how can you not know where they are?"

"She convinced him to go AWOL."

"And why won't she come in and answer the questions the DA has for her?"

"I haven't been able to ask her that question," Dane said. "But I believe the reason she won't talk to the DA is because she's been threatened."

Detective Napier sat a little straighter. "By who?"

Dane briefly explained about Brooke's unauthorized visit to the back of the Nature Fresh chicken plant, the pictures she took, and the testimony the DA wanted her to give at the hearing on Monday. "Nature Fresh doesn't want Brooke to be at that hearing, and as incentive, I think they are holding her father hostage."

Now he had the detective's full attention. "What makes you think that?"

Dane explained about Raleigh's trouble at work and how it coincided with Brooke's disappearance. "We don't know the situation inside Business Services—whether they are actually holding Raleigh and his partner at gunpoint or if the two men are just not allowed to leave. If we try to go in, we might make things worse. But if you go in, with a warrant for Raleigh's arrest . . ."

"They'd have to respect my badge," the detective agreed.

"It could still be dangerous," Dane warned.

"I can handle that," Detective Napier assured him.

"And if Raleigh is at the police station, he'd be safe," Dane concluded.

"I can't pretend to arrest someone."

"I wouldn't ask you to do that." Dane pushed a stack of papers across the desk. "We've built a case against Raleigh for you. It should be enough to bring him in for questioning at least."

The detective leafed through the papers and finally looked up. "Are we sure he didn't steal the money?"

"Not sure," Dane admitted.

"Christopher!" Neely objected.

"We trust him, but we don't have any proof that clears him," Dane elaborated. "We have a couple of good suspects. We'll be working on that so we can swap out Raleigh for the real criminal after you get him away from Business Services."

"This is very comprehensive." Detective Napier seemed impressed. "Money has been stolen, and Mr. Clayton had a motive and opportunity. That sounds like a case to me. I'll talk to a judge and see if it's enough for a warrant."

"We'll want media coverage too," Hack suggested. "People are less likely to pull out guns if they are on camera."

"I'll arrange that." The detective frowned. "I'm eligible for retirement in a few months, and this better not cost me my pension."

***

Brooke was having a beautiful dream. She was wearing the pink calico dress from the resort, and she was at a park. In a swing, there was a little girl with long brown hair, and Brooke was pushing her—higher and higher. The little girl's laughter was the most beautiful sound she'd ever heard. Then suddenly the swing was empty. The little girl was gone. "No!" Brooke screamed. "Come back, please!"

She felt a hand on her shoulder, and her eyes flew open. Hunter was standing over her with a concerned look on his face.

"You were having a nightmare."

She swallowed a sob and tried to smile. "I'm fine. Don't worry."

He still looked concerned as she climbed off the bed. "Do you want to tell me about your nightmare?"

She sighed. "It's nothing, really."

"It didn't sound like nothing."

"It's just a dream I have sometimes. I'm in a park with a little girl, and I lose her. It's a terrible feeling when I know she's gone and it's my fault that I'll never see her again." She gave him an overly bright smile. "Maybe it means that I'm going to be a terrible, irresponsible mother."

"I'm sure it doesn't mean that."

She looked out the window. It was still dreary but no longer raining. "What time is it?"

He checked his watch. "One o'clock," he answered.

"You didn't sleep long enough."

He shrugged. "I'll be okay. Are you hungry?"

"I'm starving."

Still looking uncertain, he led the way into the kitchen. "I heated up some soup for lunch. We can't risk that often, since Hack can check the power company computers and look for vacant houses with sudden increases in electricity use."

Brooke was sobered by this thought. "I didn't know that was possible. How can we possibly succeed against a team as good as my uncle's?"

"Because I'm one of them."

Their eyes met briefly. "I can never forget that."

They ate their soup in silence, and once the dishes were washed and back in the cupboard, they sat on the couch and looked out the front windows.

She stared out at the mountains and felt tears well up in her eyes. Still shaken by her dream, she wanted to turn into Hunter's arms and draw comfort from him. Over the past few days she had gotten used to constant, if pretend, contact with him. Putting her arm through his while they walked, dancing at the Plantation House, or sitting together on the piano bench. Now she had no excuse to touch him, and she missed it.

In an effort to regain some of the closeness they'd had at the resort, she said, "I feel so small without my big dresses. It's funny how fast you can get used to something."

"I don't miss my Confederate uniform," he muttered.

"Come on," she cajoled. "Admit you enjoyed being at the resort."

"It wasn't terrible," he admitted. "Except for the uniform."

"And dumb old Wilma," Brooke added. "I can't believe she was going to turn us over to those Nature Fresh guys."

"I can't believe I was worried about you volunteering to play the piano and then it was my idea to add an asthma condition that gave us away."

"It was a good idea; Wilma is just a rat."

They were quiet for a few minutes, and then Brooke asked, "Are we leaving tonight?"

"I think we'd be safe here for one more day," he answered. "But I'm not sure that's the thing to do—hide out here, I mean, waiting for time to expire on the hearing. Do you really want to live under this cloud for the rest of your life?"

She shook her head. "I don't have a choice."

"What if you did have a choice? What if we could get the proof the DA needs to prosecute Nature Fresh without endangering your family?"

"How could we do that?" she asked, trying not to be overly optimistic.

"The DA needs a witness, someone who has seen the hidden part of the chicken plant and the pipeline going into the creek, someone who can testify at the hearing—but it doesn't have to be you." He paused for a second, and their eyes held. "It could be me."

"You?" she whispered.

"It would mean hiking back up to the Nature Fresh plant," he continued. "Once I have some pictures of my own, I'll call the police to come get me and call your uncle to come get you—probably not in that order."

"But then you'll be in danger from the Nature Fresh people."

"I've been in danger hundreds of times. I can take care of myself, with your uncle's help. And I don't have a family they can use against me."

She shook her head firmly. "I can't let you do it."

"You aren't letting me do anything. I've made my own decision based on what I think is best. And a side bonus to this plan is that no one would ever think to look for us at the Nature Fresh plant."

She studied him closely. "Why would you be willing to take a risk like this for me?"

"I want you to have a happy life—to get married and have a little girl that never gets lost. I want you to play the piano and donate to chicken causes. And I don't want you to be looking over your shoulder, waiting for Nature Fresh to take their revenge."

She stared at him speechlessly for a few seconds. "I don't deserve a friend like you."

He ignored this. "And I want Nature Fresh to pay the price for breaking the law and hurting the environment—and for hiring criminals to intimidate witnesses. I want your uncle to be proud of the way I handled the whole thing. I want your family to be safe, and I want you to feel like a good citizen again."

The good citizen part was silly, compared with the gravity of the other considerations. But it meant a lot to her, and he knew it.

Her lips trembled a little. "Thank you."

"So you're in?"

She turned and looked out the window. It was wrong to involve him more than he already was, wrong to allow him to risk so much. But she needed help, and he was the only person who could provide it. So she nodded. "I am."

Hunter reached for his backpack. "Let me get my maps, and we'll make a plan."

They sat at the table in the cabin's beautiful kitchen and studied the maps. "I need you to show me where the Nature Fresh plant is, and we'll figure out a way to get in."

She pointed to a spot on the map. "Here is Willow Creek. The Nature Fresh plant is about six miles off County Road 29. We can park somewhere along here and hike in, following the creek up just like I did."

He nodded. "That should work."

She was concerned about one thing. "We've had a lot of rain since I was there, so the water level in the creek may be up enough to cover the pipeline."

He nodded. "I'll swim up the creek and take the pictures with a waterproof camera."

"You've thought of everything."

"No, things will come up that I haven't planned for, but when they do, we'll think of a way around them. That's what the army, and your uncle, trained me to do."

She shook her head. "It's more than just training. You are smart and brave."

"We'll wait until this plan works out successfully before we decide how smart I am."

He didn't actually smile, but she could tell he was pleased.

"We can't drive into Nashville on that dirt bike," he said. "We'd be too exposed, and it's too slow."

Brooke was a little sad. She enjoyed riding the bike with Hunter, having an excuse to hold him close.

"I'll go get a vehicle, and you'll stay here so if I get caught you won't."

"I'm afraid," she told him. "For you and me."

"This is the easy part," he told her. "Save your worrying for later."

"When are you going to get another vehicle?"

"In a few hours."

"And then we'll leave?"

He nodded. "We need darkness to cover our departure here and my swim up the creek. If we leave just as the sun sets, we should be able to reach the woods near the chicken plant by midnight. We'll set up a camp for you, and then I'll go up the creek and take my pictures. The moon should give me enough light." He folded up his map. "Now try to get some sleep. It's going to be a long night."

***

Dane's team spent the morning coordinating with Detective Napier, working out the details of Raleigh's arrest. Savannah made a point to stay near Neely to provide comfort and encouragement as needed.

After the detective left to go get a warrant for Raleigh, Dane pulled a chair over and sat beside his sister.

"We should hear something from Detective Napier soon," he told her. "Once Raleigh is in custody, Steamer will go to the police station and provide legal protection."

"Can I go with him?"

"They might not let you see him," Dane warned.

"But at least he'll know I'm there."

Dane nodded. "You can go with Steamer."

She smiled a little tremulously.

"If you get a chance to talk to Raleigh, assure him that with the help of the Nashville PD, we'll find out who stole the money from his company. But both of you need to accept the fact that his career may be over. The company may lose all its clients, and even the suspicion of theft will make it difficult for Raleigh to get another job in the industry."

"So we should sell the house?"

"Don't worry about that right now," Dane said. "You can discuss important decisions about your future after we get Raleigh out of jail. But I don't want him to feel like his life will be over if his company goes under. He's young. He can go back to school and start another career. But in the short term, things are probably going to have to change."

"Dinner in a Cup is doing okay," she said. "It could do better if I put a little more time into it. I might even see about branching out into other airports."

"Neely's going to be a franchise!" Steamer encouraged.

She sighed. "Maybe."

After lunch they gathered around Raleigh's desk, and Steamer set up his iPad so everyone could see. Just as he turned it on, Raleigh's face filled the screen.

"Oh!" Neely cried.

Savannah put an arm around her.

"I'm okay," Neely said. "It's just so good to see him again."

The camera zoomed out, and they could see Detective Napier, along with several uniformed police personnel, surrounding Raleigh as they escorted him out of Business Services. A reporter's voice explained that he had been arrested for embezzlement. Then the picture on the small screen changed to a shot of Neely's house.

"They're right outside?" Neely asked.

Dane nodded. "Unfortunately, the press goes with this territory. But Hack's guys will keep them back."

"It's surreal," Neely whispered. "My husband arrested and our house on the local news as the home of a criminal."

"Keep your eye on the prize, baby!" Steamer reminded her. "This was all to get your husband to a safe place. Now we can work on clearing his name."

Neely nodded. "Let's work really hard on that."

The telephone started ringing, and Savannah offered to answer it.

Neely sighed. "That will be my neighbors."

Dane glared at the phone. "Just let the answering machine pick it up."

Steamer stood and waved at Neely. "Come on, let's get to the police station."

After they were gone, Dane turned to Hack. "Okay, now we have got to find a better suspect than Raleigh. The last thing I want is to be responsible for putting my brother-in-law in prison."

Dane's phone rang, and Savannah sat nervously while he had a short conversation. When it was over, he put his phone in his pocket. "That was Detective Napier reporting on the arrest."

Savannah nodded. "What did he say?"

"When they went into Business Services, there was no evidence that anyone was being held there against their will. They met with no resistance, didn't see anyone with a gun; in fact, there wasn't even a security guard. He said Raleigh looked astonished when he presented the arrest warrant."

"So what does that mean?" Savannah asked.

He closed his eyes. "That I may have been wrong. The money missing at Business Services and the independent audit might not have had anything to do with Brooke. Which means I just got Raleigh arrested for nothing."

***

As the sun started to set, Hunter said, "I'm going to go down the mountain now and get another vehicle. Then I'll come back and pick you up."

"I'd rather stay with you," she said.

He nodded. "But it will be safer if you stay here. And I'll be able to operate faster on my own."

"Okay," she agreed reluctantly. "But hurry. I'll be a nervous wreck until you come back."

She stood at the door while he rolled the dirt bike out. Then she watched from the windows as he made his descent. When he finally moved out of her view, she sat on the couch, waiting for him to return.

It seemed like Hunter was gone forever. Brooke paced and fretted and checked the clock continually. Finally she saw headlights coming up the winding driveway toward the cabin. She had a few tense moments, since she couldn't be sure it was Hunter. But then he parked the car and climbed out. She couldn't remember ever being so happy to see anyone.

She met him by the front door and resisted the urge to throw herself into his arms. Just barely. "I was afraid you had deserted me!"

He frowned. "I would never do that."

"I know. I was kidding."

He gave her his exasperated look. "Get your backpack and stand by the door. I'm going to walk through the house and make sure we left everything just like we found it." He returned in a couple of minutes, apparently satisfied. He reset the alarm, and they walked outside, closing the door firmly behind them.

As they walked down the porch steps, Brooke examined their new form of transportation. The car was small and sleek and looked brand new. It was the polar opposite of the one they had purchased from the Cauthens. "Wow," she said, running her hand along the hood. "I was expecting something much . . . uglier."

"I'm trying to be unpredictable," he reminded her. "I figure Hack will be expecting me to buy something cheap and old. Besides, I'd rather be in a fast, dependable vehicle in case we have to outrun someone."

The thought was sobering.

He opened the door, and she slid onto the leather passenger seat. "I could get used to this."

"Don't," he said. "I have thirty days to change my mind and return it to the dealer, so as soon as this is settled, it's going back."

"It's a shame," she said.

He went around the car and climbed in behind the wheel. He reached across and handed her a spare key. "Keep this in your backpack, just in case something happens to me."

She did as he asked, although she couldn't bear to think of the possibilities that might make the key necessary. Then they started down the mountain.

"What kind of car do you drive in real life?"

"An old Ford pickup truck with over two hundred thousand miles on it," he replied. "I need my vehicle to be hardworking but not fancy."

She smiled. "Kind of like you."

He raised an eyebrow. "Does your car match you?"

"I drive a gray Honda Civic," she said. "And it's just like me—cute but boring."

He nodded without taking his eyes off the road.

"You're supposed to disagree with a woman when she says something like that." She sighed. "I haven't been a very good love teacher."

"It will probably be a while before I have to act like I'm in love again."

The thought of his acting, let alone actually being, in love with someone else was depressing. So she turned to look out the window as they made their way down the mountain. After a while she turned back to him and said, "What do you do when you're not working?"

"I'm almost always working."

"But when you're not. What do you do with your leisure time?"

"I work out."

She'd seen his chest, so she believed that, but she wasn't satisfied. "Working out is not relaxing. What else?"

"I like to play basketball."

"That's still exercise. Don't you like to watch television or play video games or something fun?"

He shook his head. "I'm even more boring than you."

She cut her eyes over at him. "And that's saying something."

When they reached the outskirts of Gatlinburg, he parked the car and went into a fast food restaurant to get them some dinner. When he got back to the car, he requested that she climb into the backseat.

"The most dangerous part for us is going to be the next hour or so. We'll be less likely to attract attention if it looks like I'm alone."

She took the sack with her sandwich and got into the backseat. Then she slumped down against the side so her head wasn't visible. "How's this?"

"Good." He started the car and ate while he drove.

"So you think we can make it out of Gatlinburg without being caught?" she asked nervously.

"Yes," he confirmed. "There's a lot of traffic to help hide us, and the fact that we're heading back toward Nashville works in our favor since no one will be expecting that."

Brooke watched out the window, tense with anxiety, until they were well out of the Gatlinburg area. Finally she said, "So, we made it?"

He nodded. "It looks that way, but I won't relax completely until we're in the woods near the chicken plant."

"Can I get back in front?"

"Yes, it should be okay now."

She squeezed between the front seats, careful not to kick Hunter and cause a wreck. Then she settled in the passenger seat. She tried to stay awake, not that she was entertaining the ever-serious Hunter, but the gentle rocking of the car and the soft humming of the engine gradually lulled her to sleep. She woke up when they were turning off the interstate.

"Not far now," he said.

She sat up straight and shivered. Turning the air conditioner vents away from her, she looked out the window, watching as the landscape became increasingly rural until it was finally nothing but trees.

Hunter found the turnoff to the chicken plant, and they drove up that road for a few miles. Then he pulled into the woods and parked the car under some trees, where it wouldn't be visible from the road.

"It's a long walk from here," Brooke warned him. "Don't you want to drive up a little closer to the fence line?"

He shook his head. "They might have guards or surveillance cameras to prevent anyone from discovering what you did. So we need to park a safe distance away."

They got out of the car, closed the doors softly, and hiked toward the creek, careful to stay off anything that even resembled a path. When they were close enough to the creek that they could hear it, but still far enough away that they couldn't actually see it, Hunter stopped and searched for a spot to set up the tent for Brooke. He finally settled on a place next to a huge rock and surrounded by trees.

"This is as invisible as I can make you," he said. He set up the camouflage dome tent under some low-hanging branches. When he finished, they sat on a fallen log and he looked up at the sky. "Some clouds are supposed to be rolling in soon, which I need to cover my approach to the chicken plant. So I'll wait here for a little longer."

She shivered again, terrified for him and honestly afraid to stay there alone while he swam up the creek.

He pulled two granola bars from his pocket and offered her one. They ate in companionable silence for a few minutes. Then she whispered, "I wonder who has been playing the piano for dinner since we've been gone."

"Probably that robotic guy," Hunter said. "He didn't have any soul, but at least he wasn't hitting wrong notes constantly."

For some reason Brooke found this comment hilarious and giggled. Once she had the laughter under control she said, "We missed the big battle—Shiloh. Doreen said it's the one where so many people die."

He nodded. "It was a turning point in the war."

She shivered again. "I'm glad you weren't there. I don't think I could stand it if you died—even just for a little while."

He didn't respond.

They were quiet for a while, and then she asked, "After this is over and I'm safe and all that . . . can we still be friends?"

He turned to face her, his expression very solemn.

She was so afraid he was going to say no and put an end to any hope she might have of a future relationship with him, so she babbled on before he got a chance. "I know you're busy flying VIPs around. I'm not asking you to marry me or anything. I just thought that when you had a weekend off instead of working out and playing basketball you could come to Nashville and we could go out to dinner."

He shook his head, and she thought she had his answer. Her heart hurt so badly she reached up and rubbed it, trying to ease the pain.

But then he said, "We can be friends—until you meet a man who can see himself married."

It wasn't as much as she'd hoped for, but it was much more than she expected. "What about you? Don't you think you'll get married—ever?"

"No, I guess I'll spend my life flying VIPs around, saving people occasionally with your uncle, and playing basketball when I have time off."

She cut her eyes over at him. "Are you developing a sense of humor?"

"I doubt it," he replied

She leaned toward him a little so their arms were touching. She felt him stiffen and then relax.

When he decided that he had enough cloud cover for his swim up the creek, he stood and pulled off his shirt. The dim light reflected off his smooth, well-muscled skin, and Brooke's breath caught in her throat.

He bent down to remove his shoes. He put his phone and his watch in his backpack. Then he handed her his gun.

"I hope you won't need that."

"Me too," she assured him fervently. She unzipped her backpack and slipped the gun inside. "You have the disposable camera?"

He patted his back pocket. "I have two, just in case one malfunctions."

They stood there, facing each other in the darkness. Finally she said, "Will you kiss me, just one time?"

"I've kissed you several times," he pointed out. His face was cast in shadows, so she couldn't see his expression.

"I know, but I want *you* to kiss *me*, Hunter and Brooke, not just two people acting like a loving couple."

"Don't fall in love with me, Brooke." His tone was pleading.

She blinked back tears, grateful for the darkness that hid them. "I'm afraid it's too late."

"I'm not husband material," he insisted earnestly. "I can't be part of your dream."

"All I asked for was a kiss."

He stood there for so long she was afraid he would refuse her. Then finally his face descended toward hers.

She waited with sweet anticipation until their lips touched. She took a step closer and put her hands behind his neck. After the briefest hesitation, his arms encircled her. She had missed being close to him, the sound of his heartbeat, his soapy, toothpaste smell.

He pulled back for a second, and they looked into each other's eyes.

"Do you want to kiss me again?" she whispered.

He pressed his mouth against her ear. "There's no question about that."

CHAPTER TWELVE

THINGS WERE TENSE AT NEELY'S house while Dane, Hack, and Savannah waited for word from the police station, where Raleigh was being held in police custody.

"So what are we expecting to happen next?" Savannah asked.

Dane answered, "The best possible scenario is that they will review the warrant, determine there isn't enough evidence to hold Raleigh and send him home."

"That's in the same category with Superman busting through a window and rescuing him," Hack said.

"Okay," Savannah pressed on. "What's the next best *reasonable* possibility?"

"The judge will set bail, and Raleigh will come home with Steamer and Neely," Dane replied.

"But if they don't let him out on bail . . ." Savannah allowed her voice to trail off.

"Then we have to prove that someone besides Raleigh stole the money," Dane said.

As the grandfather clock in the entryway struck midnight, they heard a car pull into the garage.

"It's Steamer and Neely," Hack reported. "Raleigh is not with them."

Savannah was disappointed and knew that Neely must be much more so. Savannah waited by the garage door until her sister-in-law came in.

Steamer walked through the door first. He announced, "They wouldn't release Raleigh on bail with all that money unaccounted for. But he was okay staying there after we explained everything."

Neely smiled. "The crazy thing is that he never even realized that he was a hostage."

"So he's in good spirits?" Savannah asked.

"He's tired and worried about Brooke and the company, of course, but he insists that he wasn't staying at work against his will. He says he wanted to stay so he could help them find out what happened to all that money."

Dane nodded. "I might have been wrong about the whole subtle kidnapping scheme."

Neely gave her brother a stern look. "So Raleigh wasn't in danger at Business Services?"

"We can't know for sure." Savannah looked between the siblings. "He's safe at the police station, and now we're going to figure out who did take the money, so it's really a moot point."

Dane asked, "Did Raleigh have any ideas about who took the money?"

Neely shook her head. "I listed all our suspects, but he said he doesn't think any of them could be the thief."

"Did you tell him that Hopewell is in terrible financial shape?" Savannah asked. "Someone in those circumstances could be tempted to steal."

"Raleigh said he and Finn had a deal in the works," Neely told them. "Raleigh was going to buy him out, so there would be no reason for Finn to steal, destroying the company in the process."

"So what about the three women?" Hack asked. "They all had motives and at least some opportunity."

"Raleigh doesn't think any of them had access to all the information they would need to steal money from the investment account."

"Let's set aside opportunity for now and think about who had the best motive," Dane suggested.

"The receptionist has the *weakest* motive." Hack gave his opinion. "She was fired, maybe wrongfully, and she needs money. But she'll get money if she sues, and she doesn't seem bright enough to figure out this whole scheme."

"The people from Nature Fresh could have figured out the scheme," Dane proposed, "then recruited someone with an axe to grind and an opportunity."

Savannah shook her head. "This scheme seems tailor-made for Business Services—taking money from the special holding account that only had money in it once a month. So I believe an insider came up with this particular scheme."

"Then Selma is the best suspect." Dane pulled out his phone. "I'll call Detective Napier and suggest that he bring her in for questioning."

While Dane was on the phone, Steamer said, "I know Dane doesn't want you to make a decision about selling your house yet, but once all this is settled, if you decide you want to, I think I might have a buyer for you."

Neely looked as surprised as Savannah felt. "Already?"

"I know a guy from Vegas who is moving to Nashville to pursue a career in country music. He needs a place to live, and when I told him about your house, he asked me to send him some pictures. So I did, and he loves your place."

Neely looked a little unnerved. "That's so fast."

"Don't let him rush you," Hack said with a scowl at Steamer. "You can take all the time you need."

"I'm not rushing," Steamer defended himself. "I just wanted Neely to know."

Neely said, "Tell me about this buyer."

"Now, I should warn you," Steamer prefaced, "your neighbors might feel nervous about him at first. He's a little flamboyant."

"There was a time when I would have felt bad about selling to someone that my neighbors won't approve of, but my feelings have changed."

Steamer grinned. "Good."

Hack seemed suspicious. "Who is this flamboyant buyer from Vegas who wants a house in Nashville?"

"His real name is Louis Fevere, but he's famous as Luscious Louie LeFevere—the professional wrestler."

Hack's eyes widened. "That sissy French guy who wears tacky sequined outfits and has a pet lion?"

"That's him," Steamer confirmed. "Although, his outfits—while flashy—are professionally made by a very expensive tailor, so I wouldn't call them *tacky*."

"Well, I would!" Hack countered. "And anybody that goes around with a lion for a pet has got to be crazy."

"He keeps the lion on a leash."

"Like a leash is going to protect anyone against a lion!" Hack exclaimed. "And I hope he's a better singer than he is a wrestler, or he won't be in Nashville long enough to need a house. I've seen some of his matches, and he always loses."

"He makes money whether he wins or not," Steamer replied. "And Louie gets a lot of media attention, which he's counting on to help launch his new career." Steamer glanced at Neely. "He *encourages* the paparazzi to follow him everywhere."

Neely she put a hand to her mouth. "You may have found a buyer that would actually make my neighbors miss me!"

Steamer gave her a wink. "I call that a perfect deal."

Hack muttered something unintelligible under his breath.

"Okay," Dane said. "Let's all get some sleep and start fresh in the morning."

Steamer looked around the room. "Just think, in a few weeks, a lion might live here."

"Don't tell Caroline," Savannah told him. "If she finds out lions can be pets, she'll want one of them along with her five kittens."

***

When it was time for Hunter to go, Brooke walked with him as far as the edge of the trees. Then she watched him wade out into the creek. Once he was in the middle, where the water was the deepest, he went under the water and started swimming north, coming up every few seconds for air. She waited until he was out of her sight. She felt the way she had when she'd sent him off into battle at the resort, only this time the danger was real.

Even though it was a pleasant night, she felt cold and couldn't stop shivering. Her back was aching, which she attributed to days of traveling—and part of that time on a dirt bike. She went to her little dome tent and climbed inside. Curling onto her side, she drew her knees up close, hoping that would ease the pain.

She dozed and woke up with a throbbing pain in her side. Disoriented and disproportionately afraid, she called out for help. "Hunter!" But there was no answer. Encompassed by suffering, she wept silently.

It seemed like days of anguish passed before Hunter unzipped the tent. But behind him she could see the darkened sky, so it was still night—not much time had passed.

"Did you get the pictures?" she asked urgently.

He nodded then leaned closer as he realized that something was wrong. "Brooke?"

"I'm sick," she whispered. "There's a pain in my side or my back—I'm not sure which. No matter how I move or what I do, I can't ease the pain! I'm sorry," she whimpered as the throbbing in her side intensified. "Oh, it hurts so bad."

He picked up his shirt and pulled it over his head. Then he scooped up both backpacks with one hand. "I'm going to lift you up now," he told her. "Try to help me."

"I don't know if I can." She didn't want to stay in the tent, enveloped with misery, but she couldn't imagine trying to stand and walk.

"Brooke," he said sternly. "I've got to get you to a hospital."

Her mind cleared briefly. "You have to get those pictures to the DA! Having them in your possession is dangerous."

"Don't worry about that right now," he urged. "Just hold on to me and let me lift you."

With very little help from her, he managed to get her out of the tent. Then cradling her in his arms, he started walking. The unavoidable jostling was excruciating for Brooke, and she sobbed against his chest. The jarring continued until they reached the car. He braced her against the vehicle and pulled the key from his backpack. Then he opened the door and put her gently onto the passenger seat.

She clutched her side, unable to stop the tears.

He hurried around the car and jumped in. She was vaguely aware as he turned the key and threw the vehicle into gear. They shot out onto the dirt road that led to the highway. The tires skidded in the loose dirt, searching for traction. The trees that grew close to the roadside scraped the sides, and before she passed out, Brooke thought to herself that he was going to have a hard time returning the car.

Brooke woke up as Hunter carried her into the hospital emergency room. She still felt shaky and confused, but the terrible pain was gone. She heard Hunter explaining her symptoms, and very shortly after that she was taken to a room.

A nurse helped Brooke change into a hospital gown while Hunter waited in the hallway. Then he stood stoically by her side as they drew blood, started an IV, and took some x-rays. Finally a doctor came in and told them that she had passed a kidney stone.

"The worst is over," he said. "You should be feeling much better soon."

Brooke nodded. "Thank you."

The doctor turned to Hunter. "I'd like to keep her for a few hours. We're giving her IV antibiotics to prevent infection, and she's going to be a little woozy because of the pain medication."

Brooke heard Hunter agreeing to this plan. His voice had an echoing quality, like he was far away. Her eyes were so heavy she had to close them. She reached for his hand and felt his fingers close around hers as she fell into a deep and glorious sleep.

She woke up an indeterminate amount of time later as she was being transferred onto a bed in a hospital room. The sheets were crisp and cool, and she nestled between them. Hunter was standing beside her. She whispered, "Don't leave me."

"I won't," he promised. "Just go to sleep."

The next time she woke up, her head felt like it was full of cotton. Hunter was sitting beside her hospital bed, looking worried and tired. She smiled to reassure him as her eyelids closed again.

"Hunter?" she managed with a dry mouth and chapped lips.

He took her hand. "I'm here."

Tears seeped out from the corners of her eyes. "You remember my dream about the little girl?"

"I remember."

"I know why I have that dream over and over and over. It's because I really did have a little girl, and I really did lose her."

"At the park?" he asked, and she could hear the confusion in his voice.

"No," she whispered. "I gave her away. I can't even take care of myself—how could I take care of a baby? Rex didn't want her or me. So I let a family adopt her."

He was holding her hand so tightly that it hurt, and she was thankful for the pain.

"They let me choose the family," she said. "I picked a mother who plays the piano."

He reached through the IV tubes and drew her against his chest. And then he held her while she wept.

***

When Savannah left her bedroom Sunday morning, she found Neely in the upstairs hallway with some packing boxes.

"Well, good morning," Savannah said.

Neely smiled. "Good morning."

"Were there any changes overnight with Raleigh or any news from Brooke?"

Neely shook her head. "I'm trying to consider no news, good news."

Savannah pointed at the boxes. "What are those for?"

"Steamer said I should start packing up personal items in case we decide to sell the house, and I'm trying to decide where to start."

"Let me get some fresh Spriteorade and check in with Dane, and then I'll be back to help," Savannah promised.

When she returned, Neely was standing in Adam's bedroom. Savannah walked in and looked at the blue walls and coordinating plaid curtains. The shelves were lined with trophies he'd earned in various sports throughout his youth and pictures of his smiling face as he grew older.

"I can't start here," Neely whispered.

The next room they entered had bright purple walls.

"Let me guess," Savannah said. "This is Brooke's room?"

Neely nodded. "She chose this color at the beginning of her rebellious stage in an effort to annoy me. And it worked—I hated the purple. But now, in retrospect it looks cheerful and surprisingly innocent. I wish a young teenage Brooke was still sitting on the bed right now, complaining and prepared to argue." She looked up at Savannah. "I can't start here either."

Once they were back in the hall, Neely said, "I don't know where I *can* start."

"Why don't we try a room without much sentimental value . . . like the laundry room?" Savannah teased.

Neely gave her a little smile. "I could start with the guest rooms since I don't keep a lot of personal items there, but they're all occupied."

Savannah took the cardboard box from Neely's hands. "I think we should just postpone this project until things are settled with Raleigh and Brooke. You're not even sure you're moving."

Neely nodded in resignation. "Waiting probably is the best option."

As they walked downstairs, Steamer called to them from the family room. "Dane says to come quick. Detective Napier is here."

Savannah and Neely hurried down the rest of the stairs and were with Hack and Steamer in the office when Dane walked in with Detective Napier.

The detective looked even worse than usual—like he'd slept in his clothes and forgotten to run a comb through his hair. In one hand he had a Styrofoam cup of coffee that he sipped occasionally.

"Good morning, everyone," he greeted as he sat heavily in a chair.

Neely asked anxiously, "Do you have good news for us?"

"Well, I have news," the detective responded. "At your suggestion," he pointed his coffee cup toward Dane, "I decided to question Selma Estes in hopes that she might be a better suspect than Mr. Clayton. I wasn't able to reach her by phone, so I went to her apartment early this morning. I found her body. She was shot with her own gun sometime last night."

Everyone expressed varying levels of shock over this news.

"Fingerprints on the gun?" Dane asked.

"None," the detective answered. "Not even hers."

Hack said, "So it was wiped clean."

"It's awful to think that she was here just yesterday and now she's dead." Savannah felt queasy and pressed her Spriteorade bottle to her lips.

Dane nodded. "It's possible that she's dead today *because* she came here yesterday."

Hack frowned. "So who killed her?"

"I don't know. We've started a full investigation," Detective Napier assured him. "Unfortunately, while searching her apartment, we found evidence that implicates Raleigh Clayton in the investment-fund theft."

"That's impossible!" Neely cried. "Raleigh is innocent."

"I'm sorry, Mrs. Clayton," the detective said. "And I hope you're right. But there was a transaction receipt from a joint offshore account in both their names—and a lot of cash. I didn't count it, but it's probably the missing investment-fund money. So all indications are that your husband and Miss Estes were partners in crime."

"It's obviously an attempt to frame him," Dane said.

"It's a very good attempt," Detective Napier said between slurps of coffee.

"Someone killed her and planted the evidence against Raleigh," Dane insisted.

Detective Napier smiled grimly. "I think you're right, but I'm not in a good position to try to prove that since I'm the one who presented the case against Mr. Clayton just yesterday and convinced the judge to issue a warrant for his arrest."

"So we arranged for Raleigh to get arrested to protect him, and now we can't get him released?" Neely's tone was strident.

"There's new evidence against him, and he's implicated in the murder," Steamer pointed out. "If they wouldn't set bail yesterday, there's no way it's happening today."

Savannah sent Steamer a reproving look. Then she said, "But Raleigh was in police custody when Selma Estes was killed."

"He could have arranged for someone else to kill her," the detective said.

"He hired someone to kill her but didn't think to have them pick up all that incriminating evidence while they were there?" Hack bellowed.

The detective shrugged. "That's an argument that can be made during a trial, but it isn't going to help get the charges against him dropped now. He's being held on suspicion of a felony, and we have more evidence to prove that now than we did yesterday. The murder is a separate issue."

And if they could prove Raleigh and Selma were crime partners, that made him the logical suspect for the murder as well, Savannah thought. But she kept it to herself.

"Our investigation will prove what really happened," Detective Napier said. "But right now, Mr. Clayton needs a lawyer." The detective glanced at Steamer. "One who is licensed to practice in Tennessee and who has a lot of experience in criminal cases."

Dane sighed. "Hack, can you round someone up and get them to go to the police department now?"

Hack nodded forlornly.

"So Raleigh will be in jail for . . . a while?" Neely asked.

Dane turned to his sister. "I'm sorry. We made our case against him a little too good."

"I know you can figure out a way to get Raleigh out of jail." Neely blinked back tears.

"We need a better suspect than Raleigh," Hack said. "That's what will get him out."

Detective Napier told them, "The department isn't going to let me spend much time pursuing other avenues, so you'll have to do the legwork. Find me evidence that proves someone else stole the money, and I'll push it through."

Dane nodded. "We'll come up with the guilty party."

"I want to go back to the police station," Neely said. "I'd like to meet Raleigh's lawyer, and maybe I'll get the chance to talk to him again."

Dane turned to Steamer. "Will you take Neely and wait with her?"

"I'll be glad to," Steamer said.

"Hack, send a couple of guys along. We need to use extreme security precautions."

"Don't we always?" Steamer asked.

"Even more than usual," Dane muttered. "One person associated with this case is already dead. We don't want to add more to that total."

Steamer nodded with rare seriousness. "We'll be careful."

Detective Napier said, "I'll escort them to the station and have a patrol car follow them when they are ready to come back."

Dane shook hands with the detective. "Thank you. I'll be in touch soon."

The detective nodded. "Don't drag your feet. The longer we have a suspect, the more attached we get to him."

After Steamer and Neely left with Detective Napier, Savannah sighed. "Well, what now?"

Dane was frowning. "We've got to find out who stole that money so the police can arrest them and release Raleigh."

"We're running out of suspects," Savannah reminded them. "Raleigh's in jail, and Selma Estes is dead."

Dane rubbed the bridge of his nose. "Bring me everything we've got on Hopewell, the ex-wife, the fired receptionist, and even the dead girlfriend. We'll build a case against all of them and then pick the strongest one to take to Detective Napier."

Hack seemed encouraged just by having an assignment. "I can be ready with that in an hour."

Dane nodded. "Any luck finding Owl and Brooke?"

"No," Hack replied. "He bought a car in Gatlinburg, but we don't know where they went from there."

Neely said, "I sure wish we could bring her home. I'm tired of my family being out of my reach."

As Hack swung around toward several computers he had set up along the far wall, his phone beeped, indicating that he had a text. He looked at his phone, glanced up at Dane, and said, "You're not going to believe this."

***

The next time Brooke woke up, she felt a little better. She was still groggy but less confused and more able to focus. Hunter was sitting right beside her bed, his eyes grave.

"How do you feel now?" he asked.

"Much better."

"Are you hungry or thirsty? I can get the nurse if you need something."

"I'm fine." She saw his sadness and reached for his hand. "I'm sorry I burdened you with my secret. I wouldn't have told you if I hadn't been weakened by pain and under the influence of drugs."

He nodded. "I know. Now tell me about you and Rex again, and this time, don't leave anything out."

She took a deep breath. "Six months after Rex moved in with me, I found out I was pregnant." She stared at the wall in front of her, determined to tell him everything but unable to face him while she did it. "I finally worked up the courage to tell Rex. I expected him to be unhappy or even angry. I didn't expect complete disinterest. But that's what I got. He basically told me the baby was my 'problem' and advised me to get an abortion. I found it ironic that he would work so hard to protect chickens and trees and eagles but didn't have a second thought about condemning his own unborn child."

Hunter's hand tightened around hers, offering quiet support.

"A few days later, he told me he was moving out and taking a job in California. That was it. I haven't heard from him since. He didn't care what happened to me or his child."

"Why didn't you tell your parents?"

"There were a lot of reasons. I was ashamed of the mess I'd made of my life. But mostly it was because I didn't want them to have to share the pain. It wasn't fair to make them suffer for my mistake." Her chest heaved with grief. "So I signed up for a semester at Juilliard. That gave me an excuse not to see my parents once my condition became obvious. And I did study with some amazing pianists. It was quite an honor."

"I've heard you play, remember? It was an honor for the pianists at Juilliard to work with *you*."

She savored his comment for a moment and then forced herself to continue. "Our church has an adoption service, and they arranged everything for me. The baby was born right after that semester ended. I chose not to hold her because I was afraid it would make the separation harder, but now I don't know. I kind of wish I'd gotten to hold her just once."

She looked at him through her unshed tears, and he nodded, encouraging her to continue.

"I only saw her for a second, just before they took her out of the birthing room. She had a lot of dark, curly hair." She paused again until she could trust her voice. "I flew home two days later. I thought my life would be back to normal, but now I understand that it will never be the same again."

"No," he agreed.

"I think about her every day. She's almost six months old now. I wonder how she looks and if she's happy," Brooke turned away and pressed her lips together to keep from crying.

"You gave your daughter life, which is much more than her sorry father was willing to do. You picked a good family for her, one that can give her all the things you want her to have. You chose what was best for her."

She looked back at him. "That was the perfect thing to say."

"It's the truth," he replied simply.

"Maybe you don't need love lessons after all."

He squeezed her hand. "The next time I have to fly some VIPs to California, I might just look old Rex up and beat him to a bloody pulp."

"Please don't," she said. "He's probably forgotten all about me. But if you remind him about the baby—he could make trouble about the adoption and, well, the baby's happiness is more important than anything else."

He sighed. "And I guess if he wasn't such a jerk he'd be sitting here with you now instead of me."

She smiled. "One of life's ironies."

Tired but relieved, she allowed her eyes to flutter closed. Just sharing the secret had lifted a great burden. Sharing it with Hunter had made him closer than she had dared hope.

After a while he said, "I think you should tell your parents. You'd want to know if they were dealing with something difficult in their lives—like if they had cancer or something. Wouldn't you feel terrible if you didn't find out until it was all over and knew you hadn't been there to help them through it?"

"Yes," she was willing to concede. "But this is different. It's over and there's nothing they can do but be sad about it."

"You're their daughter. They should know."

"I might be able to tell them someday, but not now. I just can't."

He didn't pressure her. "You'll know when the time is right."

Her heart swelled with love for him. Even though she dreaded the answer, she had to know and she had to know now. So she clutched his hand tightly and asked, "Be honest. Do you feel differently about me now that you know?"

"I do feel differently."

Her disappointment was profound but she was all cried out, so she just nodded in numb acceptance.

Then he continued, "Before I thought you were pretty and funny and, well, a lot of other good things. But now, after hearing your sad secret, I respect you."

She sifted through all his words and finally came to a conclusion. "You don't hate me?"

"No."

"Do you still want to go out to dinner with me?"

"As soon as possible."

She leaned over and put her hands behind his neck. "Do you want to kiss me?"

He nodded solemnly. "Yes."

She laughed and pressed her lips to his. As the kiss ended, she said, "I wish we were in the grand ballroom at Plantation House, singing 'Dixie.'"

"Please," he begged. "Could we be singing something else? I never liked that song, but now, after my brief stint as a Confederate soldier, I hate it."

She laughed. "I think of it as our song."

He frowned. "I like it that we have a song, but can't we pick something else? Like 'Jeannie with the Light Brown Hair' or 'O Susanna'?"

"I don't want our song to have another girl's name in it," she told him. "You're sure you don't want to stick with 'Dixie'? Maybe it will grow on you like I did!"

"I'll never love 'Dixie.'" He got the binder of 1800s music out of his backpack and thumbed through it. Finally he stopped at a page and read it several times.

"Did you find something?" she asked him

"How about 'Lady Mine'?"

"Read it to me," she requested.

"Don't you remember the words?"

"Yes," she said. "But I want to hear you say them. Unless you'd rather sing them."

He cleared his throat and read:

Thou art beautiful as the flow'rs
Lady mine! Lady mine!
E'en the fairest in my bow'rs
Lady mine! Lady mine!
And the azure brow of night,
With its starry wreaths of light,
Hath not eyes more pure and bright
Than are thine, Lady mine.

He lifted his eyes to meet hers.

"'Lady Mine' it is then," she managed.

He set the music aside and took Brooke's hand in his. "And now I'm going to tell you something that might change how *you* feel about *me*."

She tensed. "Go ahead."

"I sent Hack a message. Your uncle knows where we are."

CHAPTER THIRTEEN

BROOKE WANTED TO BE MAD at Hunter for going behind her back, but since she'd just confessed her deep, dark secret, anger seemed inappropriate. Besides, the kidney stone ordeal, combined with the pain medicine, had left her too weak to fight. So she just asked for his promise that he wouldn't tell her family about the baby.

"You can trust me."

She smiled. "I know."

Hunter cleared his throat and added, "There are a couple of things I should fill you in on before someone gets here to pick you up."

Brooke ignored the knot of dread that formed in her stomach and nodded. "Tell me."

"Your brother is having trouble getting out of Zimbabwe because of some tribal wars, but your uncle is getting the army's help with that."

Brooke felt mildly relieved. "Anything else?"

"Some money is missing from your father's company, so independent auditors came in and seized their books. They made your father and his partner stay at the office overnight while they tried to find the money."

"Did they find it?" Brooke asked.

"No, and your father's been arrested."

"Arrested!" Brooke cried. "He would never steal from his company!"

He shrugged. "I don't know what evidence they have against him, but Major Dane is working to getting him released."

"How long will that take?" Brooke asked anxiously.

"Don't worry about that part. The police won't be a challenge to Major Dane."

She relaxed against the pillow on her hospital bed. "So did Hack say who's coming to get us?"

A voice spoke from the doorway. "I took that assignment myself."

Hunter and Brooke turned in unison.

"Hey, Uncle Christopher," Brooke said with a tired smile. She noticed that Hunter had turned a little pale.

Her uncle walked over to the bed. "Hey, yourself. It looks like you've had a rough time."

"It wasn't bad until early this morning," she told him. "And Hunter took good care of me."

Her uncle raised an eyebrow. "Well, I'm glad to hear that. I wouldn't want things to be worse for *Hunter*. He's already facing a firing squad for going AWOL."

Brooke's eyes widened in terror. "A firing squad?"

"I won't really shoot him," Dane clarified. "But he'd better have a very good explanation for the past two days."

When Hunter didn't say anything to defend himself, Brooke decided that it was up to her.

"It's all my fault," she claimed. "I begged him not to tell you where we were—to protect my parents and your family and, well, everyone."

"We can protect ourselves," her uncle said. "And Owl follows my orders, not yours. Or he used to."

"He's a wonderful soldier, and I won't be able to stand it if I've messed things up for him with the army and you. I tried to run away so he wouldn't be involved, but he caught me. He stayed with me even though he knew it might ruin his career—"

"Brooke," Hunter interrupted. "It's okay. Stop making excuses for me."

Her uncle looked between the two of them. Then he said, "We'll talk about this later. Right now we are going to take you home." He tipped his head at Hunter. "You too."

Hunter cleared his throat. "Excuse me, sir, but I can't go with you and Brooke. I need to get some pictures to the DA," Hunter said then added another "sir" just for good measure.

Dane frowned. "What kind of pictures?"

"The ones I took of the hidden part of the Nature Fresh chicken plant and that pipe that's dumping chicken guts into the creek."

"The DA already has Brooke's pictures."

"But he doesn't have the ones I took this morning," Hunter explained. "And I'll testify for the judge so they can get a warrant to search the plant."

Brooke joined the conversation. "Hunter and I went back to the woods by the Nature Fresh plant this morning. He left me in a safe place and then swam up the creek. He took his own pictures, and now he's going to testify, making me unnecessary—worthless even." She glanced at Hunter. "At least as far as Nature Fresh is concerned."

Her uncle looked a little less angry. "That was a good idea."

"See what I mean? He's a great soldier. And brave! You can't fire him—or shoot him."

"Please, Brooke," Hunter whispered. "Stop!"

Dane's lips turned up at the corners in an almost-smile. "Okay. I have one of Hack's guys here with me. He can drive you to the DA's office to deliver the pictures. I'll call and let the DA know you're coming. If he's impressed with your pictures, I'm sure he'll let you testify at the hearing."

Hunter nodded. "Thank you, sir."

"It sounds like I should be thanking you," her uncle said. Then he turned to Brooke. "I'll send in a nurse to help you get dressed."

"Can I have a private moment with Hunter before he goes to see the DA?" Brooke requested.

Her uncle nodded. "But just a minute. The Nature Fresh people don't know that you are worthless, and I don't want them to swoop down on this hospital before Owl has a chance to get those pictures to the DA."

Once they were alone, she said. "I'll work on fixing things with my uncle."

He shook his head. "He's my commanding officer. I'll do my own explaining."

She frowned. "If you don't want me to, I won't. And at least he's promised not to shoot you."

"He was never going to shoot me."

"Are you going to come to my parents' house after you give your camera to the DA?" she asked. "I know they'll want to see you and thank you for taking care of me."

"I'm not sure. I'll have to ask your uncle what he wants me to do."

"You'll call me, though?"

He nodded. "I will."

"Then kiss me and go on. The sooner you leave, the sooner we'll be back together."

He pressed a quick kiss on her lips and then hurried out of the room. Immediately, loneliness settled over Brooke.

A nurse came in and helped her dress. Clinging to the hem of the jeans she'd worn to the hospital was a tiny leaf from the woods outside of the Nature Fresh plant. It reminded Brooke of her ordeal and of Hunter and of all he had done for her. She held the little leaf in her hand as she sat in a wheelchair. The nurse put Brooke's backpack in her lap and then wheeled her outside.

During the drive home, she told her uncle everything, starting with her discoveries at the chicken plant. She told him about the arm-twisting and threats from the Nature Fresh guys and how she met Hunter at the chicken march. She told her uncle about leaving with the Cauthens and then impersonating the couple at the Civil War resort. When she got to the part about running away from the resort, she reminded Dane that Hunter had risked his life and his career to protect her.

"He told me not to try and plead his case to you," she said. "And I promised him I wouldn't. So I'm not telling you this to make you forgive him; I'm just telling you the truth."

Her uncle nodded. "You seem very fond of him."

"I am," she admitted.

"And how does he feel?"

"I think he's . . . fond of me too. But he doesn't know how to have a relationship. So I'm going to have to teach him."

Her uncle was frowning. "I don't want you to get hurt."

"There's no point in telling me not to get involved," she said. "I am involved. And by the way, what's his last name?"

He shook his head. "His name is Hunter Ezell. But it sounds like you two have a long way to go before you know each other well enough to be 'involved.'"

***

Savannah was standing by the window in the living room, watching and waiting anxiously, when she saw one of the dark vehicles from Hack's fleet drive past the front of the house and turn into the driveway. She didn't know if it was Dane or Neely, but either way she wanted to be at the door when they walked in. So she hurried to the kitchen and arrived just as Neely stepped inside. She was followed closely by Steamer.

"Is Brooke here?" Neely wanted to know.

"Not yet, but they're on their way," Savannah said, "Why don't we sit in the family room and wait for them?"

They didn't have to make small talk for long. Dane and Brooke walked through the kitchen door just a few minutes later. Savannah stayed in the family room to give Neely and Brooke a little privacy for their reunion.

Neely embraced her daughter and said, "Oh, I can't believe you've been in the hospital!"

"It was nothing, Mom. I'm fine," Brooke insisted.

"It wasn't *nothing*," Dane disagreed. "But she's fine, or she will be when she gets through taking all these antibiotics." He put two pill bottles on the counter. "The doctor also gave her some pain medicine, although he said she probably won't need it. But it *is* important that she take the antibiotics."

"I'll make sure she takes her pills," Neely assured him.

Dane nodded and then joined Savannah in the family room. He pulled her close and let his lips graze her forehead. "Miss me?" he whispered.

"Always," she murmured back.

They heard Neely say, "Look at you with your hair all cut—and blond."

Brooke reached up and touched the ends of her hair. "It was a disguise," she explained.

Neely smiled. "I like it."

"I like it too," Brooke agreed. "I think I'll keep it this way for awhile."

"The only thing I don't like about it is that it makes you look so grown up."

"I am grown up, Mom." Brooke was gentle but firm.

Neely nodded. "You certainly are. Now come over here and sit on the couch. Christopher said he promised the doctor you would rest."

Once Brooke was settled, Neely asked, "Now will you tell us everything?"

Brooke took a deep breath and gave her recitation of the past few days. When she finished, she turned to Neely. "Now tell me about Daddy. Hunter said he was arrested."

Neely and Dane took turns explaining all that had happened with Raleigh. Savannah listened and sipped Spriteorade.

Dane concluded with, "So we kind of overthought things and had him arrested—thinking he was in danger from Nature Fresh."

"But your uncle will get him out," Savannah assured the girl with complete confidence.

"Daddy would never steal anything," Brooke declared.

"I agree completely," Neely said. "But even if the charges are dropped, Business Services may lose all its clients."

"Just the suspicion of dishonesty will be enough to make people move their accounts," Dane explained.

Steamer added, "And the money is still missing."

"So you're saying Daddy could lose his company?" Brooke asked.

"Yes," Neely said. "But we're going to be fine, even if Business Services is not. We have savings to carry us through until your dad is able to make some decisions. And to make our savings last longer, we might sell the house. We don't need all this room anyway."

Brooke looked a little shaken. "I can't say I'm thrilled about that. This is the only home I've ever had."

Neely gave her daughter an encouraging smile. "It's just bricks and wood. We'll take our love with us to a smaller place."

"And Raleigh hasn't given up on trying to save Business Services," Steamer said. "Or maybe sell it."

Savannah was surprised by this announcement. "They won't get much for the company if it has no clients."

"Anything will be better than nothing," Neely said bravely. "But I'm not going to worry about that now. I just want to get Raleigh out of jail." She looked around, "So where is Owl? I'd like to thank him for taking such good care of Brooke."

"He took his pictures to the DA's office," Brooke answered.

"Once he testifies at the hearing, the danger to Brooke should be over," Steamer said.

"We owe him a huge debt of gratitude," Neely said.

Hack was scowling. "What Owl did wasn't right. Soldiers are supposed to follow orders."

Brooke rounded on the big man, like David confronting Goliath. "He probably saved my life! Isn't that more important than orders?"

Hack blinked, startled by the ferocity of Brooke's attack.

"Brooke and Owl are . . . fond of each other," Dane said, explaining her emotional response. "And part of being a good soldier is the ability to adjust to changing circumstances. Normally I have zero tolerance for ignoring orders, but based on Brooke's glowing description of Owl's behavior, I'm going to overlook it—this time."

Brooke gave her uncle a big hug. "Thank you!"

Neely said, "So you and Owl are good friends."

Brooke nodded. "I love him, Mom. And his name is Hunter."

"Hunter," Neely repeated with a nervous look at her brother.

Brooke's voice trembled slightly as she added, "I think you and Daddy will like him a lot."

Hack got a phone call and stepped into the kitchen, where he could talk in relative privacy. He returned a couple minutes later and told them, "Owl left the camera with the DA."

"I'm so relieved," Brooke said, pressing a hand to her heart. "When will he be here?"

"He's not coming here," Hack said. "That would draw danger *toward* you instead of *away* from you, which is the entire purpose of him becoming a witness against Nature Fresh. He'll stay in a hotel under another name, protected by some of my men until after the hearing tomorrow morning."

Brooke turned to her uncle. "Did you tell Hunter he couldn't come here?"

Dane shook his head.

"No," Hack said. "That was Owl's call."

Brooke frowned. "Well nobody asked me what I thought. I'm going to call him." She got out the disposable phone he'd gotten for her in Gatlinburg.

"He's trying to protect you," Dane said. "Don't make that hard for him."

"And what is that little-piece-of-garbage phone you're using?" Hack asked.

"We bought them after Hunter left his at the resort," she replied.

"I've got your phone," Hack said. He dug in his pocket and pulled it out. Then he tossed it to her. "I'd throw that play phone away immediately."

"I won't ever throw it away," she said, although she was happy to have her iPhone back. "It has a lot of sentimental value."

Hack scowled, and Savannah had to laugh. "Don't try to argue with a woman in love," she advised.

Dane stood. "I've got to get to work finding a better embezzlement suspect than Raleigh. Steam, Hack, why don't you come with me?"

Savannah felt that Neely and her daughter needed some time alone together. So she pulled herself up as well. "I'm sure you'll have some boring research that I can do."

Once they entered the office, Dane said, "Okay, let's go over our suspect list . . . again."

"Hopewell is the most obvious suspect," Steamer said. "He has serious money problems; in fact, he's on the verge of bankruptcy. He's got an ex-wife, who took him to the cleaners and now lives the good life—with a house in Key Biscayne and a nice little business of her own. And worst of all, she still has contacts at Business Services so she can keep tabs on him and enjoy his self-destruction."

Savannah nodded to let them know she was following. "I agree that he had the best motive. But I don't understand why he would destroy his own company over a hundred thousand dollars."

"I have an idea," Hack said.

Savannah nodded. "I'm a Spriteorade-logged pregnant woman, so explain your theory slowly and carefully."

"In addition to the problems Steamer mentioned, Hopewell also has a young, but weird, girlfriend. He bought her a car and pays her rent and no telling what else. So what if she's costing him more than the relationship is worth?"

"Then wouldn't he just break up with her?" Savannah asked.

"Maybe he's tried and she won't let him—like a fatal attraction thing," Steamer joined in.

"Or maybe she has something on him and he's afraid to break up with her," Hack said. "Remember, she's cold and calculating, with a criminal background. And that's a bad combination."

"Since she works with him and lives with him, she'd have plenty of opportunity to catch him if he's doing something unethical." Steamer and Hack were in rare agreement.

"So he decides that Business Services has become a liability for him. He starts to think he should just get out—away from the demanding clients and the long hours and these women in his life who are making him miserable. He talks to Raleigh about buying his half of the business."

Savannah said, "He might get enough out of the deal to pay off his debts but probably not enough to live as well as Marjorie."

Hack nodded. "But if he could steal money from the investment fund and pin it on Raleigh . . ."

Steamer took this opportunity to make a legal comment. "I haven't read the terms of their partnership agreement, but some agreements stipulate that if one partner is convicted of a felony, his or her equity is forfeit and the other partner or partners assume full ownership."

"So if Raleigh is convicted, Hopewell gets the whole company," Dane said with a frown.

Steamer nodded. "They probably have insurance to cover the stolen money. Hopewell could reassure the clients, and maybe some would stay. Or he could sell the company. Either way he'd probably come out with more than what Raleigh could pay him for his half of the business."

Hack smiled. "And he'd still be rid of Selma and her expenses."

"All he had to do was stab his partner in the back," Steamer agreed.

"And possibly kill his girlfriend, or at least facilitate her murder," Dane added.

"Wow," Savannah said.

"This will be our working theory," Dane said. "Let's see if we can come up with anything to back it up. Because if Hack is right, Finn Hopewell is a desperate, dangerous man."

Savannah had a sinking feeling in her stomach. Hack was usually right.

Neely, with Brooke in tow, came to the office door and announced, "Adam called! The airports are open, and before long he'll be on a plane headed home."

Savannah smiled. "That's good news."

"Mom called too," Neely continued, addressing her comments to Dane. "She's upset with you for not keeping her better informed, and she wants to come here."

"I hope you told her no," Dane replied.

"I said you absolutely forbade her to come anywhere near me for security reasons," Neely assured him. "She wasn't happy."

"She'll get over it." Dane didn't sound concerned. "We've got more important things to worry about." He turned to Savannah. "Why don't you girls go to bed. Guys, let's find something that will get Raleigh out of jail."

Neely shook her head. "Now that's a phrase I never thought I'd hear."

"Get some rest, Crybaby," Dane encouraged. "Hopefully by the time you wake up we'll have it figured out."

"You're not going to stay up all night, are you?" Savannah asked.

He shrugged. "It depends on how long it takes for us to find what we need."

Savannah hated to leave him, but she was exhausted and knew she'd only be a distraction. So she stood and waved for Neely and Brooke to follow her.

***

Brooke was snuggled under the comforter in her childhood bed when Hunter called.

"It's so good to hear your voice!" she told him. She closed her eyes and pictured his handsome, solemn face.

"Are you okay?" he wanted to know.

"Almost normal," she assured him. "How about you?"

"I'm bored in this hotel room," he said. "I hate being confined. But otherwise I'm good."

"So you're going to the hearing tomorrow morning?" she asked.

"I'm supposed to be at the DA's office at eight o'clock," he confirmed. "He's going to take me over to the courthouse, where I will present my pictures and testify to their location in front of a judge. Then I'll be done."

"And you'll come here?"

"I'll discuss it with your uncle, and if he thinks it's safe, I'll come for a little while," he agreed conditionally. "But then I have to get back to Washington."

"Flying VIPs?"

"Yes."

She almost wished they were still in danger, pretending to be the Cauthens or hiding in a rental cabin. At least then she had him to herself. "But you're still going to come and take me out to dinner?"

There was a brief silence, and then he said, "That's one of the things I'm looking forward to."

She smiled.

"Now, you should try to get some rest," he suggested. "You've had a rough week."

She could tell he was ready to hang up, but she wasn't quite ready to let him go. "Hunter?"

"Yes?"

"I loved every minute of our time together."

There was a pause, and finally he said, "Me too."

"And I'm not finished with you yet!"

She could picture him making that exasperated face he used when he thought she was over-the-top.

"I'll call you tomorrow," he promised. And then he hung up.

***

On Monday morning Savannah woke up to Dane shaking her gently. She opened her eyes and studied his exhausted face.

"Did you sleep at all last night?"

He shook his head. "No, but we've come up with what we think is enough evidence against Finn Hopewell to get Raleigh out of jail. Detective Napier is coming by so I can give him what I have on our new suspect."

She sat up and stretched. "Let me brush my teeth, and I'll be right down."

When Savannah got downstairs, she found everyone seated around the kitchen table.

"You shouldn't have waited on breakfast for me," she said, embarrassed.

"We can be gentlemen," Steamer said. "But it's a good thing you got here when you did. Hack was about to eat his arm."

Hack growled.

"No point in that when I've made all this food," Neely said blithely.

While they ate, Dane said, "I believe we have enough evidence that points to Finn as Selma's partner in stealing from the investment fund at Business Services."

Neely gasped. "Finn?"

"He had the best motive: pressing financial problems. He also had opportunity," Dane itemized. "But our most compelling argument is that he has a key to Selma's apartment, which explains no forced entry."

"But that means he not only killed his girlfriend and stole from his own company—he also framed Raleigh," Neely said. "And I can't believe that. They're more than partners. They're friends."

"It will be up to the police, ultimately, to prove the case against Hopewell," Dane said. "But he was in trouble financially—to the point that he was about to lose everything, including the company."

"I hate the idea that Finn is guilty of such terrible things," Neely said, "But I guess I'd rather have just about anyone in jail besides Raleigh."

Steamer grinned. "That's the spirit."

"Detective Napier will be here soon," Dane told her. "I'm going to present him with what we've got, and hopefully it will be enough to get Raleigh released."

Neely nodded. "I hope so."

"Everybody eat quick," Steamer said. "We don't want all this good food to go to waste."

"I'm so nervous now I couldn't possibly eat anything," Neely said.

"Me neither," Brooke agreed.

Savannah held up her bottle of Spriteorade. "Make that three."

Hack grinned. "That just means more for me."

***

After breakfast Dane told everyone to meet in Raleigh's home office.

"I'll come as soon as I get the kitchen cleaned up," Neely said.

"You go on," Brooke told her mom. "I'll clean the kitchen."

"And I'll help," Savannah offered.

Once the men were gone, Savannah cleared the table while Brooke rinsed the dishes and put them in the dishwasher.

"So, Mom says you're going to have a baby," Brooke said as they worked. "I know you're happy about that."

"I am," Savannah confirmed. "I'll be a little happier when I can stop drinking Spriteorade constantly without the risk of throwing up."

Brooke's smile seemed a little forced. "It will be nice to have a baby in the family."

"Yes," Savannah agreed. "And I'm excited for you and Hunter."

Brooke's shoulders relaxed, and she gave Savannah a more sincere smile. "I am too. It's strange though. We were so comfortable together when it was just us, but I'm a little nervous about how he'll fit into my family and how I'll fit into his life."

"It won't be easy," Savannah said. "But if you love each other, you'll make it work."

Brooke nodded. "I'm determined."

Hack walked into the kitchen and said, "Detective Napier is here." He opened the door to the garage to admit the detective.

"Morning, ladies." Detective Napier looked terrible, as always.

"Good morning," Savannah returned. Brooke just nodded.

"Whenever you girls get finished with kitchen duty, come on into Raleigh's office," Hack said. Then he led the detective toward the front of the house.

"Let's hurry," Savannah whispered. "I don't want to miss this."

Brooke threw down her dish towel. "I say we just finish up later."

"Your mom won't care?"

Brooke shrugged. "What can she do? It'll be too late."

Savannah shook her head. "I hope Hunter knows what he's getting into."

Brooke laughed. "He has no idea."

Brooke and Savannah slipped quietly into the office and listened to Dane wrap up the case they'd built against Finn Hopewell.

When Dane finished, Detective Napier frowned. "Well, that's not what I'd call open and shut."

Dane winced. "I know, but it's a good start. You can check the GPS on Hopewell's car and see if he went to Selma's house that night."

"Or just call him in and grill him," Steamer suggested. "He might crack under pressure and admit everything to get a deal."

"And why would we give him a deal?" the detective wanted to know.

"To solve a murder case!" Steamer exclaimed.

Dane leaned his elbows onto the desk. "It may not be the best case you've ever heard, but I hope it's enough to cast doubt on the case against Raleigh."

Detective Napier shook his head. "Then you, my soldier friend, are an optimist."

Dane sighed. "If you don't think it's not strong enough, we can keep working on it."

"It won't hurt to try," Detective Napier said. "The worst that will happen is my captain will think I'm crazy for accusing someone new every day. And I'm retiring anyway."

Hack's phone beeped, and he checked the screen. Then he said, "A silver Lexus just pulled in the driveway." He looked a little befuddled.

"The silver Lexus owned by Marjorie Hopewell?" Dane guessed.

Hack nodded.

"Marjorie?" Neely repeated in surprise. "I wonder why she'd come here without even calling first."

"She may have tried to call," Savannah said. "We haven't answered the house phone in days."

"I forgot about that," Neely murmured.

Dane said, "I'm very anxious to hear what Marjorie Hopewell has to say. Maybe she can tell you something that will strengthen our case against her ex-husband."

Detective Napier raised both eyebrows. "I stand corrected. You are a *super*-optimist."

Dane ignored this comment and turned to Neely. "Most of us will stay here in the office to keep from spooking her. Only Hack will go with you to the door." Dane turned to Hack. "Can we watch on the computer screen?"

Hack nodded. "You can if I put a little transmitter in the family room."

"Do that now, please," Dane instructed as he moved over to one of the laptops against the far wall.

Hack walked out as the doorbell rang. Several lines of static scrolled across the computer screen. Then they saw Hack's face. "Testing," he whispered.

Dane pushed the speaker button on the keyboard. "One, two, three," he added.

"We're set," Hack said into the camera. Then he backed away as the doorbell rang again. On the computer they could see only the empty family room.

Hack came to the office door, and Neely joined him there.

"Neely, we don't want to mislead Mrs. Hopewell too much," Dane advised his sister. "Tell her we're in the office with Detective Napier, working on a way to get Raleigh out of jail."

Neely nodded and walked away with Hack.

"Close the door please, Steam," Dane requested. Steamer quietly closed the office door. Then everyone stared at the computer screen. They couldn't see Neely at the front door, but they could hear the conversation.

"Marjorie!" Neely said. "What a surprise."

"Oh Neely!" Marjorie Hopewell cried. "I've done something terrible, and I don't know what to do!"

"Come in and sit down," Neely invited.

Savannah heard their footsteps as they walked by the office.

Seconds later they came into view on the computer screen. Neely led Marjorie over to the couch and sat beside her. Hack stood in the kitchen, close enough to provide protection if Neely needed it but far enough away to give Marjorie a very false sense of privacy.

Once they were seated on the couch, facing the camera, Savannah noted that Marjorie did not look her best. Her blond hair was mussed, and her beautiful face was tearstained.

Neely said, "Now tell me what's wrong."

"I killed Selma Estes!" Marjorie cried.

Through the miracle of technology, and a very high-definition monitor, they saw the shock on Neely's face.

Dane and Detective Napier exchanged a glance.

"Well, well, well," Steamer whispered.

"Should I go in there?" the detective asked.

"Give it another minute," Dane suggested.

"You killed Selma?" Neely repeated.

"Not personally," she clarified.

Savannah saw Dane relax slightly.

"But it's my fault she's dead." Marjorie shook her head in apparent despair. "All my fault."

Neely reached over and took Marjorie's hand. "Tell me what happened."

"Finn and that girl, Selma, ruined my life. You understand, don't you?" Marjorie pleaded. "Most people see the money I got from him in the divorce and my house in Florida and my little travel business and think that I don't care. But I do care!"

"You're happy now with your new life," Neely reminded her.

Marjorie's eyes dropped to her hands, clenched in her lap. "I want my old life! The one I built with Finn. We were supposed to be together until death do us part! She took my husband away from me, Neely. Think about that for a minute. How would you feel if Raleigh came through that door and told you he didn't love you? That there was someone else?"

"I'd be devastated," Neely admitted. "I don't know what I'd do or say."

"You would feel dead," Marjorie said. "Even though your heart was still beating and your lungs were still filling up with air."

"I know it must have been terrible for you," Neely sympathized.

"I can't even describe it. I had to stand by and watch my world fall apart, and I had no control. I hated Finn for that—and Selma. I wanted them to pay for what they did. It seemed like justice."

"That's why you got such a divorce settlement."

"Money!" Marjorie scoffed. "It doesn't mean a thing! Every day I had to think about them together, eating breakfast, going to work, planning a future—just like Finn and I used to do. It tortured me. I couldn't stand it."

"So what did you do?"

Even with the slight distortion caused by the computer speakers, Savannah could hear the dread in Neely's voice.

Tears started down Marjorie's cheeks again. "I'm the one who told Selma that Finn was flirting with that receptionist, Cindy."

"And Selma made Finn fire her," Neely said solemnly.

"Yes," Marjorie said. "And after that, Selma had it in her mind that I was her friend. The nerve of that girl!"

"That was pretty nervy," Neely agreed.

"So I used that ridiculous misconception to ruin her relationship with Finn. I started taking her out to lunch about once a week. I convinced her she needed a new car and a nicer apartment. I made her suspicious of him and his motives for everything. I told her that it was only a matter of time before he left her for someone else—just like he did me. Except since she wasn't married to him she wouldn't get a big divorce settlement." Marjorie paused and bit her lip for a second. Then she continued. "I'm not proud of what I did, but I was a heartbroken, desperate woman."

Neely nodded. "I know. But how did you cause Selma's death?"

"I suggested that she could steal that money from the Sterling investment account. It was a very unsecured way of handling investment transfers. I told Finn that myself several times before, when I worked there. But he and Raleigh trusted everyone." Her mouth twisted into an ugly frown. "Too bad he couldn't be trusted with my heart."

Neely deftly redirected Marjorie to the original topic. "So Selma took your suggestion and stole the money?"

"Yes! I told her it would be so easy to make it look like Finn took the money since he was in such terrible financial trouble. I swear I wasn't trying to hurt Raleigh or cause trouble for you."

"I believe you," Neely said. "So Selma took the money on your suggestion."

"Yes. Only she used Raleigh's name on the joint accounts she set up instead of Finn's. Maybe she thought with his credit and money problems his name would invite scrutiny."

"That's possible," Neely agreed.

"Then . . ." Marjorie stopped. "I don't know if I can make myself tell you."

"You can," Neely said. "You must! Raleigh is sitting in jail for something he didn't do."

"I told Finn what Selma did," Marjorie nearly whispered. "Of course, I didn't tell him that I played a part in it."

"No," Neely's voice sounded sad.

"He was furious, of course. He said she had ruined him financially, destroyed Raleigh's reputation, and bankrupted their business all because she was a selfish little witch. I'm ashamed to admit it, but I loved hearing him say all those things," Marjorie confided. "Hearing the hatred in his voice when he spoke of Selma."

"Oh, Marjorie" was all Neely replied.

"He said he was going to Selma's place to get the money back. I followed him to her apartment. He was so mad when he went in he didn't even close the door all the way, so I could see inside. He accused her of stealing the money, and she laughed at him. She said she deserved it for having to put up with an old man like him. He said he was going to call the police. Then she pointed a gun at him and told him to leave." Marjorie couldn't control her sobs.

"Go on," Neely encouraged.

"He lunged at her, and they fought over the gun. There was a shot, and for a second I thought Finn was dead. My Finn. But then he stood up and walked out the door. He saw me standing there, of course. He knew I had seen everything. I told him I wasn't going to say a word to anyone. I thought he would appreciate it. I thought that with Selma gone he would want me and our life together back. But he didn't. He told me he didn't care what I did and he never wanted to see me again. Then he walked down the hallway."

Savannah's attention was diverted from the computer screen for just a second as Detective Napier pulled out his phone and said, "Put out an APB on Finn Hopewell. Check his apartment first and then his office. He might be armed, and he's definitely dangerous."

"I thought I would feel better when I didn't have to think about them together and happy," Marjorie continued. "But I don't feel better. I just feel empty."

"You need to talk to the police," Neely said. "Tell them everything that happened."

"Do you think I'll go to jail?" Marjorie's voice was small.

"I don't know. Probably not if you get a good lawyer."

"Will they let Raleigh go if I tell them about what I told Selma?"

Neely nodded. "I think they will."

Marjorie said, "I'll tell them. Then at least you and Raleigh can be happy."

"Do you want Hack to take you to the police station?" Neely offered.

Marjorie glanced over toward the kitchen, where Hack was standing. Then she nodded. "I'll call my lawyer on the way."

"Ask to speak to Detective Napier," Neely said. "He's the one working on Raleigh's case. He's a good policeman. I'm sure he'll help you all he can."

"They'll arrest Finn, I guess."

Neely nodded. "Yes. But maybe he can prove he shot Selma in self-defense."

Marjorie stood, and Neely did the same. "I'm so sorry," Marjorie whispered. "I wanted to hurt them; I'll admit that. But I never meant for anyone to die."

Neely gave her a little hug. "I know."

As Neely closed the front door behind Hack and Mrs. Hopewell, Dane picked up his phone. He typed a message, and then he turned to

Detective Napier. "I told Hack to drive slowly so you can get to the police station before they do."

The detective stood. "I'll be in touch." He left through the door in the kitchen that led to the garage.

When Neely walked into the office, she looked shaken. "I can't believe that Marjorie was behind all of it."

"A woman scorned," Steamer said. "They can hold a grudge forever."

"She wanted to ruin Finn's life," Neely said. "But in the process, she's ruined her own."

Dane's phone rang, and he answered it with a reluctant look. "Dane." After a few minutes, he ended the call and faced Neely. "That was Detective Napier. They found Finn Hopewell in his apartment. He'd killed himself."

CHAPTER FOURTEEN

BROOKE PACED AROUND THE KITCHEN, anxious to hear from Hunter. He should have finished testifying at the hearing by now. And they were waiting for a call from Detective Napier, telling them that her father was going to be released. That call came first.

"They're releasing Raleigh," her uncle announced.

Neely cried with happiness and hugged her brother. "He can leave now?"

Dane nodded. "Hack is still with Marjorie. She's given her statement to the police, but he's concerned about her emotional state and doesn't want her to be alone. He's waiting at the police station until Marjorie's sister can get there. So I'll take you to get Raleigh. Savannah and Brooke, you can come too if you want to."

Brooke was trying to think of a good excuse not to go when her phone rang. She glanced at the screen and said, "It's Hunter!"

"I'm done," he told her. "I gave my testimony to the judge, and the DA said he was finished with me."

"That is so great!" Brooke told him. "I can't believe my boyfriend is bringing down a huge company like Nature Fresh."

"I can't believe someone is calling me their boyfriend."

She laughed. "And my dad is getting out of jail."

"That's good news."

"Yep," Brooke agreed. "Mrs. Hopewell came to see my mom and told her that Selma Estes stole the money and that Finn Hopewell killed Selma because of it. Then Mr. Hopewell killed himself."

"Wow," Hunter said. "That's terrible."

"It is," Brooke agreed. "But at least the police know that my dad didn't take the money, so he's being released. It's finally over."

"Our part is, anyway," he confirmed. "Now it's up to the police and the lawyers and the courts."

"So are you coming here?" Brooke asked.

"Actually, I was hoping you would meet me at your apartment. While I was hiding in a hotel room last night, Hack helped me arrange a little surprise for you there."

"Sure," she said. "I'll be there in about thirty minutes."

When she ended her call with Hunter, she explained his request to the others. "So can you drop me off at my apartment on your way to the police station?"

Her mother's disappointment was obvious. "Your father will be so anxious to see you. Can't you come with us to the police station and then go to your apartment?"

Brooke shook her head. "Once Hunter shows me his surprise, we'll come straight home. That way Daddy can see me and meet Hunter at the same time."

She could tell her mother was still not pleased, but at least she didn't complain. Brooke was grateful to be allowed some space without being made to feel guilty.

"We'll drop you off on our way to the police station," her uncle agreed. "Along with one of Hack's guys as a bodyguard."

"Hunter will be there," she reminded him. "And besides, I thought the danger was over."

"Nature Fresh should have their hands full for the moment, but I never take chances," her uncle said. "So you'll have one of Hack's men to share Hunter's surprise with you."

"What about me, boss," Steamer asked. "You want me to stay here and keep the house secure?"

"That is your current assignment." Dane took Savannah's hand in his. "Are you ready to go?"

"Don't you think I should stay here and pack?" Savannah asked. "I'm anxious to get Caroline and go home."

"I'd rather you come with me," her uncle said. "I'll help you pack when we get back."

"Are you going to call Doc, or do you want me to?"

"I'll call him. I'm hoping he and Caroline can just meet us at home." Dane pulled Savannah toward the door. "The sooner we go, the sooner we'll get back."

During the drive into Nashville, Brooke was so excited she could barely sit still. She wondered what kind of surprise Hunter had waiting. She wanted so badly to look into his eyes, to feel his arms around her, and to see where life and their new love might take them.

Her uncle stayed on the phone most of the drive to her apartment. First he arranged to have Doc bring Caroline home. Brooke was busy daydreaming and only heard a portion of that conversation. Then he got a call from Steamer. She didn't pay much attention to this call either, but afterward, when her uncle was discussing the call with her mother and Savannah, she heard Hunter's name. And then she listened carefully.

"In spite of Hunter's testimony, the judge who conducted the hearing determined there was not enough evidence for a warrant to search the Nature Fresh property. He dismissed the case. It's over."

"So it was all for nothing?" Savannah whispered.

"It sounds that way," Dane confirmed.

"We did our best," Brooke said. "That's all we could do."

Savannah turned around in surprise. "I thought you'd be much more upset."

Brooke sighed. "Over the past few days, I've learned that you have to prioritize. I would have liked to see Nature Fresh punished for their crimes against the environment and helpless chickens. But I know I can't fix everything, and I'm so thankful that my family and Hunter are okay."

"That's a very mature attitude," her mother said.

"Besides, this is a happy day. Hunter has a surprise for me, and I'm not going to let a cowardly judge or stupid Nature Fresh ruin it for me."

Savannah laughed. "Now that's what I call being practical."

As they reached the street where her apartment was located, Brooke leaned forward, willing the vehicle to move faster. "I may hyperventilate before I can get there," she said, only half teasing.

She saw her mother look quickly at Dane. "You certainly have become attached to Hunter in a very short time."

A couple of weeks earlier, a comment like that from her mother would have made Brooke mad. Now she just smiled. "We lived through a lot together in the short time we've known each other. And you can stop giving Uncle Christopher those worried looks. I know you don't trust my judgment after Rex. But Hunter is different."

"I can vouch for Hunter. He's a good guy," her uncle said.

When her uncle pulled up in front of her apartment building, she saw her car, which had been parked in the same spot for a long time. Right beside it was the sporty black car Hunter had purchased in Gatlinburg.

It was a little worse for the wear, with several deep scratches marring the paint, but it was still a beautiful little car. She wondered if he'd decided to follow her suggestion and keep it.

"Just let me out at the curb."

"I was hoping I could go in and thank Hunter," Neely said.

"I want you to thank him and get to know him." Brooke was already reaching for the door handle. "But not right now. Not during my surprise."

Savannah looked at the apartment building. "We're all dying to know what the surprise is."

"I'll call and tell you later," Brooke offered as she opened the car door.

"Wait up for Hack's guy," her uncle said, glancing in the rearview mirror.

Brooke turned and saw a tall man walking up to the car. He had bright red hair and was wearing a New Orleans Saints T-shirt. She rolled her eyes. "Have you people never heard of *privacy*?"

"I've heard of it," her uncle replied. "I'm just not a big fan."

Brooke smirked and climbed out of the car. She waited on the sidewalk for the red-headed man to reach her. Then she stuck out her hand, "I'm Brooke."

He nodded. "I know."

She let her hand drop to her side. "So, what is your name?"

He seemed surprised by the question, but finally he said, "Larry."

"Okay, Larry. Let's go up to my apartment. But my boyfriend has a surprise for me, and you'd better not mess it up."

Larry's expression didn't change as he fell into step beside her. When they reached her floor, she looked down the hall, expecting to see Hunter standing outside her door. But the hallway was empty. So she hurried to her door and knocked. There was no answer. She pulled the key out of her backpack and, with trembling hands, unlocked the door.

Larry insisted on going in first, to make sure it was safe.

"I hope Hunter wasn't planning to jump out and scream 'surprise,'" she muttered. "Because if he was, you will surely ruin it." Then she smiled at the thought of Hunter doing such a thing.

There were no screams of "surprise" as she followed Larry through the door. Then she came to a dead stop just inside the threshold. The entire living room of her little apartment was now filled with a baby grand piano. The binder of 1800s music Jovette had given her was on the music rack. She dropped her backpack onto the floor with a thud and took a step closer.

When she saw the binder was open to "Dixie," she wiped away a tear, thinking of the nights she'd played while the crowds sang—and how Hunter claimed to hate it.

She sat on the bench and stared at the piano. It was obviously old and a little dusty. The name *Franklin* was barely visible in dull gold paint above the keys. It was unquestionably the most thoughtful gift anyone had ever given her. She was overwhelmed to the point of speechlessness. Running her fingers along the yellowed keys, she played a few bars of "Dixie." The piano was badly out of tune, but that just made it more endearing. She called out to Hunter but got no answer.

Larry, who had been making a sweep through the apartment, returned shaking his head. "Nobody's here," he reported.

Brooke looked around the room, confused. Why wouldn't Hunter want to be with her when she saw this fabulous surprise? Then her phone beeped, notifying her that she had a text. She smiled when she saw it was from Hunter. Then she read the words on the screen: "Meet me at our campsite, where we left our dome tent. I have an important question to ask you."

Brooke's eyes moved to the old-fashioned notes on the sheet music— the anthem of the Old South—"Dixie." Then she stared at the words displayed neatly on the screen of her phone. Then she turned to her body-guard. "I've got to go meet Hunter—I mean Owl. Do you have a car you can use to follow me?"

He shook his head. "We're both supposed to ride with Owl. Since he's not here, I need to call Hack and ask him what to do."

"He's busy at the police department," Brooke told him. One thing was for sure—she had to get to Hunter, and neither Hack nor this bodyguard were going to stop or delay her. "It's just a slight change of plans." She gave him a bright smile. "Owl's waiting for us."

"Where?" Larry asked.

"It's not far." Brooke took a single key from a bowl on her mantle and tossed it to Larry. "You can drive my car, and I'll take Hunter's." She pulled out the key that Hunter had given her. Then, clutching it in one hand and her phone in the other, she led the way outside.

Brooke walked briskly and was a couple of steps ahead of Larry when they reached the cars. She pointed to hers as she unlocked the black car with the keyless entry. Then she swung into the driver's seat and tossed her backpack onto the passenger seat. She turned the key in the ignition, and the engine roared to life. She put the car in gear, jumped the curb, and was headed down the road before red-haired Larry realized the key in his hand didn't unlock her car.

***

When Savannah, Dane, and Neely arrived at the police station, Detective Napier met them in the lobby.

"Ladies, Major Dane."

"Is Raleigh ready to go?" Neely asked.

"Mr. Clayton's release is being processed right now," Detective Napier told her. "He's already changed into his own clothes, and once they give him his personal items, he can leave. Would you like to go and wait with him, Mrs. Clayton?"

Neely nodded. "I would like that very much."

Detective Napier grabbed a uniformed policeman and assigned him to take Neely down to the floor below, where Raleigh was waiting. With a glance at Dane, the detective added, "Stay with them until they're finished, and then bring them back up here to me."

The officer looked surprised by the assignment but led Neely toward the stairs.

Detective Napier turned back to Savannah and Dane.

"So, how are things going with Marjorie Hopewell?" Dane asked.

"No charges have been filed yet. I'm not sure what the future holds for her."

Savannah felt a little uneasy about this. Marjorie may not have meant for Selma to die, but she did mean to hurt the girl—and Finn. It didn't seem right that Marjorie would just walk away and go back to her life when the other two were dead.

"Revenge is a dirty, dangerous game," Dane said. "But I'm just glad that you know who took the money and that Raleigh is being released and that I can go home."

The detective smiled, exposing his coffee-stained teeth. "It's been a pleasure doing business with you, Major. Try to keep him out of trouble, Mrs. Dane."

"I'll do my best," Savannah assured him, thinking how much her original negative impression of him had changed during the course of the past few days. "Don't retire any time soon, Detective. The Nashville Police Department needs good men like you."

The detective shook his head. "It's time for me to turn all this over to younger men and enjoy life a little."

Savannah smiled politely. "What do you plan to do once you retire—besides relax?"

"I have a fishing boat that has been collecting dust for years," he said. "I intend to use it—a lot."

"We certainly wish you the best," Dane told him.

"Here comes the recently released jailbird now," Detective Napier said.

Dane and Savannah turned to watch as Neely and Raleigh approached them, hand in hand.

It was a sweet sight, and Savannah sighed.

Then Hack burst out into the hallway, blocking her view of the newly reunited couple.

Savannah had heard of someone looking like a thundercloud. Hack looked like the whole storm.

"What's wrong?" Dane demanded.

"I just got a call from Larry, the guy you left with Brooke. She ditched him and drove off in Owl's car."

"Why?"

"She said she was going to meet Owl, but I don't like it," Hack said. "Owl called and told her to meet him at her apartment so he could surprise her with that old piano my guys helped him buy. But when she got there, Owl was gone. Larry said she got a text from him telling her to meet him. Then she tricked Larry—which I will address with him later—but anyway, Brooke is on her own without protection."

"But she shouldn't need protection anymore, right?" Neely asked as they all gathered around Hack.

Dane frowned. "The judge just dismissed the case against Nature Fresh. And they might want to tie up some loose ends."

"Like a couple of witnesses who have seen the illegal pipeline?" Hack asked.

Dane nodded. "I'm afraid she'd going headlong into a trap."

***

As she drove, Brooke pulled out her phone and made a quick call to her uncle.

"Brooke!" he answered in a near shout. "What are you doing?"

"I'm pretty sure that Hunter is in trouble," she told him. "Please come quickly to the woods by the Nature Fresh plant. You can follow the GPS on my phone to find my exact location."

"We're on our way," Uncle Christopher promised. "You stay right where you are until we get there."

"Sorry, but I can't do that," she said. "Hunter is in trouble because of me, and I have to try to help."

"Brooke!" her uncle's tone was desperate.

Wincing, she ended the call and stowed the phone in her pocket. As she neared her destination, she peered through the windshield of the little black car, watching the woods for the turnoff Hunter had used when they came together. She was afraid she had passed it and was just about to turn around when she saw the little gap in the trees.

Relieved, she pulled the car into the woods and drove along the bumpy path as fast as she dared, ignoring the additional damage the tree branches inflicted on the car's black paint. When she reached the spot where Hunter had parked, she maneuvered the car around so she could back in, just the way he had. Then she put the car keys into her backpack, slung it over her shoulder, and started walking into the trees.

She tried to move quickly, but her progress was slow. Finally she came to a clearing that looked familiar. Listening closely she could hear the creek to her right. So that meant their little campsite was to the left. She turned and walked toward the trees. First she saw the camouflage dome tent, where she'd spent several miserable hours two days before. And then she saw Hunter, standing in front of a tree a few yards from the tent.

"Hunter!" she called out as she hurried toward him.

He didn't respond.

She stared at him and noticed the awkward way he was standing—pressed right up against the tree—and that his right arm was hanging at an odd angle from his body. Then she got close enough to see that his face was bruised and his mouth was covered with clear tape. His battered eyes were full of misery.

There was a movement behind her, and she looked around to see two men. She started running toward Hunter. The men followed but didn't really chase her.

Just before she got close enough to touch Hunter, the man who had twisted her wrist outside her apartment stepped out from behind the tree where Hunter was tied. The man grabbed her arm and pulled her up short.

"Well, well, look who's here," he taunted.

"Let him go!" she pleaded. "I'm the one you want!"

He laughed. "No, you got your boyfriend here involved, and now he's in as much trouble as you are. Maybe more."

"You won!" Brooke cried. "The judge dismissed the case! We pose no risk to you now!"

"The case was dismissed by a friendly judge," the man confirmed. "But we can't risk your story coming to the attention of another, less friendly judge somewhere down the line. So today there's going to be a forest fire, set by two chicken-loving zealots. The Nature Fresh plant will burn to the ground, taking the old chicken coops and that pipeline with it. Fortunately the plant is well insured. Unfortunately, the two misguided animal activists will be caught in the fire they set and, well, they won't survive."

Brooke didn't even try to hide her fear. "You're going to set the woods on fire and then leave us here to die?"

"Exactly," the man said. "Too bad you weren't that smart the day I warned you not to get involved with Nature Fresh. If you had listened, well, none of this would have been necessary."

Brooke felt intense regret over her original decision to get involved with the whole case. "You would have let me go on with my life?"

"No, like I said, any witnesses have to be eliminated. But your boyfriend and the forest would be fine."

He turned to one of the other men. "Tie her up beside him with that organic rope." Looking back at Brooke, he explained, "It should burn away completely, along with the two of you, but if there are any traces left, it won't raise suspicion because it's made from natural materials."

The man with the rope grabbed her roughly and shoved her toward the tree. She angled herself so she landed on Hunter's left side to avoid his injured right arm. She felt him flinch as she bumped him and knew she'd only been partially successful. While the man tied her to the tree, she strained against the rope. It was a trick she'd read in a book. Supposedly this created a little room to maneuver when the person being tied up relaxed. Brooke would soon learn if it worked.

As the man finished, he stepped back to admire his handiwork, and Brooke yelled at the arm-twister, "You'll never get away with it!"

He laughed. "Of course we will. You get word that the case has been dismissed, so you convince your boyfriend to come help you destroy the Nature Fresh plant and save future chickens. The press will have a heyday. They'll paint you as a misguided girl, an arsonist, a criminal. And your death, while sad, will not generate a lot of sympathy for you or your cause. With the insurance money, Nature Fresh will rebuild a much better plant—one that will not pollute the creek. It's the best solution for the most people."

"My parents and my uncle won't believe I set these woods on fire."

"They won't want to," the arm-twister told her. "But when they find out that there are traces of gasoline and explosives in your car, your boyfriend's car, and your apartment, they will eventually come to accept it."

Angry tears seeped out of Brooke's eyes. "You can't trick my uncle."

"Well, you won't be around to find out." He turned away from her and addressed the man with the rope. "Are the fires ready to start?"

The man nodded. "Yes sir, Mr. Sperry, I've got barrels of gas and explosives all wired together. When you give me the word, I push this button," he held up a little remote device, "and that place will go up like a match."

Mr. Sperry nodded. "I'm giving you the word."

The man pushed the button, and a few seconds later they heard three explosions in the distance. Black smoke billowed into the sky.

"We need the fire to burn particularly well here too, since this is where the bodies will be found," Mr. Sperry instructed. "But we can't use gasoline because we want it to look like an accident. And we need to hurry since we don't know how long it will take the fire department to get here. So let's get started."

"Yes, sir," the other two men said nearly in unison.

"You've stacked up the empty gas cans and explosive paraphernalia by the tent?"

One of the men nodded.

"You put empty cans and some fuse wire in her car?" Mr. Sperry hooked his finger back toward Brooke.

"Yes, sir."

"And her apartment and the boyfriend's car?"

"Yes, sir," the rope-tying man confirmed. "When the police check, they will find traces of explosives and gasoline in all those places."

"Then light it," Mr. Sperry said.

The man threw a match into the tent, and the tent burned completely in seconds, igniting the dry leaves around it. The empty gas cans stacked near the tent caught fire next—popping and hissing as they burned.

Smoke and ash blew into Brooke's face, and she started to cough. Hunter fought wildly against the ropes that held him.

There was another explosion from the direction of the chicken plant, and Mr. Sperry observed, "It won't be long now before this whole place is ablaze." Then, addressing one of his men, he ordered, "Go back to the car. Start it and be ready to get us out of here quick." As that man ran off, Mr. Sperry turned to the other. "Light some of those leaves by their feet. Then we'll move back and watch from a safe distance until we're sure they're dead."

Without so much as a glance at his victims, Mr. Sperry walked toward the clearing. He stopped at the edge of the trees and looked up toward the chicken plant and the main fire. His henchman used several matches to get the leaves burning around Brooke's feet. Then he walked over to stand by his boss.

"Don't worry," Brooke whispered to Hunter. "My uncle will come and save us."

He looked at her, his eyes full of hopelessness.

She stomped on the smoldering leaves she could reach, trying to buy a little time. She had never felt such hatred for another human being as she did at that moment for the two men by the clearing. But she couldn't worry about that now. The gas-can fire had spread to include the brush around it and the low-hanging limbs of the tree above it.

Pushing as hard as she could against her bonds, she created a small amount of room behind her. She worked her right hand up and unzipped her backpack a few inches. Then she reached in. The bark of the tree scratched her arm painfully, but soon her fingers tightened around the gun Hunter had given her before he made his swim up the creek.

Hunter felt the movement and cut his eyes over to look at her.

"Gun," she mouthed.

His eyes widened. Then he moved his head backward slightly.

"You want me to give it to you?" she interpreted.

He nodded.

She frowned, thinking about his broken right arm. "You can shoot left-handed?"

He barely moved his head in another nod.

So she transferred the gun to his left hand, losing more skin to the tree bark in the process. Then she pressed herself against the tree to give him as much operating room as possible.

"I called my uncle and told him where we are. If you can just get off a shot and lead him here, that would be good," she whispered. "And if you can hit Mr. Sperry, well, that would be a bonus."

Hunter nodded. It wasn't much of a plan, but they had to try.

She felt the ropes tighten as he lifted his arm. Then a shot rang out. Through the smoke, Brooke saw Mr. Sperry whip around and look at them in surprise. Hunter had missed the man, but hopefully her uncle had heard the shot.

"He has a gun!" Mr. Sperry yelled as both he and his henchman ran for cover. "Didn't you check him for weapons?"

"The girl must have brought the gun," the other man shouted. "You want me to shoot him?"

"We can't shoot him, you fool!" Sperry hollered back. "This has to look like they set the fire to burn the chicken plant and killed themselves in the process! So go take the gun away from him!"

"He'll shoot me!" the man objected.

"*I'll* shoot you if you don't get that gun!" Mr. Sperry promised him. He pulled a revolver from his pants pocket and shook it.

"Okay, okay," the man said.

Sperry returned the gun to his pocket as his assistant moved from tree to tree, getting ever closer to the one where Hunter and Brooke were tied.

She felt the ropes tighten again. Hunter was preparing to shoot.

The man circled around and came up from behind them, so he was out of Hunter's limited range. Brooke was afraid all was lost, and then she saw a slight movement from the corner of her eye.

Suddenly a huge figure jumped out of a cloud of smoke and tackled the man who had been sent back for Hunter's gun. The two men hit the ground hard, and the one underneath let out a scream of pain. The big man turned to face her, and Brooke recognized Hack. And if Hack was there, that meant her uncle couldn't be far behind.

She looked to the tree where Mr. Sperry was hiding. He left his cover and started to run, but Steamer stepped out of the trees on the other side, cutting off Sperry's only means of escape.

Then Brooke saw her uncle. The arm-twister saw him too.

Trapped, Mr. Sperry said, "I'm so glad you're here! These two young people were trying to set the woods on fire and burn down the Nature Fresh plant. We caught them, but I'll gladly turn them over to you. I'll just hurry on out of this smoke and let you handle the arsonists."

Her uncle's laugh was not pleasant. "The only place you're going is jail."

Steamer took off his shirt and started slapping at the burning leaves by Brooke's feet

Detective Napier came trotting up behind her uncle. "I'm too old for this," he panted. He helped Hack up and put handcuffs on the man Hack had tackled.

"I think my shoulder is dislocated," the man cried.

"That's a shame," Hack remarked without a trace of sympathy.

"There's another man!" Brooke warned them. "He's in their car."

"We got him," Hack replied.

Steamer walked up to Hunter. "You okay?" Steamer asked as he started sawing through the organic rope with a pocket knife.

Hunter nodded.

Steamer saw the clear tape and paused his rope cutting long enough to grab a corner of the clear tape. "This is going to hurt."

Hunter nodded again.

Steamer ripped it off, and Hunter closed his eyes briefly but did not cry out.

Steamer resumed cutting the rope. "Man, that was close! If we hadn't heard that shot, it might have been too late by the time we found you."

"Hurry!" Hunter rasped. "We've got to get out of here before the fire spreads."

Detective Napier advanced toward Mr. Sperry with a second pair of handcuffs.

"You're making a mistake," Sperry claimed.

Hack raised an eyebrow. "I seriously doubt that!"

"Detective, if you'll get the guy with all the excuses, Hack can bring the assistant," her uncle said. "Steam, it looks like Hunter might need some help. And I'll walk with Brooke."

The ropes fell away from Brooke's arms, and the relief was dramatic. She flexed her hands to get her circulation going again. Brooke was turning to Hunter as Detective Napier approached Mr. Sperry. From the corner of her eye, Brooke saw Sperry put his hand in the pocket where he'd hidden his gun. Brooke screamed, and everyone looked at her, giving Mr. Sperry time to pull out the gun unnoticed.

Just as the rope fell off his arms, Hunter pulled the trigger. Two shots rang out simultaneously. Hunter's bullet hit Mr. Sperry in the shoulder. Sperry's bullet lodged itself harmlessly in the tree, just a few inches from Detective Napier's head.

The detective caught Mr. Sperry in a choke hold and stripped the gun from his hand. As Detective Napier clamped the cuffs on the other man, the detective said, "You've got a lot of explaining to do."

Dane looked at Hunter, who was still holding the gun in his left hand, and said, "Good work."

"Give the credit to Brooke," Hunter mumbled with his injured lips. "She brought the gun."

"We'll have to pass out credit later," Detective Napier shouted as a gust of wind blew in a cloud of black smoke. "Right now we've got to get out of here!"

They heard sirens in the distance as Steamer put a shoulder under Hunter's left arm and helped him walk away from the tree. Brooke followed right behind them, with her uncle by her side. Hack held on to the man with the dislocated shoulder while the detective dragged the wounded Mr. Sperry.

It seemed to take forever to get back to the path where the vehicles were parked, but finally they arrived. While her uncle went over to supervise loading the wounded criminals into the police van, Brooke and Hunter leaned against the trunk of his little black car.

She put her hands gently on both of his cheeks and said, "Your poor face. What happened?"

Hunter sighed. "When I got to your apartment, there was a UPS man standing by your door. He said he had a delivery for you. I never suspected a thing. I took the package and used the key Hack gave me to open your apartment. I started feeling a little woozy and sat down on the piano bench. Then I realized the UPS guy had been dressed a little odd. He'd been wearing shorts, which made sense in the hot weather, but he'd also been wearing heavy gloves, which did not make sense. Unless he needed to protect his hands from something that was on the outside of the package. I dropped the package, but it was too late."

"Did it knock you out?"

He shook his head. "It was more like full-body paralysis. But before I completely lost control of my limbs, I turned the pages in the music book to 'Dixie.' I hoped that would warn you that something was wrong."

"It did," Brooke told him. "A person with a sense of humor might do something like that to be funny—but not you."

"It never would have occurred to me. I had it opened to 'Lady Mine.'"

She smiled. "Of course you did."

"Then while I was sitting there like a slug, unable to move, a couple of his guys came in and grabbed me. They carried me out to a van parked in front of your apartment. They took my phone and waited for you to come. All I could do was watch helplessly."

"Then they texted me," she said. "Which was a mistake, since you hate texting."

He nodded.

"And the text said, 'I have an important question to ask you,' like you were going to propose—which seemed a little premature since we haven't even been on a single date."

"Very premature," he agreed. "They overestimated the stage of our relationship."

"Probably because you gave me that fabulous piano. I guess I stopped my love lessons a little too soon. We never got to appropriate gifts for various romantic occasions. If you give a woman a baby grand for no reason, what is she going to expect on her birthday and at Christmas?"

He did his best to look exasperated, which was difficult because of the abused condition of his face.

She continued, "But I *knew* something was wrong when the text suggested that we meet here. You would never bring me close to the Nature Fresh plant again. So I ditched the bodyguard my uncle left at my apartment because I was afraid he'd make me wait there for my uncle, and I didn't know what they might be doing to you."

She glanced at his face and shuddered.

"Then while I was driving here, I called my uncle and told him my suspicions. He said he was sure I was driving into a trap. So I told him to come rescue us as quickly as he could."

"And you brought my gun."

"That part was just luck. It was still in my backpack."

"We were due for some good luck." He gave her a small smile.

"But the gun wouldn't have done us any good if you weren't such a good shot!" she continued. "And with your left hand!"

His swollen lips curled into a little smile. "You've done something for me that I thought no one ever could. You've made me thankful for my shooting ability."

Brooke leaned against his chest. "And you've given me something I thought I'd never have—a baby grand. Every time I think about it I get a little bit breathless.

"I saw it in the newspaper when I was stuck in that hotel room with Hack's men. It's not in the best shape, but we can refinish it."

"I like the idea of restoring the piano to its former glory," she murmured. "I *love* the 'we' part."

Before Hunter could respond, her uncle rushed up. He gave her a ferocious look, and pointing his finger he said, "I *told* you to wait at the road until we got here!"

She faced her uncle. "And I told *you* I couldn't wait. Hunter was in danger!"

"You could have gotten yourself killed!"

"It's my fault that Hunter is involved in this," she said. "I couldn't leave him in there with," she waved toward the police van that was slowly driving away, "them!"

"You need to learn how to obey orders!"

"You need to learn how to talk to people who aren't soldiers!"

Her uncle looked shocked and hurt.

"We're all okay!" Hunter joined the fray. "There's no point in fighting about it now!"

Brooke's shoulder's sagged. She put her arms around her uncle and said, "Thank you for coming to save us. And I'm sorry I yelled at you."

Her uncle hugged her back. "I'm sorry too, but you scared me to death."

"I was scared too," Brooke said. "In fact, I've never been so terrified in my life."

"If I had been only a few minutes later, it would have been too late," her uncle said, and she felt him shudder.

"But you made it in time, and we're safe, thanks to you," she reminded him.

He nodded and then looked up at the cloud of smoke that was moving closer. "Let's get out of here."

Brooke waited until Hunter was settled in the front passenger seat before she climbed into the backseat. Then her uncle got behind the wheel and started the car.

Hunter had his eyes closed, and Brooke didn't know if he was asleep, but just in case, she whispered to her uncle, "So I guess Nature Fresh is going to get away with polluting the creek and false advertising, since the judge dismissed the case."

"They're losing this plant, at least," Dane replied softly.

"It's insured," Brooke muttered.

Hunter said, "If they can prove that the guys who burned it down were working for Nature Fresh, the insurance company won't pay. So we need to get our pictures to the insurance company."

"But we don't have our pictures," Brooke reminded him. "We gave them to the district attorney."

"I'll call the DA and ask him to find out who insures the plant and forward the pictures to them. That's all we can do at this stage."

"I'm ready to be done with it," Brooke said. "All this has almost made me not care about chickens."

Hunter raised a swollen eyebrow.

She smiled at him. "I said *almost*." Then she looked at her uncle. "Hunter needs to go to a hospital, preferably not to the same one they are taking Mr. Sperry and his associate."

Her uncle nodded. "I'll call Savannah and let her know that we're okay and have her ask your mom for a hospital referral. We'll go wherever she recommends, and if we don't see Detective Napier's patrol car parked in front, we'll go in."

Chapter Fifteen

SAVANNAH, NEELY, AND RALEIGH WERE stuck in a small room at the police station, where Dane and Detective Napier had put them before they'd rushed off to assist Brooke. Dane made the trio promise they wouldn't leave the room until he got back. At first that wasn't too difficult—boredom and extreme anxiety were all Savannah had to deal with. But now she was beginning to feel mildly claustrophobic, and worst of all, she was getting low on Spriteorade. A few more minutes and she might be throwing up—making an already bad situation unbearable.

Neely and Raleigh were huddled close together. Earlier they had been talking, catching up on all that had transpired during their brief separation. But now they sat in silence, waiting to hear news of Brooke.

Savannah's phone rang, and she glanced at the screen. It was Dane. She pressed the talk button, praying that he had good news.

"Hello!" she called into the phone.

"Hey," he replied, sounding tired. "We've got Brooke and Hunter. They're both fine."

Savannah relayed this information to Brooke's worried parents. Then she asked, "Are you coming here to get us?"

"Hack is going to take you to Neely's house," Dane said. "We'll meet you there as soon as we get through at the hospital."

"The hospital!" Savannah repeated. "I thought you said everyone is okay!"

"Hunter has a broken arm," Dane replied. "Will you ask Neely which hospital she recommends?"

Savannah quickly explained the situation to the Claytons and then asked about hospitals.

"Baptist Hospital," Neely said. "I do some volunteer work there. It's a great place."

"She suggests Baptist Hospital," Savannah told Dane. "Keep us posted."

"I will," he promised. Then he ended the call.

Savannah put her phone in her pocket and said, "Hack's coming to get us. He'll take us to your house."

"How did Hunter get hurt?" Neely asked with dread in her voice.

"I don't have any details. But Brooke is fine. Dane will bring them home as soon as they have Hunter fixed up."

Neely nodded but still looked worried.

"Christopher said she's okay," Raleigh comforted his wife. "He'll take good care of her."

"I'll just be glad when it's all over."

"We all will be," Raleigh assured her. "It's been a nightmare. To think that just a week ago everything was normal. Now Finn and Selma are dead, money has been stolen, my company's on the brink of extinction . . ."

"It's been quite a week," Savannah agreed. "But Brooke is safe, and Adam's on his way home."

"I didn't mean to sound ungrateful," Raleigh clarified. "Of course those are the most important considerations. I am just amazed at how fast things can change."

"Well, I've seen Neely face the past week with courage and inner strength. So whatever trials you face in the future, she's up for them."

Neely shook her head. "I don't feel anything but exhausted."

"It's good to know the strength is there, though," Savannah told her. "Because you never know when you're going to need it."

Hack arrived fifteen minutes later, carrying a bottle of lemon-lime Gatorade and a can of Sprite.

Savannah gave the big man a hug. "How did you know I was out?"

He scowled. "I didn't. It was Steamer's idea."

"Well, thank you double then! I know you hated to go along with something Steamer suggested."

The big man scowled while Savannah mixed some fresh Gatorade and Sprite in her old bottle and then took a sip.

"I'm addicted," she admitted. "I can't live without this stuff."

"Save it for the infomercial," Hack muttered. "Let's get you folks home."

When they arrived at the hospital emergency room, Dane registered both Brooke and Hunter, although Brooke assured her uncle she didn't need medical treatment.

"Some of those cuts on your arm are pretty deep," he told her. "I'll feel better if the doctor checks you out."

Brooke sighed in resignation. "Just make sure they take Hunter first." She lowered her voice and whispered, "He looks like he's about to pass out."

"I'm not going to pass out," Hunter muttered.

Brooke raised an eyebrow. "Apparently his hearing is almost as good as his eyesight."

A nurse came for Hunter a few minutes later. She said he was going to have some x-rays taken and then get a cast put on his arm. Brooke had fallen asleep by the time a nurse came for her.

"Have they said anything about Hunter?" she asked her uncle as the nurse led her away.

Dane shook his head. "Nothing yet."

Once Brooke's cuts were washed and bandaged, she asked to be taken to Hunter. When the nurse looked hesitant, she added mischievously, "I've been his wife for the past week."

And so Brooke was ushered into his room. Hunter was sitting on the side of the examination table. He had his shirt off, a blue cast on his broken arm, and three stitches in his upper lip. She could see the bruises on his well-muscled torso, and his face looked much worse in the harsh light.

"They hurt you so badly." She wanted to cry.

"I've had worse," he claimed.

She hoped that wasn't true. "When they let you leave, will you come to my parents' house?"

"We'll have to ask your uncle," he said cautiously.

She narrowed her eyes at him. "You've got to learn that my uncle is not your boss when it comes to our relationship."

"Who is the boss," he asked. "You?"

She shook her head. "We'll share that job."

Her uncle walked in at that moment and told Hunter, "I informed the army that you need to be put on the disabled list. You have six weeks of medical leave, and that might be extended, depending on how fast you heal. So no flying for a while. No shooting either, hopefully—if Brooke can stay out of trouble."

"I'll try," she promised.

Hunter frowned. "If I can't fly or shoot, what will I do?"

"You'll relax and rest that arm."

Brooke smiled. "Hunter doesn't know how to relax."

Her uncle didn't find her comment amusing. "That's because he's a soldier."

"It's all I know," Hunter said.

Dane said, "I remember when I felt the same way. But you can learn to be something else, if you want to. It depends on what kind of plans you have for the future."

"The army has been making my plans for so long, I don't even know how to start."

Brooke said, "Okay, maybe I *will* have to be the boss in this relationship."

Her uncle spoke again to Hunter, "If you decide to leave the army, you could go back to school or work for Savannah's Child Advocacy Center for a while until you figure things out."

Brooke gave her uncle a grateful smile. Then she turned to Hunter. "After all the time we've spent in hospitals lately, maybe fate is pointing you toward medicine. Or we could go back to our summer jobs at the Civil War resort. After we explain everything to Jovette, I bet she'd rehire us. Especially after they've had to listen to that robotic guy play the piano. It would be just like old times. I'll play while you sit by me, looking tragically romantic!"

Her uncle frowned. "Tragically romantic?"

Hunter shook his head. "You don't even want to know."

"Or you could just work for me," Brooke said. "I wouldn't mind having a bodyguard."

Hunter shook his head. "It would probably be easier to fly a plane left-handed than to keep you out of trouble."

Her eyes widened. "Did you just make a joke?"

"Not much of one," he muttered.

"You found your sense of humor!" She gave him a little hug, and he winced. She was immediately contrite. "Sorry!"

"All right," her uncle said. "Let's get you out of here before she breaks your other arm."

As they were walking out to the car, her uncle's phone rang.

Brooke waited anxiously while he talked. When he put his phone away, he was smiling. "Good news?" she asked.

"I think so," he replied. "Your brother is at the Nashville airport. What do you say we go and pick him up on our way home?"

***

When Savannah walked back into Neely's house, Steamer met her at the door. "So everyone is okay?"

"That's what we hear," Savannah confirmed. "Even me—thanks to you. I was almost out of Spriteorade when Hack arrived with fresh ingredients."

"You're welcome," Steamer said with a smile. "Where's Neely? I've got good news for her."

"She's coming." Savannah pointed toward the garage behind her.

Neely stepped inside, followed by Raleigh and Hack. "Have you met my husband?" she asked the soldier/real estate agent/lawyer from Vegas.

Steamer shook his head. "I don't think so." He held out a hand to Raleigh. "My name is Steamer. I'm glad you're out of jail, and I'm really glad you didn't steal that money."

"Steamer!" Savannah scolded.

Raleigh smiled. "It's okay. I'm glad I'm out of jail too."

"So what's the good news you have for Neely?" Savannah reminded him.

"Your son is here!" Steamer announced. "Dane is bringing him home."

Neely and Raleigh embraced, anticipating the moment when they would be reunited with both their children.

Savannah watched their emotional excitement and thought of her own daughter. Savannah was glad she and Dane had been able to come and help Neely, but she longed to collect her family and go home to their cabin by the creek—to their regular life—and begin preparations for the new baby that would be joining them soon. And maybe build a playhouse to rival the one in Colorado.

Then through tears, Neely said, "I've been so anxious to have my whole family together, but after this past week, well, it will be such a blessing."

Hack's phone rang, and after a short conversation he announced, "Dane just pulled into the subdivision. They'll be here in a minute."

Raleigh and Neely took up positions right by the kitchen door that led to the garage. Savannah stood back a little, with Steamer and Hack.

Then the door opened and Brooke stepped inside. She smelled of smoke and had an impressive bandage on her right arm but otherwise seemed okay. Brooke was receiving a tender hug from her father when Adam walked in. Savannah had never met him, but she'd seen pictures, and the family resemblance was strong. Neely embraced him vigorously, and then the parents switched children.

Dane walked into the kitchen, and immediately his eyes sought Savannah. When he found her, he crossed the room to stand beside her. He put his arm around her shoulders and asked, "Are you okay?"

"I'm fine," she assured him.

Hunter came in last and closed the door behind him. Besides the cast on his arm, he had stitches in his lip, and his face was so badly bruised and swollen that Savannah barely recognized him.

The Claytons curtailed their hugging at his arrival.

Brooke introduced him to her parents. "You've met my mom," she said. "And this is my dad, Raleigh."

Hunter held out his left hand. "It's nice to meet you, sir. Please excuse my appearance. I usually don't look this bad."

"We appreciate all you did for our daughter," Raleigh said.

Hunter glanced at Brooke. "We're a pretty good team."

"And he bought me a piano!" Brooke told them. "A baby grand!"

Neely and Raleigh both had expressions of something much like alarm.

"Wow," Savannah said. "That must have been expensive."

"It's an *old* baby grand," Hunter explained. "I got it from an estate sale, and it was really pretty cheap. It needs to be refinished and tuned and who knows what else."

"But the important thing is," Brooke interrupted him, "that I have a baby grand!"

Neely looked a little less panicked. Apparently she thought that it was better for a virtual stranger to give her daughter an *old* piano than a *new* one. "Well, that was a lovely thing to do," she told Hunter. Then she waved toward the family room. "Now, everyone come and sit down."

Savannah and Dane remained in the kitchen as the others took seats in the family room. While she and her husband discussed the events of the past few days, Savannah sipped Spriteorade and watched Hunter. He could barely take his eyes off Brooke.

"He's in love," she whispered to Dane.

He nodded. "Yes."

"So he's going to stay here and get to know his future in-laws better?"

Dane frowned. "That would be awkward for anyone, but especially for someone as shy and socially inexperienced as Hunter. I'm thinking we should take him home with us. He can work with me on cases for the Child Advocacy Center while his arm heals. Brooke can come visit him there."

"And you can chaperone?"

"I'll keep an eye on them," Dane admitted. "But I think he'd prefer that to staying here—stuck with her family that he doesn't know."

Savannah had been looking forward to some time alone with Dane and Caroline. But she felt sorry for Hunter. "That's okay with me. Are you going to tell him now?"

Dane nodded. "Right now before he reaches his awkwardness limit."

When Dane extended the invitation, Hunter looked so relieved that Savannah had to cover her mouth to keep from laughing out loud. Brooke, on the other hand, was not happy with the idea.

"But I don't want Hunter to go," she said. "I want him to stay and get to know my family."

"Your family needs some time alone," Dane said firmly. "In a few days you can come up to our place and visit. You and Hunter can take long walks in the woods, swim in the creek, fish together, and eat what you catch."

Brooke's face brightened. "He does owe me dinner."

"It's all settled then," Dane said. He turned to Hack and added, "Can you line up a plane and fly us home?"

The big man nodded. "My pleasure."

"I'd like to head back to Vegas, if that's okay, sir?" Steamer requested.

"That's fine," Dane said. "Thanks for your help."

"Yes," Neely concurred. "What would we have done without you?"

Steamer smiled. "People ask me that question everywhere I go."

Savannah heard Hack growl as she walked up the stairs with Dane to start packing. Once she and Dane were alone, he pulled her into his arms for a proper kiss.

"Your breath smells like lemons and limes."

"Get used to it," she murmured. "It's going to be that way for the next eight months."

Their tender moment was interrupted by a knock on the door. Still holding her close, he said, "Come in."

It was Hack. "The DA just called. He has the pictures of the Nature Fresh plant to send to the insurance company. But he wants Brooke and Hunter to come to his office and sign a statement. The DA said they can even do it anonymously, if you're worried about further retaliation from Nature Fresh. So is it okay to let them go?"

Dane nodded. "Send one of your guys with them. Not Larry."

Hack scowled. "I'll send two. I'll tell them to call us when they leave the DA's office, and we'll meet them at the airport to minimize the delay in our departure."

"That's fine," Dane said.

Hack grinned. "Now you two go back to . . . whatever." Then he closed the door.

"I can't wait to get home, away from all these people," Dane complained. "I want it to just be you and me and Caroline for a while."

"Too bad you invited Hunter to be our houseguest," she teased. "And Brooke."

He groaned. "Why didn't you stop me from that moment of foolish compassion?"

She laughed. "It will still be good to get home—even with houseguests," she murmured. "We've got to get started on the nursery and on the playhouse of the century."

He kissed her forehead. "I wonder where I'm going to find some baby alligators."

She pulled away. "I'm going to have to draw the line at alligators."

He grinned. "You know I won't put baby alligators in Caroline's moat. They grow up to be big alligators."

"But she is having a moat?" Savannah confirmed.

"I think it would be a cute touch and definitely unique."

"Unquestionably unique," she agreed. "I've done a few drawings. You can look at them on the plane and see what you think."

"I already called the contractor that did our addition."

She looked up at him. "You hired a contractor to build Caroline a playhouse?"

"I can't have our daughter playing in something rickety," he said. "But I want to look at your drawings. The contractor can incorporate your ideas."

Savannah shook her head. "*You* are unique. And Caroline is going to be thrilled." At the mention of her daughter's name, tears came to Savannah's eyes. "I've missed her so much."

"Me too," Dane agreed. "Now, we'd better get downstairs before Hack starts rumors about us."

"I think everyone already knows we kiss," Savannah teased him as they started for the door.

When they walked into the family room, the Claytons were watching reports of the fire on television.

"The firemen have it under control," Neely said. "But the chicken plant is a total loss."

"I can't say I'm too upset about that," Dane remarked. "Where's Hack?"

"Packing up his equipment in my office," Raleigh said.

"We'll go see if he needs any help." Dane led Savannah toward the front of the house. Inside Raleigh's office, they found not only Hack but Steamer too.

"I thought you were leaving for Las Vegas," Dane said.

"I am," Steamer replied. "My flight doesn't leave for another three hours, so we've been having an operation wrap-up meeting without you."

Hack shook his head. "He's just spouting off nonsense like usual."

"Hey!" Steamer objected. "What I've been saying is way above my usual nonsense."

Savannah laughed. "And what have you been saying?"

"Now that it's all over, I was just pointing out that those Nature Fresh guys were awfully determined to take out a less-than-credible witness."

"Brooke?" Savannah was offended on the girl's behalf. "What's not credible about her?"

"Well, she hates Nature Fresh and all they stand for," Steamer began. "She spends a lot of her spare time protesting against chicken farms in general and them in particular. So why would a judge think her testimony wasn't biased?"

"I guess that's true," Dane said.

"Just because she's biased doesn't mean she wouldn't tell the truth," Savannah countered.

Steamer continued, "And her whole story about driving to the creek for a picnic lunch after the tour was a little contrived. Then her car, which is no clunker, won't start when she's ready to leave? And her new iPhone doesn't have service. And instead of walking back to the road the way she came in, she decides to walk up the creek—having no idea how long it will take to get to the plant from that direction. And then the trees are growing too close to the fence, so she has to go under it. Then she finds an illegal pipeline and mistreated chickens and has to walk all the way back to her car and then out to the road, where her service is miraculously restored and she calls a tow truck. I mean, I'm no stranger to bad luck, but that story had so much misfortune it was nearly fantastical."

Savannah was angry with Steamer. Sometimes he took his silliness too far, and she was just about to say so when Dane asked him, "Are you saying Joined Forces set the whole thing up?"

"I'm saying that it might look that way to some people—like people on a jury."

"Brooke wouldn't lie!" Savannah defended the girl.

"She might," Dane disagreed. "At least about how she came to be where she was that day. If she thought she was helping the cause."

"If it was a setup, Joined Forces already knew about the inhumane chicken coops and the pipeline before the tour?" Hack asked.

"Probably. The chicken coops, anyway, since they are visible," Steamer said. "The pipeline is normally underwater, so that may have been a bonus."

Savannah felt uneasy. "If Brooke's lunch and walk up the creek were staged by Joined Forces, surely she'd have told us now that it's all over."

"You would think so," Dane agreed.

Steamer pressed, "All I'm saying is that Brooke's pictures weren't very good and were taken while she was trespassing on Nature Fresh property. If the case had ever made it to trial, a good lawyer would have had a field day with her on the witness stand. Heck, even a sorry lawyer would have been able to discredit her testimony."

"What difference does that make?" Savannah asked. She noticed that Dane and Hack were both being very quiet—which seemed mildly ominous.

"If Brooke was a lousy witness with an unbelievable story, why all the drama? Why would Nature Fresh threaten Brooke and start a forest fire?"

"Spell it out for us, Steam," Dane said. "What is your point?"

"What if we chose the wrong enemy?" Steamer said. "What if it's Joined Forces that has done all this—not Nature Fresh?"

"Nature Fresh is definitely responsible for the hidden chicken coops and illegal pipeline," Savannah pointed out.

"We've had attempted murder and arson. Those coops and even an illegal pipeline pale in comparison," Steamer said. "Brooke may not even have been in on it. Some of her Joined Forces friends could have suggested the picnic—maybe even provided the food. Maybe they promised to join her and then never did."

"One of them could have disabled her car and blocked her cell service," Hack added.

"And during the tour, somebody could have mentioned that the plant runs by the creek," Steamer continued. "They might have even suggested that it could be shorter to follow the creek than to go all the way back to the road."

Savannah was moderately happier with this scenario. "But why?" she asked. "If Brooke's testimony was going to be worthless, why go to all that trouble?"

Instead of answering that question, Dane said, "Steam, can you get us the news on your iPad?"

"Sure." Steamer had it set up in seconds, and images of the fire at the Nature Fresh plant filled the screen. Then it switched to the low-quality pictures Brooke had taken from behind the plant.

Savannah gasped. "How did they get those pictures?"

"Brooke said she showed them to Freddo Higgins at Joined Forces first. Apparently he made copies."

Dane pointed back to the iPad, where a reporter was describing the situation. Then the reporter introduced a spokesperson from Joined Forces, who explained that one of their volunteers had happened on the pipeline a couple of weeks before. "And since then she's been threatened with bodily harm more than once."

"Are you saying that Nature Fresh threatened her?" the reporter asked.

"I'll let you do the math," the girl from Joined Forces replied coyly. "But we hope that today's incident will finally expose Nature Fresh for the criminals they are—something we've been trying to prove for years!"

The camera swung back to the reporter. With the fire blazing in the background, he said, "One thing is for sure—we haven't heard the last of this. Now, I'll send it back to you guys in the studio."

"You can turn it off," Dane said.

While Steamer stowed his iPad in a nice, little leather case, Savannah asked Dane, "So Joined Forces set up the whole thing to discredit Nature Fresh and try them through the press?"

"Which requires much less evidence," Hack murmured. "No lawyers or court costs."

"Just a good story and some dramatic film footage," Steamer contributed. "With Brooke and Hunter as the stars of the show."

"It's a possibility," Dane said slowly. "But it's a police matter. I'll pass Steamer's idea along to Detective Napier, and if he wants to he can pursue it. We're done." Dane checked his watch. "How long have Brooke and Hunter been gone?"

"I'd say about thirty minutes," Hack replied.

"Call your guys, and see if they can give us an estimate on how much longer it's going to be. I'm ready to go."

Hack made his call and reported, "My guys are sitting in the lobby at the DA's office, waiting for Brooke and Owl to finish with their statements."

Dane pulled out his phone. "I'm going to call Mr. Shaw to make sure he keeps their names out of those statements—just in case Steamer's theory is right."

Hack nodded morosely. "We've got enemies everywhere, apparently."

Savannah watched as Dane spoke with negligible patience to a receptionist and a secretary before he was finally connected with Mr. Shaw.

Dane told the DA that there were still a lot of unanswered questions and that he wanted to be sure Hunter and Brooke were not at risk. "I'd like to see Nature Fresh pay for the things we think they've done—even if it's just through a denied insurance claim. But I really want Hunter and Brooke to be safe. So please make sure that their names are not mentioned on anything you send the insurance company. In fact, I'd prefer that the statements they're giving be shredded."

"I'll destroy the statements if that's what you want." Mr. Shaw sounded sad.

"And do you have any idea when they'll be through?" Dane asked. "We're waiting on them before we head home."

"They left a few minutes ago," Mr. Shaw said. "They said they parked in the deck and asked if there was a faster way to get there than going through the lobby. So I showed them the back elevator that goes straight to the parking deck."

Dane's voice sounded hollow when he said, "Thank you." He ended the call and brought his worried eyes up to Savannah's.

"But why would they go out the back way and leave Hack's men behind?" Savannah asked.

"I don't know," Dane said grimly. "But we need to find out."

***

As Mr. Shaw hung up the phone on his desk, Brooke watched with mixed emotions—hatred, despair, and a sickening kind of terror that she'd never felt before, even when she was tied to a tree in a burning forest. That time, she knew her uncle was on the way. This time, she had no such comfort.

She clasped her hands tightly together and forced herself to look at Hunter. He was sitting in the chair beside her. His arms and feet were bound, and his mouth was taped. His eyes were filled with such loathing that she shuddered.

Mr. Shaw smiled at her. "Well, that worked out perfectly. And no one will ever doubt your dedication to the cause, Miss Clayton."

"Lady Mine" (1846)

An admired ballad, composed and arranged with an accompaniment for the pianoforte.

1. Thou art beautiful as flow'rs
Lady mine! Lady mine!
E'en the fairest in my bow'rs
Lady mine! Lady mine!
And the azure brow of night,
With its starry wreaths of light,
Hath not eyes more pure and bright
Than are thine, Than are thine.

2. Thou art pure as mountain snows
Lady mine! Lady mine!
E'er the sun upon them glows
Lady mine! Lady mine!
But the noontide hath its ray,
And the snowflakes melt away,
And hearts—why may not thine?
Why not thine? Why not thine?

3. Thou art fair as any queen
Lady mine! Lady mine!
As the moon's resplendent sheen
Lady mine! Lady mine!
But the moonbeams fade and die
Like love's unheeded sigh,
And my hopes in sorrow lie
Lady mine! Lady mine!

Baltimore, MD: F. D. Benteen Plate No. 813 [Engraver:] Webb. [Source: 791110@ LoC]

ABOUT THE AUTHOR

BETSY BRANNON GREEN CURRENTLY LIVES in Bessemer, Alabama, a suburb of Birmingham. She has been married to her husband, Butch, for thirty-three wonderful years, and they have eight children, two daughters-in-law, three sons-in-law, and nine grandchildren. She is the LDS Family Services Representative for the Bessemer Stake and works for Hueytown Elementary School. She loves to read, when she can find the time, and watch sporting events—especially if they involve her children. Although born in Salt Lake City, Betsy has spent most of her life in the South. Her life and writing have been strongly influenced by the town of Headland, Alabama, and the many generous, gracious people who live there. Her first book, *Hearts in Hiding*, was published in 2001, and she has since published another sixteen books.